Caged in Desire

T.K. DRAKE

SINCLAIR AFFAIRS BOOK THREE

Caged in Desire

T.K. DRAKE

"Daddy is a state of mind...
I'm your daddy."
- Pedro Pascal

Author's Note

Thank you for reading *Caged in Desire*! If you're new here, welcome! If you're joining us after reading Ledger and Sloane's story, *Redeemed in Crimson, or* Margot and Jack's story, *Masked in Deception*, welcome back! When we first met Henry Sinclair we knew he had to have his own story. His energy was impossible to ignore, and we hope we've done him justice.

We want to stress that this book **heavily** features a Daddy kink between our MMC and FMC, including an age gap. There is **no** age play or DD/lg dynamic, however our MMC does refer to the FMC as "little girl".

Please do not read this if a Daddy kink isn't your thing. We understand it's not for everyone! But we are so serious. You'll hate this shit.

Caged in Desire is book three in a five book series but can be read as a standalone.

Caged in Desire
is book three in a five book series
but can be read as a standalone.

Content Warning

Please note that this is a sexually explicit romance with dark themes. Please visit www.tkdrake.com for a detailed list of content warnings and kinks. Your mental wellbeing is incredibly important to us! We can always be reached at tkdrakeauthor@outlook.com with any specific concerns or questions.

Chapter One

Light filters into my study as dawn breaks, and a soft breeze flows through an open window. The crisp autumn air filling the room is a balm to my soul. Being back home for two weeks has reminded me of how much I miss the lush greenery of the estate, a far cry from the sleek, steel high-rises I inhabit when based elsewhere in the country. Perhaps I was wrong to think being here would be tedious. I've been gone so frequently that I've forgotten what I was missing.

As always when I'm in town, the morning paper has already been placed next to my chair, crisply folded in half. After glancing at my watch to confirm I have precisely ten minutes before seven o'clock, I take a seat, light my pipe, and flip open the paper, reading the usual mundane headlines as I wait for Mrs. Potts to bring in my morning coffee and eggs.

LOCAL MAN WINS NATIONAL LOTTERY

CONDO ASSOCIATION CALLS FOR
MORE STRINGENT INSPECTIONS

THREE DEAD IN INTERSTATE PILEUP

"Good morning, Mr. Sinclair! Don't you look dashing today? You must have had a good swim this morning," Mrs. Potts says with a smile as she sets the breakfast tray down on the stand next to my chair. "I know the lap pool is smaller than some of your other residences."

"Good morning to you as well, Potts, and thank you. If only I could look half as lovely as you. But yes, it has been an exemplary morning so far," I say, causing her smile to grow even wider.

Mrs. Potts was hired by my father when I was a young child as our main housekeeper, but he decided to send her to England with me when I went off to boarding school. She wasn't allowed to live on the campus, but she was a source of matronly comfort in times of distress when I couldn't reach Mother. In fact, she's more like a grandmother to me than anything else, and despite my efforts for her to retire and enjoy herself at the property of her choice, she insists on continuing her role at the Sinclair estate. Her stubbornness extends to never calling me Henry, resulting in me having to hear "Mr. Sinclair" even at home.

"Oh, how I hate to see a suicide. Mr. Burnam. That name sounds familiar. Do we know a Mr. Burnam?"

I look behind me to see her standing over my shoulder, slightly bent down to read the paper I'm holding.

"Shall we get you a paper of your own, or would that be *too* easy?" I ask, causing her to level me with a withering expression that reminds me of my teenage days.

Hiding my smile, I look back at the paper, scanning until I find the article in question.

Mr. Frank A. Burnam found dead at 68 years old. Suspected suicide.

"Hmm...ah, yes, I believe he worked alongside the family lawyer writing contracts for either Father or Grandfather years ago. I don't recall ever meeting him, but his name has certainly shown up in a document from time to time."

"That makes sense. I don't remember seeing him around either, but I must have heard your father talk about him at some point because his name stood out to me. Either way, please let me know if he did work for the company, and I'll have some flowers sent to his family." Potts turns to leave the room but catches herself at the door. "Oh, I almost forgot, should I expect you home for dinner? It's pork chop night."

I close my eyes, massaging my temples as I walk through the day's schedule in my head. Tuesday means a brisk morning swim, breakfast and coffee while reading the paper, work at nine o'clock, dinner at six, and my weight-lifting regimen to burn off any excess energy before bed. An added wrinkle is a meeting this afternoon with my little brother, Ledger, as he has some sort of pressing news with which to regale me.

"Yes, I'll be home for dinner tonight. It's Tuesday, Potts. You know I wouldn't miss your pork chops for the world. With the weather this nice, I might dine outside."

"Well, it's been so long since you've spent this much time at home," Potts teases, "I had to be sure. In that case, I'll see you tonight. Have a lovely day, Mr. Sinclair."

"You as well, Potts. I'll see you at six o'clock sharp."

"Move the two o'clock back if you must, Linda, but I will certainly not be rushed out of my lunch meeting with the Hart Corporation. After their last delivery fell through, I'm not willing to let them off easily." I sigh, feeling a tension headache creeping on. It's only Tuesday, and my schedule isn't any lighter for the rest of the week. It might be time to move my massages up to twice weekly...or plan for another night at the club this weekend with Lori.

"Very well, sir, and I also received your next contract for review from Mr. Gregory. I left it on your desk." My secretary hovers, and given that she *never* hovers, I sense my day is about to become even more vexing.

"Whatever else it is, you may as well get it over with and tell me." Linda has been my right-hand woman for almost a decade, helping my work life run smoothly. She's also a discreet courier and fixer for my more...personal contracts and correspondence, and it's unlike her to beat around the bush.

She grimaces, and I flinch internally. "Well, unfortunately, sir, a late meeting has popped up on your calendar this afternoon at four o'clock. The Taranov family requested it, and I'm not sure who accepted the time while I was away last week. I know it will affect..."

"Thank you, Linda. That will be all."

Recognizing my dismissal for what it is, she leaves with a sympathetic smile, and I'm finally left in peace again. A four o'clock meeting on a Tuesday threatens to undermine my entire schedule for the evening. The Taranovs are longtime allies of my company, dating back to before my father, Henry Sinclair Jr., even trademarked a logo. More recently, they've been managing assets overseas, with less involvement Stateside, which makes me suspicious as to why they've shown back up with a meeting request on short notice.

I *can* take the meeting at four, and potentially be late to my evening appointment, just like I *can* do any number of things. The fact that the Taranovs scheduled a late meeting with me shows just how little involvement they've had with the business in the four years since I've taken over from my father.

This does unfortunately impact my plans to meet Ledger for an after-work drink at his club Rendezvous to "catch up on things."

I've always felt responsible for my family, especially my little brother. At first, it was the natural role of an older brother, but as time passed, it became necessary. He clashed with my father about almost everything, and I could see the damage it was causing not only to them but to Mother as well.

There was a time when I wouldn't even consider canceling on him, out of fear of how he might react, but he's straightened up over the years. Deciding to see if Ledger would mind moving our catch-up session before completely dismissing the Taranovs, I dial my brother.

Ledger answers almost immediately. "Henry! What can I do for you, Bro?"

"Good morning, Little Brother. Unfortunately, I'm calling to see if you mind moving our drinks to later this week. It appears a meeting made it past my secretary, and I have to admit, I'm curious about the reason for their urgency. If we can't reschedule, I can cancel on the..."

"No, no!" Ledger practically screams. "Don't worry about that. Just come over tomorrow. I promised Sloane a full day at home, so just swing by whenever you can."

The mention of my sister-in-law brings a smile to my face. Her ability to tame Ledger still baffles us all. He was trouble incarnate, raking about almost indiscriminately, before he fell head over heels for his wife of almost two years. "And how is my favorite sister-in-law?"

I can practically hear the smile on his face at the thought of his wife. "Oh, she's fantastic. She's at home sorting through everything she and Margot *had to have* from all their shopping in Paris when we visited last week. I know for a fact there are at least two early birthday presents for you that she's dying to see you open."

"Margot could make the most devout minimalist become a hoarder. How is our sister? Still getting along in Paris?" I ask.

Our little sister, Margot, moved to Paris almost two years ago for an internship after college and seems to be thriving, from what I hear. I didn't grow up nearly as close to her as my brother did, and even though I'm making more of an effort, she and Ledger share a closeness I doubt we'll ever achieve.

"Oh, you know how she is now, all serious and mature. I haven't decided whether it's a good thing or a bad thing yet, but she's always in good spirits when she gets around Sloane, so it's hard to tell."

"Wonderful. Well, if you're sure you don't mind, I'll let you go. I have quite a lot on my agenda today, including a two-hour meeting with Jack concerning some legal jargon for Rendezvous Too," I say, mentally rolling my eyes at the thought of dealing with Jack Carter for two hours.

Not to say I don't love Jack, but I'd be lying if I said I wasn't a bit jealous of his relationship with my family. Mother took him in after his own mom died when he was only five, and she loves him like a son. He and Ledger are as close as brothers. Being the same age, they hit it off right away and have been thick as thieves ever since. As much as I hate to admit it, they're probably closer than Ledger and I are. And he's leagues closer to Margot, who was only a year old when I left the country for school.

"Oh yes, I think he mentioned being confused about something related to that. Give him a hard time for me. I'll see you tomorrow?"

"Yes, I'll give you a more accurate estimated arrival later after I see how much disruption this meeting is going to cause."

No sooner have I ended my call than Linda is knocking on my door. "Sorry to bother you again, but the Taranovs just reached out to confirm your attendance."

I take a moment to ground myself with a calming breath before addressing Linda. I know this isn't her fault, and her persistence is part of what makes her such a good assistant, but it's occasionally trying, particularly lately. I'm not sure if she's gunning for a promotion or a raise, but she's been even more of an unrelenting presence in my life lately. "Yes, Linda, please let them know I'll be there. Make sure someone from our legal team can attend. I would prefer Danny, but if he's unavailable, I'll take Jason or Stewart."

"Of course, sir. I'll arrange the legal counsel and confirm the meeting for today." She seems as if she wants to linger yet again, but I turn to gather documents for my first appointment with Jack. Despite a twinge of uncertainty at this surprise meeting, I'm more at peace than I've been in some time. Once I know Ledger is alright, I'll be able to fully settle in, and I'll feel even better once I get back to the club tomorrow.

A knock on the door signals Jack's arrival, right on time. Routine *mostly* intact, I turn to greet him with a smile. I shake off my negative thoughts and prepare myself for what's more than likely going to be a grueling few hours of putting out another family fire.

Chapter Two

I breathe a sigh of relief as I round the corner and see Danny waiting for me outside the conference room. He's the best representation we have, bar none. While our entire legal team is excellent, there isn't anything Danny hasn't been able to work out in our favor.

"Ah, you made it. I hope this didn't inconvenience you too significantly," I say, reaching out to shake his hand.

Danny rolls his eyes with a grin. "Linda didn't leave me much choice. You know how scary she gets when you tell her no."

"Yes. In fact, I do." That's exactly why she's been such a commodity to me over the years.

"So what is this about? What's so important that the jet was waiting for me in New York at ten o'clock this morning?"

"I have no idea. Are they here yet?"

Danny shrugs. "Dunno. I just beat you here by a couple of minutes."

Taking a deep breath, I push open the door. I'm immediately surprised by an occupant I wasn't expecting.

"Mother? What's this about?" I ask, my surprise mirrored on her face as I enter the room.

"Darling, I could ask you the same thing. I had no idea you were still here. Pavel didn't mention anything about you joining us."

"Pavel? You're on a first-name basis with Mr. Taranov? Why have you never—"

I'm interrupted from any further interrogation of my mother by a portly man knocking twice on the doorframe before entering, ushering two men inside, and closing the door behind them. He's much shorter than I am, although most people are, and he has a slightly sinister aura. An expensive suit, a more expensive watch, and eyes that look like they've seen plenty of trouble in their lifetime make me believe Pavel Taranov, assuming this is him, is not someone to cross. When he sees me, he smirks before hiding it with a smile, and I see my mother's face drain of color. I'm not sure I've seen her look so distressed since Father died.

"Blanche, how lovely to see you. Surely, you haven't forgotten me. I know it's been years since we've met, but it looks like you've seen a ghost! And this must be Henry. Dear boy, I daresay I would recognize you anywhere. You're the spitting image of your father. God rest his soul," Mr. Taranov finishes, before pulling my mother into a crushing hug.

Mother blinks, and I feel like I have whiplash. Rather than the severe Russian I was expecting from his demeanor, Taranov has a soft American accent. I suppose I should be slower to judge books by their covers. *Unless...*

"Pavel," my mother recovers smoothly, and I see she has her game face on again. "I'm not sure anyone could ever forget you. I'll admit I was surprised to hear from you, but it's an absolute treat to see you. You look well! You're right, this is my eldest son, Henry."

Recognizing my cue to move to center stage, I shake the man's hand, taking the opportunity to look into his eyes and...*there.* I knew it. The hard look I saw when he first entered this room is the real Pavel Taranov. He's just excellent at covering it. Well, two can play that game.

"Mr. Taranov, it's an honor to finally meet you in person after all this time. Although I will concede, I was caught off guard by the urgency of your meeting request," I say firmly, still shaking his hand.

Finally, we release each other, and instead of answering my question, he turns to introduce his companions. "Thank you both for accepting our meeting on such short notice. This is my brother and VP of operations, Ivan. And our solicitor, Mr. Tanev." He gestures to his brother, who, despite sharing the same height, has a much slimmer build and more delicate facial structure, and his solicitor, who is even rounder than Mr. Taranov.

Mother arranges everyone around the table and I can tell she's nervous by how quiet she is. Something has really bewildered her about this meeting.

"Pavel, I am simply dying to know what brings you here today," Mother says, and Pavel beams.

He doesn't beat around the bush, and each word out of his mouth sounds like an alien language.

"Well, dear Blanche, we've come to collect on our contract! My darling daughter, Katarina, will be eighteen in a few days, and she's very excited to marry your Henry!"

Silence fills the room as I try to make sense of what he's saying. As shocked as I am, Mother doesn't seem to feel the same way. She looks confused and surprised, but not dumbfounded. *She knows something. This isn't a foreign concept to her.*

"What do you mean, an eighteen-year-old daughter, Pavel? That is absolutely not possible. I've—" Mother is interrupted by the *real* Pavel, with fiery rage in his eyes.

"You've *what*, exactly? You've watched my family's every move, had snipers and assassins trailing every one of us for years, waiting for any sign of a baby so that you could break your family's word and deprive us of our reward? You've dealt blow after blow to our side of the business, trying to ensure that we never gained a toehold, let alone a foothold in the States? Well, you certainly tried. But our business has grown despite your best efforts, and I *do* have a daughter. She's survived you, and we're ready to fulfill this contract once and for all!"

He's spitting by the end of his monologue and red in the face, his brother placing a soft hand on his forearm that's immediately shrugged off. Before I can tell him that no one speaks to my mother like that, she proves that she's capable of defending herself. Her defense is decidedly *not* a denial.

"I simply do not believe you, Pavel. I would *know* if you had any offspring. There is no way that you kept a girl confined to a house for eighteen years without so much as a birth record or a social security card crossing my desk. There is *no way* that not a single person from your payroll took my money to inform on you, *all these years!*" Mother says, indignantly.

A thick manila envelope is slid across the table while Mother stares at it as if it holds a death warrant, the scratch of the metal clasp sounding across the table like a death knell. Rather dramatic of her, considering it's *my* life being debated in a conference room right now.

"I think you'll find, Mrs. Sinclair," says Mr. Tanev derisively, "everything you could possibly want to know about Ms. Taranova is in this file. Her medical records, school transcripts, photos, and even some of her special interests are reported on in detail."

"Ah!" Mother exclaims, a smug look crossing her face for the first time since this meeting began. "The contract states that if no female was born to your family before Henry's eighteenth birthday, the deal would be void. It looks like you lost by a day, Mr. Taranov, as they share a birthday." Turning to me, she looks relieved and addresses me for the first time during the meeting, a contrite look on her face. "I'm sorry you had to experience this stress, Henry. This contract was a *stupid* thing drafted by your grandfather, and it was supposed to be *your father* who fulfilled it, but..."

"But he reneged on it, eloped with you, and punted responsibility for *his* shortcomings to his poor heir! And now it seems that you wish to do the same, Henry. I feel foolish for expecting anything else out of the slippery Sinclairs. Well, if that's the way you wish to do business, Blanche. I'll have you know that Katarina does indeed share a birthday with you, Mr. Sinclair. In fact, it seems my daughter was born to be your birthday present."

Mr. Taranov's expression darkens. "The contract *specifically* states that if a suitable daughter isn't born by the *minute* Henry Sinclair Jr.'s first son turns eighteen, the deal would be void."

Mother's posture deflates at her defeat as he slides the corresponding documents to her. "As you'll see, Katarina was born at 2:06 a.m. on the twenty-eighth of September, and Henry was born at 9:31 p.m. eighteen years earlier."

Before I can gather my thoughts, Mr. Taranov collects his things, then stands and moves briskly toward the door before addressing my mother again. "Katarina will be disappointed to wait another eighteen years before your new grandson comes of age, but I'm sure he'll be excited at the benefits of an older woman when the time comes. Let me know when your younger son is available to go over the details of his son's contract."

A low gasp escapes my mother as my eyes snap to hers. My always calm, always in control mother has tears in her eyes, and I realize the Taranov family has us well and truly on our back foot.

"How. Can you possibly? Insinuate that?" Mother asks, as Taranov smirks from his spot leaning in the doorway. "You have no proof, and I won't take the slander..."

"Sloane Olivia Sinclair, neé Johnson, date of birth June 24, 2002, blood type AB, license plate number RMFT12. Approximately eight weeks pregnant as of yesterday, if my records are correct, which they are. Based on our surveillance, we think we've narrowed down the night of conception, but your son is relentless, Blanche. That apple doesn't fall far from the tree, hmm? We're betting on this one being a boy, but based on your son's...*proclivities,* I'm sure this won't be the last."

Taranov continues as my mother's breathing quickens and her face flushes. I feel anger, yes, but also a rush of love for a fetus I didn't know existed ten seconds ago. *God.* Ledger's going to be a dad. I'm going to be an uncle. *I'm going to be an uncle.* And I'm *not* pushing this ridiculous contract off a single generation more.

As Pavel continues to taunt my mother and Ivan sits silently, looking like he dislikes everything about this shakedown, I glance at Danny, who has been speed-reading the contract. Meeting his gaze, he gives me a minute shake of his head, and I feel myself galvanize. I've been cleaning things up and smoothing the way for my family members as head of the house for the past five years, and I'm certainly not going to stop now.

I clear my throat, and everyone finally stops bickering. "I will not marry an eighteen-year-old."

Mother puts a hand on her forehead as the Taranovs' solicitor clicks his briefcase closed and Pavel rolls his eyes. "Well, then, once again, we will see you all in eighteen years..."

"I *said.* I will not be marrying an eighteen-year-old. However, we will not be carrying forth this contract any further. I will fulfill it. Come see me in a year. Send any necessary paperwork to our counsel in the meantime. And leave the dossier on the girl for our review."

With a victorious gleam in his eye, Pavel Taranov gives a mock salute and finally leaves. His lawyer follows, and Ivan gives my mother and me an apologetic look before following his brother back to whatever evil lair they came from.

Danny has worked for our family long enough to read a room, so he scurries out with a "call me later" whispered barely loud enough to hear. Taking a deep breath, I meet my mother's assessing gaze and see her looking at me with admiration and a touch of melancholy. There's no time for her emotions now, though. All I'm interested in are facts.

"Mother," I growl out. "Explain."

Chapter Three

Blanche Sinclair is a force of nature. As vexing as the meeting with the Taranovs was, it won't hold a candle to the conversation I'm about to have with my mother.

"Explain yourself," I say, walking around the table to take the seat next to her.

She adjusts herself, sitting up even straighter and lifting her chin to hold her head high, refusing to cower in the face of conflict. "Darling, I really don't have the time to get into this. I would *love* to stay and chat all day, but I do have an appointment in thirty—"

I interrupt her, slapping my hand down on the table for emphasis. "We're going to sit here and discuss this until you've told me every minuscule detail pertaining to that contract, and if it takes all night, so be it."

Her face becomes somber, and the reality of the situation finally sinks in. I'm suddenly suffocated with the enormity of what just happened. My perfectly crafted facade breaks, with anger seeping out from the cracks. I've spent my whole life training to be the heir to our family's empire. I've forgone so many of the experiences they take pleasure in, all so that I can keep our legacy alive.

"I've always done everything for this family, and now you want *this?*" I say, lifting the dossier of the woman I'm contractually obligated to marry. A woman whose name I've just learned. "Whatever you've conspired in the past has just come to light in a way that *drastically* affects *my goddamn* life!"

"Henry Charles Sinclair, don't you *ever* speak to me like that again," she says, the anger in her eyes now rivaling my own as she stares me down. "I didn't have anything to do with this contract. *This* was your grandfather's doing. How dare you insinuate that I would ever knowingly put any of my children in this situation?"

I prop my elbows on the table and rest my head in my hands, rubbing my temples to alleviate the sudden headache. "I love you, and I apologize for losing my temper, but this is important. Arguably, the most important contract I will ever fulfill. *Please...*just tell me what's going on."

She closes her eyes and breathes deeply. "I wasn't around when the contract was originally drawn up, but from my understanding, it was meant to benefit both families. *Years* ago, when your grandfather was growing the Sinclair empire, he ran across the Taranov family, and they quickly hit it off. The Taranovs were a very wealthy family in Russia at the time. They wanted to relocate their headquarters to the United States, but their strong ties to the Bratva made it difficult for them to gain any credibility here.

"Your grandfather was just that. He was an extremely credible businessman whose success was growing substantially. He was doing very well nationally. However, he lacked the funds or connections to take his trade global. The two families came together with a solution to solve both of their problems. The Taranovs would invest heavily in your grandfather's business, providing some of their foreign contacts as well, and your grandfather would help the Taranovs gain credibility in the States.

"At the time, your father was only a baby, not that it would've mattered to your grandfather. He viewed everything attached to him as an asset, including his wife and children. The contract was drawn up for your father to marry the next daughter born into the Tananov family and...well, Henry..."

She pauses, and I see the tears swelling up in her eyes as she meets my gaze. "Your life isn't the only one that was drastically affected."

"Mom..." I reach across the table with my hand out, an invitation for hers. "I'm sorry, I should have controlled my temper before I knew the whole story."

She grabs my hand and squeezes gently, blotting her unfallen tears away with a tissue.

"No, I deserved your anger. I should've told you years ago, but I genuinely didn't think it would ever affect you. When your father and I got married, the contract was amended to the next generation. Of course, I didn't know about any of this for years. You were well into your childhood before your father finally confessed how he had managed to pull the necessary strings for our union to proceed.

"As you know, the contract was to become void if there wasn't a suitable contender born by the time you turned eighteen. I watched that family for years to make sure the consequences of your grandfather's greed didn't come back to affect *my* babies."

I chuckle, remembering the things Ivan accused Mom of doing in regard to her *watching*. "Apparently, you did more than watch. Snipers, really? Assassins, too?"

"Honestly, Henry, they were *just actors*!" she says, rolling her eyes dramatically. "They almost took everything from me. I had to give them *some* trouble."

"I'm not sure I believe you."

Her face turns solemn once again, I assume from memories of her and Father, young and in love. "My darling boy, I'm so, *so* sorry you're having to deal with this. I promise you I'll do everything in my power to see this resolved."

She breaks our contact with one last squeeze to my hand and reaches for the folder containing all the information I have about my bride-to-be. Her eyes widen as she turns the first page back. "*Although* the two of you would give me absolutely extraordinary grandchildren," she says, holding up a picture of the most beautiful woman I've ever seen.

The meeting was traumatic enough that I didn't once imagine what this woman would look like, but I'm having a visceral reaction after one glance at her. My feelings of being trapped in marriage dissipate as I envision her as my wife.

An alarm on my phone lets me know I'll be late for dinner if we don't wrap this up soon, even if I could stay here all night looking at the goddess I'm going to marry. I stand and walk around to where Mom remains sitting, holding out a hand to help her up as well. She bypasses my offer, jumping out of her chair and nearly knocking me to the floor with the force of her hug. "I'm so, so sorry, son."

"It's fine, really. It's not your fault. Let's keep this between us for now, though. Our legal team can look into things before we include the rest of the family," I reply.

She finally pulls herself back from me, and the Blanche Sinclair fire I've always known and admired is back in her eyes. "Of course. We can figure this out."

I grab the folder left on the table before escorting her to her car and beginning my own drive home for dinner.

This is fine.

After dinner, I make my way to my study, dossier in hand, and recline in my chair, nursing a glass of scotch. I have thirty minutes allotted on my daily schedule for digestion after dinner, and while I would usually take this time to work on a crossword, I have more interesting information to sort through.

Opening the file, I get my second look at the woman I've been promised to. She's no doubt young, but there's a grace about her that far surpasses that of an average eighteen-year-old. Her long, light blonde hair, creamy pale skin, and almost violet eyes are entrancing.

Willing myself to investigate further, I reluctantly pull myself away from her photograph and flip to the next page.

Her academic record is impeccable. It seems she's tested at the level required for senior college coursework, which isn't surprising, considering the list of tutors she's been working with. Her instructors include some of the most decorated professors in the country.

While her academic capabilities surpass any expectation I might have had, I'm curious about the social skills she'll have after living locked away on her family's estate her entire life. If she remained hidden for eighteen years, there's no way they would let her out much, if at all. I'm first inclined to compare her to eighteen-year-old Margot. My sister was and is a kind-hearted soul, but she's always been a bit spoiled. As the baby of the family and the only girl, she always got pretty much everything she wanted. But while Margot was brilliant, she wasn't making valid points and counterarguments against famous philosophers, as my betrothed has been doing for years, based on this record. Perhaps Katarina is shyer than Margot and more of a bookworm.

Sighing, I flip through the remainder of the packet, each page humanizing her more and more. I realize this sordid ordeal must be equally as off-putting for her as it is for me, if not more so.

Although she's probably known about this arrangement long enough to wrap her mind around it all, I'm sure I'll intimidate her. At the end of the day, she's the one leaving everything she knows to move into a strange home with a man she doesn't know. *A man exactly twice her age.*

Home. I suppose I'll need to decide on a home base if I'm going to have a lady of the house. This estate makes the most sense. It's close to my family, in case she needs anything while I'm away. I pick up her picture, and my heart races as I look down at my beautiful Katarina.

Is this how Ledger felt when he saw Sloane for the first time? If there was a poster boy for anti-monogamy, it was him before he met his wife. I've envied him for longer than

I care to admit. A part of me has always longed for the love in their eyes when they look at each other, and the way they so effortlessly gravitate to one another, holding and touching without thought. And now he's going to have a baby. *A proper fucking family.*

In the back of my mind, whenever I allowed myself to imagine having a family one day, it was always here. Without meaning to, my mind wanders to this house full of the life it once had when my siblings and I were growing up, except these children running the halls have icy-blonde hair.

Walking in from a long day away, my eldest two children run past me, yelling out greetings as they race through the halls, while the youngest leaps into my arms. My stunning wife waddles into the room, well on her way to giving me a fourth child, lighting up the room with her smile. Setting the small child down to chase his siblings, I walk over to Katarina and pull her into a loving embrace, using one hand to pull her face up to mine for a passionate kiss before dropping it to her growing womb. The thought of her carrying my child again makes me ravenous, pulling her with me to the bedroom...

The chime of my phone brings me back to reality. I look at my screen and see the twenty-four-hour notice in my calendar of my scheduled meeting with Lori at Rendezvous tomorrow.

I stare at the appointment reminder for far longer than necessary before remembering that I'm in an active contract with a submissive, and we've arranged for her to fly down to meet me at my brother's sex club tomorrow evening.

I've been a member of the BDSM lifestyle for over a decade and have almost perfected my contract relationships over the years. I started with more of a 24/7 lifestyle dynamic, but my aversion to intimacy quickly became an issue for many of my submissives. With each contract, I learned more and more about what did and didn't work. My already low tolerance for intimacy took a significant hit when Father passed away five years ago, leaving me to run his empire, and it has trickled down to the bare minimum of what a healthy Dom/sub relationship can even be.

As it stands, I meet with my submissive two to three times per week at a designated location, usually a hotel or club. I hardly ever bring anyone to my residence, and I've never had someone *here.* I've been in a contract with Lori for almost a year, but for the life of me, I can't picture her face. The only face I can see is the one in the picture I'm holding. *My wife.*

Looking around the study, I think for a second that marriage might not be such a horrible thing after all. I can have the estate prepared for Katarina. My heart races at the idea of sharing a bed with her. She will be my wife, after all. Preferring to stay in my own room, I never officially moved into the owner's suite, so I can easily have it readied for her.

I suppose as of four thirty this evening, I'm effectively engaged. I need to cancel my appointment with Lori tomorrow and have Linda arrange to terminate the remainder of our contract.

Of course, we'll have our legal team working on this every free moment they have, but for now, it is what it is. If Danny's initial reaction to the contract is anything to go by, my bachelor days are coming to an end.

Chapter Four

1 year later

"Good morning, Mr. Halpern!" I greet my current events tutor as I enter the breakfast room.

He looks up from his paper with a grin on his face. "Good morning to you as well, Kat! You're in rather good spirits today."

"I must have woken up at the right time in my sleep cycle," I say, reaching for my own paper, folded crisply in half and laid out beside my place setting,

The reason for my particularly good spirits today is a salacious dream I had last night about the man I'll be marrying soon, but Mr. Halpern certainly doesn't need to know that.

"Very well, shall we go over the goings-on in the world as of late so we can both get on with our day?" Halpern asks.

"Of course."

"If you turn to page five, you'll see that the Braves lost their lead pitcher." Halpern frowns before continuing. "I know this doesn't necessarily pertain to you, but I'm somewhat of a fan of the sport and that's the team I've attached myself to since arriving in America."

"Would you like to know a fun fact about the Braves?" I ask, waiting for his confirmation before continuing. "They used to be the only baseball team you could watch on national TV because the owner of some major channels owned the Braves as well!"

Halpern fixes me with a quizzical look. "*Why* on *earth* do you know that, Katarina?"

"I know a lot of things, Mr. Halpern," I say smugly as I unfold my paper. We discuss international politics, pure drudgery, but I'll admit, it's much easier to converse with a wide range of people if you know a little about most of the hot news stories of the day.

"Anything else worth discussing this morning before we start the day?"

"If you turn to page seven, you'll see the recent deaths. It seems the owner of a property neighboring your future husband's estate passed away in his sleep last night. David Crowley. He was seventy-eight and not in the best of health, but I think it was still somewhat of a shock to his family."

"How sad. I wonder if his family was close to the Sinclairs?"

He takes one last bite of his breakfast before standing to leave. "I'm not sure. The properties are both quite large, so it's possible they didn't have much to do with each other. In any case, that's all I have for the day. Unless you've got any other hot topics, I'll see you tomorrow morning."

We say our goodbyes, and I'm left alone to eat my breakfast in peace, reading through the rest of today's paper and then finishing the daily crossword in just under ten minutes.

Like every morning, I stand from my seat just as the clock strikes eight and make my way toward the library.

I've almost sat down in my chair before I remember that since turning nineteen earlier this week, the classes I've taken every day for as long as I can remember are no more.

They've been replaced with wedding planning, dress fittings, *wife training,* and more mundane tasks. A glance at my watch confirms that I have another two hours until my appointment to choose more *linens for my trousseau.* If I didn't know how much my family stands to gain from my marriage to Henry Sinclair, I would suspect that my father's estate manager, Mrs. Nixon, was trying to bore me to death with all this incessant planning.

Usually at this time, I'd be knee-deep in small talk practice with one of my foreign language tutors, but with my new schedule, I have more free time. I barely have a moment of peace, though, before I'm regaled by the awful singing of my cousin Sasha, announcing his presence.

"My darlinggggg Katarina, she forsakes me for another...leaving me aloooooone, her poor, sad brotherrrr..."

"You sound like an out-of-tune piano that was set on fire and thrown from a cliff." I laugh, standing to receive his signature bear hug.

He's my uncle Ivan's son, though we've always acted more like siblings than cousins. Sasha was technically allowed to leave our estate, but he rarely did while we were children. He's said it's because he had everything he needed here, and he didn't want to "associate with the plebs," but I know it was at least partially out of guilt.

We grew up as thick as thieves, getting into trouble during lessons and sneaking around the house at night looking for mischief. I consider him my brother, the one person who will always have my back and want what's best for me. My smile fades as I think about how soon I'll be leaving him behind.

Sasha follows my gaze to a trio of framed photographs on the wall, of my father and his two siblings. My father is in the middle between Sasha's dad and a rare picture of their sister, Natalya. The woman whose place I'll be taking in this marriage contract.

"Did you ever meet our aunt? I don't think we've ever talked about her."

Sasha shakes his head, silent for a beat before finally breaking our silence. "I never met her. Grandfather banished her before you or I were born when he found out she was knocked up with some random man's child."

"Oh! I had no idea. Nobody ever talks about her. It's kind of weird, actually."

"I'm pretty sure everyone was banned from mentioning her name. I only know a little about her from my dad, but he was a bit closer to her than Pavel was, so it was harder for him to ignore her existence. In fact, I think they had a brief falling out over it."

I walk over to the photo to get a closer look at the young girl. "That's so sad. I can't believe her own father did that."

"Well, from the little Dad mentioned, she seemed to be somewhat of a problem child. Not that Grandfather was justified in his actions by any means."

Would my own father do that to me? I've never rebelled against him in any capacity, so the consequences of doing such have never crossed my mind. Suddenly, my gilded cage feels much smaller, and my upcoming wedding feels a lot more like a new set of shackles than it did before.

"Ah, KitKat, don't be sad. Before long, that giant of a husband will be dicking you down so hard you won't even be able to see straight, let alone frown!" He laughs as I pinch his side, following him to our favorite alcove in the back of the library.

"Must you be so crass? And must you also remind me of my wifely duties? I promise you, Mrs. Nixon has that lesson plan well in hand."

Flopping onto the plush sofa, I feel him sit beside me and reach for the tie around my wrist. As a child, Sasha was always the only person with gentle enough hands to braid my hair without causing me to scream like a banshee, and he's still the best at it now. Today, it serves as one more reminder of the simple life I'll soon be leaving behind forever.

After a few silent moments, as Sasha starts the braid, he changes his tone to ask me a more somber question.

"Is it really bad? The lessons with Mrs. Nixon and all of the wedding planning, I mean. I know the big wedding isn't what you'd pick for yourself, and I really don't know how you're being so stoic about leaving everything after all this time..."

He ties off my braid and shifts so he can see my face. His eyes are taut with worry, and I feel a pang of guilt for causing him any stress.

Smiling, I ruffle his hair the way I know he hates.

"No, it's not bad. I'm just being dramatic about the amount of time I'm spending with Mrs. Nixon. You know how she is. Stand up straighter, smile more naturally, don't ever eat garlic at a dinner with men in attendance, blah, blah. My posture is perfect! She's impossible to please." I roll my eyes and huff as Sasha laughs.

"But really, Kat, what are your days like now? I used to know where to find you—morning lessons in the library, walk after lunch, afternoon classes in the solarium, jujitsu or fencing in the evening before dinner. It's been the same for like ten years, at least. And now you're all over the place in meetings and fittings. I'm just worried about you adjusting. That's all," he says with a soft smile.

Despite being an absolute pain sometimes, my cousin has always had my best interests at heart. I can't help but tease him, though.

"All I'm worried about adjusting to is Henry's big. Ole. Dick!" I exclaim, dissolving into a fit of giggles as Sasha gags. "You're the one who brought it up in the first place, and you *know* how tall he is. It's got to be at least *somewhat* proportional!"

"I yield, I yield!" He's covering his eyes now as I cackle, satisfied that I've paid him back for teasing me in the first place.

"To actually answer your question, mornings are a little freer than in the past. Instead of lessons, I have time to relax and read unless there's a meeting scheduled, like tomorrow. I still walk after lunch. You should really join me more, by the way. It's so good for your digestion."

Sasha rolls his eyes at me, but I continue.

"Afternoons are packed with fittings and picking out details for every household item you can imagine. Did you know there are eleven categories of towels every woman is expected to have in her house? Eleven! Daytime, nighttime, pool, fancy pool...it's a nightmare, honestly. I'm still keeping up my fitness, though. That hasn't changed. I have to be able to kick your butt if the situation calls for it."

He's back to assessing me now, and I know there's nothing for it. Sasha cares about me, and he's going to worry. I think he's been a little bit concerned about my marriage since we found out about it on my sixteenth birthday.

"I just want you to be happy. This guy seems nice enough, but I hate you being a pawn in Pavel's stupid quest for greatness. I'm glad you're going to get out into the world a bit, at least."

Standing up to stretch, I reach a hand out to pull Sasha up off the couch.

"I. Will. Be. Fine. I promise. I'm excited. Nervous, of course, but who wouldn't be? And a little sad, too, to leave. I've been trapped here, technically, yes. But it's like a hundred acres and twenty thousand square feet. I don't think anyone would classify this as a prison. Besides, we found enough hidden rooms and forgotten gardens out in the grounds that it felt like we were miles away sometimes.

"I do feel happy to get to know Henry. I was always going to have an arranged marriage regardless, and all the info I've been given makes him seem like a good man. I think I'll be okay. Maybe I'll even luck out and fall in love. If not with him, then with his giant di—"

"Okay, okay! I'm so happy for you, and you've convinced me you're alright. I love you, and I'll see you later. Bye!"

Cackling, I watch Sasha scurry away from me as fast as possible.

Before I can go back to enjoying my quiet morning, I'm caught by Satan's mistress herself, Mrs. Nixon.

"Ah, Kat, there you are. I'm so glad I was able to find you. The shipment of your holiday linens has arrived for our review this evening, so I'm hoping to move up our intimacy lessons. I see you're free now. Come."

I breathe deeply, reminding myself that soon I'll be completely free of this harpy of an estate manager whom my father is obsessed with. I'm not sure where exactly he found her, but one day he showed up with her in tow, gave her a black American Express card, and allowed her to start managing almost every aspect of the house and grounds. Luckily, she mostly had more important things to do than micromanage me, and my schoolmaster had the final say over almost all of the hours in my day. But she infringed on my autonomy whenever she could, overhauling my wardrobe and renovating my suite of rooms to her taste.

Recently, though, her actions as a wedding planner have been enough to drive even the sanest person crazy. Minutiae of the wedding, my trousseau, my deportment...all have fallen in her line of fire, and I'm almost to the limit of what I'll have to endure. Luckily, I'll soon be free of her and this place, rescued by my knight in shining armor.

"Henry!"

I'm interrupted from my thoughts as Mrs. Nixon leans primly against her desk in her office, having led me across the house like an animal to slaughter.

"Henry should be the only thing you're thinking about these days, so I'm glad his name is what snapped you out of your daydreaming. Now. As I told you earlier this week, today's lesson is all about the body, and dressing it seductively to please your husband. It's important to remember it is *your job* to maintain yourself to his liking. We've already gone over how to subtly ensure your hair and makeup are his preferences, and the physical form is no less important!"

She slowly stands to circle me, eyeing my casual outfit of choice today, a pale blue and white knit skirt set that's comfy for moving about the house without getting cold.

"You're already at a disadvantage. First, no man wants a virgin. Imagine if you hadn't had me to tell you all about sex, how annoying that would be for a man to have to teach you. It'll still be trying for your husband to have to show you how to please him, but I've done what I can. Second, men prefer softer, feminine physiques, and this muscle tone in your shoulders is unseemly. Must you continue your karate?"

"It's jujitsu, and yes, it's important to me."

Rolling her eyes, Mrs. Nixon stops in front of me. "And you're going to have to get used to wearing platform heels. I can't imagine any man wanting to develop neck pain from bending over every time he wants a kiss. You're a mismatch for Mr. Sinclair in that way, certainly.

"Now, about this soft, casual aesthetic you seem to gravitate toward. I think red latex is the way to go, and we can—"

She's interrupted by her phone ringing, and when she realizes it's not going to be a quick conversation, I'm dismissed with a wave of her hand.

Saved by the bell, I practically run from her office, hoping to avoid any more sex talk for the day.

Chapter Five

After my usual morning routine with Mr. Halpern, I used my free time this morning to release some nerves on the fencing piste. My father summoned me to his office a few days ago and instructed me to be in his office at ten o'clock sharp this morning. Usually, he's hands-off when it comes to my management and maintenance, although lately, with wedding preparations, I've certainly been seeing more of him.

My relationship with my father has always been formal, and coupled with the fact that he spent most of the past nineteen years in Russia doing business, we've never been very close. He's always provided well for me and ensured I had lovely people around, so I have nothing to complain about. I do wish he would tell me more about my mother, other than the fact that she died, but Sasha says it's not uncommon for men of that generation to be emotionally stunted. They're just too busy trying to make money to do something as silly as cry. *Or connect with their daughter.*

I'm sure he won't be happy to see me in my current state, rushing from the piste to his office. My practice this morning exploded into a round-robin tournament, including more than a few of the staff who are proficient, so I'm a sweaty mess. I'm still carrying my saber, and my braid is coming loose. Finally, I arrive in the anteroom to his office, stopping with a couple of minutes to spare to catch my breath. Debating if I have enough time to redo my braid, I'm immediately distracted by two men playing chess while they wait as well.

Along with crosswords and puzzles in general, playing chess was encouraged throughout my childhood. Father considered it a more intellectual alternative to childish games, and I've gotten quite good over the years.

As I approach the men to see the board more easily, I see that the man facing away from me is tall, in a very nice suit, and has his pieces in an excellent position. He's followed a relatively standard set of moves thus far, leading his opponent into a tidy trap. The man facing me clearly doesn't play often if he's managed to get himself into this pickle. Or, perhaps, he's subtly throwing the match to ingratiate himself with Tall Man. Still, Tall Man could have made a number of different moves to leave an even more complete trap for Short Man. As it is, he's left himself ever so slightly vulnerable.

Either way, as the grandfather clock begins to chime ten times, I can't help but take up the cause of the underdog. Strolling forward, I move one key piece on behalf of Short Man.

"Checkmate!" I exclaim brightly, before continuing into Father's office, feeling as if my act of charity has been done for the day. Just as I cross the threshold, I glance over my shoulder to give a kind wink to Tall Man, just in case he's brooding over his loss. I see a flash of gray eyes filled with curiosity, and realize I've just interrupted, and lost on his behalf, my betrothed's chess match.

"Katarina, the door!"

Father's voice shakes me out of my reverie, and I give Henry Sinclair a soft smile before turning to greet my father, still somewhat flushed, and not just from fencing.

"And so, as you can see, Mr. Sinclair, everything is on pace for a lovely wedding next month. The almanac is calling for a beautiful October," Father says smugly. Although I knew an October wedding was the plan, with all my rush fittings and *linen orders,* it's very clear that Henry Sinclair has been surprised by my father once again.

He's a stoic man thus far, but a little tic in his forehead above his left eye belies his consternation.

"While I find it admirable that you've been able to organize an event of this size with such alacrity, Mr. Taranov, I'm still unclear on what exactly the rush is." His forehead throb intensifies before disappearing entirely.

My father sips his vodka and continues to talk as if I'm not here. As if the wedding date wasn't the *one* decision I've gotten to make. When offered the choice of my birthday or a couple of weeks after, I chose the latter. I prefer as many days to be feted as possible per year, thank you very much.

"It's quite simple indeed. You stipulated, very clearly, that you wished for Katarina to be nineteen years of age when you wed. If you've forgotten, I believe that I have the manuscript of that meeting filed away somewhere. On her chosen wedding date, she will, in fact, be nineteen years and a couple of weeks, meeting your requirement with room to spare. At that point, there is surely no reason to wait. Unless you are reconsidering your position? We might have to invest in a multitude of mothballs to protect Katarina's trousseau, but I'm sure it'll be as good as new in eighteen years for your nephew's wedding."

Father pauses, looking me up and down, obviously not pleased with how I presented myself for today's meeting. "If you're concerned about her appearance, I can assure you, she's usually much more put together."

"No, of course, there's no reconsidering of my position. There is still construction ongoing at the estate, which I was very much hoping to have completed before the lady of the house arrived."

Henry directs his attention to me before continuing. "I think you look rather charming today, Ms. Taranova. I was pleasantly surprised to learn you were such an avid fencer when I *finally* received an up-to-date list of your favorite pastimes." He cuts his eyes briefly to my father before continuing. "It was one of my favorite activities when I lived in England, but I haven't sparred in years, so I admit I might be a little rusty."

"Yes, Henr...erm...Mr. Sinclair, I enjoy a vast variety of extracurricular activities," I say, giving my most practiced demure smile.

"Clearly," he says, hand fiddling with something in his pocket. "I'm afraid I didn't learn about your proclivities until recently, hence the last-minute renovations. Which brings me to this." He turns back to my father, holding up a rolled paper. "Perhaps if you'll review these plans, you can advise if you have any construction contacts who can..."

Anything else he's saying fades into the background as he and my father stand to look at blueprints laid out on the desk, apparently representing extensive renovations to his home. I'm not even able to ruminate on the fact that my fiancé doesn't seem *excited* to be marrying me in a month, because said fiancé has removed his suit jacket, revealing a trim waist accentuated by a perfectly tailored, crisp white shirt. His pants are unbelted because...*oh God. He's wearing suspenders.* Now that I'm fully committed to ogling him, I luxuriate in the details of the monster of a man who is Henry Sinclair. He's taller than any of his pictures suggest, and taller still than I estimated when he was sitting at the chessboard earlier. His physique is honed, a combination of weights and cardio from the looks of it, with broad shoulders and long arms trailing down to large hands and long fingers.

My mind is flooded with fantasies of what those hands could do to me. How those long fingers would trail down my body. How they could cup my breasts fully. He could probably wrap them both completely around my waist. He's just so *large*. *So* much bigger than me. And if everything *is* proportional? Well, I can't imagine his dick fitting inside my body. I'm not sure if sex could even *work* with our height difference, but God, do I want it to. Maybe he can bend me over and take me from behind. Or I could climb onto his lap and run my fingers through his wavy dark hair as I rode him.

"Wouldn't you say, Katarina?" My father's voice snaps me back to reality. I close my mouth, which had been hanging open, and slowly pull my gaze from where it had settled on Henry's ass.

Swallowing thickly, I ignore the small smirk I see forming on his sinful mouth and try to pull it together to answer the question I'm being asked.

"I'm so sorry, Father. What was the question?"

He huffs, but before he responds, Henry interjects. "We were discussing some changes to the formal gardens on the property. I'm building an elongated addition to accommodate a few fencing pistes, enough space to have small tournaments and whatnot, but we'll have to move a fountain and relocate a family of ducks who inhabit the area. I asked your father if two pistes rather than three would be sufficient for your needs, as that would allow us to keep the fountain in situ."

"And I said," Father grumbles, "it's impossible to properly host more than ten fencers with only two pistes available, and it really should be three."

Father turns to say something to the man Henry brought with him, his solicitor, apparently, but Henry only has eyes for me. I realize he's waiting on my answer, not my father's.

"Ducks," I whisper, dazed by the smell I'm now close enough to experience wafting off my fiancé. Vanilla, tobacco, mint. I think my mouth is actually watering.

Henry smiles fully, now, and I notice a dimple in his left cheek. "Ducks it is, Ms. Taranova."

"Kat," I say, clearing my throat. "Please, call me Kat."

At this, he leans down slightly, tilting his head away from the other men in the room.

"You'll only be Ms. Taranova for a very short while longer. Please, indulge me." He pulls back with a wink and rejoins the conversation around the desk. I sit heavily back into my seat and catalog everything I can about this man I'm going to marry.

Thick hair, large shoes, back muscles flexing under his dress shirt, cuff links gleaming, and giant hands. My dreams didn't do him justice at all. I've never been so simultaneously intimidated and turned on by someone in my life.

Trying to find fault in his physical specimen, I fail. He's been nothing but polite and respectful throughout the meeting, as well, always ignoring my father's opinions to ask for my preferences and advice. It's not until he's departed with a kiss on my knuckles and a promise to see me soon that I burst into laughter, realizing that he managed to slip me what he was toying with in his pocket. The chess piece I used to beat him earlier. Holding my new good luck charm, I smile, thinking that this marriage might not be so bad after all.

Chapter Six

"I don't know, KitKat. I think Island Sand is a better shade than Pale Beige. If I were you, I would re-order all these linens."

Fixing my soon-to-be-deceased cousin with a glare, I smack his arm. "The queen herself couldn't get me to change a single thing about any of this at this point. I might not have had a say in most of the wedding planning, but I firmly believe in Pale Beige superiority. Now. Are you going to stand there rifling through things and vexing me, or are you going to braid my hair for the rehearsal dinner?"

Sasha rolls his eyes at my exaggeration, but still comes to sit with me and work on my hair. Although I'm sure that Mrs. Nixon's chosen hair and makeup minions will have me looking like a Miss America contestant tomorrow, for the rehearsal, she surprisingly agreed to let me handle simple hair and makeup on my own.

I smile, thinking of picking out things that I like, rather than Mrs. Nixon. Her style tends to be monochromatic and bland, and she moved through our home when she arrived to rip out wallpaper and paint everything gray. Father agreed when I appealed to him that the library was off-limits to her re-designing scheme. My rooms, unfortunately, weren't, and my bedroom has looked like a modern art museum for years now.

"Excuse me? Earth to KitKat! Is this braid okay?" Sasha gives his finished work a teasing tug as he snaps me out of my reverie.

"Sorry. Yes, it's beautiful. Your best work ever, I think." My smile falls, thinking that this very well may be the last time he ever braids my hair.

I move to sit at my vanity, bypassing the velvet chair to instead sit cross-legged on the counter, and face the mirror to get started on my simple makeup for the evening.

"What were you thinking about, anyway? You were smiling at nothing the entire time I was braiding," Sasha asks, taking his usual spot on the counter next to me, feet dangling off the edge as he watches me work. We've assumed these positions countless times before as I got ready for the day, always required to be dressed and painted, even if I was never going anywhere.

"Wallpaper," I answer dryly, laughing at his confused look. "I really was thinking about wallpaper! Wallpaper in the context of...freedom of choice, I guess. You know I've never been one for thinking too much about what-if. I've lived here, done my lessons, read, frolicked in the gardens, and generally enjoyed my life. You're the reason I'm still sane, of course, but overall I've refused to wallow or complain."

Sasha rolls his eyes, ignoring my censorious stare. "Yes, yes, you've been the picture-perfect princess in her castle, resigned to your fate. They should write an opera about you. Do you think you're up for singing an aria?"

Booping his nose with liquid blush as revenge, I cackle as he tries to wipe it off, only to make things worse.

"If you'll stop teasing me, I'll help you fix that. Otherwise, you're destined to have a red nose all evening. That's a long-lasting blush stain." Hearing this, he gives me his solemn attention.

"As I was saying...happy here, caged princess, blah, blah. Yes. But. I was smiling, thinking about designing my own living space. Now that nobody is trying to kill me, I'll be able to get out and about undisguised. And..." I blush, realizing Sasha might not want to hear any more of the things I'm excited about.

His eyes brighten, though, and I should have known that he wouldn't let me off the hook.

"Anndddddd...?" he asks with a devilish grin.

"I'm excited to have sex! There, now you know. A woman has needs! I know for a fact you haven't been living the celibate life in solidarity with me. Even with all your tattoos, your neck always looks like a vampire has gotten ahold of you!"

Before he can defend himself, I move on, wanting to voice a tiny fear inside me that's been growing as the wedding date has approached.

"More than sex, though...I'm really hoping Mr. Sincl...Henry likes me. We have fencing and chess in common, I know, and I think from hearing him speak to Father that he'll be kind and respectful to me. It's probably foolish. But it would be wonderful for us to care for each other. I'd quite like to be cared for—"

Sniffling, he tries to interrupt again, but I soldier on. "Not that I'm saying you don't care for me! I know you do! But you know, hopefully, you'll have your own person soon, and I can't be your number one girl forever. I guess, it might be foolish to hope that he's all he seems to be: smart, kind, interesting. I hope he's not too good to be true."

Finally, I take a deep breath and dab the corners of my eyes before moving to start on my eyeliner. Sasha, seemingly convinced that I've finally finished my word vomit, surprises me with a quiet tone, not to defend his liaisons or tease me for being a horny nineteen-year-old virgin, but to address my fears that my Prince Charming might be a frog in disguise.

"He's not," Sasha says softly, meeting my gaze in the mirror and distracting me from my eyeliner. "I didn't necessarily know when or if to mention this, and he kind of asked me not to, but I don't see the harm in it. My loyalty is to you and not him."

I fully turn to face him, makeup completely abandoned.

"Mr. Sinclair...uh, Henry, I guess...approached me after your father withheld the information he requested. You know, several months ago, he asked for more information on you than what was sent in the dossier. Less of your accomplishments, and more of your interests, desires, things that make you...well, KitKat."

Closing my mouth from where it was gaping like a fish, I feel a dark corner of my heart, filled with cobwebs from disuse, lighten up, just a bit.

"So you..."

Blowing out a heavy breath, Sasha clearly decides word vomit of his own is in order.

"So I sent him information, yes, and I would be sorry if I didn't think it was the absolute right thing to do. He came to me and just wanted to know more about you. I didn't tell him too much, honestly, because you're a treat that's best experienced live and in person, and you deserve to surprise him yourself.

"I also got to know him a bit, and I'm impressed. He's got his quirks, and he can be intense. I don't know how else to put it, and that's coming from me having grown up around our family." He joins me, laughing at this, and reaches out to hold my hand.

"I think you'll be happy with him. He'll be good to you. Plus, you can finally have someone to beat at chess all the time instead of having to lose to me!"

Having successfully lightened the mood after making me feel better, he runs away before I can smack him. "Alexsandr Ivanovich Taranov, you have *never once* beaten me at chess!"

Feeling more excitement than dread now for the evening, I finish the last bit of my makeup and give myself a final once-over in the mirror. My braid looks elegant and youthful without being girlish, and my face is enhanced but not overpowered by my makeup. If Sasha thinks Henry and I will be good together, well then...maybe I shouldn't be so nervous for tonight after all.

"Come…on…ugh!" I let out a silent, frustrated scream as the window in the staff bathroom refuses to budge.

I've never been bothered by crowds. Attending parties held by my family, wearing a disguise, has ensured my ability to mingle and make small talk in groups of hundreds of people. But tonight, well…

The evening started out well enough, with my rehearsal dress fitting like a glove and complementing my hair and makeup perfectly. I chose this dress myself, and it's different from the glittering, puffy concoction that I'll be walking down the aisle in tomorrow. My satin, corseted dress hits mid calf and has a slit up one thigh. Spaghetti straps show off my sculpted shoulders and back, and my simple white platform heels give me a little more height while meeting a million people. *Maybe Mrs. Nixon was right about the heels.*

I didn't start to feel like the world was closing in on me until Henry had introduced me to his family, then stepped away to say hello to another group. My father chose that moment to swoop in and make sure I knew how important tonight was.

Pulling me to the side with a rough grip on my upper arm, I can smell the alcohol on his breath.

"Katarina, you will *make a good impression on this family. Do you understand? I don't want to hear any of your quirky anecdotes tonight. Apply what you've learned in your lessons with Mrs. Nixon and act like the perfect wife you are going. To. Be. This is a huge sacrifice for Mr. Sinclair, and so help me, you are going to be worth it."*

Finally getting the window open, I assess the scene to make sure nobody is around to witness whatever madness I've succumbed to. Even though this is the darkest side of the house and well away from the ruckus of tonight's event, I'm mindful of any random passersby. With all the stealth I can muster, I silently climb down the trellis, careful not to tear my dress. As both feet land safely on the ground, I release the breath I had been holding and head toward the back. I'm about to turn the corner when the deep timbre of a man's voice startles me.

"I wouldn't go that way. There's an insufferable woman in red latex groping your father."

Tobacco smoke wafts toward me, the unique blend an aroma I recognize immediately. I turn slowly, knowing exactly who I'm about to face.

I open my mouth to say *anything*, but the sight of my fiancé propped against the wall, bow tie undone, with one hand in his pocket and the other holding a pipe to his lips, leaves me frozen in place.

"I don't have a runaway bride on my hands, do I?" he asks, his voice as smooth as velvet.

When I remain speechless, he blows a ring of smoke in the opposite direction of where I'm standing before pushing off the wall to bridge the gap between us. It's not until he's draping his suit jacket around my shoulders that I realize the chill in the air.

"If you're going to make a run for it, you'd better take this, or I'm afraid you won't make it far at all." His fingers brush the bare skin of my neck as he carefully pulls my hair out from where it was trapped beneath the new layer of clothing, sending sparks straight to my core.

Was I running away? I hopped out of that window with no plan at all.

Realizing my pulse is out of control, I steady my breath before finally willing myself to speak. "No...no, it's not that. I just needed a breath of fresh air, that's all."

"Likewise," he says, raising his pipe for emphasis.

We turn to face the woodland area to the west of the estate, allowing another moment of silence to pass before he places one of the hands I've thought so much about lately on my upper back and guides me to a nearby fountain. He motions toward the rim and waits for me to take my seat before sitting beside me.

"Tell me what's upset you tonight, Ms. Taranova."

I'm about to make up another lie, anything to hide my distress, just like my lessons have taught me. But his pinky ever so gently brushes against mine, where they had been sitting almost flush together on the concrete rim, and I'm reminded that this man will be my husband.

I look down at our almost intertwined hands, avoiding his gaze as I make my confession. "You're making this huge sacrifice, and there was...extra pressure put on me to make a good impression tonight. Because *I don't need to be a burden to you.*"

"A sacrifice? You think that I'm making some sort of sacrifice by marrying an intelligent, articulate, *beautiful* young woman?"

Fighting a blush, I admit to an insecurity I've had since he first put off our wedding. "Well, I know you hate how young I am, and I..."

"I do not *hate* how young you are," he says, causing me to jump slightly. He must realize how harsh that came off. Before I know what's happening, both of my hands are cocooned in his as he continues with a much softer tone. "I was hesitant at first because a nineteen-year-old has so much life to live. A life I've lived twice over. A life I couldn't justify taking from you. It's you I didn't want to burden, not the other way around."

He pauses momentarily, lacing one of his hands in mine. "Do you want this?"

Looking up to where the stars peep through the canopy of tree tops, I really think about that. Do I want this? I suppose there are worse things than being forced to marry a kind, intelligent, sexy man like Henry. But I haven't had a day of freedom to figure out what I would want.

"I don't really have a choice." I chuckle. "I'm pretty sure my family would disown me if I didn't."

"You always have a choice."

When the only response I give is a barely audible "hmm," he squeezes the hand he's holding. "Look at me."

I turn my attention from the stars to the man beside me. Once again, I'm in awe of Henry Sinclair, and our proximity makes it hard to breathe.

"I would be honored for you to take my last name, but if you don't want to go through with this, I'll respect that as well. I don't know what expectations have been set on you by your family, but I assure you I will take care of you either way."

"That's...that's very kind of you. But I'm not going to run."

"Happy to hear it. And just so we're clear, I have no expectations of you...romantically. I understand this isn't a traditional marriage, so I wouldn't begrudge you for finding companionship elsewhere."

"Oh? Oh. I see..." I say, realization hitting me like a brick wall. "And is that your plan?"

Henry gently caresses my cheek, his hand enveloping my face completely as he stares into my eyes. "No. There will be no other women."

I'm not sure if it's his hand pulling me to him or my own will, but I feel myself helplessly drawn toward him, my eyes fluttering closed as he fixates on my lips.

"Katarina?"

At the call of my name, Henry pulls back and stands gracefully, enjoying one last long inhale of his pipe before putting it out and pocketing it in his jacket.

"Shall we, Katarina?" he says, pulling me up with him before offering his arm.

I smile, linking my arm through his. "Please, just call me Kat. And you know you really shouldn't smoke. It's horrible for you. I made my cousin quit years ago."

"I'll keep that in mind, *Katarina*," he says, the low timbre of his voice sending shivers down my spine. *How is it that this man can take something as simple as my name and make it sexual?* As we walk arm in arm back to the party, I'm fully looking forward to my wedding for the first time.

Chapter Seven

The last of Katarina's things are set in the foyer as the moving team diligently places boxes in the appropriate rooms. It's been just over a week since our wedding. I felt terrible about leaving my new bride immediately after our nuptials, but she understood that I could only move so many meetings on the short notice I was given. She opted to stay at her family's compound until I was able to join her at our estate, so this will be her first night in her new home. I want to make sure she's comfortable before leaving yet again.

I'm about to go in search of my new wife when I notice a half-open box with items from our wedding spilling out. Lying on top of the pile of assorted s is a photo album, surprisingly already filled with photographs from the day.

I flip through the book, each picture a memory frozen in time, bringing me back to the day of our union.

Katarina walks down the aisle gracefully in a pure white dress that probably weighs as much as she does. With every step toward me, her beauty becomes more evident. I'm completely under her spell when she puts her tiny hand in mine and lets me lead her to the altar.

"I do," she says, and I slide the platinum band on her trembling finger. The minister continues to talk, but all I hear is the voice in my head that keeps repeating mine.

"You may kiss the bride." I haven't kissed a woman in over a decade. I hate it. My wife looks up at me, and for a moment, I think she's afraid to kiss me, too. Until she bites her lower lip. I cup her chin in my hand and use my thumb to pull it from her teeth. I use my other arm to reach around her slim waist and pull her to me as I bend down to meet her. Our lips touch tenderly, and she tastes fucking incredible. I want more. Her mouth opens to let my tongue in when cheers erupt, reminding me of our audience. I break our kiss and step back, putting some space between us as my heart races.

"You look stunning, Mrs. Sinclair," I say, as we begin our first dance, reveling in the blush that reddens her cheeks. There hasn't been time for many words between the two of us with all the fuss of the ceremony. I thought I would dread this as much as I hate being the center of attention, but I've found myself looking forward to this dance for the chance to touch her again. As I hold her close, an instinct takes over me. To protect, to provide, to...love?

All in all, the day went much better than I ever expected. It was a huge to-do, but something about Katarina's presence grounded me. We seem compatible enough, and there's no denying my attraction to her. It gives me a spark of hope that our marriage could one day grow into one of happiness.

Closing the album, I decide to bring the box into my own room before leaving for the day. I've just stored the box deep in the back of my closet when I hear Katarina's call from her suite on the opposite side of the second floor. Following her voice, I find her in her bedroom.

"Did you need something?" I ask, leaning against the doorway, taking in the sight of the chaos.

Her once spotless room is in disarray, with stacks of boxes scattered across the floor. Some are still closed, while others have clearly been rummaged through. My wife stands among them, looking confused. I can't help but notice she's wearing a very thin, very revealing cotton lounge set.

"None of your clothes are in the closet," she says, gesturing toward the spacious walk-in.

"Of course not. Why would my clothes be in your closet?" I ask, my brows creased in confusion.

"*My* closet?" I follow her gaze around the room, the gears in her brain clicking as she notes the feminine decor. "Oh. I assumed we would be sharing a room. Especially since this appears to be the primary suite of the estate."

If I had thought for a minute she would be even *slightly* comfortable sharing a room with me, I'm not sure I would've had the restraint to give her one of her own. Particularly knowing she would be traipsing around here wearing next to nothing.

"I'm practically a stranger to you, so of course, I wouldn't expect you to share a bed. I learned long ago that I sleep better alone anyway. My room is down the hall, on the opposite end of the second floor. But you assumed correctly. This is technically the owner's suite. I hope you like it. I thought about waiting for you to make the design decisions yourself, but I wanted you to be somewhat comfortable upon arriving. I was able to speak with your cousin for inspiration, but please feel free to change anything you want."

I think I see a moment of sadness flit across her face, and the idea to welcome her into my bed strikes me like lightning, but she's back to herself before I can act on my intrusive thoughts. "No, it's perfect, thank you. I'll be taking a break soon, from this," she says, motioning to the mounds of clothes piled on the bed. The way her breasts bounce as she moves makes it almost impossible to think straight. "I was wondering if you would like to take a walk or give me a tour of the estate?" I would love to show her around. If I'm being honest, I would prefer to lock us both in this room, consummating our marriage for the foreseeable future. A glance down at my watch confirms I won't be doing either. Instead, I'll be leaving shortly to hop on the jet for a quick afternoon in New York to meet with an investment board. "I'm afraid I have to leave soon, but I'm sure Mrs. Potts would be thrilled to show you around."

"Excuse me?" The unexpected sass in her voice grabs my attention from the rundown of my day going through my mind.

Looking up, I see that I've upset her in some way. I go back through what I might have said to cause her sudden change in attitude. "I assure you, Potts knows more about this place than I do. She would be a much better guide..."

"No, not that. You're leaving? *Again?* I thought the whole point of my waiting to move in was so that you would be home and that we would be here together."

I release a sigh, becoming irritated as well. "I don't have any overnight obligations for the foreseeable future, but I had to rearrange a number of things to accommodate our wedding."

"And what am I supposed to do while you're gone *every* day?" she asks, tossing down the garments she was holding dramatically before crossing her arms. The motion accentuates her cleavage, and I have to will my attention to remain on her beautiful face.

"I don't know, whatever you want!" I pause, lifting a hand in the direction of the backyard. "The pool's heated, or you can use the indoor pool. Construction on the fencing pistes is finished. There's a library, a theater. I assure you, I've added any creature comforts you left behind in your old home."

"I didn't realize I was leaving one gilded cage just to be trapped in another."

"For Christ's sake, you aren't trapped here," I say, rubbing my temples in an attempt to prevent the headache I fear will be in full force any minute now. "You have a driver, you've been added to all my accounts, go! Go shopping, get a massage, get some brunch."

"With *who?* You're the only person I even slightly know, Henry."

I look down at the petite woman fuming in front of me. If this weren't such a tedious conversation, her anger would almost be adorable. "Katarina, I'm a very busy man. As much as I would love to putz around with you all day, I have an empire to run."

"I didn't expect you to negate your responsibilities, *Mr. Sinclair.* I just wanted to get to know my husband. I was under the impression that you might share my interest in getting to know each other, but clearly, I miscalculated your intentions. My apologies, *sir.*"

This is one of the reasons I've never committed myself to a relationship, much less marriage. My fluid schedule remains packed, so I enjoy having full autonomy over any remaining free time. Allowing someone in means giving up control of my perfectly sculpted routine.

A glance at the platinum band around my ring finger reminds me that I do, in fact, have a partner. She should be my first and foremost priority as far as responsibilities are concerned. And whether it be pure obligation, or perhaps a desire of my own to spend more time together, I won't allow my vibrant wife to grow bitter and lonely because I can't find time for her.

At some point in this disagreement, we've managed to close the space between us. Now within my reach, I gently place a hand on her shoulder in hopes of calming the tension around us. "I'm sorry, darling, I know my absence isn't ideal. My next week or so is packed, but after that, I should be around more often. We can at least start with having dinner together when things calm down."

She places her hand atop mine and smiles sweetly, accepting my olive branch. Any annoyance in her eyes dissipates as she gazes up at me. "I would love that. Thank you."

My free arm wraps around her back, and I begin pulling her toward me when the shrill sound of Linda's voice pierces the air. "Henry? There you are! I couldn't find you anywhere! Mrs. Potts said you were in your room, but when I checked, you weren't there. Obviously. What are you...oh! You must be Ms. Taranova. I'm Linda, Henry's *work wife*."

I feel Katarina tense, but she holds her hand out to greet Linda nonetheless. She opens her mouth to introduce herself, but I interject, beating her to the punch. "Linda, this is *Mrs.* Katarina *Sinclair*. And the only woman to claim the title of my wife. In any capacity."

We've shifted so that I'm standing behind Katarina, my hands resting on her shoulder. Her body relaxes beneath my hold as she beams up at me, and I give her a wink before Linda responds.

"Oh, you know I was only kidding. It's so nice to finally meet you, *Katarina,*" she says before turning to me. "Are you ready to go?"

"I'll meet you in the car in a minute," I manage to growl out, annoyed at her sudden aggression toward my wife. She certainly has her faults, but professionalism has never been one of them.

As my assistant skips away, heels clicking as she makes her way down the hardwood stairs, I realize I've had a death grip on Katarina's shoulders. She turns to face me as soon as I release her. "You really have to go?"

"I do. I'll be back tonight, but it'll be late." Hurt flashes across her eyes, causing an unfamiliar pit in my stomach. Placing my finger and thumb lightly on her chin, I tilt her head to look at me. "Let me get through this next week, and I promise to keep my schedule as light as possible for a while."

She nods in agreement, but I can tell she's still upset. Taking her hand in mine, I kiss her knuckles softly. "I'll see you soon, Mrs. Sinclair."

Her pretty smile makes its appearance once again. "Goodbye, Henry."

Walking away from Katarina, I'm hit with dread for the packed week ahead of me. I've never minded the rigorous schedule and extensive travel included in running the Sinclair empire. Still, I'm suddenly craving a simpler existence—one where I'm home every day at a reasonable time to have dinner with my beautiful wife. And perhaps when I must travel, I can just bring her with me. I'm sure she would enjoy seeing the world after being confined to the Taranov compound all her life.

As I make my way to the car that will be taking us to the private airport, I see Linda propped against the back door with her arms crossed and a scowl on her face.

"It's about time," she says, as we both get into opposite sides of the back seat. Like a switch, her attitude is gone, and there's a plastered smile on her face. "Katarina sure is a pretty little thing, isn't she? I was a little confused why you would so easily agree to marry such a young girl, but now I understand why you had such minimal objection to this contract. It's probably a good thing that you have separate rooms. I mean, people are already going to talk, considering you're twice her age. Just be careful, you don't want anyone to think you're grooming her."

"That's enough," I growl, interrupting her rambling as I fasten my seat belt.

She breathes out a quiet "sorry," and I sigh, realizing how harsh my tone was.

"Linda, you've handled the contracts for every submissive relationship I've had since you've been my assistant. When have you ever known me to be concerned with what others thought of my proclivities?"

"Just be careful, Henry. This is different," she says, turning to look out her window.

Humming my agreement, I look out my own window at the estate growing smaller as we drive away.

Katerina is different, indeed.

Chapter Eight

Drip. Drip. Drip.

Placing the book I'm attempting to read down on the chaise lounge, I rise to find the source of the incessant dripping I've been trying to ignore for the past half hour.

Usually, I'm not bothered by noise. Living in a house full of staff, meetings, and then Mrs. Nixon's renovation regime, I've learned to tune out background sounds fairly well. Until today. Today, I've picked a new corner of the library to try out, and at first glance, it seemed perfect. South-facing windows, cozy furniture, a little hidden alcove with a lamp and a shelf at the perfect height for a mug of coffee. Heaven. Until the dripping started.

And unlike my usual tolerance, I find myself unsettled. Bothered. Really, really *angry* at the dripping. I know exactly what's vexing me, unfortunately.

My *husband.*

Or rather, my distinct lack of a husband since he's been gone for the past week with meetings. I know they're important, and he couldn't move them on such short notice, but still. I've tried all the things he advised. His credit card took a tiny hit because I got a head start on Christmas presents for his family, but I have more stuff than I could ever need.

I've kept to my usual routine, enjoying the lap pool in the morning and the home gym in the evening. I've walked over twenty-five miles around the grounds, meeting more of the staff and exploring the beautiful property. It's filled with follies, nooks, and crannies from past generations adding onto it, and diverse plant life thanks to the creek that runs through part of the land.

My rooms are organized, I've explored a good chunk of the house on top of my hikes around the grounds, and...I'm bored. I'm not sure what I expected married life to be, but it wasn't this. I *know* Henry has to travel a lot for work, but I thought we had a spark during our last few interactions. Maybe that was my foolish positivity, seeing things that weren't there.

Before I can figure out what to do about my absentee husband or my life in general, I have to figure out this blasted dripping. This is the perfect library corner, and I'm not going to let it go that easily. Starting from one corner of the wall closest to where I'm sitting, I follow the sound down and around the perimeter of my alcove, finding no evidence of a leak.

As I stare, flummoxed, at the wall, I realize that the little ledge where I've been placing my coffee isn't actually flush with the molding. Sighing, I add this to my list of maintenance concerns before giving up on my moment of peace and making my way back to the kitchen to drop off my dirty mug.

"Ah, Mrs. Sinclair! I thought I missed you this morning." Mrs. Potts grins as I walk into the kitchen, almost instantly soothing my earlier irritation.

Although everyone here has been kind, Mrs. Potts was the first of the household staff to *really* make me feel welcome. There's something warm about her that makes me feel comfortable and safe. In fact, I've spent much of my time the past week curled up on a sofa in the sitting room, listening to her stories.

I've learned so much from her already, from the history of the estate to the neighborhood drama.

According to her, the Sinclair family bought this land in the late 1800s when Henry's great-great-grandfather arrived from England. However, the Châteauesque-style estate wasn't built until 1947 by his grandfather, Henry Sinclair I, after the end of the war.

Their land covers a couple *thousand* acres, so neighbors is a relative term, but apparently, there is the occasional drama.

There's the Crowley family, whose patriarch recently passed away. Apparently, the children are trying to sell that land and liquidate some assets. The Gibbonses' farm borders on the northern side, and they've been complaining about all the pine cones that fall onto their property from our trees for years.

Henry's sister, Margot, and brother-in-law, Jack, own property nearby. There isn't any current drama there, but Mrs. Potts did spill some rather salacious tea about their relationship before they got married. Apparently, Jack walked quite a thin line of what would be considered consent as a masked suitor of Margot's. My jaw dropped from the beginning of that story to the end.

To the south, the Jenkinses' goats get loose from time to time and wander onto our land, although it's never been an issue because they clear the underbrush. Recently, however, some were found dead a little farther west than they usually roam, resulting in a distraught Mrs. Jenkins.

We've also gossiped like a pair of hens about the rest of the staff. Everything from simple stories, such as a driver's aunt having gallbladder surgery, to scandalous ones, like the head landscaper sleeping with both a maid *and* the pool boy.

We've talked for hours over hot tea and pastries. As much as I miss the friendships I developed with the staff growing up, I never had a source of maternal affection, and I'm finding that Mrs. Potts fills that void in addition to being a friend.

Like always, I've barely stepped into the kitchen before she's offering me something to eat. "I tried a new recipe for the sauce last night. Try this and let me know what you think."

She places a plate of cheesecake in front of one of the barstools in the kitchen and tops it with a drizzle of homemade caramel sauce. Stomach already growling, I sit and immediately reach for my fork to dig into the decadent dessert. My eyes roll back the moment the creamy bite hits my tongue. "Oh God, Potts, this is *incredible.* Forget the sauce, the cheesecake is good enough to stand on its own."

She smiles as she hops up on her seat beside me with her own plate. "Yes, this is my all-time favorite recipe. I call it better than sex with Daddy cheesecake."

"Excuse me?" I manage to cough out after almost choking on another bite.

Potts laughs, tears forming in her eyes. "It's an old joke with a girlfriend of mine, from back in my college days."

"Well, I've never had sex, but if it's anywhere close to this cheesecake, I don't think I'll ever leave the room."

Chuckling, I glance up to see she's staring at me, eyes wide, hand over her chest, clearly not as amused at my statement as I was. "You've never...you're a *virgin?*"

I can't help the sarcasm that laces my tone. "I know, right? How peculiar is it that a girl locked away her entire life, born and raised for the sole purpose of a contract marriage, didn't have sexual partners coming out of the woodwork?"

Potts rolls her eyes. "I know that, dear. I just assumed you and Hen...you and Mr. Sinclair...well, you've been married for a couple of weeks now and..."

"And what? And you assumed we were making sweet, sweet love every night? You know as well as I do that we sleep in separate rooms. Not that he's been home long enough to say hello, much less have sex."

"Hmm..." she says, thinking hard about something as she chews and swallows a bite. "Do you want to? Have sex, I mean? With Mr. Sinclair?"

"Do I want to have sex with Henry? My six-foot-six-inch Greek god of a husband? Yes. I think I would like that very much." I give a half smile and elbow her, trying to lighten the mood. "Especially if it's half as good as this cheesecake."

My joke hits its mark, both of us cackling like hyenas as we finish our desserts. As soon as our plates are clean, she puts them in the sink, then props herself on her elbows, leaning on the island directly across from where I'm still sitting. "So, do you have a plan of action to accomplish your mission?"

When all I give her is a raised brow, she continues. "To seduce Mr. Sinclair into your bed?"

I mirror her position, resting my elbows on the counter for support. "I'm not sure he sees me as much more than a girl taking up space in his home, to be honest."

Potts smirks, and I can already tell she's up to no good in that head of hers. "I don't think that's true at all, but I happen to have known Mr. Sinclair most of his life. Maybe I can help you understand him a bit more, dear."

Suddenly, I realize that out of all the things we've chatted about over the past week, Henry has never been a topic of conversation.

"You certainly know much more about him than I do. What was he like as a child?" I ask, hoping that she'll be as helpful with Henry 101 as she has been with learning about the estate.

Laughing, she grabs a chilled carafe of juice and moves toward the solarium. "Come on, dear. This is a conversation for which we need to be more comfortable."

Three hours later, we've had a light lunch, and I've laughed harder than I can ever remember. Although it seems my husband was a serious child, it sounds like he was a darling, too.

"And then he told Jack that he was a rapscallion! Can you imagine? He was only ten!" Potts says as she wipes her eyes from laughing so hard she cried.

"But you know, he was only with the other children for a relatively short time before he went away to school, and even when he was here, well..." Potts sighs. "When he was here, he was just older enough than the other boys that he wasn't really playing at their level, and with all of his father's business lessons, he was pretty isolated."

She looks out the window, deep in thought.

"I think he felt so much responsibility from an early age—to his father, his siblings, and the company. He knew it would all fall to him one day, and he was desperate to get everything perfect. His routine really started to take shape and become an integral part of his life at that time. I think it was his way of keeping control and not losing track of things. You'll see more of 'the routine' soon, as he spends more time here with you," she says, emphasizing with air quotes and another of her signature pointed looks.

"It sounds as if my husband and I may be able to bond over abnormal childhoods, if nothing else," I reply with a self-deprecating laugh. I'm wondering if I'll be able to fit myself into Henry's sacred routine at all when Potts surprises me with a belly laugh. I give her a questioning look as she waves an apology and tries to stifle her laughter.

"I'm sorry, dear. It's just that I don't think you understand what a match the two of you are. You'll ingratiate yourself here just fine, or I'll eat my hat," she says, giving me a beaming smile. "I've seen you do your daily crossword, for example, and Henry completes one every evening. I can't wait for him to see how fast you can finish. It's going to be delicious."

Her smile turns devious, and I'm a little scared at what she has up her sleeve.

"You know, his guilty pleasure as a child used to be a luxurious bubble bath. I know it's hard to imagine, and only his custom tubs are big enough to comfortably fit him these days, but he used to love to unwind with oils and bubbles. When we went to England and he hit his growth spurt, I think he grew out of the habit, but perhaps..."

I'm not exactly following. "Perhaps...?"

"I thought you were meant to have seduction lessons, my dear," she teases. "What on earth did that woman teach you?"

"Red latex…" I mumble as she continues.

"In any case, I'm saying that perhaps when Mr. Sinclair has had a particularly bad day or rough week, you might draw him a bath. He's not really one for touch, or I would suggest a head massage or neck rub…"

Cocking my head, I interrupt her. "I've touched him."

"You've what, dear?"

"I've touched him, Potts. He's touched me as well. Not for very long, or anywhere…private," I say, blushing but powering through. "But we have touched."

Mrs. Potts gives me an appraising look and a soft smile. "I don't think you have anything to worry about, darling. I think everything will be just fine."

Hearing an alarm chime, I realize it's around time for her to start dinner, and I have a video call with Sasha soon to catch up. We part ways, and as I head to my quarters, I hear her call out behind me.

"I almost forgot, dear! He loves Danish wedding cookies. Barely lets me make them because he can't eat one without eating the entire batch. I can teach you to make them from his favorite recipe if you'd like."

Turning to smile at her, I feel my plan forming in my mind already. "I would love that, Potts. Tomorrow, perhaps?"

"It's a date, Mrs. Sinclair."

Heading into my bedroom to bathe before calling Sasha, I feel as if I'm turning a page into a new chapter of my new life. I've passed Estate 101, Staff 101, and Grounds 101 in the last week, and aced them all if I do say so myself. Mrs. Potts has given me the shell of a study guide, and I've been trained my entire life to observe and adapt. Henry 101 is in session, and I'm ready for class to begin.

Chapter Nine

After a week of meetings, traveling, and unavoidable late dinners at the office, I'm more comforted than I expected to be waking up on a Monday morning at home. *Home.* I hadn't realized the estate had fully become home again in my subconscious, but clearly, all the effort that Potts has made to accommodate me hasn't gone to waste. I stretch and turn my alarm off before it can ring, don my swim trunks, and head to the lap pool. Reminding myself that I'll be home for dinner with Katarina tonight, I'm feeling more energized than usual for my first swim of the week.

I open the door to the indoor pool for my swim to find it *occupied.*

My wife, I assume, is gliding through the water at a brisk clip, making the turn at the far end of the pool to swim freestyle back to me. She would look positively Olympian with her swim cap and goggles if not for the fact that rather than a sporty one-piece, she's wearing a...less sporty two-piece. It's not a string bikini by any means, but whoever designed it obviously had both form and function in mind. It's a dusky blue, which I can imagine setting off the hue of her eyes to perfection, and is both containing and presenting her assets in a way that has the room feeling twenty degrees warmer than it is.

Seeing me as she approaches the near end of the pool to turn, she slows and gives me a beaming smile.

"Good morning Henry. It's nice to see you," she says brightly, and although I'm confused by her presence, I can't help but smile.

"Good morning to you as well, Katarina. It's nice to see you, but may I ask, what are you doing?"

Her response is lost to me as she lifts herself effortlessly out of the side of the pool, eschewing the stairs, to stand, dripping, beside me. Pulling off her goggles and swim cap, her ice-blonde braid falls behind her to her waist. I was devastatingly correct about the color of her swimsuit, her violet-blue eyes popping as she looks up at me.

"Swimming, of course! It's one of my favorite ways to start the day. You came at a great time, I was just finishing up to head to the sauna for a bit," she says, turning and torturing me with the view as she walks to fetch a heated towel from the warmer. Her shoulders are sculpted, like the rest of her, and I wonder what other activities are a part of her regular fitness regimen. I know about jujitsu and fencing, but maybe pilates? Perhaps weight lifting? I hope she's seen the home gym this week.

"Henry? Are you alright?"

She's standing before me again, wrapped in a towel, as I realize I've been lost in thought and staring. At her biceps.

I'm not sure how long I stare, only that I can't stop. My *wife* is dripping, rivulets of water trailing from her neck down, through the valley of her breasts, around the peaks of her muscles, off the end of her tiny nose...

She's not for you to ogle, my subconscious tries to tell me. But a deeper, dormant part of my soul reminds me that *she is*. She is *precisely* mine to ogle and no one else's. Reaching into the corners of my mind, I try to remember why I was leaving her alone, why I've been nothing but a gentlemanly existence promising friendship. Pulling my gaze all the way up to meet hers, I imagine a flash of fear under the weight of the no doubt predatory gleam in my eyes, replaced swiftly by heat.

I need to be careful, lest my brain continue attributing feelings to Katarina's that aren't actually hers. But if I didn't *imagine* the heat in her gaze, if she was actually lusting after me in any capacity...

My mind becomes a flip book of scenes, tearing her swimsuit off and having her here on the edge of the pool, in the sauna, sweat mixing with tears as I ravage her mouth, over my desk in my study, in my bedroom, my shower...

I'm saved as she clears her throat, pulling me out of my trance before I do something rash, like drag her over my shoulder to my bedroom and chain her there forever.

"I'm fine," I cough out, taking off my shirt and enjoying the way her eyes widen as I do so. "I just wasn't expecting anyone to be in here. Nobody ever is. Obviously. Since I used to live alone."

"Oh," she says, her face falling as she turns to leave. "I'm sorry, I can come later in the day when you're done."

"Katarina, no. I'm..." I sigh. "I'm sorry. I'm just getting used to having someone else here who isn't staff. It's nice to see you, and you have as much right to use any room in this house as I do. Please don't adjust on my account. In fact, there are two swimming lanes, so you don't have to leave if you don't want to. We can both fit in the pool."

Giving her a soft smile, she pads slowly back over to me.

"Thank you, but I really am done today, and I do want to sit for a few minutes in the sauna. I'll keep that in mind, though, about both of us fitting here."

With that, she's off, and I'm into the pool, trying to focus on my swimming form and *not* the thought of my wife in the sauna, dripping with sweat.

"Potts, may I have a word?" I ask, pulling her from the kitchen into the butler's pantry.

Following me quickly, she looks concerned. "Of course, Mr. Sinclair, whatever is the matter? Is Mrs. Sinclair ok? I told her the first time would likely be somewhat..."

"What? No, she's fine," I say, and Potts has the grace to look abashed. "At least, I have every reason to believe she is. She was fine at our swim this morning, but that's beside the point. I wanted to ask how she was when I was gone last week."

"How was she, sir? She was fine. She met the staff, took walks along the grounds, settled into her rooms..." Potts looks at me as I gently hold up a hand to stop her.

"Not what she *did.* How *was* she?"

Brow furrowed, she continues. "As I said, she was fine, sir. I do think she was a bit lonely, and she really didn't enjoy shopping or have much interest in that, although she had a marvelous time ordering swimsuits. Overall, she had a peaceful week, I should think."

"Alright, Potts. Thank you."

Leaving her in the kitchen to no doubt finish making my breakfast, I make my way to my study to read my paper. I'm just finishing a droll article on the history of the local golf course when I hear the door open.

"Thank you, Potts, I appreciate..." Pink-painted toenails appear in my line of sight below my paper as my breakfast tray is placed on the table, and I lift my head to find my wife, not Mrs. Potts.

"You're not Mrs. Potts," I observe astutely.

A small laugh is my reward for my dry humor, and I relish it.

"No, not Mrs. Potts. *Mrs. Sinclair,*" she says with a smirk. "Or Kat, as I've tried to insist."

"I'll stick to Katarina since you insist," I tease back, enjoying her smile and resolving to be responsible for it more often, before blurting out a question. "Where is Potts? Why did you bring me breakfast?"

Her smile falls, and I know I was curt. I wasn't trying to be cold, I'm...I don't know what I am. *Confused.* I don't mind her presence; in fact, I quite enjoy it, but nobody but Potts ever brings my breakfast. She's truly got me on my back foot.

"I'm sorry. I suggested to Potts that I bring it in so we could read the paper together, and I think there's an article on page eight you'll find amusing, about the…"

"Golf course," we finish my sentence together, and I place my paper down to give her my full attention. "I apologize, I didn't mean…Well, it's not in my nature to…"

I don't really have an excuse this time, so I opt for the truth and a plea.

"I don't have an excuse for being short with you. Please feel welcome to stay and read the paper and have breakfast with me. I know I gave you the same reason on Monday at the pool, but it's still true that I am adjusting to having you here, just as you're adjusting to being here. I promise to continue to try not to be a complete ass." My sheepish smile and self-deprecation seem to work as she laughs, pulling over a chair to sit closer to the table while leaving me plenty of room.

"I forgive you, Mr. Sinclair, unlike the patrons of the golf course and the concession company. *Can you imagine?*" she asks, pulling the silver dome off two plates of eggs and a third plate with fruit.

"A generational feud over a *cheese sandwich*? No, I certainly cannot imagine…"

Our discussion continues as we eat and read our papers, and for the first time in recent memory, I'm late to work.

"Well, I agree, but I do think the beavers have a right to build their dam *somewhere*. We can't just continue to relocate the beavers every ten years. How can they pass their homestead down to their children...what's wrong?" Katarina asks, as I stare at my plate.

She's right about the beavers, and her shrewd opinions about the news of the day have become more and more apparent as we've shared more breakfasts over the past few days.

"Are these different eggs?" I ask. The texture is perfectly creamy, reminding me of my boarding school days. The refectory always had the perfect eggs, and I've not wanted to offend Potts by telling her that hers were never up to snuff.

Looking up, I see a slight blush on my wife's cheeks.

"Well, yes. They are different," she says, fully blushing now. "I thought I noticed the last few days that you never finish your eggs. I asked Potts if you even like eggs, and she said yes, you've always liked them, ever since boarding school."

I continue to stare as she speeds up her explanation.

"And then I thought that perhaps the boarding school eggs were special in some way, so I decided to just call, easy enough..."

"You called my boarding school?"

"Yes."

"In England."

"Well, hopefully so."

Ignoring her cheek, I continue my line of questioning.

"To ask about their eggs, and if they do anything special to them?"

"Yes, and as it turns out, they do. They add crème fraîche and ice-cold butter. So after a few practice batches, this is my version. It looks just like the photo that Gordon sent me and..."

"Gordon?"

"Yes. Gordon, the head chef at your school. He remembers you loving the eggs, actually, and video called me yesterday to watch my technique. That's why I'm somewhat confident you'll enjoy them, although they're likely cold now that I've been faced with the Spanish Inquisition."

Licking my lips, I watch her track the movement before I speak.

"You're correct about the eggs. I tolerate them because I never wanted to upset Potts, she was always so confident in her skills," I say, finally taking a bite.

As soon as I swallow my first bite, I'm transported back to school and the morning bustle of the refectory, teeming with excitement for the day ahead.

"These are better than Gordon's, Katarina. Please tell Potts so she can—"

My wife interrupts me, and I can't say that I mind once I hear what she has to say.

"I'm afraid I refuse to give up my trade secrets, and in any case, Gordon made me swear an oath I wouldn't tell. You're stuck with me making your eggs every day, Mr. Sinclair," she says, defiantly, clearly expecting me to push back on her daily presence at my breakfast table.

Well, she's surprised me far too many times this week. Perhaps it's time to try to even the footing. And if she wants to spend more time with me, maybe she does have an interest...or it could just be yearning for companionship. Either way, having more time with her for myself is the first step.

"I'm certainly not going to stop you."

Her smile may be her best one yet as she agrees, and I consider that although she's now changed my routine twice within two weeks of being here, I can't say that I mind. As she discusses another article from this morning's news, this one about international diplomacy, I see clearly that I've underestimated her based on her age, unfairly so. I'm enjoying her company more than I could have imagined, which is a problem. The more time I spend with her, the more likely I am to put my hands on her. And once I've touched her, I know there will be no going back.

By the end of the day, I'm ready for my evening routine and bed. I told Katarina this morning that I would be late after a dinner meeting, and I find myself disappointed that I won't see her. She's only been in my life for a little over a week, and one missed dinner has me in need of an outlet to burn off some steam. Heading toward my suite to change for my workout, I don't get far before the subject of my musings falls into step beside me, taking two steps for each one of mine.

"Hello, Henry," she says quietly, and I immediately note a hint of sadness in her voice. She's dressed in her all white fencing attire, with her hair in a twisted braid around her head. She looks *delectable.*

"Hello, Katarina. I thought Sasha was going to call?" I ask, stopping as we reach the hall.

She sighs before sadly gesturing with the saber she's carrying.

"He was, but he had some kind of work thing come up and wasn't available. I figured I would try to get some practice in. I went through some footwork and bladework combos alone, but it's just not the same."

It takes everything in me not to suggest another kind of physical challenge to her for the evening. I'm about to invite her to the gym with me when she interrupts.

"Would you like to come with me?" she asks sweetly, gazing up at me with hopeful violet eyes.

I'd like to come with you, in you, on you...

"I'd love that," I say. "Although I'll wager that you'll wipe the floor with me. I meant it when I said I haven't sparred in many years. I'll change and meet you at the piste?"

She eyes me up and down.

"I can't believe they make gear your size, but yes, I'll see you there."

I change quickly and head for the piste, finding her adjusting her mask in one of the mirrors lining the long addition. Standing behind her, she doesn't reach my chest, and I can't help but lean forward to place my chin on top of her head. She stills, and her eyes find mine in the mirror before she smiles.

"Ready to get your ass kicked?"

Thirty minutes later, she's given up on "knocking my rust off," as she phrased it, and is, indeed, kicking my ass. I'm in amazing shape, but she's so damn quick, parrying and attacking before I can even use my much longer limbs to an advantage.

"I don't know what you do for cardio other than swimming," I say, bent over with my hands on my knees, mask off, and sweat dripping into my eyes from my hair. "But whatever it is, I need to keep up with your program."

Her laughter rings out as she prods me with the end of her saber, prompting me to stand up and replace my mask.

"It's called being a teenager, Henry. You might not remember since it's been so long."

I'm too winded to respond to this brat with more than a heavy wheeze. If she weren't running me ragged right now, I would spank her perfect ass so hard she would think twice about teasing me like that. As it stands, all I'm able to do is try to catch my breath before standing back up to further make a fool of myself.

"This is the last round before I'm spent," I admit.

She smirks and pulls her own mask down before immediately catching me off guard with an explosive offensive series. Retreating, I manage one riposte before she has me on my back foot again. I'm about to yield when I stumble, falling backward and landing in a heap. Her momentum carries her forward, and before she can slow herself, my long legs cause Katarina to trip as well.

Fuck.

She falls forward onto her hands and knees, but luckily, I'm there to cushion her landing. Inconveniently, she falls into a straddle. *Maybe it's convenient,* I think as we both pull our masks off and she sits up. Directly onto my lap.

Shit.

Our chests are heaving, and she's flushed with exertion and grinning triumphantly.

"I win!" she says brightly, doing a little victory wiggle that resembles a lap dance. It's enough for my dick to immediately rise to attention. I see the moment she feels it underneath her. Her smile turns into a smirk as she grinds ever so slightly onto me, just enough that I *know* it's on purpose.

Then she's up like a flash and holding her hand out to help me off the floor. She doesn't weigh enough to actually help heave me up, but I appreciate the gesture and take her hand, holding my mask in front of my crotch to hide what's now a full-blown erection.

"Good match, Mr. Sinclair," she says as she shakes my hand, then gathers her gear to head for her room. "I think with a little *vigorous training,* we'll have you in fighting form soon!"

Her laughter tinkles behind her as she leaves me to watch her go. Rock hard. Exhausted. *Entranced.*

Chapter Ten

"I'll see you at dinner tonight?" I ask, lowering my paper in an attempt to catch a glimpse of the way my husband's ass looks in his slacks as he leaves the study.

Henry turns around and smirks as he catches me ogling him. "Yes, I'll be home before dinner." He goes to leave but stops himself before he's out of the room and smiles. "Enjoy your day, Katarina."

I give him a big grin of my own, "Oh, I plan on it. I hope you do as well, Henry."

Nodding, he taps the doorframe with his knuckle and leaves for the day. It's Saturday, and I won't lie, I was half expecting—well, hoping—that he would be home for the weekend, but duty calls. Shaking off any lingering sadness, I finish the article I was reading and get changed for my morning hike.

Having Henry home more the past week has been interesting. I've had no trouble warming up to my new husband. The fact that he's the most attractive man I've ever seen only has a little to do with it. We actually have more in common than I could've dreamed, making our time together enjoyable.

I believe he's warming to me as well. We've spent our dinners together discussing current events, an activity I missed dearly during the week I was here alone. After dinner, he would disappear into his study, and it only took me a couple of days to gather the nerve to join him. The memory of the first night I followed him brings a smile to my face.

"Good night, Katarina," Henry says as he leaves for his study.

"Hmph." My arms are crossed, and my face is contorted into a pout. Not that my husband would notice, since he left without turning around.

Before I realize it, Potts is collecting the dishes. "Go after him, dear. He'll be in his study doing a crossword for the next thirty minutes." She takes my plate from my hand, trading it for another copy of today's paper. "Show him your stuff."

I sit straight, remember my worth, and march toward him, each step driven by ambition. The doors are shut when I reach his study. The thought to knock briefly crosses my mind, but I ultimately decide against it and barrel my way inside.

Henry's chair faces the wall to the left of the door. He turns his head toward the intrusion, and I see the surprise in his eyes the moment he realizes who's standing there.

"Katarina? Is there something wrong?"

"Of course not!"

His brows scrunch together, clearly confused. "Then what on earth are you doing here?"

"It's crossword time, is it not?"

He looks at the paper lying on his lap, then at the paper in my hand. "Well...yes."

"I'm here to do the crossword with you, of course!" I say with the biggest smile I can muster.

I can feel his gaze follow me as I practically skip to the chair opposite his and unfold the paper to the day's crossword. "You wouldn't happen to have an extra pen, would you?"

Without saying a word, he offers me the pen in his hand, then gets up to grab another for himself from the desk in the corner of the room.

"Thank you," I say as he takes his seat again.

He doesn't respond, but a glance up confirms I've gotten his attention. He's staring at me with a quizzical expression on his face, brows raised, blinking sporadically.

"Have you started yet?" I ask with a smile.

He shakes his head, holding up his puzzle for proof.

Smirking, I ask, "Wanna race?"

Shaking his head again, he looks down at his paper. "If you insist."

With that, I work as diligently as I can, trying to beat my best time. Potts told me it takes him fifteen minutes, and I'm usually always done in ten, but you can never be sure. How embarrassing would it be if he beat me at my own game?

"Aha!" I finish my last word and glance at the clock. Nine minutes and twelve seconds. I manage to control myself from celebrating, wanting to act as nonchalant as possible about my win, but I can't hide the smile on my face.

Without a word, I stand, lay the puzzle down on the coffee table separating us, and go to leave the room. Before I walk *out the door, I glance back over my shoulder at Henry, and his expression is one I'll never forget. Henry Sinclair is not a man to show emotion, especially surprise, but the shock painted across his face is undeniable. His eyes are rounded, brows raised, and mouth slightly open as he watches me leave.*

"Good night, Mr. Sinclair. I'll see you at the pool in the morning?"

"Yes...swim...bathing suit." Clearing his throat, he regains his composure. "I mean. Yes, I'll be there at my normal time tomorrow morning. Good night, Katarina."

My memory ends as I'm brought to a screeching halt.

"Umph," I squeak as I crash into something. I fall back, about to hit the ground, when a hand catches me.

"Oh, I'm so sorry, Mrs. Sinclair. I didn't see you coming. And I was trying to pull this...and..."

Coming to, I recognize the poor man who's fallen victim to my daydreaming. "Freddy, please don't apologize. I was the one not paying attention. I hope you're not hurt!"

Our groundskeeper, Fredrick, or Freddy as he prefers, was one of the first staff members I befriended. I run into him almost daily with as many walks as I take, and we always chat for a while if he has the time.

Freddy smiles. "No, ma'am, I'm perfectly fine. I was just trying to clear this path. I know you enjoy your hikes."

"On a Saturday? Please don't tell me you're required to work on the weekends, too."

"Only occasionally, ma'am."

"Well, if you have to work, I might as well keep you company. I was just out for a hike anyway. We can walk the path together," I say, lacing my arm through his.

He immediately concedes, allowing me to pull him along one of the many trails on the property. We walk for miles, stopping occasionally to clear any growth in the passageway, while he shows me places special to Henry and his siblings growing up.

He shows me a tree Henry's sister fell from as a child, breaking her leg. Apparently, that's where her husband, Jack, proposed to her earlier this year. A little farther down into the forest is a clearing of land where Ledger, Jack, and Margot would play baseball. As we make our way back to the house, he points out a dock where their father used to take Henry and his brother fishing as young boys.

With every passing story, I miss Sasha more and more. It's impossible not to think of my own childhood and all the memories we made outdoors. When we make our way back to the house, I give Freddy a hug goodbye, insisting he go home and take the rest of the weekend off.

Still missing my cousin, who I've hardly talked to since moving away, I search for Mrs. Potts in hopes of some companionship, only to learn she's out running errands. I grab my current read, trying to shake off the melancholy once again, and head to the back veranda. I'm well versed in letting things roll off my shoulder, but when a crack of thunder sounds the minute I sit down, I give up on being cheerful for the day.

After a rather dreary dinner, Henry excuses himself like always and heads to his study. I would typically follow him and show off my crossword skills, but I've had enough of his mood this evening.

With a sigh, I decide to call it an early night and head to my room to lie in bed sulking with a box of candy and some trashy reality TV shows. Unfortunately for me, Henry's study is between me and my sulking. As I turn the corner, the open doors shine like a beacon. This is the first night in almost two weeks I've seen them open. I want to walk past them with my head held high, but I can't keep from peeping in.

Passing by, I allow myself a glance and...wow. Henry stands leaning over his desk, arms spread wide to support himself. He's clearly upset about whatever he's looking at. His suit jacket lies over the back of his chair, and his crisp white shirt is on display. The top two buttons are undone, allowing the slightest bit of his chest hair to peek through. His sleeves are pushed up to his elbows, leaving his muscled forearms on display. His normally well-kempt, thick black hair is disheveled and falling into his face, where he's clearly been running his hand through it.

I realize I've gravitated into the doorway when he looks up at me. "Katarina, I'm afraid there will be no crossword for me tonight, but you're welcome to do yours if you'd like." He lifts a hand in the direction of my usual seat, and I see there's a paper and a pen laid out for me.

With a catch in my breath, I look back at my distressed husband, any irritation I had from dinner gone. He's looking down again, raking his hand through his luscious hair. I can't stop myself from moving closer.

Approaching the desk, I realize he's staring at a map. "What's this?"

"It's a map," he says without looking up.

"Thank you, Sherlock." I roll my eyes. "What's the map of?"

This time, he does look up. "My, er, *our* property."

I squint my eyes, hoping that will help, but looking at it upside down, it's impossible to read. I make my way around the desk and try looking over Henry's arm, but that's no good either. Finally deciding to just go for it, I bend down slightly and shimmy under his arm to get a front row view of this map.

The moment our bodies align, I feel him tense up. Luckily, he can't see my face right now because I'm sure he wouldn't appreciate the way my eyes roll back briefly at the feeling of his large body behind mine. He's so close, his scent so strong. I take a deep breath, inhaling the scent of mint and vanilla, his after-dinner scotch, and something unique to him, but something is missing. I'm not sure if it's just my imagination running away with me or him actually smelling my hair, but I swear I feel his head lower slightly as he inhales as well.

To my disappointment, Henry adjusts to allow some space between our bodies, then clears his throat, clearly requesting an explanation for my actions.

"Sorry, I couldn't see it properly before. So what's upset you?"

A moment of silence passes us while I survey the map, immediately noticing several familiar landmarks, until Henry finally concedes with a sigh. "A neighbor of ours passed away recently and—"

"Oh yes, Mr. Crowley. I sent his family some baked goods last week. It's so sad what happened. I know he was elderly, but to just pass out of the blue like that has to be hard on his..."

The sound of Henry's fingers strumming on his desk makes me realize that not only am I rambling, but I interrupted him to do so. "Oh God, I'm so sorry. Please continue."

"Like I was saying, his children sold the property, and the new owners insist that we have our property lines mixed up. Their surveyor is claiming an additional three hundred acres," he says, pointing at a spot on the western side of the property.

I run my fingers along the paper, imagining the hike I took last week on this part of the land. Cross-referencing the distance key on the map with how many miles I hiked, I confirm there's an error on their end. "What year is this map from?"

Henry pulls back the corners of the map, looking for a date. "I'm not sure, this is the one they brought me."

I walk him through to the corner in question with me still calculating what could take an extra half of the distance when it hits me. "I think they're missing the entire peach orchard. This must be an old map. There has to be something in the family archives letting us know when this land was annexed."

Henry lowers his head to get a better look. "You're right. How did you...?" Turning to look at me, he pauses when he realizes how close we are now. I track his gaze from my eyes to my parted lips, to my neck, then back up. "How did you know that?"

"I like to walk..." I breathe, barely a whisper.

"And the archives?"

"I like to read..."

Henry's gaze traps me in place as his gray eyes search mine. When he finally breaks the silence, his voice is lower than usual. "Very good, *Katarina.*"

Arousal floods my core. I'm not sure how he knows my panties are soaked, but he must. His expression turns almost devious as he raises a brow, the corner of his mouth lifting to form a smirk. "Should we start searching for them?"

"Huh?"

His smirk transforms into a smug grin. "The maps? In the archives?"

All I can do is nod and dazedly allow him to lead me to the library.

After hours of research and stacks of books from the archives, I've finally found the information we've been looking for.

I'm sprawled out on the floor, barefoot, with a blanket wrapped around me, and my hair pulled back in a braid.

"I think I found it!" I call to Henry, who's propped against the wall reading a book of his own, his attire even more relaxed than earlier.

"The peach orchard was annexed by your grandfather in 1962, the same year they built the greenhouses." I hand the book to him, then grab another one from the stack. "The property lines were surveyed later that year, and a new map was commissioned, including the additional acreage."

Flipping back a few pages, I find a picture of the map that was drafted five years prior and match it to the one on Henry's desk. "I think the map they gave you must be from 1957."

Henry follows my lead, taking up his earlier position of enveloping my body in his long arms, as he joins in comparing the maps. "This is it!" Without warning, I'm being lifted in the air and spun around. The smile on his face is one I've only ever seen once before, briefly, as we were dancing at our wedding.

Caught up in the moment, I wrap my arms around him and laugh.

I stumble when he sets me down on my feet. At his full height, he's a good foot and a half taller than me. Throwing my head back to look up at him, I'm met with awe painted on his face as he stares down at me. "Thank you, Katarina, you don't know how much time and trouble you saved me tonight."

"Seriously, it was nothing, but you're welcome." I give him a little squeeze since my arms are still wrapped around his waist. When he returns it with one of his own, I realize he hasn't let go of me either. *He's hugging me.* Henry Sinclair is *hugging* me.

I can't stop myself from resting against him, the top of my head barely reaching his chest, where his heart beats nearly as fast as mine. The moment lasts both forever and for only a moment before he's pulling away with a soft smile on his face.

From the corner of my eye, I see an empty ashtray and realize his missing scent is tobacco. I'm trying to think of the last time I smelled it on him, but I can't quite recall. "Did you stop smoking?"

He shrugs. "You told me I should quit."

*Oh...*I look up at him with wide eyes, speechless.

"Good night, Katarina," he says, tucking a piece of hair that's fallen from my braid behind my ear. "I'll see you tomorrow for a walk? Maybe we can check out the property lines in question."

"I'd love to." I smile, gather my blanket, and make my way out of the study. "Good night, Henry."

Chapter Eleven

"Katarina!" Knocking louder on her bedroom door, I wait for her to appear. I know it's slightly earlier than her normal wake-up time unless she gets up much earlier than necessary for her morning swim. And usually we don't swim on Sundays, but...

The door flies open, and a terrifying creature resembling my wife stands before me.

"What. Is. Wrong with you? It's four o'clock in the morning! On a Sunday!"

She's as I've never seen her before. Her braid is puffy around her head and frizzy along its length, there are sleep marks on the right side of her face from a pillow, and her pajamas, if they can be referred to as such, are askew. Tiny shorts not quite high enough to meet her pajama tank as it rides up her abdomen, showing a delicious sliver of skin and hinting at...

"Henry!"

"Hmm, yes?" I reply, forgetting why I'm here in the first place.

"If you don't tell me why you're here right now, I'm going to attack, and I promise you, since I have the element of surprise, I will win."

I can't resist a smirk at the idea that she thinks she could bring me to the ground, with a foot and a half on her in height and weighing at least one hundred and fifty pounds more, too.

"As fun as that sounds, and as terrifying as you are right now looking like an angry kitten, I was seeing if you were ready for our walk."

Long seconds pass as she blinks up at me.

"A walk. At four o'clock. In the cold morning air. On a Sunday. Sundays are meant for sleeping in!" she exclaims, already moving toward her closet to change. I knew she wouldn't be able to resist a walk.

"Well, it's ten past four now that we've been having this riveting discussion for so long, and I want to stop by the kitchen and make sure my pack is adequately stocked for the day before we leave. So it'll likely be more of a four thirty in the morning walk, depending on how quickly you can get ready."

Wandering through the open door clearly meant as an invitation, I avert my eyes slowly from where I can see her changing in the closet. A flash of a hot-pink sports bra and matching panties, cut high on her hips, is all I allow before reminding myself I am a gentleman, not some pervert ogling unsuspecting women. She is my wife, however...

"You can look, you know. I am your wife."

I glance back up to see her crossing the room in just her bra and panties, rummaging around in her nightstand before walking back into the closet.

I look and immediately regret it. I promised myself after almost losing it at the pool the other day that I would keep my hands to myself until she's ready. She's my wife, but she's still young, and she's only recently had her entire life upended. *And if I ever get my hands on her, well. If she knew the things I wanted to do to her, she would probably run.* She doesn't deserve me lusting after her while she tries to acclimate to her new home, but I can't help it. She's all I can think about. And if she does decide one day that she wants to take our relationship to the next level, I'll certainly be waiting with open fucking arms.

Before I can follow this line of thought any further, she's back in front of me, fully dressed in walking gear that's perfect for the weather and the distance I'm hoping to cover today. Even if I have to slow my stride for her to take two steps for every one of mine. At least.

"You look like you've been dropped directly into an English moor. Perfection," I say, kissing her knuckles as she smiles.

"I wanted to be curled up in that bed for at least four more hours, so I hope whatever you have for me at the end of this walk is better than a *moor*," she sasses, and I laugh with her as we make our way to the kitchen to grab a quick bite before heading out the door.

A few miles into our walk, the first tendrils of daylight start to peek above the horizon.

"It's beautiful out here," Katarina says softly. "I haven't been out this early, but the sunrise is spectacular. Thank you for bringing me, even if I was a little grumpy about being woken up. I expected you to work again today and really did plan to sleep in a while. When we agreed to go on a walk, I thought it would be much later."

"I wouldn't say you were grumpy," I reply, enjoying the small smile she gifts me. "I *would* say you resembled a gremlin more than anything else, and I was very briefly afraid for my life, though."

Smirking, I revel in the shocked look on her face as she makes an adorably indignant sound.

"First of all, I have never once looked like a gremlin..."

"And I appreciate you joining me out here. I had forgotten about how special this land is, and how many secrets and adventures it holds. You've already realized it in the short amount of time you've been here, and it's helped me remember. So I owe you a very big thank-you," I say, hoping she can see the sincerity on my face.

I mean every word. Having traveled for so long, I had neglected the estate, including the land and the staff. Katarina has helped me rekindle my love for being here, and she deserves to feel my appreciation.

As usual, she deflects the compliment immediately, a deep instinct of hers that I don't understand. She does, however, accept the wrapped egg-and-cheese biscuit I hand her from my pack, making grabby gestures with her hands like a little raccoon.

It's such an adorable action that I'm distracted from where I'm walking and stumble over a tree root, managing to turn and land sitting down in the dirt rather than falling on my face. Katarina is immediately in front of me, looking at me with concern.

"Henry, are you okay? Let me help you up," she says, reaching out a hand for mine.

She still hasn't learned that she won't be any help in getting me up, but I place my hand in her tiny one anyway, feeling amusement at the barely there tug I feel as she gives all her effort to pulling on my arm. It's endearing that she tries so hard to help me.

Back on the move, she polishes off two biscuits before waving off a third.

"If I eat any more, I'll get sleepy, and then you'll have to carry me the rest of the way," she jokes, pulling off her jacket and wrapping it around her waist.

"That wouldn't be a problem," I say. "In fact, we're approaching an area that gets notoriously marshy when it rains like it has recently, so I'll be carrying you for a while anyway."

Her head snaps up to look at me with an indignant expression. "I'm not going to let you carry me around like some overgrown toddler. Besides, you'll get tired, and I don't want to burden you...ooomph!"

Picking her up and cradling her bridal style before she has a chance to deny me, I point out the deep mud I'm currently trudging through. Mouth hanging open, she stares at me, then at the squelching mud, then back at me, tightening her grip around my neck.

"I'll admit this is a superior mode of travel to mucking about in that. Thank you for carrying me. I hope I'm not too heavy." She sighs, relaxing her head against my chest.

I can smell her from here, no perfume today, just a mixture of her shampoo with her underlying musk.

"If you didn't already know, you're a slight thing. You'll never be too heavy for me to carry, wherever you need to go," I say quietly, and we continue toward our destination.

Sitting in the shade of a magnolia tree, we've made it to our destination at the edge of the orchard, but I refuse to let her explore until she eats. I'm already starting to understand the fine line between not hungry and hangry, and for my own health, I'm determined not to cross it again. Although it's certainly been a task to keep her from looking around the greenhouse beside us. She briefly read about it in one of the books we looked at last night from our archives on the property and has been excited about exploring all morning.

"You're not telling me that you and your cousin actually spent three months living in the woods behind your house as children?" I ask, incredulous as Katarina laughs, recounting another of her and Sasha's adventures. She described him as more of a brother, and it's clear that's exactly how they grew up. It occurs to me that she must really miss him, and I need to invite him over for dinner. Perhaps a standing invitation with Ledger, Sloane, Margot, Jack, and Mother. A big family dinner once or twice a month.

"That's exactly what I'm telling you," she says, swallowing another mouthful of soup from the tureen I packed this morning. "Although we spent every night inside, and had our meals packed from the kitchen...and I think we always had at least one bodyguard discreetly trailing us in case we got off the marked paths. But yes, for three months, we spent most of our time in the woods pretending we had been shipwrecked."

Eating my own soup, I listen as she describes their efforts to learn survival skills, working their way through a large portion of the Eagle Scout handbook and reading everything they could get their hands on. I'm pleased to hear that she knows so much about wilderness survival, especially if she'll be spending so much time walking the estate. She finishes regaling me with their outdoor adventures and moves on to their obsession with mermaids, telling me about their intricately choreographed synchronized routines performed to precision.

Thinking of a young Katarina, giving her all to perfectly execute a mermaid swim routine, I can't help but smile. It reminds me of Margot, trying her hardest to perform the Rose Adagio. My parents went too far indulging her, but I know it's impossible not to spoil only daughters, at least a little.

"You two sound like my sister. I can't imagine how much your parents must have enjoyed watching the two of you and your hijinks."

Her face subtly darkens as she fusses with her soup, and I realize I must have broached a sensitive subject. *Her parents.* Of course. I saw how cold her father can be at our rehearsal dinner, and if she was close with her mother before she died, she surely would have mentioned her. This is a harsh reminder of how little I know my wife, but I've already resolved to make more of an effort, and there's no way to learn more except to ask.

"Were you close to your parents when you were younger?" I ask softly, avoiding the obvious fact that she and her father aren't close now.

After a pause, she blows out a breath before turning to give me a sad smile. "My mother died giving birth to me. And my father, well. The episode the night before the wedding wasn't a one-off. He isn't, and has never been, overtly cruel or abusive. It's just that he's very matter-of-fact. So no, I wouldn't say we were close."

Looking at me, she must see the confusion and sadness on my face, imagining a small Sasha and Katarina putting on a performance for household staff only, instead of a cozy family scene like the one I grew up with. Immediately, she tries to gloss over my concern.

"He was fine, Henry. Truly. He would certainly never shy away from telling me he was proud of my school accomplishments, particularly when I started to take the advanced courses. And he was thrilled I was able to pick up languages so quickly. He considered it a huge asset. Plus, we had a wonderful team of nannies and tutors when our dads were traveling, and they would check in with us through the staff to make sure we were behaving. And I *think* he was proud of the way I conducted myself at the wedding, so it all worked out in the end." She polishes off her soup and turns to rummage around in my pack for the cookie I promised her once she was done.

"I was proud," I say quietly after a moment, and she stills but doesn't turn around. "I've certainly never seen a more beautiful bride, nor one who held herself with so much grace and poise throughout what was an excruciatingly long, ornate affair. I couldn't keep my eyes off you. You had a smile for everyone you met, just as radiant at the end of the night as you were at the beginning of the day."

As I suspected, this compliment is deflected as well, with her murmurs about the hair and makeup team and basic manners glossing over the fact that she had been, in fact, a young woman faced with quite a challenge. One that she has risen to with aplomb. If I had expected any sort of spoiled, self-assured confidence from my young wife, I was clearly mistaken. My knee-jerk reaction to compare her to my sister was unfair because as much as I love my sister, she was coddled and spoiled to a degree that made her late teens and early twenties sometimes trying, as she felt she always knew best.

Katarina is humble. *Too humble.* She hasn't been told what a marvel she is. Certainly not often enough to understand that she's an extremely accomplished young woman and should be proud of *herself*, first and foremost.

As she continues to rave about all the people who helped her be camera-ready for the wedding while she eats her third cookie with her left hand, I reach for her right. Sunlight catches on my wedding band, and for the first time, I've become so used to its presence that I forgot it was there. Katarina pauses her story as I kiss her knuckles, silently entreating her to stop her diatribe, attributing her success on our wedding day to anyone but herself. When I leave our hands connected and place them back down on her thigh, she gives mine a squeeze.

My wife hasn't had enough people in her corner to support her and ensure she knows what an incredible woman she is. She might not have wanted for anything materialistic in her childhood, but it's clear there was a void where emotional support and love should have been. Someone should have been taking better care of her.

It just so happens that for the first time in my life, I find myself thrilled at the prospect of being responsible for taking care of someone. As a friend or...more, I can make her life easier and encourage her in all of her pursuits. God, she's perfect. She deserves someone in her corner, and the ring on my finger reminds me it's my duty to be there.

Instead of feeling like a foreign weight, my ring feels solid and warm, providing comfort and protection. Exactly what Katarina needs and what I'll strive to give her, whether she realizes she needs me or not.

Chapter Twelve

Henry stands from his seat when I finish my dinner and holds out his hand. For the past week, he's been waiting for me so that we can leave together to do our nightly crosswords. In fact, since our walk last weekend, he's been doing a lot of things differently.

Blushing, I think back to a few days ago...

A perfunctory knock and my bedroom door flies open, startling me out of my pain-sleep haze.

"Katarina? Are you alright? Why didn't you come to the pool this morning?"

I look up from my nest in bed to find Henry, still in his swim trunks. Based on the time glowing from my bedside clock and the fact that he appears to be dry, it seems he waited around ten minutes before coming to find me. Wincing, I sit up as he catches my facial expression and takes a quick step forward to try to figure out what's hurting me. I decide that trying to be discreet will be useless. After all, we are married…

"I'm okay. But I started my period last night, so I'm bloated and I have awful cramps. Usually, my first day is the worst, and then I'm back to mostly normal by tomorrow. So I don't think I'll swim today, or get up to much at all, honestly…" I look up to see if he's grossed out or mad that I'm making a big deal out of it.

He sits on the edge of my bed-nest and takes my hand, kisses my knuckles lightly, and toys with my wedding band.

"What helps?" he asks, and his gray eyes look so intense in the darkness of my room that I'm confused by his question.

"Wha?"

A knowing smirk tells me he knows I'm distracted by his shirtlessness and warm presence in my bed, even only at the edge.

"What helps your cramps? Have you taken ibuprofen? Do you have a heating pad? Chocolate?"

My face must show confusion at which woman in his life he's taken such care of to know period remedies because he laughs and immediately dispels my jealousy.

"You forget, I have spent a little time around my sister, as she experienced such things, particularly when home for the holidays. And I assure you, prior to menopause, my mother was never shy about making sure we boys knew exactly the pain that women go through. She thought it was very important that we all know how to 'cherish and care for our future goddesses,' as she would say," he finishes quietly, still holding my hand and waiting for me to tell him what I need.

"Heat always helps the most, but I can't find where I packed my heating pad. It might have ended up in a box destined for storage, I'm not sure. My ibuprofen in the bathroom has expired. And yes, I'm craving chocolate. Specifically, the variety bag of truffles and dark chocolate, and hot chocolate with peppermint sticks. And truffle fries, although that'll be more of a lunchtime thing. I can get all this later after I sleep just a bit longer, though—" I'm cut off by another kiss to my knuckles and a no-nonsense glare.

"Stay here, see if you can rest a bit more before the sun comes up. I'll make sure you have everything you need today."

And he did. I dozed a bit, waking up to find different sizes of heating pads, chocolates, my favorite gummy candies, and a mug of hot chocolate resting on a warmer on my bedside table.

Henry's voice carries from the hallway, head poking in as he sees I'm awake again, and smiles at me. Holding up one finger, he goes to end his call.

"Nope, Linda, I won't be in today. I don't care what you tell people. Tell them I have the flu, very contagious, too tired to call in from home. I'll probably be back tomorrow. We'll see." Ending the call, he tosses his phone onto the bed before helping me sit up and adjust my heating pad. He hands me my mug, placing a peppermint stick in as he does.

"You didn't have to do all this or stay home with me. But I really, really appreciate it," I say, inhaling the rich aroma of the hot chocolate.

Sitting next to me on the bed, he hands me the remote. "You're welcome, although I disagree. I think I absolutely had to do all of this, as you are, in fact, my responsibility these days. Now, take this ibuprofen and show me what your unhinged reality TV favorites are up to."

My smile at the memory turns into confusion as we arrive at the study, but there's only one paper laid out on the coffee table. Henry picks it up and pulls out the crossword to hand to me.

"Here, you can do it tonight. I'll finish reading where I left off this morning," he says, taking his seat and flipping through the pages.

I sit and look down, moments passing as I stare at the empty puzzle. I look up to see Henry still lost between the pages of today's news. My first thought is to share this with him and work on it together, but there isn't a good seating arrangement to make that comfortable.

The idea to sit in his lap springs into my mind. Two weeks ago, I wouldn't have considered acting on this, but things have been changing between us. Deciding to just go for it, I get up, round the table, and plop down sideways on his lap.

"Katar...what..."

I can feel him tense. This is pushing the boundaries of our relationship, but if we're ever going to become more than friendly roommates, someone has to do it. As much as he's flirted with me lately, he's never taken physical touch this far. Smiling, I interrupt his rambling with a soft, "Hi."

Still tense, he sets the paper down beside him and smiles, "Hi...erm, what are you doing?

"I thought we could do this together," I say, holding up the paper. The longer we sit here staring at each other, the more I lose my resolve. I want to be bold and stand, well, sit my ground on his lap. But the silence is uncomfortable, even for me. "I'm sorry, I'll get up..."

"No, wait..." Henry finally relaxes, wrapping an arm around my waist to pull me a little closer. "I would say get comfortable, but you finish so fast, I don't think it necessarily matters."

"I would imagine comfort directly correlates to how fast I finish, but then again, I've never tested that theory." I wink at him and wiggle slightly on his lap as I settle in, feeling him grow hard beneath me.

"Christ, Katarina," he murmurs, barely audible, as he adjusts himself as discreetly as possible in our position.

Feeling accomplished that I've successfully rattled my husband, I lift my wrist to start the timer on my watch. "Shall we get started?"

"Eight minutes and twenty-two seconds!" I squeak, "My fastest completion time yet!"

Henry sets the completed puzzle down beside us. "Well, you did have help. I'd like to take *partial* credit for your victory."

"*Our* fastest time yet."

My excitement quickly dies as I realize I have no good reason to be sitting on this man's lap any longer. As if he can read my mind, Henry pulls me closer to him. "When did you get so good at crosswords?" He tightens his grip, letting me know he wants me to stay.

"Lots of time alone in my ivory tower, I suppose." I pause when he flinches, forgetting how uncomfortable it makes him that I was contained for eighteen years, largely because of the threat of his mother, real or not. "No, really, I've just always liked puzzles. Sasha used to read the comics to me when I was young. When I asked him what the crossword was, he told me it was a game. And I loved games. I obviously couldn't complete them at first, so I asked almost everyone I came across for help. It became such a routine for the staff that they would seek *me* out to help before starting their work for the day."

Henry laughs, an action becoming less and less rare as of late. "There's still so much I don't know about you."

"Me? You're the one who's a mystery! I feel like I hardly know anything about you," I say, nudging him. "Except how poor a chess player you are."

"What would you like to know?"

"Anything? Everything? Just start from your first memories and keep going."

"I'm afraid I haven't lived a very exciting life. My role was predestined from the moment my father found out he was having a son. As far as first memories, I don't remember much about life before my brother. I was four when Ledger was born, and I quickly adapted to the role of big brother. We had a normal childhood until I was around nine. Within two years, Jack had moved in with us, Ledger had started school, Margot was born, and I was preparing to attend boarding school.

"I never objected to leaving for England, and I was able to come home often, but my family's life carried on while I was away, so I felt like an outsider. Still, I enjoyed being around them when I was home. I know you've only met them briefly, but they're a great time. Mom certainly never showed any bias toward my siblings, even with my long stints away, and I was, without a doubt, the pride of my father."

As I sit, listening to Henry recount his life, realization hits me like a train. I'm not the only one of us who grew up in a cage. Henry's walls might have been invisible, but he knew his bounds, and he never dared to cross them. At least I was able to discover who I wanted to be within my confines.

I caress his face, my hand small against his cheek. "What are some of the happiest moments you can remember?"

I expect him to have to think about that question after such a strictly regulated life, but he answers immediately. "Fishing with Father and Ledger, holding Margot for the first time, winning back-to-back championships in college." He places his hand atop mine. "Dancing with my wife on our wedding day."

My breath falters as my eyes shoot directly to his, where he's staring at me with a gaze so sharp it could cut glass. *This is your chance, Kat,* I keep hearing over and over in my mind. *He clearly wants you. Make a move. Do something.*

Hopping off his lap, I walk to the record player in the corner of the room, then start flipping through the vinyls stacked beside it. I sort through a variety of rock bands and a handful of classical options before landing on one with the song we danced to at our wedding. When I go to take it out of its sleeve, I realize it still has the plastic on it. I make quick work of opening it, placing the disc on the platter, and setting the stylus on the track before walking back over to my husband.

"Dance with me?" I ask, holding my hand out in invitation.

Henry accepts my hand and stands, pulling me with such force that I crash into him. The moment my body meets his, I feel peace I've only ever felt in his arms. He's by far the most attractive man I've ever seen, and his body exudes sensuality. There is no denying my sexual desire for him. But when he's holding me against him, it's not only the physical aspect of a relationship I crave. When I'm wrapped in his arms, I find myself comforted in ways I never imagined this arranged marriage would allow.

He takes my hand in his, his other arm wrapped snuggly around my waist, and leads the dance. Placing my free hand on his chest, I continue to ask about his life. "Alright, so...back-to-back championships? What did you play?"

"Football."

"Do you mean soc—"

"American football." He clarifies before I can ask the question. "I played quarterback pretty much all my life. When I had breaks from school, I would play on travel teams here in the States, and Father had the best coaches training me while I was in England. I could've easily gone pro, but I had more important things to do. The day of the draft, Father gifted me with ownership of the team most adamant about recruiting me. 'Why play for a team when you can own it?'"

"Oh, that's...did you *want* to continue playing?"

Henry smiled down at me. "I wouldn't know. It was never going to be an option, so I never opened that door."

Now that's something I can relate to. "And what about women? Have there been any special girlfriends in your life? Were you with someone when you found out you had to hitch yourself to me?"

His laughter startles me. "God, no. I don't know if you've realized it or not, but I stay pretty busy." He pauses, a huge grin growing on his face as he winks at me. "More than that, I've never had the time to focus on a relationship the way someone deserves."

"You've been great with me lately."

"You're my wife. It's my responsibility to take care of you."

His voice drops, and suddenly, thoughts of him taking care of me in more *intimate* ways cross my mind. "So you've *never* been in a relationship?" I ask, trying to clear my head before I completely overheat.

I feel Henry tense up slightly. "Well, yes. I've been in relationships."

"Okay...explain."

"My relationships have been more contractual by nature, and not in the same way ours is."

"You mean, like, *Fifty Shades* BDSM contractual?" I'm only half serious, but that's the only situation I can think of that would require a contract.

"Yes," he deadpans.

I'm at a loss for words. There's an emotional warfare going on inside me where jealousy, curiosity, and arousal are all fighting for control. "Oh. Well then..."

Picking up on my change in posture, Henry pulls me toward him. "Katarina, if you ever want to know more, all you have to do is ask. I'll tell you everything. But that's all my past. And no woman I've ever been with holds a candle to my wife."

As if his words weren't enough to make me blush, the look in his eyes causes me to shy away from his gaze.

Henry gently takes my chin in his hand, lifting my attention back to him. "Why do you always deflect my compliments? Don't you know you're the most stunning woman in the world?"

Henry smiles softly when I shake my head. "You are, Kitten. Inside and out. Both the most beautiful and most fascinating woman to have ever walked this planet." He pauses to push a strand of my hair behind my ear, his hand still supporting my chin. "And you're all *mine.*"

Chapter Thirteen

After years of routine and relative satisfaction with a life driven by work, racing home from a late dinner meeting to tell my wife good night is not something I expected of myself. But as I throw the car into park and stride purposefully to Katarina's room, I'm more content than I've been all day.

The past two weeks have been odd, for me at least. To have someone in my space and not feel an ounce of resentment has shocked me, although when I mentioned to Potts it was nice to be home and seeing more of my wife lately, she didn't seem surprised at all. It's taken some effort to move things around and not have as many travel days or late meetings, but I think Katarina and I have benefited from our time together.

As I've gotten to know her more and more, her intelligence and maturity have astounded me. Her daily discussions keep me on my toes, and I know if I try to speak about anything I don't grasp fully, she has no qualms calling me out. Yesterday, for seemingly no reason, she teased me with questions about the inner workings of electricity until I had rambled for ten minutes and finally had to say, "I don't know, Katarina," which seemed to delight her.

She's someone I can consider a good friend now. I'm certain she wants more, but I won't be the one to make the final move. She's inexperienced, and this is all new to her…There cannot be an ounce of doubt in my mind that she desires me for me, not out of obligation. After Linda's petty comment about grooming, I decided that no one would have a leg to stand on with accusations that I coerced my wife in any way.

If she wants me like I think she does, she has to be *dripping* for me. I'll continue my little touches and encouragements as she gains confidence to take what she wants. Approaching her door, I smile, thinking of her curled up in her nest. My kitten loves blankets but gets hot when she sleeps, so I bought her an undersheet cooling system that allows her to have the feeling of sliding into a cool, crisp bed constantly. At this time of night, she's probably burrowed under a pillow, one foot sticking out…

A high-pitched whine stops me in my tracks as I reach Katarina's door. Forgoing knocking, I try to turn the handle only to find it locked. Briefly, I consider her lying inside, injured, and despite the fact that this door is solid wood, I think I could bring it down with my shoulder.

"Ughhh, more, pleaseee."

That doesn't sound like a distressed noise, and I realize when I hear a faint buzzing exactly what my kitten's up to. She's getting herself off. Or becoming frustrated while trying to, if her moans are anything to go by. Not only sounds of pleasure, but adorable little growls and frustrated groans that make me think perhaps she's not an expert in this activity. *I wonder if she's ever made herself come at all.*

"Mmm, Henry, please, please, please..."

I release the handle as if burned and step back, hitting the far side of the hallway and placing my hands on my knees. She sounds so *frustrated,* and it pains me not to go in and help. I could. God, I could burst through the door and just *help* her get off. It wouldn't take much, one, maybe two fingers inside her, touching places that her little fingers can't reach. Maybe a whisper of pressure on her clit, and she'd be coming apart beautifully for me.

Imagining her chest flushed with desire, mouth open on my name, violet eyes wide and teary with pleasure, I've decided she *needs* me. My hand is back on the handle, ready to put my shoulder into this door and help my wife in a way only I can, when she shrieks and throws something at the door. Jolting back, I hear a buzzing sound. She must have gotten so frustrated that she flung her vibrator across the room.

This was exactly the wake-up call I needed, because *what* am I doing? Running my hands through my hair, I take long, quick strides back to my room, fighting the urge to slam the door behind me. Locking myself in, I pull on my hair as I lean heavily against the wall.

What was I about to do? Burst into her room and pretend I'd be able to keep myself from fucking her? Pretend I could resist her perfect little body if it were spread out for me? She'd be mine whether she was ready or not, and who knows if she's ready for me in that way. My wife's been flirting with me lately, but that isn't consent to losing her virginity to her beast of a husband bursting into her room after missing her during his late meeting like a lovesick teenager.

I barely stop my fist before it hits the wall, shocked at my own outburst. Trying to be rational, I remind myself exactly how long it's been since I've fucked anything. Moving to the shower, I turn on the icy spray to try to deal with the hardest erection I've ever experienced, but I know it won't work.

I haven't been with another woman since I found out we were to be married. And going from routine sex to complete celibacy is not for the faint of heart. I always had my fist, of course. I tried hard to avoid disrespecting her by imagining her, not knowing if she felt that way about me or would only want friendship. I tried my best to imagine the bodies of former partners, or just the most generic female form I could, but it was always her. I've fantasized about this woman for a year, but never in my wildest imagination were her moans that fucking sexy.

As I turn the temperature of the spray up from the unhelpful cold, my mind is filled with images of my wife's icy-blonde braid wrapped around my wrist as I fuck into her from behind, my thighs keeping her spread wide for me. I imagine her tiny cunt stretching around me, the whimpers from around her gag, barely able to take me.

I'm close to coming when the scene in my mind shifts, and I feel pleasure shoot up my spine.

Instead of my usual position with my subs—tied up, doggy style underneath me...Katarina's in my lap, her hands are in my hair, and she's looking into my eyes as I thrust slowly up into her, taking my time. Her nails scratch down my back, harder as they reach lower, causing me to groan into her mouth as I kiss her. She never stops caressing, trailing teasing touches over my abs, and the light catches on her diamond bedecked ring finger, my claim on her obvious to everyone.

My thrusts are slow but deep, wordlessly conveying my intention to make her understand that she's mine. Over and over and over, I drive into her as she writhes beneath me. Her soft, breathy moans are getting louder as I bring her closer to the brink of pleasure. "More," she begs. "Mmm, Henry, please, please, please..."

Keeping a consistent angle, I increase my intensity. Her breathy little moans become screams as I drive into her faster, harder, deeper. "You asked for this." Her tight little cunt is squeezing me like a vise. "Come for me, Kitten," I whisper into her ear, biting at her before pulling back to look into her eyes. I wrap my hand around her tiny neck and squeeze, applying just enough pressure to restrict her air flow. Her pussy flutters around me, milking my own release as she comes undone.

My fantasy fades, and I'm met with the evidence of my release painted across the shower wall. I groan, looking down at my still hard cock, obviously not getting the idea that all he's going to get right now is my large hand and vivid imagination.

I get ready for the night, making quick work of drying off, putting on some boxers, and brushing my teeth, then turn the lights off and get in bed. I would normally read for a bit, but I arrived home later than expected, and I know if I don't get to sleep, it'll be hell to pay in the morning.

My room has always been a safe place for me to unwind, but looking around now, it's both too large and too suffocating at the same time.

Closing my eyes, I'm immediately met with visions of my wife. My imagination works on overdrive, sending image after image of her, each one more erotic than the last.

I enter our room to see Katarina's small, naked body right where I left it, tied to my bed, waiting to be used. Passing by her, I leisurely walk to the closet to undress, taking a moment to come down from the day. Her confines really only allow her to lie on her back, but my day was especially grueling, so I'm in need of a rougher fuck. "On your hands and knees, wife," I say, unlocking her chains, allowing her to adjust so I can take her from behind. I grab the base of my cock and line myself up to her soaking cunt...

Katrina greets me at the front door, wearing only her lingerie. "Let me take care of you," she says, sinking to her knees. She makes quick work of my belt and unfastens my pants, then pulls my briefs down, allowing my cock to spring free before wrapping her hot little mouth around the head...

Looking up at the clock, I see thirty minutes have passed. I *really* need to go to sleep *now*. "For the love of everything, stop thinking about your wife," I tell myself, closing my eyes again and trying to force thoughts of what my day will look like tomorrow.

I'm at my desk, sorting through paper after paper of the quarterly financials. Something isn't adding up, but I can't figure it out. Katarina walks into my office with a brilliant smile on her face. "Can I help you with anything?" She skips over and drops down on my lap, flipping through the expense report. "Here!" she says, almost immediately finding the error.

"God, you're incredible," I lift her out of my lap and onto my desk, her knee-length skirt teasing me as it rides up her thighs. Goose bumps pebble on her legs as I slowly trace my hand higher and higher up her thigh, stopping only when I'm met with soaked lace. I pull down her panties and pocket them before dipping my head under her skirt to get a look at her perfect pink pussy. She's leaking, and I've never wanted to taste anything more. I move closer, my face flush to her core, and lick from her opening to her clit, reveling in the way her entire body shakes.

I'm propped up on my elbows, looking down at Katarina, my cock still buried to the hilt in her perfect cunt, our bodies slick from perspiration after hours of exertion. She lifts her hand and pushes back the wet hair that's fallen in my face. "I love you, Henry." I close my mouth around hers, kissing her. My tongue moves with hers in the same rhythm as my languid thrusts...
"I love you, too, Kitten."

Opening my eyes again, I see that another thirty minutes have passed, and I'm no closer to falling asleep. If anything, I'm more wound up than I was before I got in the shower. All I can think about is the woman at the end of the hall. I've tried my best to give her time and space. I've tried being a gentleman. But *fuck* do I want her. I want her more than I've wanted anything in my life. She's my goddamn wife, for fuck's sake. The irony that I both have her and don't have her at all doesn't escape me.

"Fuck!" I yell, throwing the bedside clock at the wall, the crash loudly echoing through the room.

Dammit. Pull yourself together, Henry.

I'm pacing back and forth in my room, working through my breathing exercises, when I hear a knock on my door and Katarina's quiet voice.

"Henry?"

Freezing, I hold my breath to avoid making even the smallest of sounds.

"Henry, are you okay?"

I remain still, hoping that if I just remain silent, she'll go away.

I think I've successfully avoided her until the door handle turns. "I'm fine, Katarina." It kills me to speak to her with a harsh tone, but I need her to leave. Having her in my room is something I *cannot* deal with right now.

The handle stops moving. "Are you sure?"

No, no, I'm not sure. What I want is for you to open that door, run to my bed, and throw yourself on top of me. What I'd really like is to fuck you into the mattress until dawn and then snuggle up against each other and sleep in.

"Yes, go back to bed."

"Good night, Henry." Her voice is nothing more than a whisper now.

"Good night." *Kitten.*

As I hear the echo of her steps down the hall, I'm flooded with shame. My sweet girl came to check on me after I threw a tantrum like a child. I have to do something about this. It's clear my need for her isn't going away, but I refuse to push her into something she doesn't want. Her friendship is more valuable than any other I've had, and I won't lose that because I can't keep my dick in check. As much as I want to storm into her room and impale her, it has to be her. She has to be the one to initiate the change in our dynamic.

I know she's attracted to me. I see the result of her desire every time her skin pebbles when we touch or when her pupils dilate as I'm staring into her eyes. I see it when a whispered tease causes her pulse to rise, and when she bites her bottom lip when she talks to me. Maybe she just doesn't know that her feelings are reciprocated. Tenfold. Perhaps *I'm* the one who hasn't been clear with their intentions. Maybe I just need to ramp up my seduction.

With a clear plan of action, I'm finally able to unwind. Holding a pillow, I drift to sleep, knowing that soon it will be my beautiful wife in my arms instead.

Chapter Fourteen

Henry's week has been increasingly busy, and it's obviously stressing him out. The first night he was late, he called several times, apologizing for not making it to dinner. I must have missed him coming home and was dozing off when the startling sound of his yelling and a crash woke me up. I went to his room to check on him, but he sounded angry. So I let it be.

Before we could discuss it the following morning, he found out about an incident at one of the foreign offices and immediately jetted away to help with damage control. To make matters worse, he had to rearrange all of his meetings, meaning next week will likely be stressful as well.

When he let me know he'd be able to come home today, I think I squeaked out loud in excitement. It's only been two nights, but I miss him. Deciding to be thankful that this dilemma hasn't derailed our entire weekend, instead of being pissy that I'll be spending most of the first half alone, I get up and prepare for my Saturday morning walk.

Since our first walk together, I've enjoyed waking up a little earlier to catch the sun rising over the vibrant autumn leaves. Even if my husband isn't here to carry a backpack filled with treats, the air is crisp, the views are stunning, and life is good.

I've almost made it back to the estate after a lovely hike when I hear the rustling of leaves behind me. At this time of the day, the staff aren't usually wandering about, especially on a weekend. The next logical explanation would be wildlife. I've walked almost daily and haven't come across anything predatory, although I'm aware of the risk, having grown up on a large estate myself. I'm trying to calm down, but the sound keeps getting closer and closer, and I can tell it's not a small animal. The memory of the Jenkins's goats crosses my mind, and I have to force myself not to break into a full-out sprint back to the house.

I slowly reach behind me for the Swiss Army knife Henry keeps in the bag. *Remain calm; some animals react to weakness.* I breathe deeply, gripping the blade for dear life. I'm almost to the clearing when I finally gain the nerve to turn around and gasp. A man stands not ten feet away from me. Despite the age-old man versus bear debate, I'm actually relieved. I've taken enough self-defense classes to know how to take someone out, and with the little weapon I'm holding, I'm confident enough in my ability to defend myself.

"Who are you, and why are you following me?" I ask, no need to beat around the bush now.

I hold the knife out when he tries taking a step toward me, causing him to raise his hands in surrender and back away. "I'm sorry, Mrs. Sinclair. I didn't mean to startle you, ma'am. I've been stepping in for Fredrick for a while and wanted to get an early start on my chores for the day."

I place my free hand over my chest, breathing a sigh of relief. "Oh, well. You certainly startled me, Mr....?"

"Oh my apologies, my name is Thomas, but most people call me Tommy." He extends his hand, slowly making his way closer to me, but stops a few feet short.

I'm torn between greeting him...or running to the house, but finally decide on the former of the two. Because how would he know Fredrick's name and specific role unless he was telling the truth? *Right?*

Taking a few steps of my own, I return his gesture with a smile, shaking his hand firmly. "Nice to meet you, Tommy. And welcome! Please call me Kat. I can't tell you how glad I am that you aren't some wild animal waiting to rip me to shreds!"

"Of course. Well, Ms. Kat, I guess I need to get back to it."

I watch him leave, not wanting to turn my back again, but the moment he's out of sight, I practically run back to the house. Slamming the door shut, I sink to the floor when I'm safely inside. I'm not sure what it was about the interaction, but something about it has me on edge.

Triple-checking that I've locked the door, I decide a bath would be a nice way to both warm up and calm my nerves. Walking into my room, I'm so deep in thought about what oils I'm going to use in my bath that I completely miss the package on the bed as I go to the en suite bathroom to get my water started.It isn't until I come back in to grab the bottle of lavender oil on my nightstand that I notice the small parcel on my bed. It's wrapped in beautiful pale blue paper and tied with a silver ribbon. Henry has left me enough gifts lately, all wrapped in the same style, so I immediately know who it's from. I scurry over to the bed and pick up the card lying next to the box.

Kitten,

I'm so sorry I've been gone the past couple of nights. Trust me when I say I've missed you. Hopefully, this helps with your lonely nights, better than the last one.

Henry

My curiosity piqued, I make quick work of untying the ribbon. Lifting the lid, I get my first glance at the mystery object inside. I pick it up, turning it in my hand. A black silicone rose, with a little button on the side. I click it, only to be startled by aggressive vibrations, and I drop the toy back into the box. Fumbling, I finally manage to click through the settings and turn it off. I've only ever had one vibrator. A little pink bullet, I believe, is what it's called. One of the younger maids I was chatty with back home gifted it to me for my eighteenth birthday. It broke a few days ago, not that it was ever helpful in the first place. The memory of its death plays in my head.

I'm lying in bed, tossing and turning. Missing him. Wishing it were my bed he would climb into when he got home late. What kind of lover would he be after a long day? Would he be hard and fast, just wanting a release to help his stress? Would he take his time, wanting to lose himself and forget all the day's troubles in the throes of passion? Would he want to take me from behind for the best leverage, or would he want to lie back and let me ride him?

Before I know it, my core is aching with what I've come to know is arousal. An ache I've yet to figure out how to ease on my own accord. Not from lack of trying. I grab my vibrator from my nightstand, turn it on, and place it between my legs, hoping that this time it will work.

My mind drifts to visions of Henry busting through my door, needing me as much as I need him. I'm lying out for him atop the comforter in my most alluring lingerie. He grabs my ankle and pulls me to the edge of the bed, my knees resting on his forearms as he unfastens his pants. He gives no warning, just thrusts into me, pausing only briefly. A growl leaves his lips as his head falls back. Before I can adjust to him, he's driving into me at a brutal pace. But I want more...

"Ughhh, more, pleaseee," I beg. "Mmm, Henry, please, please, please..."

Nothing. I throw my useless toy against the wall.

No...

I'm doing the mental math, trying to line everything up, refusing to believe that there's even a possibility that the reason I didn't hear Henry coming home Wednesday night was because I was in the middle of a failed attempt at orgasm that resulted in the death of my vibrator.

Oh God. Was *that* why he was angry that night? Because he didn't want to hear me masturbating? *Actually, that makes no sense. He just bought me a new one.*

Was *he* sexually frustrated as well? Surely, he knows by now that I'm interested in him. I thought he would pick up on my flirting, but I suppose, as intelligent as he is, he's still a man.

How do I let him know, besides flat-out saying *I would like to have sexual intercourse with you?*

Turning off the water, I look down at the clawfoot bathtub, and I'm reminded of Mrs. Potts's words.

"In any case, I'm saying that perhaps when Mr. Sinclair has had a particularly bad day or rough week, you might draw him a bath..."

Smiling, I step into the scalding water and plan my seduction.

"Katarina?"

Perfect timing. I turn the water off and wait for him, sitting on the ledge of his large bathtub, fiddling with the strings of my new black bikini.

My heart rate spikes at the sound of his door opening. I'm not entirely sure what I'm expecting from tonight, but one thing is certain: our relationship will not be the same when we leave this room.

His footsteps echo from his room into his bathroom while I sit for what seems like an eternity. *If he doesn't come in soon, the water will get cold.* I'm about to get up and let him know I'm here when the door opens and he comes walking in, completely naked. I've seen him with just his swim shorts on, so I know how ripped he is, but damn.

Thankfully, he's still looking down, unfastening the watch from his wrist, giving me time to ogle him properly. All six foot seven inches of him. Saying he's the archetype the gods modeled themselves after doesn't give justice to this man's body. I trail my gaze from his broad shoulders to his prominent chest, the perfect amount of hair accentuating his strong pecs. Continuing, I count eight abs before his happy trail thickens between where his Adonis belt tapers down to his...Oh God...His flaccid dick swings heavily with each step he takes. Already bigger than anything I could imagine. *And I have imagined.*

Of course, that's the moment he chooses to notice my presence. Eyes wide, mouth in an 'O,' cheeks reddening. I would be embarrassed, but he looks just as shocked as I am. "Katarina? What on earth are you...?"

"Bath!" I interrupt, pointing at the tub full of hot water and essential oils.

He looks from the bath back to me, his eyes darkening as he takes me in. His thick cock is growing impossibly larger. "Kitten. What are you doing in my bathroom?"

"I wanted to give you a bath. Wash your hair..." I say, playing with the string of my bottoms, refusing to look into his eyes.

I can feel him getting closer. "And why are you wearing that scrumptious little bathing suit to do it?"

"In case I got wet..."

"Oh, Kitten, there's no doubt about that."

He steps over where I'm still sitting on the edge of the bath and chills pebble on my skin at the soft brush of his hard length against my arm on his way. He tilts his head back, groaning as he sinks farther into the hot water.

Pulling myself together, I grab his shampoo from where I had it waiting on the floor beside me and turn, putting my feet in the water for a more comfortable position as I wash his hair. Before I know what's happening, two large hands are wrapped completely around my waist.

"Join me," he says, giving me no time to protest before pulling me into the bath with him.

"What are you...Eek!" I land on his lap, my legs on either side of his. "I was going to wash your hair!"

"Then wash it." He gently takes my legs and wraps them around his waist, then draws my body flush to his. "But don't think you're going to come into my bathroom wearing what could barely be described as scraps to cover that body I've been imagining for weeks and expect me to do any less than hold you like this."

I lather my hands with his shampoo and raise my shaking arms to massage it into his scalp. He's so close like this. One of his arms is locked around me, keeping my body pressed against his while the other explores. His gentle traces start at my neck as his hand makes its way down at an excruciatingly slow pace, stopping to rest between my breasts. His breath against my neck is electric. He tilts his head forward, almost resting it on my shoulder for me to wash the back side. I'm not sure how I managed to wash his hair at all.

"All done," I whisper. "Time to rinse."

Taking the handheld spray, I turn the water back on and begin rinsing the shampoo from his hair. Still holding me against him, Henry leans his head back slightly to avoid getting water in his eyes. His erection was resting against my core, but the new angle causes it to rub against me, sending chills through my body, despite the scalding water. It's only separated by the thin strip of fabric from my bathing suit. All it would take is a slip, and he would be...

"Thank you," he whispers as he raises his head, his hair dripping water onto his face, and stares into my eyes with an intensity that takes my breath away. He's the most beautiful man I've ever seen.

The memory of the kiss we shared at our wedding crosses my mind, and I find myself drawing closer to him, dying to feel his lips on mine again. I'm a hair's breadth away from tasting him again when he turns his head at the last minute, placing a chaste kiss on my cheek.

I swear the water turns to ice around me as rejection makes my blood run cold. The tension filling the air dissipates, leaving a thin silence. "I should go."

The water splashes around us as I hastily exit the tub, covering my body until I can get a towel, all of a sudden feeling exposed.

"Katarina!"

I don't look back, keeping my composure long enough to get out of his room before closing his door and running as fast as I can to lock myself in mine.

Chapter Fifteen

I'm sitting at my desk as Linda drones on and on about the upcoming annual charity gala that the company puts on the day before Thanksgiving. She's going over seating arrangements when my mind wanders to the memory of Katarina and me in the bath. The memory that's been playing on repeat for over a week.

"Katarina?" I call out. My wife is the first thing on my mind as I walk through the door. When I don't get an answer, I walk up the stairs and check in her room, only to find it empty. Deciding to rinse off after a long flight before I go looking for whatever my wife might be up to, I head to my room.

I never used to mind traveling, but I haven't been away overnight since Katarina moved in, and it almost killed me to be apart from her. It feels so good to be home. However, the problem of her not sharing my bed remains. I've half a mind to say screw it and just tell her how I feel instead of playing the potential long seduction game.

Undressed, I walk into the bathroom, my focus on taking off my watch. Looking up to grab a towel, I'm met with the mouthwatering view of the woman I've been thinking about nonstop for the past three days.

"Katarina? What on earth are you..."

Goddamn, she looks like pure sin in her black string bikini. I can feel my erection growing with each passing second.

The next thing I know, she's in my arms, straddling me in the bath, massaging my head as she washes my hair. This is much better than the cold shower I was planning on taking. I can't help but touch her. I want to pull the scraps of cloth from her perfect, perky breasts. Despite the hot water, her nipples peak out from under her bikini. I want to see what shade of pink they are. I want to pull them into my mouth and suck until I leave them marked with bruises. Bruises that trail from her perfect breasts to her...

"All done," she breathes, "Time to rinse."

I lean back, and the new angle forces my cock closer to her hot little cunt. If we weren't already in a tub of water, I know I would feel how wet she is.

All I'd have to do is slide this flimsy strip of material over, and I would be lined up at her entrance. I could drive inside of her right now and officially make her mine. Consummate this marriage right here, right now.

She's so close to me, our eyes locked, and she's moving closer. God, I want to kiss those lips again. The kiss we shared on our wedding day wasn't long enough. I want her to open up for me.

But I can't. Turning at the last minute, I kiss her cheek.

I was such an idiot. She left that night, and things haven't been the same since. I wasn't rejecting her. If she hadn't left, I one hundred percent would've fucked her in that bath. If she had just let me explain...I don't kiss women. It's not her or something she did. I just *don't*. It's written into every contract I've had as a dominant. Our kiss on our wedding day felt like a once-in-a-lifetime lightning strike, but I know now that it completely shifted my perspective on the act.

It's an intimacy I haven't allowed myself to indulge in, but I would learn for her. I *want* to kiss her. *I want everything with her.* I would've done it that night in the bath. It's just my first reaction to deflect. I should've gone after her that night. I should've burst into her room and kissed her so fervently that she would never mistake my desire again.

If she knew how rare it was for me to allow touch, for her to wash my hair so intimately, she wouldn't have felt the rejection of her kiss quite so acutely. But that's my fault, once again, for not expressing myself clearly. The gala will be the perfect opportunity to show her how proud I am that she's mine, and just how much she owns every ounce of me.

"Mr. Sinclair?" Linda's shrewd voice brings me back to the meeting.

"I'm sorry, what is it, Linda?"

"I was just asking if you were going to bring a plus-one."

"Of course I'll be bringing a plus-one," I say, lifting my left hand to flash my ring.

Linda rolls her eyes, her attitude peeping out more and more as of late. "I just didn't know if you were planning to bring your *child bride*."

Suddenly, my attention is completely directed at her, my predatory reflex kicking in at her insult. Before I can say anything harmful, she speaks up again.

"You know what I mean, it's a very important night for the company. I know she is an extraordinary piece of eye candy to have on your arm, but you'll be dealing with tycoons in the industry, and she *is* so young. I would hate for them to think poorly of you because she just doesn't have the proper schmoozing experience..."

My sudden outburst of laughter stops Linda from her rambling. "If you'd ever had a conversation with my wife, you would know how absurd your statement is."

The anger in her eyes is impossible to miss, and I know if I don't shut this down quickly, it will turn into a nightmare.

"Linda, please make sure Mrs. Sinclair is properly documented as my plus-one. For this event and everyone moving forward. You're excused."

She gives a curt nod before leaving, and I rub away the tension headache threatening to form.

After all of the chaos of the past two weeks, I'm beyond ready for the gala and a chance to show off my wife. I can't change the fact that Katarina felt rejected, but I can make sure she knows exactly how proud I am to have her on my arm.

Leaning back in my desk chair, I imagine what it'll be like to finally have a plus-one to an event like this. Although these galas are for a good cause, I've never enjoyed them. I'm an expert in showing up, donating to whatever deserving cause there is, dancing with ladies of all ages with a smile on my face, staying an appropriate amount of time before sneaking off home or to the club...but I've never had a confidant there with me. Someone with whom to make wry observations about other guests, to hog all my dances. These events can be a lonely business, particularly when it feels like everyone wants a piece of you.

I can't stop thinking about my wife these days, and although I have another meeting in five minutes, my mind wanders to the gala.

Collapsing into giggles, Katarina leans heavily on me as we sneak into a hallway off the ballroom. Finding what seems to be an overflow storage room for disused holiday decorations, we sneak in and I sit her down on a table.

"My feet huuuurt, Henry. I knew these heels were a bad idea." My wife slurs her words just a bit, showing off her champagne indulgence. By next year's gala, if I have my way, she'll be drinking sparkling cider.

Kneeling before her, I hear her breath catch and can't help but smirk. Undoing the clasp around her ankle, I gently pull one platform heel off before moving on to her other foot. Her thigh-high slit tantalizes me, but I have an easier path to pleasure for her right now. Digging my thumb into her arch, she collapses back onto her elbows with an almost pornographic groan.

"Ohhh fuckkk, that feels good, Henry. Please don't stop..."

"Language, Kitten. Just because we're out doesn't mean I won't punish you."

Moving my ministrations up her calf to her thigh, because I can't help myself, I realize she's been gallivanting all night with no panties.

"Mrs. Sinclair, have you had no panties on all night? That's quite naughty. I think you might need to be punished."

She pulls herself up off her elbows and raises one eyebrow defiantly.

"What are you going to do, spank me?

The harsh alarm on my phone jolts me back to the present, hard as a rock and late for my meeting. It's going to take me a few more minutes to cool down before I can walk into a conference room, but any time I can spend with Katarina is worthwhile, even in my imagination. Perhaps we can recreate the scene in real life at the gala. Thinking of how perfect her dress will be for clandestine touches all night, I ready myself for the last meeting before getting to leave for dinner and the relaxing comfort of *home.*

With Mrs. Potts and Katarina holed up in her dressing room finishing her hair and makeup for this evening, I admire the dress I've just snuck in to hang on the window's curtain rod. I told my wife that she could pick any of the gowns in her closet for this evening, but I lied. From the moment I saw her in her dusky periwinkle swimsuit the first morning she came to the pool, I knew she needed a gown in this color. *And lingerie, and sweatpants, and a cocktail dress.* I may have gone overboard, but once I figured out the exact color code for the hue that makes her eyes sparkle, well. It's not my fault; it's so easy to order custom colors of things.

The gown is a strapless satin, with a structured, corseted waist that tapers to the floor, accompanied by a slight train. A showstopping thigh-high slit makes it dramatic and will show off her perfect legs. Matching platforms, as comfortable as possible, and teardrop diamond earrings will complete the look. She's going to be magnificent on my arm, and her dress will only enhance her beauty.

My laughter when Linda expressed concern for Katarina's ability to mingle with the rich and famous was sincere, as I can't imagine anyone better suited to the role. I can feel the hearts in my eyes as I think of how quickly she's bewitched the staff, truly caring about their lives and making an effort to get to know them. She knows precisely how to balance asking thoughtful questions of someone with subtly directing the conversation in any direction she pleases, and I can't wait to watch her work the room tonight. People will be eating out of her hand in no time.

A throat clears, and I turn from the dress to see the woman occupying my every thought. She's *exquisite.* Covered by a dressing gown, for now, her hair simple and out of her face. Potts discreetly takes her leave, and I approach Katarina in a daze before reminding myself I have seduction to accomplish and can't be caught off guard. She's eyeing me apprehensively, and I need to show her how proud I am to be hers tonight.

"You look beautiful tonight, Mrs. Sinclair," I say lowly, brushing a kiss over her knuckles. "I hope you don't mind that I took the liberty of having a dress made for you this evening, and that you'll do me the honor of wearing it."

I see her decide not to be *too* mad at me, and I'm rewarded with a smile. "It looks like a beautiful dress. Thank you, Mr. Sinclair. But, Potts left, and it looks like I'll need some help with the zipper..."

"I was, perhaps foolishly, anticipating that you might allow me to be of assistance?" I ask, showing her the vulnerability I feel. I've seen her in nothing but a tiny swimsuit, and she's seen all of me, at this point. Although I'm not pushing for an immediate return to the intimacy we shared in the bath that I fucked up, I long to see her...

She drops the robe she was wrapped in, and I feel my mouth drop open. Mrs. Potts obviously delivered the package containing her matching lingerie, and she's wearing it to perfection. *Beyond perfection.* A lacy corset in the same custom periwinkle, with a barely there thong to match. Walking past me, swaying her hips, she stops just in front of the dress and looks at me over her shoulder.

"Well?"

Sassy girl. *That'll get you spanked sooner than you realize.*

Taking another deep breath, I cross the room, reaching over her to pull down the dress and hold it open for her to step into with my arms bracketing her hips. Zipping her up, I catch her eye in the full-length mirror in the corner of the room and make no attempt to hide my blazing desire for her. Maybe all this isn't necessary, and we could just stay in…

"Do you have shoes for me, as well?" she asks sweetly, and I huff a laugh at how well she's able to play me now.

"Yes, brat. Go sit, and I'll bring them to you."

Grabbing the box off the bed, I follow her to her settee and kneel before her, mirroring my fantasy from my office. Pulling her left leg onto my knee first, I delicately place her foot into the shoe and clasp the ankle strap. Before she can pull it away, I grab her ankle and hold her in place. Looking up from my vantage point, and feeling incredibly at home on my knees before her, I lick a tiny stripe up her instep before kissing her inner ankle and releasing her foot to grab the other.

The heat in her eyes is unmistakable, along with the goose bumps rising across her skin. I repeat my worship of her other leg and stand, pulling her with me. Arranging us before the mirror with her in front of me, I'm awed by the perfection I see. Her toned leg is perfectly framed by the slit in the dress, diamonds glittering at her ears, plush lips slightly parted as her eyes meet mine. My frame towers over her, left hand protectively across her lower stomach, as if daring anyone to approach what belongs to me. As she delicately places her own left hand on mine, her rings glisten, a reminder to everyone tonight what she is.

Mine.

Chapter Sixteen

David Wiltshire, on his fourth marriage. Six kids total between the first three wives and another on the way. He enjoys golfing and boating in his free time. Ha, no surprise there.

Jonathan Beaumont operates mostly from France after marrying a French model. Only on his second wife. His children have been estranged since he changed his will. Fan of sailing.

Nathan Ellis took over his father's empire around the same time as Henry. Engaged to a European heiress. Recently took a hiatus from the company to take his yacht around the Caribbean.

"There were several salacious rumors about that hiatus involving more than one illegitimate child." Henry reaches across the back seat and rests his hand on my thigh, squeezing slightly. "Katarina, you'll be fine."

"I didn't realize I was speaking out loud, but of course I'll be fine," I say, giving him my most polished, charming smile.

Henry chuckles, pulling my hand from my lap and kissing my knuckles. "I know you will be. You've been mumbling the whole ride, though, and I don't want you to stress yourself out about tonight. You're already going to blow everyone away."

"Hmm, perhaps. Henry?"

"Yes?"

"Do you have a boat? It seems there's a trend among your peers when it comes to aquatic hobbies."

Henry's laughter deepens. A sound I've grown to love above most others. "Yes, we have a boat. A very nice, very large yacht."

The car stops, and my husband hops out with haste I've yet to see from him. I take my time to unfasten my seat belt, and before I know it, my door is pulled open and Henry has extended his hand to mine.

He pulls my hand to his mouth and bends down slightly to kiss my knuckles again. When he hovers just a moment longer than before, his hot breath against my skin sends chills through my body. "Mrs. Sinclair."

When he's successfully helped me out of the car, he bends his arm, allowing me to loop mine through, and leans down to whisper in my ear. "Your beauty is otherworldly, Katarina. I don't think I'll be able to tell you enough how stunning you look tonight."

"Henry! It's great to see you!"

A man who looks to be around the same age as my husband walks up and pulls him into a hug, much more familiar than the greetings of stiff handshakes we've been receiving since walking inside. "And who do we have here? This lovely lady can't be the mysterious wife we've heard so much about, can it?"

"Ah, Charles Dawson, it's been too long. This is indeed my *incredibly* lovely wife, Mrs. Katarina Sinclair."

The man turns his attention to me. "It's a pleasure to meet you, Mrs. Sinclair," he says, shaking my hand.

"The pleasure is all mine, Mr. Dawson, and please, call me Kat," I say with a smile.

"In that case, call me Chuck. I'm not sure if Henry has mentioned me. We went to school together in England and got into our fair share of trouble," he says, squeezing Henry's shoulder.

"Of course he has. I believe he's mentioned your hobby for picking locks, having come in handy time and time again."

"Oh, so you do remember me!" He chuckles, looking at Henry. "When I found out you were married, I thought you must have forgotten about me. That's the only plausible reason I wouldn't have received an invitation. But now that I've met her, I believe you were just trying to keep Kat's beauty hidden lest you have some competition."

Chuck winks at me, and I can't help but smile. He's a rather charming man, and not terrible on the eyes either. If not for my Greek god of a husband, I might call him handsome?

Henry pulls me against his body so fast, I'm surprised I don't have whiplash. "That will be enough, Dawson. We've got to make our way to our seats soon anyway."

"Ugh, I hate this part of these events. An hour of boring speech after speech before we can get to the fun part of the night," Chuck says, not seeming to notice Henry's caveman behavior. "Again, it's a pleasure to meet you, Kat. I hope you'll save a dance for me later?"

"I wouldn't count on any dances with *Mrs. Sinclair*," Henry says and pulls me away, placing a hand on the small of my back in an obvious act of possession.

As he guides me through the crowd to our table, his fingers trail lower and lower. His touch has been constant but modest since we've arrived, but by the time we reach our table, he's practically groping my ass.

It's been over a week since the incident in the bath, and I've been doing my best to avoid him, but I've missed his touch. *I've missed him.* Whatever feelings of rejection I've felt since then have all but disappeared. After countless touches, countless compliments, and the way he *looks* at me, he's made his desire clear.

"Thank you," I say when he pulls back my chair.

"Come here, *wife*," Henry says, pulling my chair against his, throwing his arm around my shoulders, and leaning his head close to mine. "You're the most beautiful woman in the world. Have I told you that tonight?"

"Only about twenty times," I breathe out.

"Mmm, so not nearly enough," he whispers in my ear before slowly trailing his nose down the curve of my neck and placing a kiss on the edge of my bare shoulder.

"You're the most beautiful. Stunning. Extraordinary. Breathtaking. Brilliant. Goddess of a woman. To have ever.

Existed," he whispers, each word punctuated with a kiss as he makes his way back up my neck.

The kisses are chaste in nature, but the combination of his words and his breath on my neck sends a flood of arousal to my core.

When he pulls back to look at me, his eyes are level with mine and darker than I've ever seen them. "And you're *mine.*"

Oh. Dear. God. I can't breathe. And I'm going to leave a puddle on this chair if I don't do something fast. "Erm...I should probably freshen up before this starts," I say, doing my best to stand gracefully in my current state.

The powder room is surprisingly empty, allowing me my choice of stalls. I rush to the one farthest from the entrance and close the door behind me, breathing deeply to calm myself.

I've finally gotten my heart rate down when the door creaks open. Heels click on the marble floor in different cadences, indicating multiple women. Wanting to avoid any small talk, I wait for the sound of stall doors closing before making my exit, but it never comes. All I hear is the faucet turning on, and I've waited long enough that it would be awkward to leave now.

"Any chance we can hide out here until the dancing starts?" a woman asks in a husky voice.

"Ugh, I know. I *hate* these stupid ceremonial speeches. Like, everyone here is already going to donate, just take our money and let us be!" another woman replies, her tone lighter and airier but no less grating.

The screeching laughter threatens to do serious damage to my eardrums, but their voices are distinct enough that I can confidently assume there are only two women.

"Did you see Henry?" Husky asks. "I mean, did you see Henry and his *wife?*"

"Yes! Have you heard the rumors?" asks woman number two.

"That he knocked her up? Yeah, right. You know as well as I do that Henry Sinclair *never* goes bare. Not even with him being so particular about his women being on birth control. He made my doctor send him a notarized confirmation that I had undergone the implant. Not that you can't feel it in your arm regardless."

I'm frozen. I obviously can't leave now, but I'm suddenly aware of any noise I make. Not that I can breathe anyway as I listen to these women discuss having sex with my husband. Something I've been longing for but that he keeps avoiding.

"Same girl, same. There just has to be more to this story. She's *so* young. There's no way she's experienced enough for him. He doesn't even accept applications from partners with less than five years of experience in the lifestyle. In fact, there's a renowned submissive at one of my favorite clubs who had had ten years of experience but only two partners, and he didn't give her a chance."

"Maybe he just finally fell for someone? I mean, have you noticed how handsy he's been all night? Have you ever known him to be so touchy?"

"Ha! Funny. Minimal touching, no kissing, minimal eye contact. He has so many rules against intimacy. Honestly, it's really a wonder he's such a sought-after Dom."

"You've seen the man. He's built like a god! Who *wouldn't* want a chance at that? And his *cock*...I've yet to come across one bigger. *And* goddamn can he fuck. Even if it was only from behind, I've never come so much in my life."

"You too? I thought maybe it was just me, but you're right, I certainly didn't mind not kissing when he was dealing out one orgasm after another. I wonder if this has anything to do with his last sub, Lori? He terminated their contract early, and I heard she made a huge deal about it."

"You know we all tried to be the woman to get him longer than his standard one-year contract, so whatever it is that she did, I'm certainly jealous."

"Ugh, they're about to start. Let's go."

They're out in a flash, but I've lost my ability to breathe yet again. Henry told me about his past with BDSM and was clear that he would tell me anything I wanted to know. I really should've asked him. I would've preferred to hear his explanation of things instead of from two of his past partners.

He apparently wasn't touchy with them, but did he care for them? Did he bring them to the home we now share? Did they swim in my pool or eat at my table? Did they sleep in his bed?

I'm trying to convince myself that what we have is different. He touches me, and he certainly makes eye contact. He won't kiss me, though, so maybe I'm no different. After all, our relationship is just another contract, isn't it? At least he personally chose those women. He had no choice with me. And he certainly hasn't tried to fuck me.

Music bleeds into the powder room, signaling the start of the ceremony. *Breathe, Kat, breathe.*

Summoning all the grace I can, I hold my head high and make my way to the front. I can feel the eyes of everyone at each table as I pass, threatening my composure.

I practically fall into my seat when I finally reach my chair, but Henry immediately reaches for me. "Are you alright? You seem flushed." The concern in his eyes is evident as he rubs his thumb across the top of my hand.

"I must have had too much champagne. I should be fine in a minute," I say, reveling in his touch as he wraps his arm around me and pulls my head to him, kissing the top before letting his hand rest on the back of my chair.

His hand finds my arm, stroking tenderly up and down throughout the ceremony, calming my nerves. Making me believe I *do* mean something special to him after all. By the time it's over, I'm feeling much better about things and ready to spend the evening dancing with my husband.

That is, until I hear a familiar husky voice.

"Henry! How are you, darling?"

Turning, I see two gorgeous women, both built like models with legs for days. I'm sure they're much closer to Henry's age as well. They both look young, but there's an air of maturity there, too.

If my husband is shocked to see them, he hides it well. "Hello, Val, Melissa," he says, holding out his hand to greet them. It's as stiff a welcome as he gave every middle-aged man, but it still ignites a burning jealousy in my heart.

"And who is this?" the woman with the higher-pitched voice, Melissa, asks.

Henry smiles down at me. "This is my wife—"

"Mrs. Sinclair." I interrupt, holding out my hand. Henry raises an eyebrow and smirks. My introduction clearly amuses him, but he doesn't say anything.

Each woman shakes my hand and introduces themselves. Not knowing I was eavesdropping on their previous conversation, they recount their relationship with Henry as "old friends," and to my dismay, he doesn't correct that when they leave.

Whatever resolve I felt during the ceremony is gone as Henry leads me to the dance floor, and by the time I'm in his arms, I'm fighting tears.

My husband immediately senses my change in demeanor, something I would typically find charming, if not for my current emotional crisis. "Kitten, what's wrong?" he asks, his tone gentle.

"I'm just not feeling well tonight," I say, placing my head on his chest so he can't see the tears welling up in my eyes. "I just want to go home."

"Let's go home then."

He doesn't hesitate, doesn't ask if I can make it a little longer. He doesn't protest that this is *his* gala and he shouldn't be leaving this early in the night. He just leads me to the exit and helps me into the car.

The ride home is quiet, especially after I pulled my hand away when Henry tried to hold it. He patted my thigh and apologized that I wasn't feeling well. He hasn't tried to touch me since.

He's been perfect, actually. The entire night, he's been nothing but attentive and caring. Flirting with me and complimenting me. Driving me insane with his touch. Taking care of me and putting my needs before anything else.

I shouldn't be reacting like this to a silly conversation, but what I overheard was the last straw breaking through six weeks of emotions I haven't been able to even understand fully, much less deal with.

The car is barely parked when I fling open the door, running to my room before he can follow. My youth is already a sore spot for him. I don't need him to see me falling apart over his exes like a jealous, immature schoolgirl.

I'm on my bed crying my eyes out when I hear a knock on the door.

"Katarina? Are you okay, darling?" His voice is soft, but I can hear his concern.

I do my best to calm my crying so my voice doesn't come out shaky. "I'm fine, Henry, just not feeling well."

"Is there anything I can do for you?"

Yes, hold me. Kiss me. Take me back to your bed and make love to me.

"No, I'll be fine, I promise. Good night, Henry."

The door handle turns slightly, halted by the lock. "Good night, Kitten."

Chapter Seventeen

Tonight didn't go as expected at all. I didn't anticipate being back in my bedroom this early, and I halfway hoped that when I did get back, I wouldn't be alone.

Thoughts of my beautiful wife cross my mind, and I'm tempted to walk down the hall and listen through her door for any signs of life for the fourth time tonight. Ultimately, I decide that she's probably sound asleep.

She was a dream tonight, and the gown I chose made her look like the goddess she is. Even with her six-inch platform heels, she was a tiny little thing, still barely coming to my chest.

Tomorrow is Thanksgiving, and though we don't have an early morning, I need to be as well rested as possible to deal with my family. This is the first time in years we'll all be together for the holiday. It's my nephew LJ's first, and Mom is planning on a big spread.

It's not that I don't want to see my family. I find myself missing them more lately than I ever have. But I've managed to keep Katarina to myself since we got married despite their begging. I know that tomorrow will be a lot for her, especially after whatever upset her today.

I had hoped she would ask to leave early, but I wanted it to be so I could bring her back into my bed and fucking ravish her. Not because she wasn't feeling well. If I were any less of a man, I would've done it anyway. I would've thrown her over my shoulder before she could get out of the car and carried her to my room, even kicking and screaming.

This charade of ours has gone on long enough. As soon as we get through this weekend, I'm consummating my goddamn marriage. I just have to hold myself together a few more nights, and she'll be beside me. For good.

A glance at the clock confirms I have more than enough time to read for a bit before bed. Sighing, I reach into my nightstand and grab my book and reading glasses, calculating how long I can read so I still get a solid eight hours of sleep. I might not have been planning to sleep much tonight, but since the opportunity is presenting itself, I'll take advantage. I'll need to get as much as I can now because once I get my hands on her...

I've barely had time to open my book when the creaking of my door opening catches my attention. The room is dimly lit from the lamp on my nightstand, but the vision at the entrance of my room is as clear as day.

My wife is propped against the doorframe in a sheer white silk nightgown, biting her lip.

"Katarina?"

Without a word in response, she slowly makes her way toward me, each step flaunting the shadow of her naked curves underneath her gown. My breath hitches when she gets to the edge of my bed, hopping up on the mattress and climbing to me on her hands and knees. *She's such a natural fucking submissive.* My cock twitches when I think of all the positions I'll be able to take her in. I've seen how flexible she is, and I'll be able to fold her up like a pretzel while I manhandle her.

I sit up straight, laying the book down to hide my erection under the covers, but it does no good. She doesn't hesitate to move the book when she reaches my lap. Her eyes search mine as she straddles me, and I can't focus on anything but her plump, glossy lips only inches from my face as she tilts her head toward me.

"Katarina, what are you doing?" I ask gently, wrapping my hands around her arms before she closes the distance between our mouths.

If she wants this, I'll give it to her. I'll give her everything *either* of us can imagine and so much more. I'll make it so fucking good for her, going nice and slow for her first time, worshipping her body like she deserves.

The heat in her eyes cools, and she sits up, stiffening in my arms. I can see her desire fading as her pupils contract, although the vein in her neck tells me her pulse is only increasing. Concern replaces my own desire as I try to figure out what's happened.

"Val and Melissa were subs of yours," she says flatly.

I certainly didn't have that on my *why is my wife upset* bingo card. "Yes."

She's searching my eyes for more, but I'm not sure what she's looking for. "They said they were *old friends* of yours, and you just went along with it. You didn't think to tell me?"

"I haven't thought about those two women in years, and certainly not sexually." I've honestly forgotten about sex with anyone other than imagining it with her.

"Well, I have. I got to hear all about it when I went to the ladies' room before the ceremony." Her little body is shaking, but she swats my hand away when I try to steady her. "They went on and on about how well you fucked them and how you made them come *so many times*."

"Katarina..." I try caressing her cheek, but she pushes me away again.

"They did say it was practically a miracle that you were touching your *inexperienced young wife*. And they *did* defend against the rumors that you'd only married me because you'd knocked me up. Apparently, you're quite the stickler for birth control."

She pauses to laugh, her expression turning manic. "Funny, don't you think? Knocking me up would at least mean you were attracted to me enough to fuck me in the first place. They even mentioned they were jealous of me. Bet they wouldn't be if they knew you were *forced* to marry me."

"Katarina."

"Oh! I was meaning to ask!" And if smiles could kill... "Have either of those women been in my house? Or I guess any others...You apparently have a hard stop at a year, so I'm sure there have been *plenty* more where they came from. I just want to know where any women might have been whoring around naked in *my* house so I'll know which rooms to completely renovate."

"Katarina!"

My voice is loud enough to finally startle her into silence. I cup her cheeks gently. "Kitten, I'm so sorry you had such a negative encounter, and I want to hear all about it. But you knew this about me. I wasn't hiding any of this from you. So can we please calm down and talk about this rationally?"

She nods, her arms still crossed, lips in a pout. Fucking adorable.

"What would you like to know?"

"Did you have little pet names for all of them, too?"

"Technically, yes, I called them all "pet." You were right about there being quite a few of them. I've had one a year for over 10 years, and names can run together, plus the one-offs during my breaks. I felt more comfortable referring to everyone as the same thing."

"You say *my* name."

"I do." I squeeze her hand. "What else?"

"Were any of them here?"

"No, I've never brought a woman here. I would have them over to various other residences across the country, but I haven't even done that in years. I'm afraid the only living women you'll have to worry about 'whoring around naked' in your house would be my mother and sister. You can take that up with them tomorrow when we see them."

Her little smile brings me some relief. I hate for her to be upset about something as insignificant as my past contracts. They mean *nothing* to me, so they shouldn't burden her. "What else?"

"They mentioned you don't like inexperienced submissives. I'm not even sure I could be a submissive at all, but I'm certainly inexperienced."

"I don't want you in the same capacity as I wanted them. I want you *completely*. I don't need to have that style of relationship with you to be satisfied. I just want to take care of you. And your inexperience just means I'm the only lucky bastard who will ever get to do that."

"Does that mean you'll be intimate with me?"

"Excuse me?"

"They said you have things written in your contract like *minimal touch, minimal eye contact, no kissing*. Are you going to be like that with me?"

Thinking back to all the rules I had with my subs, I can't imagine missing out on those things with my wife. I wish I could touch her all the time. I wish my obligations would allow me to always be with her. I certainly can't imagine not being able to look into her remarkable violet eyes. And her lips...I've dreamed of tasting those again since our wedding day.

"I don't want to be. You're special. It's different with you."

"You say I'm special, but they have a piece of you that you refuse to give to me," she says, hanging her head.

Finally allowing me to touch her again, I hold her face in my hand, tilting it back up to match my gaze. "Katarina. Intimacy is just not something that comes easily to me."

"So you'll never kiss me?"

Lifting my other hand from where it rests on her thigh, I tuck a strand of fallen hair behind her ear before cupping her face. "Of course I will."

Her voice is barely a whisper, and if I weren't so close to her, I would miss it. "Then do it...please?"

I freeze. Why do I feel like a teenager kissing a girl for the first time? I suppose because this isn't just *any* girl. It's *the* girl.

I didn't even realize I had a "dream girl" until I met my wife, but she's all I've dreamed of since before we even got married. She's all I've dreamed of since I saw her picture.

"Ugh, will you at least fuck me then, so I can at least say I've had as much of my *husband* as his past *whores* have had?" Whatever calm she had is replaced by an attitude rivaling that of earlier.

I slowly trail my hands down her neck before resting them on her shoulders. "I've given you my last name. Why can't you see how much more that means?"

Still straddling me, she shakes away from my hold. Apparently, she doesn't want me to touch her, but sitting on my lap and teasing my already weeping cock isn't a problem. "Exactly. I'm your *wife*. Why won't you fuck me?"

"Language, little girl." Squeezing my eyes shut, I do my best not to raise my voice, but her temper is starting to wear on me. "Not a single woman has ever had what you have."

"Well, they were pretty explicit about how your *cock* felt, and you've definitely not given me *that!* Am I supposed to spend the rest of my life celibate? To sit around, thankful that you grace me with your touch?"

Still frozen, I furrow my eyebrows as I try to understand what she's feeling right now. Her emotions have been all over the place tonight, and I don't want to overstep. I'm about to reach for her when she huffs, jumps off the bed, and marches out of my room, slamming the door as she leaves.

Chapter Eighteen

"It's hard to believe we used to be her size." Henry's sister, Margot, sighs and looks at me wistfully as I try on another dress in the third boutique we've been in today.

I was slightly intimidated when Margot reached out to ask if I'd like to go shopping after Thanksgiving with her and Henry's sister-in-law, Sloane, but I shouldn't have been. It crossed my mind briefly after our wedding that I should reach out and try to build those relationships, but things have felt so busy since moving in that I just haven't had the chance. Between settling in, getting to know the staff, and working on my plans to seduce my husband, I've been a bit preoccupied.

Spending time with the whole Sinclair family during the holiday itself was a whirlwind, with lots of attention on Sloane and Ledger's baby, Ledger Jr., so I wasn't the main attraction. I was able to mostly avoid being in Henry's proximity between the men watching football and the women cooing over the baby and discussing Blanche's pickleball team.

Today, they immediately set my mind at ease, taking an interest in how things are going in my household without making me feel like they're prying. I know Margot grew up in society, but even so, I don't think her interest in me is from being trained how to make small talk. I think she actually cares. Sloane is a sweetheart, and we've trauma-bonded over our insular childhoods—although at least she was allowed out into the world.

I've laughed more than I have in a long time, but as Sloane echoes Margot's sentiment with a sigh, I realize they might also be living vicariously through me today.

"Neither of us was ever *that* small, and you know it. But no, I can't remember a time when I fit into every sample size in this store," Sloane says wistfully, absentmindedly rubbing her belly.

Both women are pregnant, Margot with her first and second, and Sloane with her second. Even though Margot is having twins, Sloane is a little farther along and popped earlier with this pregnancy, so they're roughly the same size for now. As soon as I suggested stopping at a maternity store, both of them cursed me and said they were counting on me to be their avatar for the day, so here I am. They have impeccable style, so I really can't complain.

"I like it, but don't you think it's a little..." *Much,* I try to say before Margot interrupts.

"*How* does every color work on you? Have you ever done a color analysis?"

Sloane rolls her eyes, but agrees. "Tell the salesperson we'll definitely take this one. Then can we go eat lunch? Ledger keeps texting me that it's been too long since I've eaten, and

I hate agreeing with him, but I think he's right. There's a great Mediterranean place a few shops down, if that's okay?"

I forgot that Ledger tracks Sloane's every move, so of course, he knows we haven't eaten yet. *Must be nice having someone who's that obsessed with you.* Agreeing to stop for lunch, we send our purchases to the car with my driver and make our way to the restaurant, ordering one of everything so we can graze. With a round of mocktails ordered along with our appetizers arriving, Margot gives me a solemn look.

"Kat. It's been wonderful getting to spend time with you today. I think you're a great match for my brother. You're funny and lovely and smart and blah blah. But I'm going to be completely honest with you."

I pause with my tzatziki-topped pita chip halfway to my mouth before placing it back down onto my plate. *Alright, Kat, you're fine. This is what all your training has been for. Whatever she's about to throw at you, you can take it.* I raise an eyebrow and gesture with my hand for her to continue.

"Henry has always been stoic and averse to having anyone in his space. He hasn't spent much time at the estate in years. He's never brought a woman around the family. Even at family gatherings, we can tell when he's had his fill of social time and is ready to leave. What I'm trying to ask is...is my brother truly treating you well? Not that I think he wouldn't, just, is he cold? Are you lonely? We can come around more, or you could come visit—" Margot says, interrupted by Sloane.

"You could babysit LJ any time!" she says brightly, before giving me the same soft, concerned look that Margot is.

Phew, this is a lot better than anything I thought they might have to say, maybe judgment about our age difference or concern for my family's motives.

"You're both so kind to be concerned, but truly, Henry and I are navigating things fairly well, I think, for our first month of living together," I say, and Margot and Sloane share a slightly skeptical look. They still have old "routine" Henry in their minds, and I can't blame them.

"We have breakfast and dinner together most days unless he has a meeting he can't move. We swim together in the morning and do our crosswords together in the evenings. Oh! He took off work when I got my period and watched reality TV with me all day. That was fun!" My smile at the memory fades when I see the looks on each of their faces. Mouths open, shock evident.

"What? Did I say something *that* crazy?" I ask.

"Yes!" both women yell in unison, causing the attention of the restaurant to briefly settle on us before the noise level buzzes back up to normal.

Margot glances at Sloane, then speaks first.

"It's not that we aren't happy to hear that, it's just that we are *so* surprised. We all kind of assumed it would take him much longer to open up to the idea of sharing a space with you and deviating from his routine," she says.

Sloane nods. "I haven't been around that long, but I know Henry has never missed a day of work. Even when LJ was born, he took meetings at the hospital. I think he was holding the baby for one call and said it was LJ's 'first ever million-dollar deal' or something," she says, rolling her eyes.

"Once when we were all home for Christmas, he couldn't swim one morning because Jack threw up in the pool, and it had to be sanitized. He didn't speak to Jack for a month," Margot adds.

"Speaking of Jack!" Sloane exclaims as Margot blushes. "Why don't you tell Kat and me all about your recent excursion to Rendezvous Too, hmm?"

Henry had mentioned to me that Margot and Jack had just taken a trip to New York, but he hadn't given me any details.

"Oh, did you two go to check on the club?" I ask.

Sloane laughs and gestures at Margot to speak. "I haven't even heard the full story, and I want *all* the details. I told you that you'd love it."

Margot must see the confused look on my face and decides to take pity on me.

"Sloane once fucked Ledger in front of a crowd at Rendezvous, so she suggested I try it one day. Jack finally agreed, so we went before I get too big to travel," she says, draining her mocktail and taking Sloane's out of her hand.

Trying to keep my face blank, I think desperately for something to say.

"That sounds amazing!" I say brightly.

"He fucked her while he held expansion talks with some of his closest business associates," Sloane says, and Margot shrugs.

"I sat in his lap for around an hour while he fucked me and mostly ignored me." She sighs. "It was amazing. I thought I'd be nervous with everyone watching, but I felt like a goddess. I think everyone in the room either wanted to be me or be Jack.

I don't think we'll make a habit of it, by any means, but it was very special."

I think about sitting on Henry's lap while he languidly thrusts in and out of me, holding me like a cherished object. My vision morphs into him rutting into me, raw, then filling me up while all of his former submissives watch with envy. The satisfaction I feel even from my daydream is heady, and I wonder if Henry would ever feel proud enough to show me off in that way. Hearing Margot explain more about how proud Jack was to show everyone that she belonged to him sounds so intimate.

The words are out of my mouth before I can think twice.

"Do you know if Henry has ever, um, claimed someone like that? At one of the clubs, I mean," I say quickly, before shoving a huge bite of food in my mouth so I can't say anything else.

Sloane chuckles. "Oh no. Ledger told me that Henry never did anything like that in front of a crowd. His only public scenes were tame, with him staying fully dressed, thank God. You know the first time I ever saw him was during a scene at the club? He really didn't come around much after that. I saw one of his submissives make the mistake of touching him at the bar at Rendezvous once. I could tell he was so mad. They immediately left, and Ledger told me he ended the contract. Ow! What was that for?"

Margot is giving her a look that could kill, and Sloane realizes before giving me an apologetic cringe.

"I'm sorry, Kat. I did *not* mean to bring up a sensitive topic. I can't believe I..."

"It's fine," I say, giving her what I hope is a reassuring smile and ignoring the nausea building in my stomach. "I know about the...contracted women. And we've discussed it a bit. Our relationship is not following along the same lines. He enjoys when I touch him, for example, even if he won't actually fuck me."

The entire restaurant turns its attention to us again as Margot and Sloane have both dropped their glasses, which shatter on the tile floor. Before the server can finish cleaning things up, Ledger bursts through the door with LJ strapped to his chest in a baby carrier. His eyes scan the room before quickly zeroing in on Sloane, and he rushes to our back corner table.

"Angel, are you okay? Your heart rate spiked like crazy and..."

He quiets as he sees that Sloane is okay and eyeing him with a bemused expression. "I'm fine, as you can see. But thank you for keeping such a close eye on me." She accepts a kiss on her forehead before giving one to the baby, and Ledger says hello and goodbye before going back out to what I assume is his mobile command unit set up outside.

"Sorry about that. He's a lot, I know," she says, sipping the replacement mocktail the server brought. "But I can't say that we necessarily overreacted to that piece of information you just gave us. You're telling me that in the month that you've lived together..."

"Nothing?" asks Margot. "Not that I really want to know much more than I already do about my brothers' sex lives, but I can try to think of you as my girlfriend I'm talking to and not my sister-in-law."

I grimace, appreciating that she's willing to talk to me about this but also regretting that I slipped up and admitted my husband would rather stay celibate than have sex with me. Oh well. It's better to have girl talk than go to Sasha for advice. In for a penny...

Giving them a brief rundown, I breeze past the initial awkwardness and separate rooms, giving more details about our friendship and flirtations. The bath scene has Margot jokingly fanning herself with her hand, and Sloane's jaw drops when I tell her about our suggestive gala evening that ended in tears after the sub encounter and discussion.

There's a brief silence after I finish as we all sip our drinks and pick at the baklava we ordered for dessert. It feels good to have gotten some of my feelings out into the world since I didn't really want to confide my sexual woes in any more detail to Mrs. Potts. But now that both of these pregnant women are staring back at me, *obviously no celibate marriages there,* I start to regret being so vulnerable. Before I can apologize for dumping on them and suggest we hit the romance bookstore next, Margot speaks.

"I think both of you want the other to make *the* move," she says.

When I give her a quizzical look, she laughs. "Think about it, Kat. You're inexperienced, younger, and I can understand the urge to compare yourself to Henry's past partners. Although it's clear he's placed you in a different category. So, of course, you want the validation of him being the one to make the move. The *sex* move."

What she says makes sense, but I can't help but ask. "Why won't he? He has the upper hand in practically every way, and he knows I won't turn him down. It's embarrassing to admit, but I've begged him to take me to bed at this point. And I know he wants to. He's been pretty vocal lately."

Sloane pipes up, "I think you're underestimating how confusing this is for him, too. His relationships have really only ever been one way, and you've already flipped a lot of his norms on their heads. He knows he has the upper hand, but I don't think he wants to use it. If I know Henry at all by now, I think he wouldn't want there to be any inkling of taking advantage of you."

I blow out a deep breath and think about what they've said. It makes sense, but there's one piece that doesn't fit.

"That's all well and good, ladies, except for the fact that I *have* made it abundantly clear that I'm all in and completely on my knees for it of my own free will. If the bath didn't do it, and me bursting into his room and straddling him didn't do it..."

Margot jumps back in, eyes lighting up as she seems to have a realization. "With the bath, you purely shocked him, and the bed was an emotional night. He wouldn't have done anything if you were upset. But you're exactly right about two things. You're going to make it *abundantly clear* that you want him and..."

"And...?" I ask, eyebrow raised as Margot picks up her glass for a toast, urging Sloane to do the same.

I raise my own glass to toast what I hope is the coup d'état that will finally win my husband's cock, and the victory clink rings out in the restaurant as Margot delivers her closing argument.

"You're going to get on your knees for him."

"I can't possibly accept all of these, Margot," I say as she adds *another* of her designs to my growing pile. We're in her warehouse on the property she and Jack have next to Henry and me, and I feel confident I have one of every lingerie set to ever be sold by Le Reine. She built the lingerie brand herself, but stepped back into the role of creative director to spend more energy on life with Jack and less on the day-to-day operations.

"You can, and you will, darling. When your sister-in-law slash soon-to-be best friend designs lingerie, you're guaranteed a spot on the free-corsets-for-life list. Now. I have an absolute showstopper—just enough to lift and tease yet also tantalize. What's your absolute favorite color, if you could pick anything?" she asks, rifling through another rack of lace.

Although I know it's unlikely she has anything exactly like it, I tell her. "It's a kind of dusky periwinkle, not really too gray or blue but not too purple, either."

Popping her head out of the rack, she comes over to sit next to me on the couch at the end of the space. Ledger kidnapped Sloane for some family time with LJ, so it's just the two of us now. She pulls out her phone to show me a picture I've never seen before, of Henry and me at the gala. It looks like it's before my run-in with the witches from his past. We're sitting at the dinner table, and he's already pulled my chair closer to his to cage me in with his arm across my back. It looks like he's said something into my ear, and I've turned to look up at him. He's so much taller than me, even sitting down. I look up at him adoringly, and he looks down at me like he wants to eat me. What a fun night, at least in the beginning...

"Kat!"

"Huh? Sorry...yeah. That is a picture of Henry and me?" I ask, wondering why Margot is showing me.

"I was asking if this is the color? I saw more pictures of the two of you and loved your dress. It made your eyes pop," Margot replies, eyeing me like she knows I was thinking nasty thoughts about her brother.

"Yes, that's it," I say, and like a whirlwind, she's off. Her production facility in New York will be dyeing a number of garments for me, apparently, not just lingerie, in the color she's calling Kat's Kream.

"They'll dye them tonight, dry tomorrow, and ship overnight to be here in two days. He won't be able to resist you. You can mix the pieces in with some of the others we already bought. Keep him guessing!"

Smiling at her enthusiasm, I give her a big hug as I stand to leave. "You'll never know how much I appreciate this, Margot. You and Sloane have both helped me so much. But can we please revisit the name you've given my favorite color? Please?"

Cackling, she waddles to her car as my driver opens my door. "When inspiration strikes, you don't fight it, Kat! If you can come up with a better name, be my guest!"

Armed with roughly a thousand shopping bags full of tools with which to seduce my husband, and more on the way, I head home to take an everything shower and start phase one of my plan. Time to play dirty and finally get what I want.

Chapter Nineteen

"Henry, can you help me please?" Katarina calls from her suite. She's been quiet, but not avoiding me as judiciously as she was during Thanksgiving, so I'm hopeful that some girl time helped after the gala fiasco. Walking into the closet, I see bags strewn about from the shopping trip she indulged in with Margot and Sloane.

"Katarina, where are y..." I freeze mid-sentence when I see her, facing away from me on her tiptoes on a step stool, reaching for a box on a high shelf. She's wearing clothes that I've never seen her in, high-waisted, cutoff jean shorts with what looks like one of my dress shirts. Her sleeves are rolled up, and the hem is tied tightly around her waist. With her braid trailing down her back and her muscular legs shown to every advantage while she stretches, she looks exquisite.

"I can't quite reach this box," she says, then gasps as she begins to tip over backwards. Rushing to her, I catch her bridal style with time to spare, relishing how light she is in my arms and seeing the lacy bra she's wearing under my shirt. Before I can

react to having her in my arms again, she pops out of them to stand beside me and point.

"It's that box. Can you get it for me, please?" she asks sweetly, and I oblige, moving the unnecessary stool out of the way to grab what she needs from the high shelf. Handing it to her, I see it contains...sex toys? All shapes and sizes. One looks like it might be a tentacle, Jesus. Before I can ask her about them, she's in her bathroom, shutting the door with a breezy, "Thank you!"

Time for another cold shower.

"What are you doing?" I ask as my wife bends over to place her hands on her ankles, feet spread wide, and forehead almost to the floor. I came to the pool this morning to find her wearing what can barely be called a swimsuit while she pornographically presents herself to me. I swear I can see her pussy lips around the scrap of fabric.

"It's Pilates! I'm trying to incorporate more functional movement. You know I love swimming, and I don't plan to stop, but I want to keep my flexibility and mobility into my old age, so I'm going to diversify my fitness," she says brightly, deepening her stretch. "I've been working on my splits, and I'm really close!"

Jesus Christ.

"You're nineteen years old. I don't think old age should be on your list of concerns." I sigh, preparing to dive in and hoping the water will distract me from all of my blood rushing south to my dick.

She pops back up with enough momentum that I see her full breasts bounce. That top is nowhere near sturdy enough for her to swim in.

She drops down into a deep squat, pulsing and shifting her hips back and forth as if sitting on a low bouncy ball. Or my dick...

"Fair enough!" she says. "But Sloane also said having mobile hip flexors really helped her bounce back after giving birth, so I just figured it was prudent to start working on it now!"

I gawp at her for a long second before turning and diving into the pool, finding absolutely no respite from my dick or thoughts of the siren on the bank full of my baby.

Fuck me.

"Henry!"

I sprint to Katarina's suite, her scream pulling me from sleep at two o'clock in the morning. Bursting through her door, I see her sitting in bed, pointing at the corner, terror all over her face.

"What is it, Kitten?" I move to the corner in question, ready to kill.

"A spider!" she says with a shaky voice. "A big one. I saw it scurry all the way across my ceiling and over there!"

I look thoroughly, and finding no spider, turn to reassure her that there's nothing when I see her sleeping attire. High-waisted thong, barely there tank top, nipples poking through the thin material. All in her perfect shade of periwinkle. She's looking at me with tears in her eyes, shining violet in the moonlight, so I press a chaste kiss to her forehead and shuffle quickly to the door to hide my immediate erection.

"No spider. You're safe. Go back to sleep."
Fucking hell.

"Shhh," I hear softly as I walk into the den after coming home early from work.

Sloane must have dropped LJ off for some "Aunty Kat" time today, because my wife is rocking my nephew as he sleeps, drool visible on her shoulder.

"I just got him asleep. He was fussing," she whispers, before looking down adoringly at the little blond Sinclair.

Rooted to the spot, I watch them rock for the next thirty minutes, Kat closing her eyes and humming, a serenity about her that resonates in my soul.

Finally, I run a hand through my hair and move from my spot, heading straight for the shower.

God. I. Am. Fucked.

"Brother, I think we have enough wood to last all winter. Even if we lived in Alaska, which we do not," Ledger observes, sipping his cider and watching me work.

Jack agrees. "Yeah, man. Are you working to chop some for like an old lady around here, or a homeless shelter, or something? My schedule is full because your sister is pretty fucking insatiable, but I can probably find some time to help for a good cause..."

Thwack.

Leaving my axe deep in the log I'm currently working to split, I observe my pile as I pull down my suspenders to take off my shirt underneath. As soon as I do, I see steam rise from my skin, hitting the cool crisp air, and a cheer rises from the deck where the women are sitting around a firepit sipping their drinks. Luckily, they're too far away to hear us as I turn to threaten Jack.

"If you keep making jokes about fucking my baby sister, so help me, these babies will be the last you ever give her," I say menacingly, but Ledger already has him in a light chokehold.

"You still can't talk about her like that, man, even if I am happy you're together," Ledger says, before releasing Jack.

"Fine, fine. But my question stands. Why so much wood? Are you trying to prove to Kat you can provide for her? Show her what a daddy you can be, taking care of things?"

Picking my axe back up and brandishing it briefly at Jack to shut him up, I resume my chopping, enjoying the burn in my muscles as I get a steady rhythm going. I decide to cut straight to it.

"Your wives are ruining my life," I say.

"What?"

"How?"

"My baby angel would never..."

I push through the log, finally, and turn to grab my scotch off a stump.

"Your wives took Katarina shopping after Thanksgiving, and since she got back, she's been flouncing around my house in scraps of clothing. Doing stretches. Holding babies, for fuck's sake!" I polish off my scotch before moving to take a seat across from the guys around the smaller fire we have burning away from the house.

They both stare at me for a beat before bursting into laughter.

"Oh, I wondered when you would come to us for help, big brother," says Ledger. "I didn't expect you to be down this bad when you did, though."

Jack stops laughing first, but only to make more jokes at my expense. "Are your joints starting to creak from trying to keep up with her? You might need to join her for daily stretches."

"Did she finally tell you about her student/professor fantasy? She told Sloane she was nervous to bring it up, but..."

Perhaps sensing that I'm seconds away from reaching for my axe again, Ledger elbows Jack, and they give me more sober looks.

"Really, bro. Sloane and Margot told us a decent bit about their time with Kat. Are you planning to be celibate forever? Are you punishing yourself or her at this point?" Ledger asks.

Sighing, I realize I could use some perspective and decide to be honest.

"It's not about punishing either of us. It weighs on me a bit. The age difference. I told myself I wouldn't give anyone a chance to say anything untoward was happening. To make sure she was comfortable here and with me before I tried anything. I wanted to make sure she wanted me, and not just fleetingly or for sex. I want her to *need* me. For everything," I say, and neither of them is looking at me like I'm crazy. Yet.

Jack speaks up first, and being with my sister seems to have made him at least a little wiser. "Margot made it sound like you guys have become really good friends first, which is always a good thing. Not as good as *childhood best friends, but...ow!*"

Ledger's smack shuts Jack up before he gets himself hit, but he echoes the same sentiment. "We all know you aren't just interested in her physically, man. She's clearly super fucking smart, and it's cute that you guys do all your little nerdy stuff together. She seems extremely mature for her age. Where's the problem? Something happened at the gala, Sloane said. But she wouldn't give us details."

Well. Might as well lay it all out there, even if I'm about to sound like a giant douche.

"At the gala, Katarina overheard two of my former submissives discussing our marriage, my disdain for intimacy, and some of the intricacies of our contracts..." I begin.

"Yikes, dude."

"Damn."

Ignoring their interruptions, I soldier on. "After she came back from the bathroom, she said she didn't feel well, but I didn't pry. The two women in question came over, and I introduced them as old friends. She recognized their voices and knew who they were."

"Jesus Christ, brother."

"Yeah, you might have to go the masked route, man. I suggest a full face balaclava and...ow!"

This time, it's my hand to the side of Jack's head that shuts him up, but I continue.

"She got upset even though she's known about my history for a while, and I gave her the chance to ask any questions she wanted. I think it just reminded me of how young she is, this flash of immaturity." I sigh.

Ledger speaks up next, and I'm surprised by his serious tone.

"Her reaction has absolutely nothing to do with her age, Henry. Come on. Any woman would have reacted the same way. I mean, at least tell me you ran after her when she went to make you jealous. How did she do it? Dancing with other men? A little flirt with the bartender? Sloane dancing for even one second with one guy at Rendezvous was enough to make me lose it after we had a similar fight."

"What are you talking about?"

"After Kat got jealous, the natural response is to try to make you jealous, you know, a taste of your own medicine. What did she do after the women left?" he asks.

I pause, thinking back to that night. "She stayed quiet during the ceremony, then told me she wasn't feeling well as we started dancing, so I brought her home. She went straight to her room. I assumed she was sick until she came to mine and told me how she felt."

Two sets of eyes stare at me, blinking like owls in the night.

"What?" I ask.

Jack shares a look with Ledger before scratching his stubble and answering. "Well, it's just that it seems like a kinda reasonable response, you know? You guys were in public, and she got faced with your experience, which is always different from talking about it. She held it together as long as she could, asked to go home, then came to you to talk about it."

Ledger rolls his eyes to the sky. "Dude. Sloane tried to get revenge when this happened to us. She went to grind on some asshole on the dance floor! I had to drag her out, then grovel on my knees. It sounds like Kat's maturity is not a real problem."

Well, fuck. That makes *me* the problem. I shouldn't be surprised since I don't exactly have experience navigating meaningful relationships, but I'm thirty-seven years old. I should have been able to react to Kat's feelings in a more reasonable way.

"Let's say you guys are right. My wife is perfectly mature, and I'm not in danger of taking advantage of her. Now what? I've rejected her too many times. Now she's just teasing me to torture me?" I ask.

"I don't think that's it, bro. I think she still wants you. But she wants you to want her more. It takes two to tango. I think it's time to give as good as you're getting," Ledger says.

I raise an eyebrow.

Jack explains, "It's time to get back to the pursuit, Henry. Before you fucked it up. But not just seduction. Sexually, mentally, physically, emotionally. All of it, man. And you cannot reject her again. You need to be ready to finally kiss her. And for God's sake, fuck her."

"Don't say fuck and a pronoun referencing my wife in the same sentence, Carter!" I stand and make to grab him, but he's a hair faster, running back to the deck and the women.

"It's Sinclair now!" he yells over his shoulder, and I shake my head as I pull my shirt back over my head.

"I have faith in you, Henry. You've already let her past so many of your walls, and I don't think she's let you down yet," Ledger says, pausing as we make our way back to the house. "I do think Jack was right about one thing, though, brother."

"What's that?"

"I think you give off big daddy energy. And with the age gap, come on. It's right there. You'd be a fool not to at least give it a try. Here, let's try. Hi, Daddy," he says, in what I assume is meant to be a seductive voice but sounds like a drowning, high-pitched rat.

He gets a step on me before I can goose him, and we race back to the house. Seeing my wife laugh with Margot, Sloane, and Jack as Ledger hides from me behind a chair fills my heart. I can see now the game she's playing, with her tight periwinkle sweater and sweatpants, a sliver of her abdomen teasing me.

If that's what she wants, she's gonna have to earn it.

Game on, Kitten.

Chapter Twenty

"Yes, Father, I know. No, everything is going well."

"And you're making Mr. Sinclair happy?"

"Yes, Father."

"Good. Don't disappoint me, Katarina."

Click.

Sighing, I fall face down on the bed and toss my phone toward the pillows. This week has been exhausting. I've been implementing all of Sloane's and Margot's suggestions, to no avail. Well, to almost no avail. I've at least been successful in flustering my husband, but nothing further.

The only silver lining has been how close I've gotten with my sisters-in-law. Meeting his family at our wedding was one thing. Everything that weekend was all painted smiles and practiced words. But since Thanksgiving, I've felt like I actually have a family. Really, for the first time in my life. Not that Sasha isn't incredible, but one brotherly figure doesn't necessarily replace the real thing.

The thought of Sasha reminds me that he'll be arriving later tonight for a short visit. His absence is one of the other things that's thrown me off lately. I was prepared for his physical absence after my wedding, but he's hardly even replied to my texts since I moved.

The sound of a knock against my doorframe reminds me it's been open this whole time. I wasn't exactly *expecting* my father to call and give me the *It's almost been two months since you've been married, and you better be making your husband happy* speech.

"Are you alright?"

I don't have to look to know who's at the door. My husband's voice is etched into my soul at this point, considering how often it runs through my imagination.

"Yes," I respond, my voice muffled by the comforter.

"Who was that on the phone?"

"My father."

The edge of the bed dips, his scent somehow surrounding me regardless of the fact that my nose is buried in the covers.

"What did he want?"

I flip over onto my back as dramatically as I can, spreading out like a starfish, "He wanted to make sure I was *making Mr. Sinclair happy,*" I say, staring up at the ceiling. I know if I were to look at Henry, I would tear up. A weakness I really don't want to show right now.

"I *am* happy, Kitten. Happier than I can recall ever being...Katarina?"

When I dare to glance at him, he's propped against my headboard, looking down at me with that intensity I've seen time and time again. That intensity that leads to *nothing.*

Sighing, I pull myself up and join him, leaning against the frame. "Yes?"

"I'm sorry. I'm sorry for my part in this." He reaches out, taking my hand in his. "I liked where our relationship was going, and I would like to continue down that path."

"Yeah, me too," I whisper.

He lets go of my hand and wraps his arm around my shoulders, pulling me slightly toward him. I don't even realize I've laid my head on his chest until I recognize the heartbeat I'm listening to isn't mine. Sitting together like this is just so natural. Like a couple of lovers in a routine embrace.

His ringing phone breaks the silence, drawing us out of our moment of bliss. "Ugh, I have to leave soon," he grumbles, declining the call.

When I try to shimmy away, he tightens his grip on me. "I'll be home for dinner, and then crosswords? I've missed my partner."

Smiling, I nod. "I'll be here."

Sloane:

Is it happening???

Margot:

Please tell me you're about to get laid.

Margot:

Actually, spare me the details…Of my brother's pipe laying.

Me:

Well, not exactly… But he did apologize. He said he "liked where we were going and wanted to continue down that path." And then we cuddled for a minute. Before he had to leave :(But he said he would be home for dinner and crosswords.

Me:

Any suggestions on how to seduce a man over crosswords?

Sloane:

Call the paper and have them make one with only the most suggestive terms??

Margot:

Wow, Sloane, you're starting to sound like Ledger. How about we start with something normal, like a slutty dress?

Sloane:

Whatever, Margot, it's called efficiency. LOL

Me:

I've barely been wearing any clothes all week! And it's December! I'm going to turn into a snowman soon if he doesn't make a move. Anyway, my cousin Sasha is going to be arriving tonight for a little visit. So I don't want to take things TOO far and then not be able to do anything about it for a few days…

Margot:

Hmm, what's your seating arrangement like when you two nerds do your crosswords?

Me:

Usually, I sit sideways on his lap.

Sloane:

Holy shit.

Margot:

God, my brother's an idiot. You've been sitting on the man's lap, and he hasn't made a move?

Sloane:

Hey, don't be mean. Not all men just go for it like your husband did! Henry obviously values consent.

Margot:

Mm-hmm... Hey, didn't my brother STALK you?

Me:

GIRLS! REIN IT IN HERE!

Margot:

Sorry, Kat. Okay, you can't sleep with him tonight. But you need to make sure he knows you REALLY want to...May I suggest straddling him for your puzzles tonight?

Me:

And then what? "Henry, I would love to have sex with you tonight, but can we pause this while my cousin is here? Could you maybe pencil me in for eight p.m. on Tuesday?"

Sloane:

What about a date? That's what led to Ledger and me doing it the first time!

Margot:

Wait a second…are you telling me you gave it up after the first date?

Sloane:

Idk, are you telling me you gave it up to an anonymous man in a mask at a club?

Margot:

Touché.

Margot:

Yes, a date. Make him take you on a date. I'm not sure if he deserves you putting out on the first date.

Well, he technically already put a ring on it.

That's true… But if you want to drive him *wild*. Make him wait.

"Under eight minutes!" I squeal, wrapping my arms around Henry as he fills in the last word.

I'm in my usual position, sitting sideways across his lap. I thought through every possible way to make it work, straddling him while also working on the puzzle, but came up with nothing. I even used the desk chair in my room to visualize it, until I leaned too far back and toppled over, chair and all.

Ultimately, I decided to transition to said straddle after completing the crossword. Which was all fun and games until now. I had at least ten different segues rehearsed and ready to go, but can I think of a single one of them now? Not a chance.

As if he can read my mind, Henry spins me around on his lap, adjusting my legs around him. "There, that's better," he says with a smirk.

Oh God, I'm melting. Despite nearly freezing to death for the past week, I decided on a short little linen dress, and it's completely pulled up to my waist. To make matters worse, the lacy thong I chose has migrated to the side, meaning Henry's trousers are the only thing separating me from the monster cock I know is hiding underneath.

I'm a squirming mess, to be honest. But the more I try to adjust, the harder he grows beneath me.

"Stop that," he teases with a smack to the back of my thigh. His teasing ignites confidence in me, and I make even more of an effort with my wiggling.

"I said stop that, Katarina." This time, there's no humor to his tone. But despite his words, he pulls me down onto him.

Somehow, my confidence remains, and I make a show of biting my lower lip. "Or what?"

He growls a warning, but I don't back down.

"What are you going to do, Daddy? Spank me?"

We're both up in a flash. Henry carries me effortlessly to his desk before spinning me around and bending me over the cold, smooth wood. I welcome the heat from his body as he leans over me, trailing kisses from the back of my shoulder to my nape.

"You want me to spank you?" he asks, his breath tickling my ear.

I can hardly *breathe,* much less talk.

Wrapping his fist around my braid, he pulls my head back. *Hard.*

"I asked you a question, little girl." His other hand rubs circles around where the hem of my dress rests mid-thigh.

Chill bumps erupt throughout my body even though I feel like I'm on fire.

"Yes, sir."

Still holding on to my braid with one hand, he slowly makes his way up my thigh with the other. "Mmm, I don't think you know what you're asking for, Kitten."

"Henry...*please!*" I beg. I don't know what I'm asking for, but I *need something*.

His hand trails higher, and I feel the cool air on my ass as he lifts my skirt. He runs his hand up and down, squeezing slightly, massaging me.

Swat.

He chuckles darkly as I squeak, my body jerking involuntarily. "I told you that you didn't know what you were asking for, but you insisted."

The pain from his slap feels like a hundred needle pricks, each sending shocks of pleasure circuiting through my body. It's like walking outside into freezing air, when your first breath is painfully cold but soon grows invigorating.

"Another," I beg.

I expect him to take a moment, but he strikes me almost immediately. I can't help the high-pitched moan I give in response. He must take that as a plea for more as he strikes me over and over, alternating sides and placement.

I feel like I'm floating in the clouds, more aroused than I've ever been before. I know if I widen my stance, I would feel the result of my arousal dripping down my legs.

"More, Henry...*please!*" I cry. Begging for what? I don't know.

"Please, what? Tell me what you need from me."

"I...I don't know," I say, rubbing my thighs together for some relief.

He lets go of my braid and uses that arm to wrap around my waist while the hand he's been using to spank me explores again. Slowly, he runs his fingers from my ass, around my hip, to the front of my thigh. He's barely reached the hem of my panties, but his touch causes my body to shiver.

"Do you need me to take care of that ache between your legs, Kitten?"

His fingers hover over the lace of my panties, tracing featherlight circles over my clit as he waits for my response.

"Mmm, yes. *Please!*"

He rips the dainty fabric from my body and slowly traces one finger up and down my pussy lips before spreading them open with his thumb.

"Oh God!" My body shakes as he makes soft circles around my clit, the sound of my wetness amplified in the quiet room. With his hand in front of me, I'm pushed back against him, and I can feel his covered erection rubbing against my bare ass. His hand from my waist reaches up and squeezes my breast, the pressure almost painful against my pebbled nipple.

"Mmm, you're *soaking* my fingers, and I'm not even inside you."

The finger on my clit trails down to circle my entrance, and I've never felt so empty in my life. I'm about to beg him to put something, *anything*, inside me when his other arm comes behind me, rimming my *other* hole.

"Don't worry, little girl, I'm going to fill both of these up before long."

It's sensory overload. I feel like every nerve ending in my body converges on my core. I'm familiar with this buildup, but I've never been able to let it wash me away. He moves his hands back to their previous positions, but they're rougher than before. He's alternating between circling and pinching my clit while he does the same thing with my nipple.

I'm so close. I know I am. I've never gotten myself this far. I can feel my pussy fluttering as my body tenses up.

Henry leans over me, pulling me even closer to his body. "Let go, my kitten," he whispers before latching onto my neck and...*ohhh*.

My body convulses underneath him as he bites or sucks or whatever he's doing to my neck, and what feels like a lifetime of pressure explodes out from me in waves.

He holds me tight until my orgasm wanes completely, whispering words of praise in my ear as I lose myself in pleasure from his touch.

"That's it, Katarina. That's my good girl. You come so beautifully for me. My perfect, gorgeous girl."

When the last wave ebbs, he pulls my skirt down and turns me around to set me on the desk. Pulling up a chair so that we are sitting eye to eye, he cups my face,

"How was that, Kitten? Are you okay?" The concern in his gaze melts my heart. He's just given me my first orgasm, and he's worried.

I smile as wide as I can, considering I'm still half in orgasm la-la land. "Wow...I want to do that again," I say, pulling a legitimate laugh from my husband.

"Anytime, darling," he says, kissing the tip of my nose. He pulls back just enough to look into my eyes, searching them before turning his attention to my lips and leaning into me. I can *just* feel his mouth against mine when the doorbell chimes through the house, startling us both.

Grabbing the back of my head, he gently pulls my forehead to his. "I'm guessing that's your cousin?"

"Probably so."

"Then perhaps not *anytime,*" he says before sitting back in his chair and helping me off the desk.

I'm at the door by the time I realize he's still sitting in his chair. "Are you not coming?" I ask, straightening my dress and slicking down my hair, trying my best to make myself look presentable.

He smiles loosely, "You go ahead, I, um, have a bit of a situation here. I don't want to greet your cousin with a cum stain on my pants."

My skin flushes red with embarrassment. "Oh God, Henry, I'm so sorry. I didn't mean to get my...on you."

"Not yours, Kitten."

The heat I feel changes from embarrassment to desire as I make sense of Henry's words. *Did I really just make him come in his pants?* I'm opening my mouth to ask when I hear my cousin calling.

"KitKat?" Sasha's excited yell echoes down the hall as I stand frozen in place in the entrance to the study.

Henry nods his head toward the door. "Good night, *Katarina.*"

Chapter Twenty-One

My nerves flare as I wait for Katarina to finish dressing and come to my room. When I told her we were going on a proper date this evening, she was so excited that I thought she would levitate off the ground. It made me realize that I haven't even approached the lengths I'd like to go to spoil her and show her off. Selfishly, I've been enjoying our cozy little bubble and routine we've developed here at home. I need to step my game up, though. She deserves the best.

A million ideas came to mind for our first official date, from elaborate trips overseas to a theme park she's been not-so-subtly hinting about wanting to visit. I decided to table my idea of having a hedge maze built for a game of chase. *Perhaps that will be an anniversary present in a few years...*

No, I decided to keep things simple tonight. I'm taking her into the city to one of my favorite restaurants at a member's club that should have dancing this evening. Instead of coming home, we'll stay in a penthouse suite downtown and enjoy the nighttime views from the balcony hot tub. *I hope.* Since our explosive encounter a couple of days ago when I finally snapped and put my hands on her, we've been apart as she's spent time with her cousin and I've dealt with business. Tonight, though, she's all mine, since Sasha has to go back to...whatever or whoever he's doing.

A knock on my door draws me out of my thoughts, their subject finally gracing my presence. She's a dream, wearing the outfit I laid out for her earlier, but holding the dress up at the chest.

"I find myself once again in need of a zip, Mr. Sinclair. Would you mind terribly? But close your eyes. I can't have you privy to all my secrets at the beginning of the night," She demands in a coquettish tone, and I sigh in relief that there won't be any awkwardness between us this evening.

"Of course, Mrs. Sinclair. Thank you for wearing the dress I picked for you tonight," I murmur into her neck, as I feel for the zipper of the corseted dress. She'll need a coat until we get into the restaurant, but I didn't want her to get hot dancing. "And the jewelry, and the shoes. Hopefully other things..."

I hope I'll have the chance to see if she wore the lingerie I chose for the night.

"I wasn't aware I had a choice. When clothes appear hanging in my room, it generally means the decision of what I'll wear for the evening has already been made," she teases.

Nipping her shoulder, I spin her around in my arms to look into her eyes. "You always have a choice, Kitten. But that doesn't mean there wouldn't be consequences if you ignore what I pick for you."

Heat flashes in her eyes, and I briefly consider the merits of staying in tonight and fucking my wife on every surface of the house before moving outside to the grounds, but then I take a deep breath. This is not the point of tonight. Well, maybe later. Not right now. Right now is about treating her like a queen and showing her off.

"This place is amazing, Henry! What year did you say it was built?"

Katarina seems pleased with my choice of venue for our night away, an Art Deco-style supper club that's been a favorite of our family for years. It was built in 1927, and I explain it's the best vantage point in the city as she takes in the sleek brass accents throughout the lobby. Once they've taken our coats, we're led by the maître d' to my preferred booth in a back corner, with the best view in the house and a modicum of privacy provided by a half wall.

All eyes are on us as we make our way through the restaurant filled with business associates, people I've known my entire life, and a few town gossips. The lovely thing about this club, though, is that conversation between parties who did not arrive together is *highly* discouraged. Everyone can see Katarina, feel my obsession as I lead her through the restaurant with a hand low on her back, and see us sit closely on the same side of the booth...but they can't approach, talk, or touch. No Chuck Dawson pawing at my wife, no blabbing submissives to make her feel less than or question my utter devotion. Smirking, I see the envious looks on every face we pass.

She doesn't know any of these people or the restaurant rules. She's too busy admiring the architecture of the building, the decor, the ambiance, and the view. No, the peacocking is pure selfishness on my part. *Look, everyone. Don't you wish she was yours? Too bad.*

"Oh, Henry, the view is wonderful! The sunset is going to be beautiful," Katarina says before looking up at me with those bewitching violet eyes.

Bending down, I give her a tiny peck on the nose before gesturing for her to sit in the booth.

"Not as beautiful as you, darling."

Before long, we're cozied up with glasses of champagne, toasting our first date. *Being a longtime member here has some benefits, since nobody is bothered about checking Katarina's ID.*

"To you, Kitten, and to thousands more dates for us," I say, clinking our glasses. Her eyes well with tears, but her smile tells me they're happy ones as she sips her champagne.

The server arrives, and I make quick work of placing our orders for the evening.

"French onion soup for both of us to start, then we'll each have the tenderloin. Rare for me, medium for my wife. I'll have the broccolini on the side. She'll have mashed potatoes with gravy and steak fries. For dessert, one slice of the chocolate ganache cake and one crème brûlée. Thank you."

He scurries off as I turn to see Katarina looking at me with an eyebrow raised.

"Did you think perhaps I might want to see a menu or decide what I wanted to eat myself?" she asks, but I can tell by her tone that she's not truly upset.

"I did not consider that, no," I say, earning a swat on my arm. "I know what you like, and these are the dishes on the menu you'll like best. If you aren't satisfied by the end of the meal, I'll get you whatever you want."

With no rebuttal to that, but a hungry look in her eyes that I'm not sure is only directed at the food, she continues asking about the history of the building, and we watch the sunset as our conversation flows. It's not lost on me how smart she is. No topic is too dry or obscure for her to make interesting. By the time we finish our soup and our main course arrives, she's migrated closer and closer to me and is practically against my side.

"I think it might be hard for us to eat our steak sitting so close together," I tease, but she's eyeing her steak with an odd expression on her face. "What's wrong?"

She gives me an embarrassed look. "I love steak, but usually, I don't cut it myself. Something about it just grosses me out, even if it's tender."

Thinking back, I realize Mrs. Potts has pre-cut Katarina's steak when we've had it at home. Internally grinning, I realize this gives me the perfect opportunity to take care of her.

"Come here," I say, and she gives a delightful little squeak as I pull her sideways onto my lap, pushing the table back slightly with my foot to accommodate her. "You can sit here, and I'll cut your steak for you. How does that sound?"

She blinks up at me and inhales deeply, looking peaceful and right at home on my lap. Nodding, she smiles as I cut and feed her the first piece of steak, and the little moan she gives tells me it's cooked to her liking. We pass the rest of our meal like this, me feeding her little bites and chatting about various subjects. It's torture having her in my lap, but I love it. With my arms around her, I feel like I'm protecting her from the world. Nothing can upset her or harm her as long as she's right here where she belongs.

"What made you choose this hotel for tonight?" Katarina asks as we make our way inside the suite, tired but feeling less full after dancing some of our dinner off at the club.

Hanging our coats and popping open the champagne that was on ice when we arrived, I pour two glasses. "Take a look on the balcony and you'll see."

Her gasp tells me she found the infinity hot tub on the deck, and I move to follow her and catch a glimpse of her surprise.

But *fuck me.* She's the one doing the surprising. My kitten has managed to unzip herself and drop her dress, showing me that she didn't wear the lingerie I laid out for her because *she's not wearing anything.* Downing both glasses of champagne, I lean onto a deck chair as she slowly submerges herself in the water, looking every bit a siren in the moonlight.

"Come in with me?" she asks with a teasing raised eyebrow before tipping her head back into the water to wet her long hair.

I've given up trying to deny her, and I feel like a teenager again as I kick off my shoes and step into the water fully clothed, refusing to waste time stripping before joining her.

I crowd her against the edge, slowly placing one hand on her neck to hold her still while my other softly trails across her collarbone, dipping lower to slightly graze a peaked nipple. I feel her sharp intake of breath against my hand as she tries to turn her head, and I tighten it, just a bit, to keep her where I want her.

Her fluttering pulse against my thumb makes me groan as I dip down to taste the nipple I've been teasing, before giving it a nibble and relishing in her squirming as I do. Moving my hand to hold her jaw, I tease her lower lip with my thumb once, twice, before I can't handle this torture a second longer. I need to taste her more than I've ever needed anything in my life.

Kneeling to be eye level with her, I softly brush my mouth against my wife's. She's still, as if worried any enthusiasm might scare me off, but any reticence I felt at crossing this line of intimacy is gone. I need her lips. I need her cum. I need her in my lap every day so I can feed her and take care of her. I need my seed in her womb so she can grow my babies.

But first, I need to taste her. My second brush is firmer, and she tries to chase my mouth, but my hold on her jaw is firm. Teasing her just a little more, I run my tongue across her lush lower lip, reveling in her tiny gasp, which is my undoing. My hand leaves her jaw to join the other in her hair, bending her head to the side so I can finally claim her mouth.

She parts perfectly for me, letting my tongue in to dance with hers, and I groan deeply at the taste of my wife. Sweetness from her dessert, a lingering hint of champagne earlier, and a flavor all her own that I know with certainty I'll be dreaming of on my deathbed.

It feels like I've reached a new plane of existence when she winds her arms around my neck and wraps her legs around my waist, trying to get as close to me as possible. I leave the sanctuary of her lips for just a moment, trailing hot kisses down her neck until I miss her lips too much and return to give her more teasing pecks.

Finally, with one last nip at her bottom lip, I pull back to find my wife looking thoroughly debauched. Lips reddened and eyes glassy, she looks like a dream.

"Please," she says, and my kitten has tears in her eyes. My mood changes from elation to concern in a heartbeat, and I cup her face in both hands.

"Darling," I whisper. "What's wrong?"

She sniffles to keep her tears from falling and takes a fortifying breath before breaking my heart.

"Please don't kiss me, then take it away again. You kissed me at the wedding, and I was beginning to think you never would again, and I—"

I cut her off with my lips on hers, pulling her tighter to me and rising out of the hot tub. Water cascades off us as I stride into the suite. Pushing her into the wall just inside, I grip her thighs tightly and swallow her gasp of pain. Finally pulling back, I try to give her every ounce of the honesty she deserves in my gaze. I can feel her trembling, and I know she's wet and cold, but she needs to hear this now.

"Katarina. You will *never* go another day without my lips on yours. It was my misplaced fear that had me holding back from you, but that's no excuse. You'll get tired of me kissing you before you ever have to beg me again. It's more likely that you'll be begging me to stop."

She's breathing heavily but no longer on the verge of tears, and before long, one side of her mouth turns up in a soft smile. Leaning toward me, she reaches for a soft kiss that I readily give her, but when I try to deepen it, she pulls back.

"Put me down, please," she says, and I do, although I'm confused. I certainly thought we were heading for a potentially consummative night, but she's walking away from me toward the bathroom, toned ass swaying back and forth torturously.

"I'm going to warm up in the shower, then can we cuddle and watch some reality shows until we fall asleep?" she asks, and I start slowly stripping off my wet clothes.

Giving her what I know is an irresistible smirk, I move to join her in the bathroom. "That sounds perfect, Kitten. Can I join you in the shower?" It'll be the perfect chance to get my hands on her again, and she can familiarize herself with my body more so that she's as comfortable as possible before we...

"No, thank you," she says primly before stepping underneath the rainfall showerhead and closing the non-frosted shower door.

Before I can ask why and whether something's wrong, she continues.

"You can watch, though, if you'd like," my wife purrs, and I stare gobsmacked as she lathers up her hands to wash.

Even without anything else happening, this is already one of the best nights of my life. Sitting down on the bathmat outside the shower, I settle in for Katarina's show. As she writhes beneath the water, I feel my desire for her sharpening beyond any feeling I've ever experienced. I would burn down the world for her if I thought it would make her happy, even if it consumed me. I'd have to rise from the ashes to ensure she was taken care of, but I'd do it again and again.

The last bit of my restraint hangs on by a thread as I watch her wrap her hair in a towel, dry off, and lotion herself, all while showing me every inch of her body. I'm hit with a sudden urge to rip her towel off and fuck her on the counter. I want her first time to be sweet and respectful. I want her to feel cherished and loved and special, knowing it's not how I've ever fucked before. But she's toeing a dangerous line by teasing me like this. The longer we go, the less I want to respect her and the more I want to ruin her. We're losing the chance for a soft consummation as I get closer to losing control.

I need to keep my desire more tightly locked in its cage. *Otherwise, I'm afraid we'll both burn.*

Chapter Twenty-Two

Last night was everything I could've dreamed of and more, but I'm left more confused with our relationship than ever before.

After our amazing night, I wanted to take Margot's advice to not give it up on the first date. But after the orgasm he gave me a few nights ago in his study, I was desperate for more. I wanted him to take me right there in the hot tub. The way the fabric of his wet clothes felt against my naked skin, the way he held me tenderly yet firmly in his arms, the way his kiss took every strand of my DNA and altered it permanently. I was barely hanging on by a thread.

I knew that if I didn't put some distance between us, I would have given him everything. And I want to make him burn for me. I fled to the shower with strict instructions for him not to join. I half expected him to ignore them, but he was a perfect gentleman, waiting and watching, then handing me a heated towel before leaving to let me get dressed.

He had my favorite guilty pleasure show ready with snacks when I walked back into the bedroom, and had somehow managed to dry off and put on some lounge clothes of his own. My husband in gray sweatpants and a white T-shirt is a masterpiece who belongs in the Louvre. My decision to make him wait would have gone out the window had he come on to me, but again, he respected my wishes. We curled up in bed together, falling asleep quickly.

It was one of the best nights of sleep I can remember ever having. And judging by the fact that he didn't so much as flinch at the sound of his alarm, I would say it was for him as well. "*I* sleep *better alone anyway,*" I murmured as I nudged him to wake up. *Yeah, right.*

I woke up with his very obvious erection poking my thigh, and my intrusive thoughts had me nearly pulling the band of his sweats down to wrap my hand around him, but he needed to get up and get ready for a work call during the drive home, so I didn't push anything.

He did kiss me good morning, though, and I'm not sure I'll ever get over the joy I feel from that connection. Regardless of what he thinks, I can't imagine a day when I would ever tire of his mouth on mine.

In fact, I wish he was kissing me right now. Or that he was here with me at all. A kiss, a game, our sweaty bodies moving together in a way I've never known before. Anything really. Unfortunately, his one work call turned into two more, which turned into more, and what was supposed to be a lazy Saturday has turned into a full workday for Henry.

I'm trying to remind myself that I'm strong, and I'm capable of entertaining myself, but after last night, I'm addicted to having his full attention. I know he's a very important man, but I'm important too, dammit, and it shouldn't be such a competition for a sliver of my husband's time.

Making myself a coffee, I take it to the den and sit in my favorite armchair facing the large windows out the back of the property. Although it's a frosty day outside, the fireplace in this room makes it a perfect cozy place to read. Cracking open the newest book suggested by my sisters-in-law, I forget about my earlier frustrations.

I'm two coffees in and making a third when Henry strides into the kitchen looking like he's had a long morning—hair tousled from running his fingers through it, two buttons of his shirt undone, and forearms exposed from his rolled sleeves.

He doesn't say a word as he crosses the room, picks me up, deposits me on the counter, and kisses me like he's been waiting to see me all day. *Maybe he has.* Or maybe I'm just being horny and emotional and irrational because he's busy today. I melt into him, accepting the fact that my husband might be as crazy about me as I am about him.

He breaks our kiss, breathing heavy as he rests his forehead against mine. "I'm so sorry I've been occupied all day, Kitten." He pauses to nip and kiss down my neck, then pulls back just enough to look into my eyes. "Everything should be sorted. I was thinking we could..."

Before he can finish his thought, his phone rings again. "Dammit..." he grumbles, looking down to see who's calling. He runs his hand through his hair, sighing. "This shouldn't take long. I'm sorry *again.*"

I'm flooded with guilt from my selfish thoughts earlier. Here I am, getting to cozy up and read by the fireplace while my husband has had to deal with work all day. Hopping down from the counter, I head over to grab the mug of coffee I just poured when Henry holds his phone to his chest and points at my mug. "How many is that today?"

I hold up the number three and smile innocently.

Without saying a word, Henry takes my coffee, pours it in the sink, and hands me a bottle of water. He's got his phone up to his ear again, but his attention is solely on me. Rolling my eyes, I grin. "Yes, Daddy."

I can almost see his skin flush at the effect of my words. He literally growls at me, the grip on his phone tightening as his other hand flexes at his side before turning to march off to his study.

Still standing, propped up against the counter, I grin when I hear the sound of his doors slam. I thought maybe the other night was the perfect combination of events, but now I *know* what words cause his undoing.

A daddy kink was *not* something I saw coming, especially knowing how he's battled with the concept of our considerable age difference. Oh, I can have fun with this.

It makes sense, though. From the moment I moved in, he's gone the extra mile to make sure I was comfortable and taken care of. Even before our wedding, he had my happiness in mind as he made renovations to the estate that would soon be my home.

I shudder, thinking of how he had me bent over his desk, spanking and soothing my ass. The way he calls me *little girl* when he's so close to losing his wits.

As a girl who grew up with few choices in life, the irony isn't lost on me either. I appreciated the way he picked out everything for me on our date, from my clothes to my food. How comfortable it was sitting on his lap as he cut my steak and fed me.

The difference is crystal clear to me, though. He's not doing any of this to control me. He's doing it to take care of me. My thoughts and feelings matter to him. In the two months I've lived here, he's paid such close attention to me. He knows what my preference would be when the moment presents itself. In fact, he respects me so thoroughly that in the passion of any moment we've shared, he waits when I say wait.

Making my way back to my cozy nest of blankets by the fire, I pick my book back up and wait for Henry to come get me. I can't help but smile thinking about the dirty things we're going to get into tonight. He may not realize it now, but he's just left his king open.

"Ha. Ha. Ha. Very funny, girls," I say to myself, having just realized my sisters-in-law recommended to me a MMF forced marriage book. Picking up my phone to shoot a text to the group chat, I realize the time. I've been reading for hours. And Henry hasn't come to get me.

Laying my book down, I unburrow myself from my cozy cocoon and go to check on my husband. When I see that his study is open and empty, I head to his room. *Our room?* Will he expect us to sleep in separate rooms after last night? If he tries the excuse of not sleeping well with me again, I'm going to show him the video I was able to take of him completely knocked out, full-on spooning me, while his alarm blared.

I knock on the cracked door of his room before entering. It's quiet and peaceful, with the afternoon sun filtering in through the window. Everything is immaculate, and I know that even if he didn't have a team of housekeepers on staff, his room would be clean. Just like Henry, everything in his life is organized and structured.

His room is adorned in cool, dark tones, a far cry from the light, feminine way he had mine decorated. Do I even have a place here? He's let me into almost every aspect of his life, but is this last sanctuary of peace too much? Walking to the side of the bed opposite the one I know he prefers, I lie back, imagining what it would be like to sleep here every night.

A grunt from outside reminds me of my mission to find Henry. Hopping off of the tall bed, I make my way to the window and see the man himself. Out in the snow. Chopping wood. Shirtless. *Goddamn.*

Grabbing my puffy coat, I make my way out to him. "Henry? I think we have enough wood to make it through winter," I say, the scene getting sexier with each step I take closer. Despite the snow, Henry is dripping with sweat. I watch as flakes catch in his chest hair, his muscles flexed and swollen with the blood that's been pumping through them. His hair, disheveled and wet, falls into his face.

"How long have you been out here?" I ask, approaching him slowly, like a wild animal I'm trying not to startle. "I thought you were going to come get me."

He freezes mid swing the moment he sees me. Pausing momentarily before continuing his motion, he hits his mark and sends pieces of wood flying to the ground. He runs his fingers through his hair with a sigh. "Katarina, what are you doing out here? It's freezing, and you're not wearing a scarf or hat."

"I came to find you. I missed you, and I'm sorry your call was so bad. I..."

"It wasn't just the call," he mumbles, putting another log on the chopping block. He swings the axe and finds his mark again. I watch as he repeats the motion, each swing splitting the wood with both precision and accuracy that only come from years of practice.

When he finally takes a moment's reprieve, I make my move.

"Is there anything I can do to help?" I ask. Closing the gap between us, his scent— vanilla, mint, and his natural musk—strengthens, intensified from the sweat.

When he shakes his head, I drop to my knees, only an arm's length in front of him.

Game.

"You've had such a stressful day. Please let me help..."

Set.

His curious eyes search mine as I look up at him. "*Daddy.*"

Match.

The curiosity in his gaze wavers as an edge of darkness takes over his expression. He turns from me, pacing in the opposite direction. "*Fuck!*" he yells into the woods, his hand rubbing the back of his neck.

He marches back over and lowers to his haunches in front of me, taking my jaw in his hands. "Say that again, little girl."

I can't control the devious smile and gleam in my eye as I watch him unravel before me. "I said, let me help take some of that stress away, *Daddy*."

All I can do is squeal when he throws me over his shoulder, marching us toward the house.

Chapter Twenty-Three

"Please let me help...Daddy."

All rational thought leaves my brain the moment she says those words. Every encounter we've had plays through my head like a crescendo leading up to this moment. The way her delicate fingers send tingles through my body every time they touch me. The way her mouth molds to mine when we kiss. The way she fell apart so beautifully in my arms when she came days ago.

She knew what those words would do. I could tell by the little twinkle in her eye and her smirk that she knew *exactly* what she was doing. I should've mounted her right then and there for being such a little brat. Painted the goddamn snow with her virgin blood as I tore into her tight little cunt.

I'm damn near jogging as I make my way up to my bed with my wife thrown over my shoulder. I can hear her squealing from behind me, her words barely intelligible as she pleads for me to set her down. I'm done with her clever little taunts. She asked for this, and I'm more than fucking ready to oblige.

Regardless of whether she fully knew what she was asking for or not.

Reaching the top of the stairs, I glance down the hall that leads to her suite. A room she'll never sleep in again. She'll be warming my bed for the rest of her life, and if she protests, I'll chain her to it.

It doesn't take any time before I'm kicking through my door, tearing her coat off, and throwing her on the bed. *Our* bed. She squeaks again when she hits the mattress. By the time she's stopped bouncing, I've managed to rid myself of my pants. Her gaze turns from surprise to pure lust as I stride toward her, my painfully hard cock bobbing with each step, eager to fill her up.

Reaching the bed, I grab her ankle, pulling her toward me just enough to be able to find the waistband of her yoga pants. In one quick motion, I pull her pants and panties off. I can see the outline of her pink nipples pebbled beneath her thin cotton tank top. Reaching up, I rip the flimsy fabric right down the middle, her perky breasts springing free as her chest heaves with her deep breaths.

Her mouth opens, but before she can say a word, I flip her over onto her stomach, pulling the ripped top down to her wrists to bind them together. I place a hand on the small of her back to calm her shaking, as I use my other to fist my cock. Lining the tip up to her entrance, I can't help the groan that escapes me when I feel how soaked she is. I ease my head in slowly, just enough to stabilize myself so I can let go and use my free hand to push her head down into the mattress before I...

Thrust.

"Fuuuucking fuck." I growl, throwing my head back once I'm buried to the hilt. I've never felt anything so tight in my life.

Her screams are muffled as I drive forward, the force of my thrust pushing her even further into the comforter. I know it hurt her. I could feel myself prying open her walls as I breached her forbidden channel. It's a fight for my life not to immediately start fucking into her, but I want to give her a moment to adjust to my size.

"Oh, my poor girl, does that hurt?" She tries her best to nod with my hand forcing her head down. As I lean forward to whisper in her ear, the angle forces me deeper, resulting in more screaming and squirming beneath me. "Fucking *good.* It should hurt because you saved it for me, didn't you? Because it belongs to Daddy."

Her deep, animalistic scream echoes as she clenches around me.

"You need to get used to this cock, and quickly, *wife,* because you're going to be full of me more often than not," I say, pulling away and giving her a few half thrusts. She's wetter with every stroke, and it doesn't take long before she calms, her frantic screams transforming into moans of pleasure.

"Isn't this what you wanted, little girl? You wanted Daddy in this pussy, right? You wanted it *so badly* that you pushed and pushed. Now, you're going to lie there and fucking take it."

With that, I plunge into her with all the force I have. I've given up on trying to hold her face down since it's hardly softening the sounds of her moans. Combined with the sound of our skin slapping as her wetness coats my cock and the bed, it's music to my ears.

"You want to know how to help Daddy with stress? It's just like this. Letting me fuck into that tight little cunt of yours as hard as I want. *Whenever I want, Katarina.* There won't be an inch of this estate where you'll be safe from me."

She grips me like a vise at my words. "Oh, do you like it when Daddy talks to you like that? You do, because you're my dirty little girl, aren't you, Katarina? You get off on the thought of letting Daddy have his way with you?"

I know she can't talk right now. Not with how fast I'm fucking into her. But she's trying her best to nod. And her cunt is about to cut my blood flow off by how hard it's squeezing me. It feels *so fucking good*. Better than anything has ever felt. In fact, I didn't know pussy could even be this good. Still, something is missing.

Looking down at my tiny wife, writhing on the bed beneath me, I realize I need more of her. I need her eyes and her mouth. I need her hands on me. I need her skin. Her chest against mine so that I can feel her heart pounding in a synchronized rhythm to my own as we bring each other to the edge of release.

After I make fast work of untying her arms, I pull out of her slowly, fighting my better judgment with every inch to stay buried inside her forever. I'm barely out for ten seconds, but it feels like a lifetime.

I quickly turn her over and pick her up, holding her weight with one arm while my other hand guides her back down on my dick. She's so light in my arms, so easy to move up and down my length. My own little personal sex doll, but with a beating pulse and a hot little pussy that clings to my cock for dear life as I bring her down to meet every thrust.

"Mmm, Kitten, you're crying so prettily for me. Does it still hurt?" I say, licking away her tears one by one. "Because nothing's ever been in your pussy before, has it? And Daddy's too big…"

I grab the back of her head, fisting her hair in my hand and bring it toward me, driving my tongue into her mouth the second our lips meet, stealing her moans and whimpers. Her hands are everywhere on me, scratching, grabbing, rubbing. I want to be able to do the same.

"Umph!" She breathes as I slam her into the wall, freeing up one of my hands to run over her perfect, soft body. For the first time since this started, I pause to take her in. She's the definition of debauched. Her hair is a tangled mess, her face is flushed, and her eyes are hooded. *She's stunning*.

I can't stop looking into her eyes. I'm not…I've never. *Fuck*. I want to stare at my wife until she knows every piece of my soul. I want hers. I want to break her on my cock until she aches if she's not full of me.

I slow my thrusts, angling my hips so that I hit both her clit and that sweet spot inside that has her shaking every time I rub across it. I can feel fluttering around me as her body tenses.

I didn't expect her to come this first time, but I can feel how close she is. Breaking my pace, I drive into her as hard as I can. This time, when I'm buried as deep as I can go, she doesn't scream. Instead, the sexiest moan I've ever heard falls from her lips as her eyes roll back. "*Fuuuck, Daddy…yeeesss.*"

The pictures rattle as I fuck her into the wall like a rabid animal, groping and biting every part of her I can reach, but I can't bring myself to stop. She's fucking begging me for more. Moaning my name. Calling me Daddy. "Please, He-Henry.

Harder, right there. Oh God, *yes!* More Daddy, more. *Harder, faster.* Fuck! *Yes, Daddy. Oh God,* yes!"

I'm about to lose my resolve. My balls tighten as they slap against her ass, tingling with every thrust.

"You're squeezing me so tight. Do you want something? You want my cum, Kitten?"

She's barely holding it together, her words broken. "Thought...you...didn't...witho...condom."

Shit, I haven't had one thought about that this whole time. I've never gone bare before, but I knew the moment I pulled off her pants that I wasn't going to have anything separating me from her. And why should I? I didn't think much further than that, but looking down at my wife, writhing on my dick, all I want to do is fill her up.

"You're my goddamn *wife*, Katarina. *Mine.* Nobody's ever been inside this perfect cunt other than me, and nobody ever will. I'm going to fill your pussy up with so much fucking cum, little girl..."

"Not...on...birth..."

Her entire body shakes because she's *right* there.

"I know," I whisper in her ear, pinching her clit as I bring my lips to hers, kissing her with every ounce of passion I have to give.

"Goddammit, fuck!" I growl, pulling away from her mouth as she detonates in my arms, ripping my own orgasm from me. My cock pulses, shooting ropes of hot cum inside her.

When she finishes screaming her release, I carry her to the side of our bed, still buried inside her, admiring the way she trambles after the first orgasm she's ever had with something inside her. After I lay her down, I place a hand on each of her perfect thighs. I squeeze, then trail my thumbs higher to spread her open. *Fuck.* Her inner walls are gripping me so tightly that it's hard to pull out. Just a little bit of fluid leaks from where we're connected, a creamy pink...her blood mixed with my cum.

As I finally pull all the way out, she winces, but I'm mesmerized by the evidence of the consummation of our marriage. I've never seen my cum inside anyone before, and I feel a caveman buried deep in the back of my brain roar. My wife's pussy is red and swollen but still looks so small compared to what I know was just buried deeply inside. She's so pink and cute that I can't help myself. This is my reward for being the first to have her, and I want it.

Before I can question myself, I tell her not to move as I reach for the pocket of my pants, long forgotten at the side of the bed. Leaving no angle unphotographed, I capture my essence leaking out of this perfect woman. *Fuck,* that's beautiful. I doubt a day will ever go by that I don't look at these pictures. Pushing on her thighs to open her up more for me, I lean down and lick some of our juices that have escaped and dripped down her thighs.

Christ. I'll have to be careful, or I'll be addicted to the coppery taste of her blood. *As big as I am, this might not be the only time she bleeds...*

Using my middle finger to gather the rest of what's leaking, I gently push it back inside where it belongs. I know she's sore, but I can't stand the sight of it escaping. Once I'm satisfied, I look up at my wife.

We're both covered in a sheen of perspiration from our exertion, panting, hearts beating out of control. "You're such a good fucking girl," I say, wiping strands of hair stuck to her face.

Taking my hand in hers, she brings my fingers to her mouth and sucks them to the back of her throat. The vision of her lips wrapped around my cock makes me insatiable. My cock never really softened after I came, and now it's back to needing a release.

"*Fuck*!" I say, throwing my head back, but before I can collect my thoughts, I feel her trying to get up.

"Where do you think you're going, little girl? I'm not even close to being done with you. I'll let you pick the next hole I fill, but your pussy is already swollen and damn near bruised, so I highly suggest either your mouth or ass."

Katarina freezes, and I growl, "You pick or I do."

"Mouth," she says, barely louder than a whisper. "But I don't..."

Before she can finish her thought, I flip her around so that her head hangs off the mattress. Fuck, she's a masterpiece laid out in front of me.

"I'll teach you how I like to be sucked off later. Right now, just keep your mouth open so I can fuck your tight little throat."

That's all the warning she gets before I'm thrusting into her, and my dirty girl does a great job of flattening her tongue and breathing through her nose. She gags as I thrust deeper, but she keeps her jaw wide and teeth away from my shaft. I feel a white-hot bolt of rage down my spine, and reach forward to place a hand around her throat.

Squeezing, I growl out, "Your throat is almost as good a cocksleeve as your cunt, Katarina. If I didn't know for a fact that nobody had ever touched you, I wouldn't believe you've never had a dick there before."

She tries to mumble something, but she's cut off as I stop holding back and truly let go, rutting into her. She probably can't breathe, but she's going to have to wait. I'm so close, and I...

My vision goes hazy as I feel her touch. I forgot she wasn't tied up, and I've never allowed anyone to touch me or look at me before. My rules apply at all times during scenes, not just during sex.

My wife's little hands explore. One massages my ass cheek, digging in with her nails, and the other...*fuck me*, the other has found my balls. Once, twice, by the third time she's caressed them and applied the slightest bit of pressure, I'm on the edge. Glancing down, I see her eyes looking at me, filled with tears but also with love, devotion, and passion. Before I can stop myself, I'm roaring my orgasm as I come deep down her throat.

Even with no warning, she swallows it like the perfect girl she is. I can't remember the last time I came that hard twice in under half an hour, but I've also never allowed someone to have so much of me. Pulling gently out of her mouth, I see that she's shivering, but still looking up at me, never breaking eye contact.

"You did so good for me, my perfect girl. Let's get you into the bath, Kitten," I whisper, picking her up and carrying her into my bathroom. She's given me the greatest gift, the most transcendent experience of my life, and it's time to make sure she feels as cherished as she should. It's time for her to understand she is *mine* and she is *loved.*

Chapter Twenty-Four

Everything is hazy as Henry carries me into the bathroom and places me on a cold counter. I don't know why I'm trembling. I'm not cold, I'm...hot? Everything hurts, and my heart has slowed down a bit but still beats way too fast to be healthy. I'm wrapped in a fluffy, warm towel and slowly blink as my surroundings come into focus a bit more.

A naked Henry is bent over his giant bathtub, fiddling with the temperature as it fills with water. I admire his muscles as they flex and stretch as he works, noting with pleasure that my scratch marks on his back are red and don't look like they'll be fading any time soon. Finally satisfied with the bath, he turns around to find me grinning at him and smiles back at me, although I can't quite decipher the look he's giving me.

"Well, hello there, Kitten. Glad you're back in the land of the living," he says, coming to stand before me and bracing my hips with his arms on the counter. A sweet peck on the lips is all I get before he pulls back to scrutinize me, his gaze starting at the top of my head and slowly working its way down. "How do you feel?"

"Everything hurts, and I'm dying," I manage to rasp out, my throat feeling like it's been grated from my screams.

"Hmm," he says. "I'm glad we're not overreacting." He holds his serious face for only a second before laughing as I smack his arm. "But really, Katarina. Let me have a look at you and then we'll get in the bath, okay?"

"Okay, what do you mean have a loo..." I'm cut off by him pulling my towel away and then repositioning my butt on the very edge of the counter. Before I can ask what he's doing, he's grabbed each of my feet and put them on the counter by my hips. I squeak because he's displaying me rather lewdly, but before I can voice my protest, he's kneeling before me, eye level with my pussy.

Raising an eyebrow at me, he turns his intense gaze to my core and licks his lips before letting out a low growl.

"I want to make sure you didn't tear, Kitten, or this bath will sting more than it has to," he says, gently using a finger to part my lips and get a better look. I flush, knowing that there's more of his cum leaking out, but he doesn't seem bothered. He looks his fill, gathers some of the leakage onto his finger, and licks it off as he stands.

"I think you're okay. Let's get you in the bath before you catch a chill, though."

With that, he lifts me and sits us both into the whirlpool. Low jets are already on, creating a frothy, soft layer of bubbles on top of the water. I keep my legs wrapped around his waist until he sits in the middle of the tub, then he rearranges us so that I'm leaning back against his chest. One long arm holds me tightly to him across my stomach, and the other spans my cheek as he cradles my head.

He's holding me like I'm the most precious object to him in the world. I want to talk to him, but I'm too tired. Maybe just a little catnap...

Too soon, I'm woken up from my dreamlike state by hands roaming all over my body. Up and down my stomach, over and across my thighs, back up to pass over my breasts with a featherlight touch. I think about moving or saying that I'm awake, but I'm enjoying my little rubdown too much. Every part of me is sore, but a deep place feels satisfied where I've only ever felt frustration. I start to smirk, thinking about how sex is completely underrated, then I hear Henry whispering into my neck.

"My beautiful, perfect wife. *Mine.* Made for me, *only for me.* Took me so well, even though I know it hurt. Better than anything I've ever felt. Such a tough girl. *Fuck.* Never had anything like you in my life. You fell apart so beautifully, giving everything to Daddy. You'll have anything you want, Kitten. Any house, any trips, as many babies as you want. *Anything.* Anything for my perfect girl."

He keeps murmuring, and tears gather in my eyes as I realize this man *loves me.* Like *loves me,* loves me. Even if he didn't say it tonight, I know it's true. I can't hold back a sniffle and he stills behind me, stopping his long stream of praise.

"Tell me how you feel, Mrs. Sinclair," he whispers, kissing my temple and never pulling back, just resting there so I can feel his lips on my skin.

"I'm overwhelmed, Mr. Sinclair," I reply honestly. "I had no idea sex was like that. Nothing could have prepared me for that."

Shifting me slightly to perch sideways on his thigh, he faces me and traces the planes of my cheekbones, jaw, and lips with his hand before cupping my jaw again.

"It's *not* like that, Katarina," he says seriously as he stares into my soul. "It's not...it's never been anything close to that. I'm not sure I have words for what we just shared. I do know that you absolutely own me. Every part of who I am is yours."

Touching his forehead gently to mine, he kisses me languidly, as if he has all the time in the world and this is all he wants to do. He never stops caressing me, as if he can't get enough of the feel of my skin. I can understand the addiction because feeling his naked body behind me has the first flames of arousal burning in my core, fighting against the soreness and ache already there.

As I start to squirm on his lap, he pulls back and chuckles. "Are you okay, Kitten?"

Rolling my eyes, I pout. "No! I've been trying to make myself orgasm for years, and you've just made me come twice in the past few days!"

His eyes turn dark, and I try to think of what I've said to displease him.

"Let me make myself perfectly clear, little girl. There will be no more attempts to orgasm by your own hand. Do you understand? All of them are mine, and I promise I'll give you more than you could ever want. I'll take care of you. But they are *all* mine, not yours. Understood?" He finishes, staring so intently at me I'm not sure what he would do if I said no.

I nod, sensing this is not the appropriate time to be bratty, and am rewarded with another kiss as we stand from the bath. After a quick rinse in the shower, we're dried off and heading for my bed. Briefly, I panic, thinking he's taking me back to my own suite to leave me, but he immediately explains himself.

"We'll sleep in here tonight since I was not expecting your all-out seduction. I told myself you'd never sleep in here again, but I don't feel like changing those linens, and the bed is probably still wet. Not that I would mind sleeping covered in your juices, Kitten, but I don't think you'd be comfortable," he says with a kiss to my temple. "We'll have to get a waterproof throw for the future. An oversight on my part, but I've never had someone in my bed before."

He walks me through my room and sets me on the smooth, cool counter in my bathroom. I flinch, expecting it to be cold against my bare ass, but his naked body is already crowding mine, making me burn in ways I didn't know I could. His hand caresses my face, eyes staring deeply into my own. "What did I ever do to deserve you?"

With a light kiss to the top of my head, Henry gently begins working on my tangled mess of hair. "Wow, I believe some would refer to this as the princess treatment."

"Well, I made it this way. The least I can do is help you brush it out." He chuckles at the way I grimace as he works. "I could tell you I'm sorry for messing it up." He pauses to pull back and look at me, a devilish glint in his eyes. "But the truth is, I've never seen your hair look better than it did as you lay on my bed, freshly fucked and sated."

His lower timbre reminds me of our recent proclivities, which has my pussy aching again. "Oh," I breathe out, trying my best to remind myself that I do *not* need anything inside her again right now. *Especially* with the way my husband fucks...

"What are you thinking about?" he asks as he sets the brush down, and I realize I've been lost in my head.

"Just wondering what else I can get out of you right now," I say with a smile.

Henry settles between my legs again, his skin sending sparks into mine at every point of contact. Using both of his hands, he cups my face and tilts it up so that we're looking into each other's eyes. For a moment, he just stands there, tucking my hair behind my ears before stroking my cheeks as his gaze pierces into my soul. "You must not have heard me earlier in the bath. Katarina, my darling, there's nothing in this life or the next I wouldn't do for you."

His lips come down on mine, and I immediately open to let his tongue in. I expected him to ravish my mouth with the same intensity I've been used to tonight, but instead, he's gentle. His kiss is slower and deeper than ever before. The passion is there, but it's born from a place of love. Not breaking our kiss, he effortlessly lifts me into his arms and leads me into the bedroom with my legs wrapped loosely around his trim waist.

Setting me down on the edge of my bed, I expect him to go get in on the other side, but instead, he spreads me open on the edge like he did on the counter earlier and kneels between my legs.

"What are you...oh *fuck,*" I whine as he licks from my ass all the way to my clit, giving it tiny kisses as I moan.

Chuckling, he murmurs between my legs as he alternates licking me and sucking on my lips.

"You have the most delicious pussy," he says, lapping at the arousal that's already started leaking out. "I know you worked yourself up in the bath, Kitten. This will help you sleep."

"I'm so sore, though, Henry, I don't know if I'll be able to..."

A harsher suck on my clit makes me cry out, almost sobbing at the pleasure and pain.

"Shhh, little girl. Don't tell me what you can or can't do with *my* pussy. You don't make decisions about your orgasms, remember? You agreed that I do. So be quiet and let Daddy take care of you."

He stops his assault on my clit, soothing me with gentle licks. "If you're impressed with how many orgasms you've had in the past few days, just wait until you see how many I can pull from you in the next hour."

With that, his tongue becomes intentional, circling my clit with precision as he feasts on my pussy. The sensation is unlike anything I've felt before. Compared to the slower buildup from when he was inside me earlier, my core tightens almost instantly. I can't help myself as I reach between my legs, grip his hair, and pull his head into me.

He's persistent with his strokes. He's not going slow, but he's not rising to meet the frantic way my body demands as I shake and writhe around him. I feel like my heart will pump right out of my chest, and he's taking his goddamn time. *"Faster p...please."*

To my dismay, he completely stops, chuckling against my core. I'm sensitive enough that his every breath blows just enough air to have me jerking. "Such an impatient little kitten I have," he growls, using a hand to flatten my stomach against the bed. "Now, be a good girl...lie back and take what Daddy gives you."

He continues his circles, this time even more languid than before, but the pressure from where his hand rests on my lower stomach makes it feel...more. It doesn't take long before I'm coming undone as this orgasm sends waves of pleasure washing through me for what feels like forever.

When I've finally stopped trembling, Henry stands, smiling down at me as he places my legs on the mattress. I relax under the sheets as he circles the bed, climbing in beside me. I'm about to snuggle up to him when he pulls the covers back, exposing my still naked body.

"That puts us even for the night, but I won't settle for anything less than a 2:1 ratio."

I'm about to question him when he yanks my legs up over his shoulders, peppering a line of kisses from my belly down back to my core. "That's at *least* two more for you tonight, little girl, so you better lie back and let me eat this delicious cunt until you fall asleep."

I lie back as my husband keeps his word. I hold out as long as I can, but my body was already exhausted from the way he fucked it earlier this evening.

I'm drifting into a blissful sleep when I feel the bed dip beside me. Henry's strong arms wrap around me, pulling me into his body before placing a kiss on my temple. "Sleep well, Kitten." Then I'm falling away into a sea of warm skin, mint, vanilla, and my husband.

Chapter Twenty-Five

The dim light of a snowy winter's morning filters through the curtains as I slowly blink myself awake. Realizing that I'm not in my own bed and I'm not alone, I smile and turn my head to look at my precious wife nestled in the crook of my arm. God, she's perfect. Last night wasn't what I would have imagined for our first time together, but she reacted to my monstrousness with a ferality all her own. *My kitten, indeed.*

After wearing us both out, I'm not surprised that I slept like the dead, but I've never felt so relaxed and peaceful in bed as when she's in my arms. She's facing away from me, using my bicep as a pillow, with both of her hands holding onto my much larger one. Her perfect ass is pressed against my hip, and based on her deep breathing, she's exhausted and still fast asleep.

Unable to resist her, I gently roll to fully spoon her. Her only response is a little sleepy groan as she burrows further back into me. I'm not sure how I'm going to make it the rest of my life feeling so overwhelmed by this need to care for her. Dropping my face to the crook of her neck, I smell our bath oils, her natural scent, and *me.* She smells like me, and I suppress a groan at how possessive it makes me feel.

Everything about how Katarina makes me feel is overwhelming. I expected us to be compatible, given how much time we've spent together getting to know one another, but having experienced the nuclear power of our coupling, well...she can't get away from me now. She's utterly *mine.*

As if she can sense my thoughts, my wife squirms against my hard cock pressed into the crevice of her ass. I wish I knew what she was dreaming about. Maybe pushing into her slowly in missionary, staring into her eyes and cradling her face between my hands. Or perhaps railing into her from behind, legs spread impossibly wide to accommodate me between them. Or maybe...

Gently moving my arm that she's lying on, I hinge my elbow to allow my hand access to caress her breasts. Just barely skimming over her soft skin before moving to slowly circle a nipple that quickly pebbles under my touch. As Katarina's hips continue to move in tiny circles against me, I can't wait any longer to feel her again. After lifting her top leg up and over my knee, I move my dripping length to fit against her pussy, making sure to push every inch against her clit on the way by.

Fuck.

I can feel remnants of her cum leaking out from what a mess I left her in last night. It's plenty of lubrication for her as she rubs herself up and down my cock like such a good girl, taking what she needs. Based on her moans, I can feel she's close to coming, so I pinch her nipple harder and move my other hand to her clit to help her along.

She keens, and her eyes pop open, looking so cute and confused about where she is and what's happening, before she turns her head slightly to meet my gaze. Seeing me and then realizing she was grinding back and forth on my cock, her eyes roll back into her head as she lets go. Her low, almost painful moan of relief is music to my ears, and the gush of wetness that accompanies her release is necessary to make this part a little more bearable for her.

"Good morning, little girl. What were you dreaming about while you were riding Daddy's cock, hmm?" I rasp into her ear, nipping on her neck just beneath. Holding her in place, I continue to thrust between her lower lips and rub lazy circles around her clit. She's sore, so it's going to hurt when I push inside her, no matter what, but the least I can do is make sure she's as wet as possible.

She squeaks as I give a firm tap to her clit and tries to close her eyes, but there's no escaping me. She's going to look at me while I fuck her. I want to see her wince in pain, her pupils dilate in pleasure. I need to watch her react to everything I say to her, so I can make sure she knows that I mean every word.

"Katarina," I growl. "Eyes on me. You're going to be a good girl and look at me while I fuck you."

Her eyes widen as I position myself at her entrance, and she tries to squirm away.

"Henry, I'm so sore, please n..." she whines as I push slowly inside. She's wet, but I know it still hurts, so I go slowly, not stopping until my hips are flush against hers. Her eyes are wide and full of tears, and her thighs are shaking, but she did as I asked and held my gaze the entire time.

"Shhh, it's okay, Kitten. You can cry. I know it hurts. But you take Daddy so well, and you've been grinding on me all morning. I had to be inside this perfect pussy of mine," I whisper darkly, savoring how blown her pupils are, her body pliant beneath me and no longer resisting. Giving her slow, deep thrusts, I roll my eyes back with a groan at how tight and wet she is. *My wife is the perfect little fucktoy.* I told her exactly what she had unleashed yesterday when she chose to push me over the edge. It's time for her to get used to being full of me.

Kissing her temple, I stop for a moment as deeply as I can, savoring the slight fluttering of her walls around me, before pulling out. Turning her fully to her back, I grab an ankle in each hand and pull her down to the center of the bed. Holding her legs wide for a moment, I admire her glistening center, a little red now from my attention this morning, flushed and throbbing. Pushing back, endlessly thankful for how flexible my wife is, I bend her in half, holding her feet by her head before entering her again in one long motion.

Her scream mingles with my shout and echoes throughout the house, no doubt painful pleasure for her but pure nirvana for me. This angle is deep as hell, allowing me to bump against her cervix in a way she'll have to learn to love. Leaning down to lick her tears away, I hold myself deep and stare into her eyes with my forehead against hers.

"Do you feel that, little girl? That's me as deep as I can go, right where I belong. And it reminds me that I need to apologize for last night, something slipped Daddy's mind," I tell her sweetly, kissing her deeply because I can't wait a moment longer to feel my lips on hers again.

Her curious gaze has me continuing, and fuck if she isn't still sweet when I'm hurting her.

"I let you fall asleep empty last night, Kitten. We took our bath and washed all of Daddy's cum away. I promise it won't happen again. We're going to keep you nice and full," I groan as she clenches around me. I'm glad that even if her brain tries to tell her she should resist, her pussy can't lie to me.

Her legs are shaking on my shoulders now, and if she comes, she's going to drag me with her.

"Daddy, I need. Ughhh..." She struggles to speak, and it's adorable watching her fight to try to stay present instead of going under the wave of pleasure that's about to crest.

"What do you think you need, hmm?" I tease, bending down to pull a nipple into my mouth as the pace of my thrusts increases.

"I need birth control if you're going to...if you're going to keep...ungh!"

She screams her release as her legs tighten around my head, and I follow her, just as I knew I would.

"Look at me," I growl out, and I force myself to maintain eye contact as I fill her up with a deep moan, instead of letting my eyes roll back the way I want to. I let her see how utterly gone for her I am, how much pleasure she gives me, and how she's absolutely, one hundred percent, not getting what she's asking for.

Smirking down as she lets her legs fall limply to the side, I sit back on my heels but don't pull out.

"You're not going on birth control. You're my wife, and now that I know what it looks like when my cum drips out of you,

I need your pussy full of me all the time. But I've seen the way you are with LJ. Don't even try to deny you'd love a baby."

She clenches around me *again,* and I know I have her.

"Like I said, I'm sorry you didn't go to bed dripping last night, but it won't be happening again, little one." I kiss her forehead and gently pull out. The surprise on her face when she sees my still hard cock, covered in the combination of our releases, is adorable. "Now come here. It's time you learned how to suck Daddy's cock like a good little wife."

She's lying on the bed so peacefully as I look down on her from where I've sat back on my knees. I take one more look, sweeping over her tiny body before scooping her up in my arms. When I've made my way to the edge of the bed, feet planted on the floor, I set her down between my spread legs.

"On your knees, Katarina."

She obeys beautifully, dropping to her knees and staying there. Just looking up at me with her pretty eyes and waiting for my next command. I pull her hand from where it's resting on her thigh and wrap it around the base of my cock, reveling in how her fingers don't touch.

"I know you can take Daddy's cock down the back of your throat, but we're going to start slow today," I say, moving her hand up and down my shaft, still lubricated by the mixture of our cum. "Move your hand, just like this, for the parts that you can't reach with your mouth."

She's a quick learner, taking no time to figure out the exact pressure and motion I prefer. "That's a good girl. Just like that," I say, looking down to see her biting her lip, her attention alternating between my eyes and my cock.

"Alright, now open that pretty mouth of yours and stick your tongue out. You can see how much you can take, but if you want to focus on the head for a minute, that's fine too. Urgh..."

Before I can finish, her hot mouth is on me, much deeper than the head. She swirls her tongue around and then hollows her cheeks and damn near sucks the soul out of me. My head falls back involuntarily. "Goddammit," I say, panting. "That's it, *fuck* good girl."

She's doing such a good job working me with her mouth and tongue, alternating between sucking and licking off the cum coating my cock, replacing it with her spit. I'm *pleasantly* surprised with how willing she is to lick off her own arousal. She guzzled me down like a dream last night when I spilled down her throat, but you never know what someone is comfortable with. I'm glad she doesn't mind, though, because now she knows how fucking delicious she tastes. *How delicious we taste together.*

When I finally get enough control of myself to open my eyes, the vision below me is *well* worth it. She's looking up at me through hooded eyes, wet from tears as she works me up and down, her drool dripping down my length and pooling in the dark hairs at the base of my cock.

"That's it, dirty girl, get me nice and sloppy. Get Daddy's dick good and wet."

She's moved both of her hands to my thighs to prop herself up as she bobs up and down. "Here," I say, taking one of them and wrapping it back around my base. "Use this and your mouth at the same time. Work me with your hand just like I showed you earlier."

She finds her rhythm immediately, bringing me so close to the edge in no time. If I hadn't just emptied myself in her tight little cunt, I would be shooting into her embarrassingly quickly. Even now, I don't have long.

"Fuck, you're good at this," I say as her enthusiasm increases, sucking and squeezing me harder and faster as she goes. "If I didn't know you were Daddy's virgin, I would think you've had plenty of practice..."

Pressure on my taint cuts me off mid-sentence. I've completely forgotten how to think, much less speak, when her dainty little fingers start rubbing back and forth from the edge of my asshole to my balls. I didn't even feel her lift her hand from my thigh.

"Goddammit, Katarina. *Fuck*!" I yell, throwing my head back when she takes my balls in her hand and squeezes.

Grabbing the back of her head, I push her down on my length to keep her from moving as I shoot my hot cum down her throat. I look down at her as I find my release, my cock pulsing over and over. I realize when she starts squirming and trying to push herself away that I've cut off her airway for longer than intended, but I'm not letting her up until she's swallowed every last drop of me.

She jumps back when I finally let go of her head, breathing almost as hard as I am after that life-changing experience. Before she can get too far away, though, I've picked her up in my arms, positioning her to straddle my lap as I capture her mouth in a searing kiss. After we're both breathless, I hold her head to mine for a moment, letting my heart slow, before giving up. I lie back on the bed, pulling her with me.

"That was outstanding, Katarina," I say between breaths. "How the fuck did you learn to suck a dick so well?"

She sits up, using her hands to prop herself on my chest. The thought of her riding me crosses my mind. A position I haven't had in years but now suddenly crave.

She looks down at me with the most adorable, innocent smile. Ironic, considering what her mouth was just doing. "I read *a lot* of magazines. Did you like it?"

Grabbing the back of her neck, I pull her face to mine, hugging her against my body with the other. "I swear, that was the best I've ever had." She smiles her cute little smile and "hmms", laying her head on my chest as I stroke her hair. Closing my eyes, I think back through my life before this woman came barging in, and I'm starting to realize it really wasn't a life at all. With one last squeeze, I pick up my wife and walk her out of her room to my bathroom for us to clean up for the day. Excited for what's to come for the first time in years.

Chapter Twenty-Six

"Yes, thank you very much for coming, it would have meant so much to him to have you here," I say for what feels like the thousandth time today. It's probably been at least a hundred, if not more, considering how popular Pavel Taranov was in certain circles. Everyone here has been on their best behavior, at least outwardly, but there's an undeniable undercurrent of tension in the air. The graveside service was drawn out, speech after speech from Father's business associates and cronies about what a wonderful man he was.

Eh. He was fine, I suppose. I can't say that I'm terribly sad, or that I'll miss him, because truthfully, my life won't change much with him gone. He was never very present during my childhood, didn't take much of a personal interest when he was around, and spent most of his free time traveling with his women or indulging in an ever more absurd hobby. I mean, *collector's goats,* really?

As soon as we received the news, Henry went into full daddy mode, and I've never been so turned on or thankful for him.

As I see him coming back toward me with another fresh glass of liquid courage to help me through the drudgery of the evening, I think back to how he handled yesterday and smile.

Giggling on Henry's lap, I move my chess piece. "Checkmate!"

"Ughhh..." he groans into my neck, taking a long sniff of my hair. "How do you win even sitting on the wrong side of the board? I'm beginning to think you're cheating, Mrs. Sinclair."

"You forget Occam's razor, Mr. Sinclair," I tease, kissing the tip of his nose. "The most straightforward explanation is that I am simply that much better at chess than you."

We've been in a sex-haze for two days now, and I don't know how either of us will come up for air anytime soon, considering that we can't keep our hands off each other. I've given up on trying to continue to tease Henry with my new wardrobe for now, since he prefers for us both to be naked with only a blanket wrapped around us if needed. He's eyeing his desk as if he has devious plans for me, and I'm about to tell him I need lunch first before there's a knock on the study door.

Wrapping us tighter in the blanket, he calls for Potts to enter.

"So sorry, dears," she says kindly. "Kat, your phone has been ringing. I retrieved it from where you left it charging in the kitchen. Here you are, love."

Dread fills me as I see missed calls from Sasha, various employees of my father's, and Uncle Ivan. With shaking hands, I show Henry before calling Sasha back. He answers on the first ring, and I breathe out a heavy sigh of relief that he's okay, and put him on speaker.

"Hi, KitKat, I'm glad you called me back," he says in a quiet voice.

"Sasha, I'm so glad you're okay. What's going on? Why is everyone calling me?" I ask.

"I hate having to be the one to tell you this, but it's your dad…"

After his brief description of my father being found dead overnight, he asks if we can fly in as soon as possible. Apparently, the will requests burial soon after death, and things are underway for tomorrow. Already, business associates and distant relatives based Stateside are en route to my family's estate.

"I…uh…" I don't know what to say, looking up at Henry for guidance.

"Yes, Sasha, we'll be there on time. We'll fly tonight or tomorrow, based on what my pilot thinks of the weather. If he deems it unsafe, though, we won't risk it. No, don't prepare any rooms, we'll stay in the city. Thank you, but I'll have a car meet us at the airport. No, I'll fly my representation up separately in the event he's needed. Yes, of course. I'll make sure she texts you. Goodbye."

With that, he hands me back my phone and gives me a gentle kiss on the forehead.

"I'm so sorry, Katarina. I know you weren't close, but he was still your father. Are you okay?"

Confused about both the news and the fact that he's already handled the most important travel plans with Sasha, I reply with my own question.

"Umm…I think so? I might be in shock."

"That's a perfectly reasonable response, darling. Let's get you into a bath, okay? I'll take care of everything, don't worry."

And he did take care of everything. My husband arranged for us to fly on his jet this morning, along with a hotel suite and a rental car. He also had Danny fly up for legal meetings with my family later. Last night, while I was in the bath, he packed for me, bringing a perfect, weather-appropriate mixture of formal and casual clothes in muted mourning colors, comfortable underwear and shoes, and my morning and nighttime skincare necessities. The hotel was stocked with my favorite shampoo and conditioner this morning when we arrived, and he had a lovely woman come in to dry and curl my hair so that I didn't have to fuss with it before the burial. When he put my heels on my feet and they were comfier than usual, he told me somewhat sheepishly that he had added his mother's favorite cushioned insoles to try to improve their wearability.

He's also been checking in on my emotions without smothering me. His encouragement to allow myself not to be that sad over my dad's passing felt like the permission I had been waiting my whole life to hear from someone.

"He wasn't there for you when you really needed him, Kitten. You can respect his memory without forcing yourself to feel feelings that he didn't earn while he was here." God, this man.

He's taken care of everything, especially me. I smile as he finally reaches me and hands me my glass.

"Hello again, Mrs. Sinclair. What's that smile about?" He asks, placing a possessive hand on my hip and steering me toward the butler's pantry, away from the hustle and bustle of the reception.

"I was happy to see you, and I was thinking about how comprehensively you've taken care of me the past twenty-four hours. I couldn't have done it without you, Henry. Thank you," I say with a wide smile.

He finishes herding me into the pantry and closes the door with a quick flick of the lock behind him. "You're welcome, Kitten. I find taking care of you to be my favorite pastime. And you never have to do anything without me ever again," he says seriously. "In fact, consider it expressly forbidden. Now, spread your legs. Bend over, hands around your ankles."

Shocked, I snap my head up to look at him as he places our glasses on the counter. "Wha…"

Clearly not happy with my delay in following instructions, he holds me around the waist, pushes my elbows down onto the counter, and kicks my feet apart, before using his free hand to gather my pleated midi skirt. Holding it above my waist, he tucks it underneath my elbows, exposing me completely.

"Henry—" I gasp out, but he interrupts me.

"Tsk, tsk, tsk…you just told me I take such good care of you. Who am I, little girl?"

"Daddy…" I whisper in a low moan.

"That's right. And you're going to let Daddy check on his pussy, aren't you? I haven't had you since the flight, Kitten. I need to see what we're working with," he says quietly, kneeling behind me and opening me with his thumbs.

"Ah…I knew I should have inspected you sooner." He uses the slightest pressure to rub up my opening, and I realize I'm *leaking.* His cum from earlier was as deep inside me as he could get it, but clearly, it's made its way out throughout the morning. "Your poor little pussy is leaking my cum, and you know that's not where it's supposed to be. You should have come to me earlier for help, Katarina. You know Daddy can fix this."

I whine before he shushes me.

"You have to be quiet, Kitten. We don't want the hundreds of people in mourning out there to hear what's happening, do we? I didn't lock the door."

His thumb is barely rubbing me now, and I feel my legs start to shake as I breathe out another low whine. I can't help it. I don't care who hears.

"Shhh, it's okay. You're okay. Just relax. I'm so glad I took a look, darling. I can fix this."

I almost collapse in relief, expecting him to fuck me again and fill me back up, and I'm so, so ready for him when I hear him unfasten his pants.

I'm still waiting when I hear a low groan behind me, and I look upside down between my legs to see Henry...*jerking himself off*?

"What are you doing?"

He gives me a wicked smirk. "I'm gonna fill you back up, Kitten. We identified a problem, and Daddy has to take care of his girl."

I whimper, hoping to elicit some sympathy, but clearly, this is a game that Henry is just starting to play because all he does is laugh.

"Let's make sure you're nice and open for me."

He uses his thumb and middle finger to spread my pussy open, and I feel the thick head of his cock at my entrance. I'm so desperate for him to thrust into me and give me relief that I rock back slightly onto my heels, causing just an inch to slip inside. I want to fuck myself on him, anything to take this edge off, but before I can, he's coming. His head drops between my shoulders, and both hands grab my hips roughly.

He lets out a long, low moan that has me trying to clench onto the tiny bit of cock that he's given me. "That's my good fucking girl," he says, kissing a trail down my neck as he pulls out and sits back on his heels. "Keep this nice and deep for me, okay? But if you feel it all leaking out again, let me know." Taking his long middle finger, he pushes his cum as far into me as he can before standing up and giving me a light slap on the ass.

Helping me stand, he straightens my skirt before pulling me in for a quick, hot kiss. His rakish smirk is irresistible, and I know even if he didn't make me come just now, he'll make it up to me later.

Wandering back into the fray, I see that my uncle's gaze follows us across the room, again. With everything going on, we've only briefly spoken, but I'm sure there will be a long meeting sometime later. He's been keeping a very close eye on Henry and me, though.

Danny has met with my family's representation, and a large portion of assets were left to me in my father's will, something that I'm sure Uncle Ivan will have plenty to say about. At this point, I really don't care about any of it. Other than perhaps a nest egg for myself in old age and trusts for my children, I don't need or want any of my family's money.

Sasha finally finds me just as Henry takes a call from work. Seeing that I'm in good hands, he tells Sasha not to leave me alone and kisses my temple before moving away to find a quieter spot. He crushes me into a hug, and all of my emotions seem to come at once as I realize just how much I've missed Sasha.

"Hey, KitKat, don't tell me *I'm* the thing that pushed you over the edge into tears today. Come on, let's go chat in the library for a minute," he says once he realizes I'm sniffling back tears.

Making our way quickly to the library, I see him send a quick text before turning his full attention to me.

"I'm okay, really," I say, dabbing my eyes with the handkerchief he hands me. "I just miss you so much, and I think it all hit me when you hugged me. I'm really okay with all of this going on. You know Father and I weren't particularly close."

"No, you weren't," he agrees, eyeing me carefully. "I'm glad this gave me a chance to see you. I've been under my dad's thumb all evening, which has been a nightmare. I've been looking for you, though. I wanted to ask you. How are things going with Mr. Sinclair?"

Blushing, I know there's no way to hide the pink creeping up my neck to my cheeks.

"He treats me very well, and I'm happy. We've been getting to know each other more lately, which is nice," I say, sipping on a bottle of water Sasha grabbed when we left the reception.

Seeing the still serious look on his face, I put my water bottle down.

"What?"

"I'm going to ask you this once, and I promise to take whatever you say seriously and never ask you again," he says.

"Sasha, what on earth," I begin, but he continues.

"I saw the two of you in the butler's pantry, Kat. I was in the silver vault, uh, finishing up a call. If that's a consensual interaction, fine, I'll let it go. But I have to make sure he's not taking advantage of you. He's a lot older than us, and…"

"I promise you, Sasha, it was consensual," I say, smiling in relief that all my cousin wants is my happiness and not to judge me. "I know the age difference is a thing, and not everyone understands it from the outside, but it works for us. We're incredibly compatible, and he takes such good care of me."

He breathes out a heavy sigh before laughing.

"God, that was fucking awkward to ask. And look, I know you're compatible from when he and I collaborated before your wedding. I just had to make sure that with all the sex stuff…I wanted to make sure he loves you, KitKat. You deserve the whole world. And if that includes kinky sex stuff, I can tell you a few things that…"

"Nope! We're good!" I say, at the same time that Henry opens the library door and joins us, before locking it behind him.

"No discussion of sex with my wife, if you please, Mr. Taranov," he says, handing me a glass of ice water and pressing a quick kiss to my lips. He's holding a plate of fruit and cheese balanced on another container, which looks like it has…

"Dranikis!" I exclaim, pulling the container from his hands and popping one into my mouth. The crispy potato pancake is one of my favorite childhood foods.

"I saw you eyeing them earlier and grabbed some in case you were feeling peckish," Henry explains, laughing when I give him a dramatic kiss on the cheek and proclaim him my hero.

Sasha has been watching us quietly with a small smile, and when I turn back to him, I can see in his eyes that he feels comforted to see me safe with my husband. He gives me a wink, then winces and scratches the back of his head. As he does, I see what looks like a fresh tattoo trying to peek out below his cuff.

"Sasha, is that a new—" He quickly cuts me off and changes the subject to something much more serious.

"I didn't necessarily want to be the one to tell you this, KitKat, but the coroner sent his final report over earlier today regarding your dad's death. The official cause is suicide."

I know my confusion is written all over my face, and Henry immediately sees it.

"What is it, Kitten?" he says, taking the empty draniki container from me.

"I just don't think that's possible. Father and I might not have been close, but if there's anything I would ever swear to, it's that he wouldn't kill himself," I explain.

Obviously tired of not touching me, Henry pulls me onto his lap.

"Sometimes people have hidden demons, Katarina. The human mind is capable of terrible things at a moment's notice, in some cases," he says softly. "But if you feel strongly, I certainly believe you."

I look at Sasha. He cocks his head to the side, then nods.

"I have to agree. I don't think Uncle Pavel would do it. He had a lot to live for and was making plans with my father right up to the last hour before they found him," Sasha says, and I can tell he's got something else to say.

"What else is there, Sasha?"

"Well..." he says, again scratching his neck in a nervous tic. "He had a piece of paper in his hand when he died. Nobody saw it when he was found here, but they included it in the report."

Henry and I both wait for him to tell us what might be the only clue to my father's death.

"The only thing written was a name, in his handwriting. *Natalya.*"

Chapter Twenty-Seven

The past seventy-two hours have been a whirlwind, to say the least. Being pulled out of my perfect, magical, otherworldly sex bubble that I had only just created with my wife is one thing. But having to leave our bubble to attend her father's funeral and play politics with her family, well. That's grated on my patience in ways I couldn't have comprehended three days ago.

As we approach the gates to her family's estate, I pull the hand I'm holding from her lap to my mouth, kissing her knuckles and enjoying the smile she gives me as she turns to me in the back seat. She's been a trooper during this trip back to her gilded cage, playing the part of the grieving but strong daughter perfectly. And she is strong, certainly, even if she isn't necessarily grieving. Maybe grief for a paternal relationship that could have been, but I hope she doesn't hold any guilt over that. It wasn't her fault that Pavel Taranov didn't see what a lovely daughter he had in front of him. In any case, she has a daddy now to take care of her. She won't ever feel unloved again.

After the burial and reception yesterday, we had a tense but pleasant dinner with her uncle Ivan, cousin Sasha, and various other distant family members. Following dinner, Ivan requested to speak with me in his office alone, but I could see that Katarina was flagging. By the time we made it back to our hotel, it was all I could do to get her showered and tucked into bed before she was fast asleep. I watched her for a while, trying to make sure she wouldn't have any nightmares, before allowing myself to drift off too.

Now, we just have to listen to the summary presented by the lawyers from their meeting earlier this morning, get through my meeting with Ivan Taranov, and get back to the jet to go home. I've blocked off more time working away from the office and taking a lighter load, utilizing the company's family grief policy, although, of course, as CEO, I set my own schedule. Still, Danny assured me that the feedback from my absence has actually done the business some good, as perception of me has shifted to a family man who's caring for my new wife. Apparently, my willingness to do something other than work makes me seem "more well-rounded and stable", he says.

Not everyone is taking my absence well, though. I had to hang up on Linda yesterday when she wouldn't stop blowing up my phone with calls and texts. She can't seem to understand that Katarina is my priority now, and work is well down the list, orders of magnitude below my wife. After trying to patiently explain that my work had mostly been divvied up to lesser executives, I lost it when she told me I no longer had my priorities straight. I told her my priorities were exactly as they should be, and if she called or texted me even once in the next ten days, she was fired. So far, she hasn't.

"I'm very ready to get this over with and go back home," Katarina says softly as we take off our coats and make our way to the conference room for our meeting with the lawyers. "I miss our bathtub, our bed, our crosswords..." She blushes, and I know what she means. *I miss doing nothing all day but lying around naked and fucking on every surface we can think of, too, Kitten.*

"Ah, there they are. Now we can begin!" says a portly man who I believe is the Taranov counsel. I nod to Danny, who gives me a smile and a wink, signaling that this shouldn't take long and won't be too painful.

Katarina's uncle is looking at us intently, and I sincerely hope he's ready to man up and ask his questions when we meet in his office in a few minutes, because I'm tired of him staring at my wife, uncle or not.

"As we briefly discussed yesterday, there were really no surprises in the will. If you'll all turn to page three hundred and ninety-four of your packets..."

After thirty-five minutes and many signatures from everyone in the room, our legal business is thankfully adjourned. Katarina made it clear to me that she had no designs on her family's business shares or a seat on the board, although I offered to fight Ivan tooth and nail for whatever she wanted. We looked over big picture finances on the way here, and seeing provisions for herself and future children taken care of, her only concern was if it would benefit me to absorb any of her father's stake in the company.

My sweet girl, thinking of how to help me even in her own stressful time. She'll be rewarded for that. Ultimately, Danny said that since it was a minority stake, the benefits down the line likely didn't justify fighting now and adding any stress to Katarina. As such, the meeting was relatively simple.

Now, as I sit with an ankle over my knee in Ivan Taranov's office, I find myself nearing the end of my patience with his scrutinous gaze. I decide to cut to the chase in an attempt to get out of here as soon as possible. The quicker we can fly home, and I can be in my house with my wife on my cock, the better.

"Mr. Taranov, I thank you for your hospitality in hosting my wife's father's funeral the last two days, and for your willingness to swiftly conclude the legal matters," I begin magnanimously. "I hope that you'll forgive me for asking that we settle whatever other business you have with me quickly as well, as Mrs. Sinclair and I are tired from the whirlwind of travel and anxious to be home again."

There, I can play nice. He can state his peace, and we can leave.

"I'd like to offer you the chance, and encourage you to take it, to sell my niece back to me," he says placidly, as if he didn't just throw a bomb on my doorstep.

I remain seated, not because I'm not enraged, but because I know the benefits of staying coiled and ready to strike, rather than brashly making a show of my size. But what the actual fuck is wrong with this guy?

"I beg your fucking pardon," I spit out, unable to keep the vitriol from my tone. A cloud of red descends across my vision, and it's only the reminder that the documentation of our marriage is legal and binding that keeps me sane. He can't have her back. *Mine.*

Sighing, Ivan sits back in his chair, looking ragged from the toll of the past few days.

"I can't put it any clearer than that, Mr. Sinclair," he says. "You were forced into a business contract by my brother, with my much younger niece, who you objected to. While I'm sure the two of you have made the best of it, there's no denying the natural incompatibility that accompanies such an age difference. I can't imagine you have much in common, and surely, you don't want her having to deal with you in your old age while she's still spry. Not very fair to her, I'm sure you agree."

This fucker is sitting behind his desk, as serious as a heart attack, calmly explaining to me why it's a ridiculous idea for me to keep my wife. I'm obviously doing too good of a job hiding my emotions because he continues.

"I won't deny that we've missed her, and her place is here. I'm sure she misses her home, and we can certainly compensate you for your time and emotional distress in this whole nasty business—" He's cut off as I interrupt him. We're done here.

"That's enough," I snarl, finally standing and making my way to Ivan's desk to lean heavily against it and place my face as close to his as possible.

"I beg your pardon?" he asks, and this guy must be an imbecile not to read my face and body language right now.

"That. Is. Enough." I'm whispering by the end, belying my rage. If I walk out of this office without killing this man, I should win a medal of honor for my restraint. I go through two cycles of breathing exercises before I think of Katarina waiting for me to join her to fly home. Taking her home is the only thing grounding me to this planet right now.

"I will say this, and you will listen, and you will never speak of this conversation again unless you have a death wish," I say lowly, making sure I have Ivan's eye contact so that he can see that I mean every word.

"I would kill you and anyone else on this planet a thousand times over if it meant keeping my wife. You're lucky I don't kill you now for insinuating that I do not covet her, cherish her, *love* her." My voice cracks, just a hair. I've known that I love her for a while, but saying it out loud magnifies it in my heart and soul. I can't believe I haven't told her yet. That ends today.

Continuing, I keep my voice even, having learned from my father at a very young age that men aren't threatened by yelling as much as they are by control.

"She is happy, *we* are happy, and this prison you kept her in, even with good intentions, is no longer her home. My home is her home, and she will blossom there. This gilded cage will be no more than a memory soon, and although I allow her unlimited access to Sasha because she loves him like a brother, if I catch so much as a hint of you all sniffing around ways to get her back, it all stops. Do you understand? It. All. Stops.

"She is mine. No one will take her from me while I breathe. I categorically deny every. Single. One. Of your pathetic attempts to undermine our union. We have everything in common, we bring out the best in each other, and I'll make her so happy every day that I live that she'll be sustained by my love well after I'm gone. I'll know immediately if you or anyone from your team tries to contact her. If you have business to conduct with her, you can reach me via my lawyer."

Forgoing any sort of goodbye, I turn and stride quickly from the office to the adjacent sitting area, where Katarina sits reading a book. Her face is twisted with concern, and I know she can see every bit of my distress.

"Henry, what…?" She begins to ask, but I shake my head, picking her up to wrap her legs around my waist and carry her to the waiting car.

Smelling her hair, I feel my heart rate start to slow, but every nerve fiber still feels soaked in adrenaline.

"Plane," I whisper. "Everything is fine, I promise. Just. Let's get in the air. Please."

She clutches me tighter and clings to me even in the car. The drive to the airfield is blessedly short, and before I know it, we're high enough in the air to be cleared to move about the cabin.

Immediately, I stand, pacing with my hands on the back of my head. Instead of time and distance from the Taranov compound making me calmer, they've had the opposite effect, allowing me to perseverate on the fact that that *asshole* even had the thought to take my wife. Let alone speak it out loud to my fucking face.

"Henry?" Katarina's soft voice brings me back to the present, and I realize I'm behaving like a beast, growling and thrashing about. The last thing I want to do is scare her. Walking back to her seat, I kneel on both knees in front of her and put my head in her lap. Immediately, her fingers start to play with my hair and scratch at my scalp, and I feel some of my tension untwine itself from my spine.

Taking a deep breath, I stay between her legs but lift my head enough to look into her eyes. She's wearing one of her custom periwinkle designs from my sister, a cashmere travel set that makes her beautiful violet eyes pop. *Fuck, I hope our girls get those eyes.*

"He wanted..." I hear my voice crack with emotion for the second time today. Clearing my throat, I try again.

"He wanted you back," I whisper. "He wanted you back, but he can't have you back, Katarina. You're mine."

Her soft smile is free of judgment, and I bask in it.

"I know. I heard," she says, without any trace of guilt in her voice at eavesdropping.

Chuckling, I take her left hand and kiss the pad of each finger before repeating myself on the right.

"I *knew* there was no way you wouldn't be listening to that meeting. What was your trick? A loose floorboard that allowed sound to travel underneath? A secret room in the broom closet next to the office?"

That earns me a small laugh along with a shake of her head.

"Nothing that fancy. Old-fashioned ear to the door. Works more often than you'd think," she says, voice tapering off at the end. "Henry, you said..."

Keeping my gaze locked onto hers, I make myself as transparent as possible in the hope that she'll be able to see directly into my heart. If she does, she'll find herself looking into a mirror. *It's all her.*

"I said a lot of things, Katarina, and I meant every single one of them. None more so than the fact that I love you. *I love you. I love you.*"

I find it hard to stop saying it once I start, especially considering the tears from her eyes. I wipe them away with my thumbs before cradling her face and pressing the softest kiss to her lips, then pulling back to look at her once more.

"I meant it all, Mrs. Sinclair. As harsh and murderous and psychotic as it sounded, multiply that by a hundred and it won't touch the truth of it. *I burn for you.* I *would* burn for you. Anyone. Anything. Any entity who dares to utter the mere *suggestion* that you won't be mine for eternity will not meet the same benevolence as I just bestowed upon your uncle. Your family, my family, nobody on earth would be spared if they took you from me."

Even in the midst of my admission of exactly how far I would go to hoard her to myself like a dragon over his treasure, she looks at me with adoration and, I hope, with love. She's not shrinking away from me at all, but rather leaning into my hands. *My perfect girl.*

"I'm never letting you go, Katarina. Not even if you asked. I would follow you to the ends of the world and bring you home. My *wife. Mine.* We're going back home, back to being happy, and I'm going to take care of you forever. You're going to have *my* babies, and we're going to fill our house with so much joy, Kitten. I promise you, you'll never need or want for anything."

She's crying now, but her smile is huge as she launches herself at me, almost knocking me backward off my knees with the force of her exuberance. After she's tried to crush me with her hug, she pulls back to kiss me, then looks in my eyes.

"I love you too, Henry."

And that's all I need. *Forever, that's all I'll need.* Continuing to murmur into her ear as we make our descent, I refuse to let her go when the stewardess tells us to take our own seats. If the landing is bumpy, I'll just hold her extra tight. Eventually, I know I'll have to physically let her go. She'll need the bathroom, or she'll want a girls' night with her sisters-in-law. For the foreseeable future, though, I have no plans to unhand her.

Her uncle, the stewardess, anyone who wants me to let go can fuck right off.

Mine.

Chapter Twenty-Eight

The relief I feel as we walk through the door is unmatched. *Home.* It's an interesting feeling. While we were gone, visiting the estate where I spent my first nineteen years of life, I spent the entire time longing for the house I've lived in for barely two months. It's also an interesting feeling to leave there knowing that I have no place there anymore, regardless. Since my father's passing, it's Uncle Ivan's now. Until Sasha inherits, I might as well be an outsider. Especially after Henry's profound threats.

I realized days ago that my husband loves me. It wouldn't have taken a genius to figure out how he feels. He says those three words every time he goes out of his way to tend to my every whim, or when he touches and kisses me with such passion it lights my body on fire. Or when he looks so deeply into my eyes that I think he's found my actual soul.

Of course, hearing him say them out loud was incredible. Especially hearing him declare his love for me to someone else. If any doubt in my mind existed about his devotion to me, it's long gone after hearing him threaten my uncle. I know I've always had Sasha on my side, but I've never had someone care for me to the degree Henry does. Someone who would face the world if it meant my happiness. Someone who hasn't stopped touching me since I told him I loved him too.

Turning in Henry's arm, I raise to my tiptoes and wrap my hands around his neck, pulling him down to meet me in a kiss.

"Henry, I need to shower," I say, but he doesn't let me go, just stands there looking down at me like if he blinks I'll disappear. "Did you hear me, Henry? I need to—"

"Yes, I heard you," he interrupts. "We can go shower."

"We? Ahh!" In a flash, he scoops me up bridal style in his arms and makes his way to our bathroom.

When he gets to the shower, he pauses, his attention alternating between me, the shower, and the bath, before setting me down on the counter. "Are you sure you don't want me to run you a warm bath, Kitten?" he asks, rubbing his hands up and down my arms as he searches my eyes like he will find the answer there.

"What would you prefer? Shower or bath?" I ask, letting my hands rest on his chest, reveling in the way I can feel his heart beating. "Honestly, if you could pick, which one would it be?"

He finally gives in with a sigh. "Truthfully? A shower, just so I can get you in our bed faster." He tries to give me one of his smirks, but it comes out as a weak imitation after the emotional roller coaster of today.

"Shower it is, then!" I say, hopping off the counter and squeezing past him to get the water turned on and the temperature set. I make quick work of shimmying out of my clothes, then turn back to Henry in just my matching bra and panties. I almost swoon seeing him leaning casually against the counter, looking at me like I'm a piece of meat.

His hair is disheveled in that way it always is when he's been running his hands through it. I can't help myself from reaching up to do the same, pulling a groan from him when I start massaging his scalp.

The longer I spend playing with his hair, the more I start to realize how little my husband is ever taken care of. He looks out for everyone he cares about without question, giving everything of himself for those he loves. And he never requests anything in return. I'm sure it's partly because of how proud he is, putting on a front for everyone that he's got everything under control. He's spent the better part of his life perfecting his facade. And while he's obviously inclined toward caring for others, he deserves to receive it in return.

He groans in protest when I move my hands from his hair to start unbuttoning his shirt. I half expect him to grumble, but he doesn't say a word the whole time, just meets my gaze as I undress him. Pulling his shirt off, I run my hands from his broad chest to the band of his pants, then drop to my knees before working on his belt.

His dick is half hard by the time I've freed him of his clothes, and I place a gentle kiss to the tip, causing him to growl my name in a warning I heed. Before he can toss me over his shoulder like the caveman I know he is, I step back, removing the rest of my clothes and checking the water.

"Just right," I say with my hand held out in invitation.

He follows, shutting the door behind him, and stares down at me, as if he's waiting for my instruction. "Um, can you sit?" I ask, pointing toward the built-in bench. "I don't *mind* having to climb to reach your head, but it would be a lot easier if you just sat down."

He arches his brow but ultimately follows my instruction, taking a seat and looking at me for further directions. All I wanted to do was wash my husband, but I'm frozen in place as I look down at where he's manspreading, legs out wide with his cock lying heavily on his thigh. I can tell the moment he notices my ogling. He winks, then leans down with his forearms propped on his knees to look up at me, waiting.

I make quick work of lathering myself up, enjoying the way his erection grows as he watches me. I'm not sure what he was expecting, but sudsing up my hands with his soap seems to confuse him. "Were you expecting a lap dance?" I ask as I begin washing him, starting with his shoulders and working my way down.

"Erm, well, I've had a woman in my lap more times than I've had a woman washing me," he says, pausing to chuckle when I narrow my eyes at him. "Don't worry, Kitten. Both of those are from you and you alone."

I dip my head to hide the smile forming on my face, and continue washing, taking extra care to tease around his private bits for payback.

I've barely finished when I'm being pulled up from where I'm kneeling between his legs. He lifts me around effortlessly, placing me on his lap. "Kiss me," he says, pulling my face to his.

"Wait!" I protest, trying and failing to resist him. "I was going to wash your hair!"

With his hand still around my head, he rests his brow against mine, "Kiss me, Katarina," he says, his voice barely a whisper.

I don't hesitate this time. Holding his face in my hands, I bring my lips to his. The passion in his kiss doesn't escalate. Instead, it's slow and steady, as if we have forever. And I suppose we do.

I'm so lost in the kiss I don't even realize we've left the shower until he's laying me gently on the edge of the bed. When he finally breaks our connection, I scoot myself back, allowing him room to join.

I'm propped up on my elbows as he crawls between my legs. Grabbing one of my ankles, he begins peppering a series of kisses up my calf, pausing as he reaches my knee.

"My love, you astonish me," he says as he places my leg around his waist before closing the distance between us.

I have no choice but to fall back on the mattress as he climbs on top of me, his hands caging my face as he looks down at me. My arms instinctively wrap around his neck as we stare into each other's eyes.

"Henry?"

"Yes, Kitten?"

"Make love to me..."

He freezes, a panic briefly flashing in his eyes. "Katarina, I've never. I don't—"

"I know." I interrupt, caressing his cheek as I smile up at him, unable to stop myself from letting out a little giggle. "I haven't either."

His serious expression shifts as he grins down at me, shaking his head. "You're ridiculous, you know that?"

"Yeah, but you love me anyway."

"Fuck yes, I do."

He moves one hand to guide his cock to my entrance, groaning when he feels how wet I am. I'm preparing myself for him to thrust into me with his usual force, but he takes his time, rubbing my arousal up and down the length of my pussy, before slowly pushing his way inside. It's not the usual pain with pleasure sensation I'm used to, but it *is* painfully slow.

"*Fuck*," we say in unison when he's seated as deep as possible inside me.

He begins moving immediately, pulling out only halfway before thrusting deeply again. Each time, he hits my G-spot perfectly. Combined with the friction on my clit from the pressure of his groin against mine, it takes no time before I feel that familiar coil form within my core.

"I love you, Katarina, and I hope you never doubt that for a second. If there is one thing you can be sure of your entire life, it's my love for you," he says before crashing his mouth to mine.

Torturing me with a languid pace, he teases, pulling almost all the way out before devastating me with each thrust back in. With one hand holding his weight, he lets the other explore, his touch gentle as he worships my body with his fingers and mouth. The combination of everything is overwhelming.

"Fuck, you're squeezing me so tight," he says, shaking with restraint. "I can't hold out much longer, Kitten. I need you to come for me."

He lowers his hand between us, using his thumb to rub circles around my clit. Once, twice...I writhe under him as my orgasm crashes into me, sending ripples of pleasure from my core throughout my entire body.

"That's it, love. Come on my cock. *Fuck!*"

I'm still shaking when he thrusts into me one last time, his body going still as he pulses inside me, painting my walls with cum. I'm still shaking when he drops his head to rest against mine, telling me over and over how much he loves me. He rolls us so that I'm lying on him, both of us breathless as we lie entwined in each other's arms.

He sits up, bringing me onto his lap, the change in position causing his dick to slide out of me in the process. My sadness over our broken connection is short-lived when I notice the wet strand of arousal connecting me to him.

"See something you like, Kitten?" he asks, kissing the top of my head when I nod. He strokes his hand up and down my back, and I try to reciprocate, but my limbs aren't cooperating.

"Ugh, can't move," I mumble into his chest.

With a chuckle, he wraps both of his long, strong arms around me. "Not a problem for me. I actually prefer when you can't."

"You're ridiculous, Mr. Sinclair." I roll my eyes.

I look up to see my husband staring down at me with amusement. "Yes, but you love me."

"I love you *very* much."

Chapter Twenty-Nine

"I don't know, Daddy. I thought it looked better the other way around."

I know for a fact that Katarina is teasing me, making me switch the orientation of our stockings and garland draping the fireplace in my study at least three times in a row. But she looks so distracting in her red silk pajamas that I've happily obliged her Christmas decorating whims all day.

We started with homemade Danish wedding cookies, and I'm more convinced than ever that I need to get back to my usual gym routine or I'll have a stomach bigger than Santa's. My wife is a wizard in the kitchen, particularly when it comes to baked goods, and everything she puts in my mouth is better than the last. I know it makes her feel like she's taking care of me when she feeds me, and she's right. There's nothing like smelling something delicious wafting from the kitchen while I'm on a work call and having her burst into my study to stick something in my mouth.

She's been on a Christmas spirit tear, and we've already gotten our bedroom, study, and sitting room decorated. Trimming the big tree in the sitting room earlier while music played softly in the background felt like a fever dream, like I couldn't possibly be lucky enough that this is my life.

I switch the stockings one last time, then box her in with both of my hands on the mantel.

"Seeing you in your monogrammed pajamas with my 'S' prominently displayed in the middle is an aphrodisiac, Kitten. As is seeing these stockings on the mantel," I say, nipping her bottom lip between my teeth, then pulling back so I can look into her beautiful eyes.

"The stockings are sexy?" she asks, clearly confused as I bend down to kiss her again.

"Mm-hmm," I murmur into her neck, then kiss my way up to her ear. "Only two this year, and there's plenty of room. Next year...who knows?"

Her hands reach under my pajama top as she moans, raking her nails down my abs and pulling a growl from me at the sensation. I'm about to throw her over my shoulder when the doorbell rings. Both of us look at the other, confused, since we weren't expecting anyone, but before I even reach the door, I hear Jack's voice as he cracks jokes at my expense.

"I told you, they probably won't even hear the bell from the sex dungeon...Oh! Hi guys!" he says, having the decency to look sheepish as I open the door.

"Hello, you two," Katarina says sweetly, stepping under my arm to usher them out of the cold. As it turns out, my sister and Jack were out shopping and decided to stop by and say hello.

Sighing, I tuck my hard cock up into my pajama bottoms and resign myself to family time instead of family-making time.

Our evening ended up being lovely. We played Christmas Clue, and I wiped the floor with everyone else, even Katarina. As we're brushing our teeth for the night after Jack and Margot finally left, I can't help but tease her.

"I'm just unsure how you manage to have such an analytical mind, destroy me regularly in chess, and simultaneously be so bad at Clue." I bend over laughing again because it's unbelievable how bad she is.

Yawning, she finishes with her teeth and smacks my ass on the way to the bed.

"It's not my fault! After Sasha and I came to literal blows when we were nine, it was banned in my house! I'm not even bad. I'm just rusty. You just wait," she says as she yawns again and climbs naked into her side of the bed. *Fuck,* I'm glad we both agree that skin to skin is our preferred way to sleep. "I'm going to read that rule book front to back and dig into strategy online. You'll never beat me again!"

Pressing a kiss to her forehead, I tuck her in.

"I'm sure you're right, Kitten."

Sleepily, she reaches for my hand as I move to leave the room.

"Are you not coming to bed?" she asks.

"I'm going to go do the usual walk-through and check the alarms, darling," I say with one more soft kiss to her lips. "I'll be back before you know it."

"Mmm," she mumbles, turning and burrowing into the plush comforter. "Come back soon so you can ravish me. Margot and Jack ruined the moment earlier."

Chuckling, I promise I will as I go to walk through the house, knowing she'll be asleep well before I make it to bed. Usually, I do this earlier in the day since nobody else comes in or out. Margot and Jack were a deviation from the routine, though, and nothing is as important to me as keeping Katarina safe. After my walk and checking that the systems are armed, I finally make my way back to my sleeping wife. Pulling her to me, I breathe in the scent of her hair, shampoo mixed with Christmas aromas from our time in the kitchen today.

She feels like home and hope, and I drift into a deep sleep.

Blinking, I turn to my bedside clock to see it reflecting 2:00 at me. I'm not sure what's disturbed my sleep, as usually I have no issue sleeping through the night. Especially now that Katarina is my personal heating pad, keeping me cozy. After going to the bathroom to relieve myself, I come back to bed but stop to admire my wife.

She's sprawled out like always, half on her side and half on her stomach, with one leg tucked up to her chest and the other stretched behind. Normally, any movement from me in the night also wakes her, but she indulged in a fair bit of mulled wine with Jack tonight, so I'm not surprised she's out like a light.

My wife is a work of art, I can't help but think. White-blonde hair pale in the moonlight, full lips and breasts, a little tummy pouch that I'm proud of, because she's been spending too much time on my dick to work out as much as she used to. Long legs for her height parted just enough to see her perfect cunt, glistening slightly in the light peeking in from the window.

I'm fully awake now, and so is my cock, hardening immediately as we stare at our favorite place. A devilish idea comes to mind, another of my firsts that I can give to Katarina. I told her that I would use her whenever I pleased, and after thinking about adding stockings to the mantel earlier, I can't believe I let her go to sleep without being full of me. Time to fix that.

Slowly, I move onto the bed, the mattress dipping slightly beneath my weight but redistributing it well. With one knee inside her straight leg, I use the other to gently bend her top leg *just* a touch more, and she doesn't stir at all other than a tiny twist onto her stomach, opening herself up for me. Parting her lips with my thumb and middle finger, I use my other hand to slide one exploratory finger inside.

Fuck. She's so tight and warm, my perfect little girl always ready for my cock. Keeping one finger deep inside, I slowly rub her clit until I feel her moistening around me and opening up around my finger. Crooking my finger inside, I give her G-spot a few solid strokes before pulling some of her wetness out to coat her entrance. Spitting on my cock, I've lost all patience. This will have to be wet enough.

Pressing against her little hole, I have to stop myself from groaning as I slowly but steadily push in. She's still so *goddamn* tight, even with me fucking her multiple times a day. By the time I'm seated against her ass, looking down at her serene face, I'm already close to coming. Since I'm not in any hurry, I stay deep without thrusting, watching her eyelids flutter and her breasts rise and fall slowly as she breathes deeply in her sleep.

Testing her, I pull almost all the way out, then plunge slowly back in, but she sleeps on with the minimal jostling. I'm not sure if I'd rather see the shock on her face as she wakes up with me inside her or her confusion tomorrow morning. The idea of her waking up a little sore tomorrow, sticky between the thighs and not knowing why, has me unable to stop myself. I can't help but groan, hitting her cervix as I come deep inside my wife.

My noise has finally woken her, and as she sleepily blinks her eyes open, I see her realize something's hard and inside her, and her eyes open wide in panic. She tries to kick me off, and I see her open her mouth to scream. Quickly covering her mouth with my hand, I lean over so that I'm in her field of vision and she can see who's fucking her.

"Shhh, Kitten. It's me, okay? It's Daddy. It's okay, you can go back to sleep," I say, and when her eyes light up in realization of what's happened, they roll back as she groans and comes on my still hard cock. Her squeezing the life out of me pulls me under, and I fill her up once again with almost painful thrusts.

Easing myself out of her, I see that she did as I said and fell right back asleep. Pulling the comforter over us both, I join her quickly, feeling much more settled than earlier with my wife full of me by my side.

Bleary-eyed, I wake as I feel Katarina stirring beside me. She's curled on my bicep as usual, but flips over to face me and drape her arm across my chest, playing lazily with my chest hair. Turning my head to face her, I see her eyes are still squinty with sleep as she nuzzles into my side. Marital bliss has made my wife less of a morning person, and I can't blame her. I never want to leave a bed that she's in, either.

"Good morning, Mrs. Sinclair," I say, kissing her temple and inhaling her scent. "How did you sleep?"

She yawns before her face scrunches in thought.

"Alright, I suppose. Although I had the weirdest dream that you..." Her eyes pop open as I move between her legs, throwing the comforter away and spreading her wide for me to inspect.

"That I *what*, darling?" I taunt, dipping two thick fingers into her pussy to coat them in our cum before pulling them to my mouth and tasting our combined flavor. *Delicious.* Even better when it's been marinating all night.

Her mouth drops open in shock, and she tries to feign outrage as I lower myself and get to work licking to clean her up properly.

"You *fucked me* while I was asleep? Why? *Unghhhh...*"

Finishing my meal, I decide not to finish her off since she's going to question me this morning. Sitting back on my haunches, I mindlessly grab one of her tiny feet to rub.

"Well, you fell asleep very early last night. Before you had a chance to perform your *wifely* duties, in fact. So since you were so tired, I decided to let you sleep," I explain. "You came for me, you know," I say with a smirk. "So good even in your sleep that I filled you up twice."

When I lean over to kiss her languidly, she moans as my length brushes up and down her clit, and I forget my earlier reasoning for not making my wife come. Pushing into her quickly, I set a brutal pace and drag both of us over the edge in record time.

"Tell me what you're thinking," I say, pulling back to get a full view of her face as she scratches my back.

She bites her lip before squeezing her walls around me where I'm still buried deep. I groan, and she *laughs at me*. I've created a monster. A sexy, confident *monster.*

"I'm not sure why I think that's so hot...but it is," she says, before digging her nails harder into my back. "In fact, perhaps I'll return the favor one morning."

The thought of waking up with her hot mouth already around my cock has me subconsciously thrusting again, and I realize we're probably not leaving the bed today. *Maybe I'll retire, and we can stay in bed forever.*

After a very late brunch, Katarina heads to her room to call Sasha and then take part in a Christmas planning group video chat with my mother, Margot, and Sloane. It's amazing to consider what Christmas will be like this year with us all together as a family. LJ will be the center of attention for his first Christmas, but not for long. By next year, there will be at least four little Sinclairs to dote on. *At least.* Taking my coffee in hand, I send a few emails while admiring the view from the windows looking back toward the end of my wing, where Katarina's rooms were.

It seems like a lifetime ago that she had her own bedroom and a separate space away from me. *Never again.* We've already been talking about the best use for her room, and it can be whatever she wants as long as I have a chair in the corner to be in her presence. I'm just about to go find her and see how her calls are going when I see a fluttering of a curtain in the window a few rooms down from her bedroom. Moving quickly to the second floor, there's an open door to a room that connects to Katarina's old one, the original owner's suite of the house. I think my parents used it as a nursery, but it's been a storage space since my mother moved out. Imagining it as a nursery once more, I think that for Christmas I'll add renovations to my list of gifts for my wife. We can create a suite that suits both of our tastes, rather than her having to deal with my masculine decor.

For now, though, I shut the open window that allowed the curtains to flutter outside. I have no earthly idea why it would be open in the first place. I don't think Katarina ever really entered this room other than a cursory glance when she first moved in. After she commented on being creeped out by too many doors into her bedroom, I ensured the adjoining door was tightly locked. Perhaps Potts pulled some of the Christmas decorations out of here yesterday and thought the room could use airing out? Although I'm certain I checked this door when I made my rounds last night.

I'll start by asking Potts if she came in here yesterday and go from there.

"Henry?" Katarina calls for me from our room. I give the nursery one more glance, planning to make some calls this afternoon and get the ball rolling on renovations. Maybe as part of her present, we can pick out finishes in Italy in the spring, before she gets too far along to travel internationally. Before I can get fully lost in my daydream, I shake myself out of it and go to find my wife.

Chapter Thirty

This is shaping up to be the best Christmas I can remember. Father's estate manager always hired out the house decorations when I was growing up. Everything was always very "corporate Christmas" with neutral colors and crystals. Very little green or red was allowed. This year, not only was I allowed a hand in our decorations but Henry actually let me spearhead the entire theme of the house. I've also been able to spend more quality time helping Mrs. Potts bake all of her classic Christmas treats. It's been such a fun activity working with her to perfect recipes, then being able to gorge on the fruits of our labor.

It's especially fun when Margot and Sloane come over to help us "taste test." They're both swiftly approaching their third trimester, and Potts and I are more than happy to indulge them. When all the baking is finished, the four of us will stack a mound of treats on a plate, grab a pitcher of non-alcoholic eggnog, and cozy up by the fireplace, gossiping away.

The only negative is how pudgy I'm getting. Not that Henry seems to mind. No, the softer I become, the more insatiable he is. He calls it *happy weight* and insists it makes me that much more attractive to know he's making me happy. *He* hasn't gotten soft, though. I don't know when he finds the time to exercise since every spare moment he has is spent buried in my pussy. Not that I'm complaining.

I made the mistake *once* of mentioning how I've put on a few pounds to my very pregnant sisters-in-law, and they've never let me live it down, insisting that even if I gained twenty pounds, I would still be smaller than they've ever been. When I tried defending myself, Sloane hit me with, "Well, does Henry seem to struggle at all to throw you around?" She's got me there.

I'm in the middle of wrapping some last-minute presents when my phone buzzes with a text from the man himself.

Henry:

> There will be a car there in five minutes to bring you to my office.

> Wear a dress or skirt. No panties.

> Make sure you're ready when it arrives.

> I need you.

This is the first day he's back in his office since my father's funeral, and I'm missing him as well. I've enjoyed having him nearby in his study every day, knowing all I have to do is knock and he would put aside his task to tend to me. Although I never had to. He never let too much time pass before coming to find me. Sometimes just to make sure I was okay, and sometimes because he needed to be inside me.

I make haste, changing into a plaid skirt and matching sweater, along with some stockings and platform boots. I barely have time to look in the mirror before the car pulls up. Sighing, I throw my hair up in a clip and walk out as put-together as possible, considering the amount of time I was given. One thing I've learned about my husband is how much he values punctuality.

As I'm escorted through the building up to his suite, I try my best to act the part of a confident CEO's wife, but inside, I'm a nervous wreck. I've never actually been to his office. I've heard some names thrown around and met a partner here and there, but I have no idea what my husband's daily work life *really* consists of.

I can feel everyone's eyes on me as I pass by, and I'm starting to regret not taking the extra time to make myself more presentable.

"Good morning, Linda!" I say as I reach his assistant's desk. She's one of the only people I've met, although I wouldn't say I enjoyed it.

She notices me, and if looks could kill...As if to prove my point, her expression is one of pure disgust while I stand there with a smile planted on my face, waiting for her to speak. Thankfully, Henry calls me into his office, saving me from the awkward exchange.

I don't know what I expect from my husband's office, but it's like any other space of his. It's minimalistic, with a hint of personality, whether that's his own doing or an interior designer. Clean without being sterile. His desk faces the door, and behind his desk are floor-to-ceiling windows, boasting an incredible view of the city below.

The frustration on his face fades almost immediately as I walk in, a huge grin taking its place. "Kitten! Come sit."

I practically skip to him, just as excited to see him as he is me, and drop down hard on his lap. I think this has actually been the longest we've gone without physical contact since the night we consummated our marriage. My arms reach around his neck instinctively as his find my waist, squeezing me close before turning me so that my back rests against him.

"God, I've missed you," he growls into my neck, before sucking and kissing from my ear to the spot he knows drives me wild. He smirks as chills erupt through my body. "Did you do what I said? Hmm? If I reach under this skirt, will I find *my* cunt bare for me?"

I nod, but he doesn't notice. His attention is on my thigh, where his large hand slowly slides up past my skirt to test for himself. The moment his fingers find my naked, soaking wet pussy, he actually whines. I snap my eyes up to see him looking every bit as sad as he sounded.

Noticing my confusion, he chuckles. "Sorry, darling, I was hoping you wouldn't have minded that particular bit. Not because I don't love it when you walk around bare and waiting for me, but I really wanted a good reason to spank that bratty ass of yours."

"Bratty? I'll have you know, I've been a very good girl." I pause to bite my lip, giving him my most seductive eyes. "But you know I love it when you spank me, Daddy."

"Mmm, little girl, you better watch yourself or you'll be raw for days." He makes quick work of his belt and pants, his already weeping cock springing free from its restraint. "Now be a good girl and sit on Daddy's cock."

With that, he lifts me and guides me down slowly until his wide head is in, then thrusts up into me with brutal force. I grab the desk in front of me, expecting him to continue driving into me, but he just sits there. I wiggle my hips to let him know I've adjusted and would very much like for him to continue fucking me senseless, but all it does is make him laugh.

"Since you're *such a good girl* and *not a brat at all,* how about you be good and sit on Daddy's lap while he finishes his work?" I cross my arms over my chest and huff, acting every bit the brat I just denied being. "Oh, come now, Katarina. Daddy has some very important things to do today."

To my *extreme* dismay, Henry does just what he said. He sits and works with me impaled on his cock. Eventually, I give up hoping for him to relieve the ache growing between my legs, and lay my head down on his desk, using my arms as a pillow.

I must drift off because before I know it, I'm being startled awake by the sound of Linda letting the door slam behind her as she walks into the office. Sitting up straight, I wipe the drool from my mouth as discreetly as possible. But it's no use. She's smug as she catches my vulnerability. *If she only knew you were sitting on her boss's cock, maybe she wouldn't...*Oh.

I tense, remembering that my husband is very much inside me while his assistant sits only a few feet across the desk from us. Henry strokes my thigh in calming circles, sensing how uncomfortable I am. We listen to Linda drone on and on about his upcoming schedule for the holidays, and just when I've relaxed a bit, I feel the smallest thrust.

I'm doing my best to hold myself together, but my heart rate is rapidly increasing as Henry's shallow, languid strokes rub against my G-spot over and over. Out of nowhere, he drives forcefully into me, masked by a change in his posture. Luckily, he coughs over my squeak, and Linda is none the wiser, but he's toeing the line now.

From his new position propped on his elbow against his desk, it's easier to hide how deep he's going. It just looks like he's swiveling his chair as he listens to her agenda.

I squeeze his thigh in warning, as if he couldn't already tell how affected I am by my pulse, but my gesture causes the opposite reaction I was looking for. Instead of stopping this madness, Henry snakes his fingers slowly up my leg until he reaches my throbbing clit.

My entire body spasms at his touch, and this time, Linda does notice. She halts her rambling and stares at me quizzically, waiting for an explanation I certainly can't give her.

"Katarina? Are you cold, darling?" my *lovely* husband asks, pure victory upon his face.

I nod, looking between the two with my practiced smile.

"Linda, would you mind getting my wife a blanket from my closet before you continue?"

This time, his assistant puts on a fake grin as she follows my husband's command, tossing it to us. Henry wraps the large throw around us, the cover giving him more freedom for his debauchery. At least I'm able to hide my mouth with the edge of the blanket, which is a blessing as Henry increases his speed with both his thrusts and around my clit.

Try as I might to keep myself from orgasming with my husband's assistant a mere four feet away, my body betrays me. The coiling pressure in my core is undeniable as he works my pussy. I know he can feel how I'm fluttering around him, my telltale sign that I'm about to fall over the edge.

Henry leans down, his warm breath blowing against my sensitive neck, and God, I want his mouth on it. Instead, he closes in to whisper in my ear, "Is Daddy's good girl going to come on his cock like this, or am I going to have to bend you over my desk and fuck you good and rough while she watches?"

His words do the trick. I try to maintain a casual facade as pleasure shoots through me in what seems like endless waves. Thankfully, Henry adjusts us and speaks up to get Linda's attention. "That's about all I need to know for now. If you'll leave that with me, I can look through it and let you know what I can and cannot make. I plan on spending most of the next few weeks with my family." I don't miss the glare she gives me at that last part. I try to figure out what I've done to this woman to deserve such resentment, but I keep coming up blank.

"Oh, Linda!" Henry says, catching her as she's opening his door to leave. "Cancel whatever meetings I have today after four o'clock. Mrs. Sinclair and I have to run an errand for my mother this afternoon."

It turns out our errand is picking up a gigantic playhouse that Santa is bringing to seven-month-old LJ, who, to my knowledge, isn't even crawling yet. I didn't even know Henry owned a truck, especially not one so big that he has to pick me up to put me in my seat.

We have a lovely evening, walking through the shopping center, lit up with Christmas lights and decor. The cold weather is perfect for snuggling up to each other with hot cocoa as we walk around, dipping into store after store, finding way too many last-minute presents. It's frivolous, but I've never gotten to enjoy the whole holiday shopping experience before, so I don't feel too bad. Our night ends with a fantastic dinner at a cute little taco restaurant with holiday-themed margaritas. Well, Henry ordered them and then gave them to me.

Walking into our home, Henry is loaded with bags. "Time to get these wrapped and ready to take to your mom's house tomorrow!" I say.

"Yes, darling," he sighs, winking and going to grab our wrapping supplies.

We're hours into wrapping when Henry holds up the "I heart boobies" onesie I bought for LJ. "Really?"

"He's a Sinclair man after all! It's only fitting." I'm barely able to stifle my laughter, knowing that he, Ledger, and Jack all have matching shirts already wrapped up.

"Touché."

"Oh!" I hop up, remembering the matching boobie rattler I have in a bag in my room. Well, *old* room.

I practically sprint there, eager to show Henry the toy. Turning right at the top of the stairs, I realize how strange it is to go this way. I haven't been here in weeks. I'm several steps into the room when I freeze, a bloodcurdling scream leaving my lungs at the sight of my destroyed room.

I've moved most of my belongings to mine and Henry's suite, but plenty of things were left behind, all of which are thrown about the room. The mattress is leaned against the bed frame, cut in half, all the drawers are pulled out, the curtains torn down, the pillows shredded, and clothes strewn about.

I'm still frozen in place when I hear Henry running down the hall. "Katarina?" When he finally reaches me, he wraps his arms around me and pulls me to him. When he's taken in the state of the room, he turns me around, holding my head and angling it up to him to search my eyes while his are wide with fear. "Katarina, are you okay?"

He holds me there a moment after I nod, making sure for himself that I'm okay, then tucks me behind him as he assesses the destruction.

"Who do you think could've done this?" I whisper. When he doesn't answer, I start going through a list of people who might have access to the house, when a name stands out. "Do the groundskeepers have keys to the house?"

He nods. "I don't think Mr. Frederick would do this. I've known him most of my life."

"No, I love Freddy!" I say, earning a warning glance from Henry. Rolling my eyes, I continue. "I don't think it's him, but the replacement he had while he was away kinda gave me the creeps."

"Replacement?"

"His name was Thomas or, erm, Tommy. He said he was helping Freddy..." My heart rate spikes again, thinking of that day in the woods.

"There's been no other approved groundskeeper," Henry practically growls, fisting his hands by his side. He pulls me along as he walks around, careful not to step on anything, then opens the door to the creepy storage room that sits against mine.

"Did you open this window?" he asks.

I could just be hearing or seeing things, but all the windows in this room are in fact closed. Sensing my confusion, he walks over to one of the windows and pulls it up.

"I know for a fact I locked these a few nights ago, so have you opened this window?"

"I've never opened either of them. I've hardly ever even come in here."

He pulls out his phone, looking frantically through it, apparently not pleased with his findings. "Fuck!" he says, throwing the device against the wall.

"Henry, are you...?"

"The surveillance has been tampered with," he says, pacing back and forth now, his hand running through his hair. "Alright, I've already got our bags packed in preparation to leave tomorrow. We're going to go to Mother's tonight and stay until I deem it safe. I'll send someone for anything else we might need later on."

Before I can respond, I'm in his arms as he strides to our room, grabs our bags, and carries me out the door.

Chapter Thirty-One

"Alright, girls! This next gift is only for our eyes, so come over here, and we'll open them together!"

My mother gathers Katarina, Sloane, and Margot over in a corner by the tree, mostly hidden from my brothers and me on the couch. Whatever they tear into has them all howling with laughter, and Mom catches my eye with a wink. Sloane grabs my wife's arm to say something in her ear, then throws her head back, laughing even harder. This Christmas Eve has been more stereotypically magical than any that I can recall since my childhood, and I'm feeling particularly sentimental watching Katarina.

We've talked about the lack of emotional connection that she endured as a child, although Sasha and some members of her father's staff helped. If there was ever any concern of how she would handle my family, who on the best day can be *a lot,* I knew after Thanksgiving that she was fitting right in. Being here in my mom's house has been a storybook holiday so far, and I'm doing my best to keep Katarina's mind off the break-in at our home. We still aren't any closer to figuring out who's behind it, but my wrath will ensure that whoever it was will never have a chance for a repeat once we catch them.

The girls pack their secret gifts away again, and Margot and Sloane, both fairly pregnant at this point, sit heavily back down on the couch. Jack and Ledger swarm them, putting footstools in front of each and handing them a drink refill. Ledger places a plate of sweets between the girls, and Jack glares at him before putting down his own plate of sliced fruit. I understand for the first time the urge to cater to a woman's every need, and I can't imagine the way that feeling must amplify when she's carrying your child.

My wife is still with my mother, deep in conversation by the tree, so I decide to leave her to her own devices for a bit. Catching her eye, I give her a saucy wink, and her blush is captivating. I love that she still blushes for me, even after the debauchery we've taken part in. Standing, I wander toward the kitchen, pouring myself another drink and grabbing another Christmas cookie before sitting at the breakfast table. My brothers join me, satisfied that their women are taken care of.

"I'm gonna guess that by the wink I just saw, you finally managed to overcome your crippling fear of sexually disappointing your wife and...ow!"

The back of Ledger's hand makes satisfying contact with Jack's head, but he still grins at me, and honestly, I can't do anything but laugh.

"What Jack is *trying* to say is that we're sorry for not checking in more often, and we'd like an update on you and Kat," Ledger says, glaring at Jack.

Jack, recovered from his head wound, continues.

"Is she pregnant?" he asks, and Ledger's head hits the table with a thud before lifting it to give me an apologetic look.

"What?" Jack asks indignantly. "We had a whole plan, Ledger. You can't act like we weren't gonna bring it up at some point."

I sip my drink as Jack gives me a very passionate yet clearly rehearsed speech. Ledger drains his glass and pours himself another before shrugging his shoulders in a "what can you do?" way.

"So, Henry, our fearless family leader. What we're trying to say is that we would really like to have the cousins all close in age. We love Kat, Mom loves Kat, and Sloane and Margot are basically obsessed with her. It's obvious she's sticking around, which is great, but if she's not already pregnant, we need to get you guys on a PIP."

Frowning, I ask, "You want to put my wife and me on a performance improvement plan?"

This is apparently the funniest thing Jack's ever heard, and I wonder exactly how many eggnogs he's had this evening.

"No, silly. A prompt impregnation plan. Margot has already threatened my balls if she doesn't get a break after the twins are born because she wants to be in top shape for the monstrosity of a wedding she's planning," Jack says, before Ledger interrupts.

"Sloane has also made me promise her a break after this one, although I think she forgets how cute they are when they're tiny and fresh. Granted, I am looking forward to her having periods again..."

"The point is," Jack continues, "if you want in on this first round of grandkids, the time is now, bro. Otherwise, you might have to wait a few years to jump in. Now, if she's on birth control, I know it might seem impossible. *However,* Ledger and I were once in your position in dire straits, and there are...creative paths you can take. If it's a pill, you can actually get exact dupes online and switch 'em out. Easy peasy."

I make eye contact with Ledger, expecting another commiserative glance regarding Jack's birth control lecture, but he's nodding along.

"If it's not a pill, that's more complicated, but we know a very discreet doctor...anyway, if she's *not* on birth control and she's not pregnant, Ledger has a turkey baster so you can really get in there and..."

"Jack," I say, stopping him short of what I think was about to be a suggestion to turkey baste my semen into my unknowing wife. "Thank you very much for his informative discussion. I don't think I'll need the turkey baster just yet, but it's good to know it's an option. Although I think I'll buy a new one rather than borrow Ledger's."

Draining my own glass to try to keep pace as Ledger pours refills, I decide there's no reason to deny my truth to my brothers. If I have my way, we'll all have plenty more reason to spend time together as one big family. And I'll definitely need their advice if I'm lucky enough to be a dad.

"There's no birth control, and to my knowledge, Katarina isn't pregnant. *Yet,*" I add, and Jack and Ledger both smirk. "It's not something that we're preventing or something that we're actively working toward at this time. We've been married barely over two months. Give me a chance."

Margot calls for Jack, who's up and back into the living room like a rocket. Ledger sits quietly for a moment with an ear to the door to see if Sloane calls out too, but she doesn't. He stays with me as we sip our drinks until his eye catches on a framed family photo that Mom has in her kitchen. It's the six of us at Christmastime when Margot was a baby, and we're all smiling around the tree. Well, as much as our dad ever really smiled. Ledger has his own demons he's had to deal with, due to our dad's pressure on him throughout the years, and he breathes out a heavy breath before turning his attention away from the photo to eye me.

"You know," he says quietly, "I was absolutely terrified of fucking up LJ the way Dad fucked me up. As excited as I was to get Sloane pregnant, as *obsessed* as I was to create something that belonged to just us, born out of our love...I was terrified, Henry."

Ledger looks up with tears in his eyes and a huge smile on his face.

"But it's *the best,* brother. It's so good that I don't know how that bastard never realized it. I'll never understand, but that's not my problem anymore. I can't imagine treating LJ the way he treated me, or you for that matter, and I barely even think about him anymore unless I see his picture." He's wiping his eyes as Sloane finally calls for him.

As we both stand, he pulls me into a tight hug.

"If you ever wondered at all if you'd be like him, don't. You won't. You'll be amazing, and so will Kat. You know you can always call me if you want to talk, big bro. Trust me, when that first teething scream hits, you'll want every trick I have in the book," he says with a watery laugh. Clapping him on the shoulder, I make Katarina a plate of food before I head back into the living room to take care of my woman, only to find a round of what looks to be Christmas Pictionary in progress.

Jack has managed what I think is supposed to be a stocking, but it's skewing phallic in shape, and everyone is laughing and making increasingly bad guesses while he gets more and more frustrated. The harder he tries, the more it just looks like an avant-garde, or perhaps diseased, dick.

Seeing the back of my wife's head on an oversized loveseat in the corner, I head straight for her, only to find her cuddled up and holding a sleeping LJ. Bending down to press a kiss to her temple, I add a soft one to LJ's forehead for good measure. *And maybe good luck.*

"Hi," she whispers. "Oh yay, a snack! Fruit and pigs in blankets? My hero."

She winks at me and adds a mouthed, "Thank you, Daddy," and I fight the urge to hand the baby back to my brother and abscond with her upstairs like a caveman.

Sitting beside her, I feed her small bites since her hands are full with the baby. Eventually, the Pictionary game becomes less raucous and fizzles out with everyone lying around eating and halfway paying attention to various Christmas movies on TV.

I'm scratching Katarina's scalp with my arm around her shoulders when I notice both Jack and Ledger, across the room from each other, lying in Margot's and Sloane's laps and softly talking to their bellies. Having Katarina in my life has changed me already in so many ways, but fuck if seeing my brothers and their families doesn't prove exactly how much I was missing out on before.

I don't know if I've ever felt the flames of jealousy lick up my spine as acutely as they do at this moment. Perhaps as a child, watching Ledger and Jack act more like twins than friends or even brothers. Or maybe when they would play as Father pulled me into another lesson or meeting. Now, though, is an entirely new level of need. Taking a deep breath, I move my fingers from my wife's scalp to LJ's, gently petting his soft blond hair and marveling at the sleepy coo he makes before sucking on his pacifier twice and falling back asleep.

God.

Katarina leans her head further back onto my arm and turns to smile sleepily up at me.

"I can take him if you're tired, Kitten," I say softly, offering her a break.

She shakes her head even as her eyes close.

"Absolutely not. I don't get to see him enough as it is. I need to stock up on snuggles while we're all here together," she replies.

Have I really been hoarding her from my family to the point that she thinks she doesn't see the baby enough? I'll have to make it a point to reinstitute weekly family dinners at the estate. Potts would have a field day with everyone coming over more often.

LJ stirs a little more, and Katarina whispers reassurances that I don't understand, murmuring softly in Russian. She's so good with him, and with his blond hair and gray eyes, he could easily pass for ours. *Fuck, I wish he was.*

Fully enveloped in my daydream now, I think about what she would look like pregnant, how if she thinks I smother her now, she'd have another thing coming. Flashes of possibilities fly through my brain. Wheeling her into a hospital suite, her struggling through the pain of labor to bring our child into the world, sleepily gazing at me with a smile while our baby lay on her chest.

I feel a tear trail down my cheek as LJ decides to make his presence known, and I'm snapped out of my fantasy. His plaintive wail makes Sloane and Ledger's heads snap up immediately, and my brother practically teleports across the room to pull him gently from her arms.

"No offense, guys, but I think it's feeding time," he explains, giving me a knowing look and understanding smile like he knows why I'm trying to hold it together. He takes the baby as he and Sloane say their goodnights and head upstairs.

"I think he's right," Jack says. "I'm peckish too. Feeding time. Come on, Princess."

Rolling my eyes as my wife betrays me by laughing at Jack's crass joke about *my baby sister*, I give her a tiny pinch. She swats me back, and in our tussle, she ends up straddling me on the loveseat. Mom went to bed a bit earlier, so we're alone in the room, the soft glow of the tree creating a perfect Christmas ambiance.

She notices my tear streaks, of course, and concern fills her beautiful face.

"Henry? Are you okay?" she murmurs, and I give her a soft kiss before pulling her into me in a crushing hug and burying my face in her neck. Taking a few minutes to compose myself, I breathe her in as she rubs tiny, caring patterns on my neck. Finally pulling back, I take a moment to look at her.

"I love you," I say quietly. "I love you so very, very much."

Her lips turn up at the corner as she traces my cheekbones and my browline, following a path down my cheek and underneath my bottom lip.

"I love you too," she whispers. "Will you take me to bed?"

I stand with her in my lap, and she wraps her legs around my waist. I turn off the lights before moving toward the stairs.

"You can have the bathroom first for your bedtime routine. I might take a quick shower before we—"

She interrupts me as I put her down near her side of the bed, then turn to shut the door behind us.

"I'm not tired, Henry. Lock the door," she says, and my brain doesn't compute what she means.

"You wanted to sleep..." I turn around to find her pajamas on the floor, leaving her in a red corset, stockings, and a garter belt.

"I never said a word about sleeping. I asked you to take me to bed," she purrs, climbing onto the bed and kneeling, elbows down and ass high in the air. "Please lock the door, Daddy."

Following her instructions and reminding myself to spank her later for being a brat, I lock the door and unwrap the best present I've ever received.

Chapter Thirty-Two

Rolling over to an empty bed, I frown, realizing that it's Christmas morning and my husband is nowhere to be found. Looking at my phone, I see it's almost nine o'clock, and I know for a fact that Blanche said under no circumstances was she appearing for stockings and unwrapping the presents that Santa brought until ten. Slowly showering and going about my morning routine, I see fresh snow out the window and plan to cajole all non-pregnant people into a snowball fight later this morning after brunch. Before I can dress myself, the door to our bedroom opens, and I squeak, wrapping my towel tighter until I see my husband come through the door with a plate of pastries and two steaming mugs of coffee. His eyes darken as he places everything on the dresser, then locks the door behind him.

"Good morning, wife. Merry Christmas," he says, approaching me slowly and appraising me like I'm about to be his breakfast instead of the pastries. Deciding to tease him, just a little, I drop my towel to the floor before moving to pick up a pastry.

"Merry Christmas, Daddy," I say, biting into the flaky dough without realizing it's cherry-filled. The filling shoots out of the other end of the pastry and ends up dripping between my breasts as I gasp. In a flash, Henry kneels before me, licking me clean. Just as he's pulling a nipple into his mouth and reaching between my legs, Blanche's voice rings out from downstairs.

"Darlings, it's almost time for stockings! I have mimosas!"

Huffing a long breath out against my belly button, I giggle at Henry's frustration. He rises slowly to his feet and kisses my forehead before handing me my towel.

"Laugh now, little girl. We'll handle you later," he says. "Be downstairs in ten. Wear a skirt with a thong."

Sticky and even hornier than I was last night, I pick out my festive ugly sweater and pleated skirt set and head down into the hustle and bustle of the morning. With five minutes to spare, I make my way to Henry, who already has my plate fixed and a mimosa for me. He's burping LJ after a feed, and seeing how huge he looks holding the baby makes me want to kneel and present myself right here, family be damned. He must see the look on my face because he bends to give me a quick, hot kiss.

"Eat," he says, and I do. Brunch is delicious, and chatting with the family about Henry as a little boy at Christmas distracts me until it's time for stockings and presents from Santa.

Everyone oohs and aahs over what Santa brought, and when the boys pull Blanche outside to show her the new luxury minivan they bought her, she loses it and hugs everyone.

"Oh my goodness, room for *all* my grandbabies," she cries. "I'm so happy, and there's room for more!"

"Hell no, Mom," Margot yells as she goes inside. "I told you I'm taking a break after this! Maybe permanently!"

Ledger nudges Sloane, who immediately slaps his arm away from her. "Absolutely not, do not nudge me! Long break. Don't even look at me, mister!"

We all go inside out of the snow and spend the afternoon eating far too much and lazing about, mostly just enjoying each other's company and reminiscing about the Sinclair children's childhoods. While Jack and Ledger perform some dramatic reenactment of a gaming console feud from years ago, Henry and I head to the kitchen to put our dishes away and refill our drinks.

I can hear the girls howling with laughter as Blanche involves herself in the drama, but before I can rejoin them, I'm pressed over the kitchen island.

"Spread your legs," Henry growls in my ear, and the clinking of his belt has me practically dripping.

"You cannot be serious," I hiss. "Your family is on the other side of that wall."

And they are. If they walked in, they wouldn't technically see anything since we're on the other side of the island, but it would be apparent what we were doing. Asking if Henry was serious was the wrong thing to do because my feet are kicked apart, thong pulled to the side, and face pressed into the counter before I can even think.

He notches himself at my entrance, then uses the hand not pressing me into the counter to cover my mouth before thrusting into me in one long, steady push.

A scream isn't the sound that tries to escape me so much as a long whoosh of air, the pain of the stretch magnified by the fact that he didn't really prep me.

"I would've had you dripping had you not sassed me, little girl," he says darkly into my ear, and if cozy Christmas Henry from yesterday had me forgetting who my husband is, well. He's reminding me now.

"I'm sorry, Daddy," I say underneath his hand. Either he hears it or feels it because his grip on me tightens, and I earn a kiss on the temple.

"I know you are, Kitten, and once I fill you up, your punishment will be over. You just have to take a little more."

I can still hear his family in the other room as their story winds down, but Henry never falters, the pace of his thrusts increasing as we get closer to being caught. Finally, with a low, tortured groan, I feel the warmth of his cum exploding within me. I didn't come, and I know that was part of my punishment. Still, it's nice to be full of him even if I don't know how I'm going to avoid leaving a stain on my skirt or the couch.

Pulling out, he rights my thong and spins me around, the look in his eyes feral as he claims my mouth in a searing kiss. His tongue is dancing with mine, and he has two hands full of my ass when a low whistle breaks our spell.

"Hot damn!" Jack says, holding LJ in one arm and grabbing a bottle from the fridge to warm with the other. "Don't mind me. Actually, Henry, mind if I watch? Your sister is *extra* freaky these days, and I can barely keep up with her, so I could use some ideas."

The tic in Henry's jaw tells me Jack is in mortal peril, and only the human shield of LJ is protecting him.

"Katarina, take the baby from Jack and handle his feeding, please," Henry says. I comply, and Jack must be looking for a fight for how readily he hands LJ over.

As soon as the baby is safe in my arms, Jack makes a break for it, and Henry tears off after him outside and into the snow. By the time I've finished the feed, all three boys are wrestling in the snow, laughing and having what looks to be a grand time.

Sloane asks if I want her to take the baby, but I tell her I'm okay for now and end up sitting back on the loveseat. Before long, Blanche comes to sit next to me, not offering to take the baby, just giving me a smile.

"How are you doing, really, dear? I'm glad to have the two of you here for as long as you need, but I know how it is to prefer your own home. Henry has been beside himself that there's no more information about what happened," she says, kindly patting my leg.

"I've been holding up," I reply truthfully. "All the holiday cheer over the past couple of days has been such a nice distraction, and it's been nice to spend more time with all of you. I was honestly nervous, more so than at Thanksgiving since we're all staying under one roof. But everyone has been so welcoming."

Blanche gives me a soft, contemplative look when she replies.

"It's easy to be welcoming to someone such as yourself, Kat," she says cryptically, but when I raise an eyebrow, she explains herself.

"I always wondered what kind of woman, or man, would snare my Henry," she says, eyes sparkling. "I assumed a woman, but really, anything can happen, and as long as my babies are happy." She waves a hand dismissively and sips her wine.

"She'd have to be very strong, I always thought, to deal with him. He's got a great strength within him, but a softness, too, that nobody ever really sees. Whoever captured his heart would be soft where he's strong, but with a steel spine to hold him up when he needed it. She'd have to be whip smart and willing to put him in his place now and then. I had begun to worry this woman didn't exist," she continues, reaching over to rub her fingers through LJ's blond hair.

"It's an absolute marvel that the woman Henry needed was someone I tormented for years. And I'll always feel terribly guilty for my part in your adolescent imprisonment, Katarina, please believe me."

There are tears in her eyes, and I do believe her, but I sense a but coming.

"However," she says, "the thought has crossed my mind that perhaps the fire of your upbringing was what steeled your spine for him. You're absolutely perfect for each other, and it just seems impossible that he's found such happiness. You have no idea what peace you've brought me."

I eye her shrewdly, trying to reconcile the very kind things she's saying with the fact that she thinks it's marvelous that she scared my father into imprisoning me for nineteen years under her murderous threats.

What an interesting woman, Blanche Sinclair. Regardless, I choose the high road and smile.

"I love him, Blanche. He brings me peace as well. Being here with your family has been like coming home," I say.

"They're your family too, dear," she replies, looking relieved that I'm not calling her out.

The boys burst in, having shed their shirts, and stand dripping in the entryway. They're all striking, but my husband is a god. His lush hair is wet with snow, my favorite piece roguishly flopping over one eye. His chest heaves with exertion, dark chest hair trailing down his abdomen, happy trail pointing down...

"...for watching him, you're such a natural. You'll be wonderful with your own."

I close my mouth, which had been hanging open, and hand LJ back to Sloane, who I think was thanking me for watching the baby.

Henry inclines his head to the staircase, and I follow him up, feeling the effects of earlier finally dripping down my leg. He opens the door and allows me to enter first before closing and locking the door behind him and resting his forehead against it. I've seen this body language before. He's trying to stay in control.

I'd prefer he lost it.

"Daddy?" I say in my sweetest voice, and the whiny groan he releases goes straight to my core.

Oh yeah. He's about to snap. *Yes please.*

"Is everything okay?" I ask, quietly starting to pull off my clothes.

By the time he's turned around, I'm naked, and that damn piece of hair is in front of his eye again. At this rate, I might be the one to lose it.

"You're very young, Katarina." He cocks his head and regards me as he peels off his socks, pants, and underwear.

"I think both of us are very well acquainted with my age, Henry," I reply evenly, curious about where he's going with this. The appearance of his hard cock, heavy and already weeping, as it springs free from his briefs, gives me a fairly good indication of what's in store.

"You've been coveting my brother's baby all weekend, being a huge help to everyone where he's concerned. Giving Ledger and Sloane such a break that I think they'll be sending you fruit baskets for a year," he says, slowly backing me against a wall now, his hard length pressed up my stomach and almost between my breasts with our height difference. Cupping my jaw, he traces my lips before holding me in place by the neck.

Looking down at me, he regards my hips, my waist, before giving me a devilish smile.

"I'm afraid it won't be comfortable for you, carrying my babies," he murmurs. "They're bound to be huge. LJ was nine pounds. And you're such a tiny thing," he whispers against my ear, pressing hot kisses down my neck.

Gasping at his words and the sensations, I try to keep my mind in the reality of the moment instead of floating away.

"I think you're underestimating me, Mr. Sinclair," I rasp out. "And not for the first time, if you'll recall."

He pulls back from my neck to look at me with so much love and pride that I almost forget what's being said.

"You're absolutely correct, Mrs. Sinclair," he whispers, giving me a quick, hot kiss before regarding me seriously again.

"I do think, based on your cycles, you'll be ovulating soon. If you don't want..."

"I want," I say clearly.

Henry blinks at me owlishly for the better part of thirty seconds.

"I want your baby," I clarify. "Please, Daddy. I know I'm nineteen, but you're certainly not getting any younger..."

I squeak as I find myself thrown onto the bed, barely bouncing once before Henry is on top of me and inside me. He's feral, absolutely unhinged in his pursuit of giving me what I want. I smile before giving myself over to the pleasure, happy to receive the best present of all.

Chapter Thirty-Three

The days we've spent at Mom's house have been some of the best of my life. Our security system hasn't been sorted out yet, and we've had to stay longer than intended, so the entire family decided to stay in solidarity. It's coming up on a week of us being here, and I don't feel smothered at all. I can't recall the last time I've spent this much time with my family, and I don't know if it's because I have my wife at my side, but it's been therapeutic. A peace I didn't realize I was missing until now. Katarina seems to be enjoying herself as well, lazing about with Mom, Margot, and Sloane.

Since the snow has melted, Ledger, Jack, and I left early this morning to run before the girls woke up. I've run ahead of them since my wife isn't quite the late sleeper that Margot and Sloane are, and I'm hoping we can have a moment of quiet together to do our daily crosswords before we have to leave for the morgue.

A couple of days ago, a man was found dead on our property, and authorities have asked us if we could help ID the body. We aren't suspects, considering our alibi is airtight, thanks to the video evidence of us being here for the past week. Additionally, I had already reported the break-in on the day we left, so it's pretty clear to the authorities that we're not involved.

By the time I reach the kitchen, Katarina is sitting at the table, dressed with today's paper in her hand. She accepts my sweaty kiss but demands I go get a quick shower, insisting that we can do the crossword in the car on our way.

"That's him, Henry. That's the man I was telling you about. Tommy or Timothy or whoever," Katarina says, eyes wide as she stares at the dead body in front of us. "Do you think he was on his way to break in again? What happened to him?"

"We aren't sure, ma'am," the medical examiner says. "The body shows no signs of an attack. There are no aberrations or wounds. There were no signs of internal bleeding during the autopsy. The quick toxicology report didn't show any signs of drug use, but we'll have to wait several weeks for the more comprehensive testing results. As of right now, all we know is that he died approximately four days ago."

"That would've been Christmas. All the staff knew we would be gone." Katarina says, still staring at the lifeless man. "So maybe he didn't want to do us any harm, just wanted to get something from the house. But what? And why would *my room* be the first place he would look?"

I wrap my arms around her and pull her into my chest. "Darling, there's no way to understand some people. We don't even know if it was him in the first place. I'll admit, he's my first suspect, but his death is strange."

"Where was he found?" Katarina asks.

"I believe near the western border of the property," the examiner says, flipping through the charts. "Yes, western border, in front of a greenhouse."

"Hmm, that's not even close to where I ran into him that one day. I was walking back home from a loop around the pond in the southeastern corner."

I move my hands to bracket Katarina's shoulders, sensing how uncomfortable she is. "Well, if that's all you need, I think we should be on our way."

The examiner shakes both our hands and tells us he'll be in touch with the reports of the other tests they ran, and bids us goodbye.

When we get back to the house, Mom greets us with a spread of lunch, letting us know the rest of the family, including LJ, are napping. We both join her at the breakfast table, munching on some leftovers, when she hands Katarina an envelope.

"This is addressed to you, darling."

Katarina looks as confused as I am as she takes the piece of mail from my mom. "Um, that's strange. The only person who knows I'm here is Sasha, and he's hardly one to send Christmas cards."

"Ah yes, your oh-so-charming cousin! You should have invited him to join us. He seems like he would be a great compa..."

Katarina's gasp stops Mom from finishing her thought. Both Mom and I wait for *anything* from her, but she just sits there, eyes wide. When she starts shaking, I decide I'm done waiting.

"Kitten?" I take her wrists in my hand and rub calming circles with my thumbs. "What is it?"

She slowly brings her eyes to meet mine and hands me the letter in her hand.

All you'll ever be is his whore.

Go home, or else.

Two lines. Eleven words. It's such an insignificant amount of ink to make such an impact.

Mom takes the letter from my hand after I've gone still as well. "Oh fuck!"

Mom's sudden burst of profanity causes Katarina and me to fall out of our stupor as we snap our attention to her. I'm not sure what's going through my wife's head right now, but my brain has finally started working again as I lift her out of her chair and march her up the stairs to our room. I don't give a damn who I wake up in the process.

As soon as we get in the room, I lock the door behind us, then toss her maybe a little too roughly onto the bed. I don't care at this point. Not even her fucking adorable little squeak will change the darkness I've spiraled into since reading that letter. She watches me pace back and forth for God knows how long, probably too scared to say anything. I'm sure I'm a sight right now: hair disheveled, shirt untucked, and barely holding on to my sanity.

I'm racking my brain, trying to figure out who might be after her, and the only person who fits all the clues is her uncle. Ivan Taranov. The man who was weird as fuck at our wedding and at her father's funeral. The motherfucker who tried *buying* her back from me. Who in their goddamn mind does something like that?

I'm trying to figure out how to strangle the bastard to death right fucking now, but he's so heavily guarded I wouldn't stand a chance. There's a reason they were able to keep Katarina hidden for so long. Nobody has dared to say anything, but there's no denying they at *least* have strong ties to the bratva. His men would gun me down before I even stepped foot on that compound uninvited.

Realizing I'm going to have to take my time and politic my way to her uncle causes me to see red. Spinning, I slam my fist into the wall, the impact breaking through the drywall. "*Fuck!*" I yell. I fall back against the wall, blood dripping from my hand. My heavy breathing is the only sound in the room.

My wife's pensive voice breaks the silence. "Henry, are you okay?"

She's sitting back on her knees at the edge of the bed closest to me, her arms wrapped around her waist, as if to protect herself. As if to fucking protect herself from me. I sigh, realizing how I've scared her with my little tantrum, and pull myself up from the floor.

"No, Katarina. I'm not okay," I say, stroking her hair with my uninjured hand when I reach where she's sitting. Her hands find my chest, rubbing up and down to try to soothe me. *Try.* "Someone is threatening my entire world, and I don't know how to get to them."

"Wait? You know who it is?" she asks, looking up with wide eyes, her movement paused.

"I have a good idea who it is. I think it's your uncle, Katarina."

"Henry, you can't be serious!" she says, pulling back from me. *Fucking pulling away from me.*

I'm pretty sure there's smoke coming from my ears as I lunge at her, grabbing her hips and yanking her back, flush to my body. "Yes. I am serious. And I'm trying to figure out a way to get to him without being shot down in the process."

"Love, I don't think it's him. I mean, he's always been sort of strange, but why don't you just talk to him? I can reach out to Sasha."

"Fuck, yes!" I say, remembering my cousin-in-law. Sasha and I have gotten close enough over the past few months, and I feel certain he wouldn't do anything to hurt Katarina.

I plant a long kiss on the top of her head before pulling back to look into her beautiful violet eyes. "Stay," I say as I turn to leave.

I'm going to the Taranov compound right fucking now, and I have a lot to arrange before I arrive. Starting with the jet, then

I'll probably need to get Danny in to make sure I don't do anything traceably illegal, then...

"Excuse me?" the tiny woman says from behind me.

Turning, I see that she's hopped off the bed and stands a few feet away. Looking up at me, she's pouting with her arms crossed. She's mad, and it's fucking adorable.

"Yes?" I smirk.

"Where do you think you're going? And what the *fuck* do you mean by 'stay'?"

I can feel my dick growing harder with each word from this brat's lips as I tower over her, walking her backward. "Language, little girl."

For every step I take toward her, she takes two back until she hits the bed, losing her balance and falling back onto the mattress. I bend, caging her in with my arms and hovering over her, my gaze never leaving hers. "I'm going to figure out who is threatening my *wife*. And *you* are going to stay in the goddamn room until I get back. Is that clear?"

She narrows her eyes at me, trying to shove me, to no avail. She pushes with all her might, not forcing me to move in the slightest.

"I said, is. That. Clear?"

"You can't just keep me here, Henry! I was locked away for nineteen years, and I am *not* going to be caged again! Not by you or anyone else!"

Her words flip a switch in my brain. I'm *not* anyone else. I'm her fucking husband, and she better believe I'll do whatever I have to to keep her safe. I'll burn the entire fucking planet down to keep her safe. Picking her up by her perfect ass, I toss her back on the bed, giving myself room to crawl on as well.

"Oh, Kitten, you have no idea the lengths to which I would go to keep you safe. I'll lock you in a cage and keep you hidden so that I'm the only one who knows where you are. You're lucky I'm not tying you up and leaving you that way until I return. I'll keep you safe until we catch whoever this is or whoever else may want to come after *my wife.*" With every statement, I move farther down the bed until I have her trapped against the headboard. I stop inches from her face, close enough for her to see the fire burning in my eyes. "I'll make sure to come and fuck you, though, Kitten. I'll keep you full of my cum, just like I promised."

I crash my mouth to hers, my kiss as violent as my headspace right now. She tries to shove me off again, but it only makes me kiss her harder, biting and sucking on her lips and tongue. The blood from my hand now smeared all over her face where I've grabbed her makes her look every bit as animalistic as I feel. She bites back on my tongue, hard, the taste of metal filling my mouth.

"Mmm, fuck, baby," I growl. "You know, you better be glad I'm in such a hurry or I would spank that bratty ass of yours."

Try as she might, she can't help the moan that escapes her mouth or the way her eyes roll back at my words.

"There's my girl. Now be a good girl and let Daddy fuck you into this mattress before he has to go kill your uncle."

Chapter Thirty-Four

It's been hours since Henry left me locked in my room at Blanche's, and I'm losing it. First, being confined to *a single room* is totally different from having the entire estate and house to explore when I was growing up. Second, it hurts a lot more that it was Henry who did it. I can understand his urge to protect me, and it's kind of hot that he got so worked up over me being threatened. *Not sure what it says about me that I think it was hot...*

I've never seen him as infuriated and inconsolable as he was before he left. Wild eyes, hands that seared every inch of me they touched...it was as if he needed to consume me so he could ensure I still existed and wasn't a figment of his imagination. I told him before he left that the easiest way to make sure I was safe was to take me with him, and that I would sit quietly on his lap the entire time. He looked at me hotly, as if considering it, before groaning and saying I was safer here.

We're all trapped here together, as Henry has exercised whatever power he has as head of the family to call in a crap ton of security. He's also ordered Ledger and Jack to keep all of us girls and the baby within their sight at all times. Even though the threat was against me, Ledger and Jack were shaken up at the thought of anyone nefarious getting close enough to the compound to put a piece of mail in the mailbox.

Currently, Ledger is downstairs eating with everyone and will bring something up for me when he finishes and takes Jack's place. Sitting on the bed with my arms crossed, I continue my stare down of Jack.

"She really didn't know who you were? Like not even an inkling of an idea?" I ask, still trying to wrap my head around his and Margot's love story.

He continues spinning in the desk chair he's commandeered, but grimaces at my question.

"No, she really didn't know. I know it's fucked up."

"She didn't recognize your...you know..."

Stopping his spins suddenly with both feet on the ground, he gives me a horrified expression.

"Are you crazy! We absolutely, positively, certainly *cannot* talk about my dick. Henry would cut it off and keep it as a reminder for anyone who looks at you wrong! No! Not happening!"

He resumes his spinning, and I laugh, happy for just a moment to forget about all the scary things that have been happening. The pit in my stomach that's been festering since the break-in has me feeling almost constantly nauseous, especially now that we know whoever did it was likely coming for me specifically. Clearing my throat, I try to appeal to Jack again.

"Don't you think only giving me *one room* is a little excessive? I mean, truly, Jack. What's the worst that could happen by letting me have the run of the house?" I ask in my nicest, totally not up to anything voice.

Ugh, I don't want to pull out the big guns, but I miss LJ. I should at least have the girls to chat with if I'm gonna be kept cooped up for God knows how long.

"I got so used to being around everyone," I say honestly, even if I am trying to manipulate Jack. Desperate times...

"You'll see them all soon, I'm sure," he replies, although I've gotten his attention, and he's stopped spinning.

"Yeah, I guess. I just," I sigh quietly before meeting Jack's gaze. Regardless of whether he lets me out or not, he and I have some childhood trauma in common, I think. "I just never got to have the feeling of truly fitting in somewhere until I got here, you know? I had Sasha and the staff, and that was *it*. But here, it's like I know we all care about each other and have each other's backs. It's the best feeling in the world."

Rolling my eyes, I sniffle and then laugh.

"Henry locked me in here, and I'll bet the girls are downstairs playing board games! Or planning LJ's first birthday. Maybe his next nursery redesign. Or something for Margot's wedding! And I'll miss it up here with you, no offense," I finish.

"It's my wedding too," he grumbles quietly, before sighing. "Alright. You win. Only because I miss Margot so much, though. Not because your little speech cracked my rock-hard, tough guy exterior."

Laughing, I pop up from the bed and squeeze him in a side hug before he opens the door for me and gestures for me to head out first. Almost skipping through the door, I make a quick turn into the hallway when...

"Ooomph!" A masculine grunt comes from Ledger as the plate he was carrying crashes to the ground. He puts his hands on his hips and regards Jack and me with what strikes me as very disappointed dad energy.

"John Flynn Carter Sinclair. Katarina I-don't-know-your-Russian-middle-name Sinclair. Exactly why are you leaving this room when our fearless family leader Henry expressly told you not to?"

Blinking up at him, I realize I'll be turning around and heading right back to prison. Great. The urge to stomp my foot like a toddler is real.

"It's Pavlovna. The kinda feminine form of her dad's name. Russian thing but not really a middle name, per se."

Ledger and I both turn to stare at Jack, who has picked up the sandwich that was meant for me from the floor and is already halfway through eating it.

"What? I know things. You get a Russian sister-in-law, you try to learn some shit. Good sandwich, by the way, brother," he says, taking another huge bite, unbothered as ever.

Ledger closes his eyes, sighs, then looks down at me.

"Come on, Kat, let's get you back in your room per Daddy's orders," he says, and I choke on air.

Any hope I have of hiding my reaction is gone as I cough, and Jack unhelpfully smacks me on the back as Ledger doubles over in laughter.

"Holy fuck, I didn't know he had actually taken my advice. That motherfucker," he wheezes as he ushers me back inside. "I cannot wait to tease him about this."

I flop down on the bed dramatically and scream into a pillow, glad to be of amusement to the family but upset and bored at being quarantined once again.

"I'll have to go remake your food since Jack ate it off the floor like a dog..." Ledger begins.

"Rude!"

Ignoring Jack, Ledger continues. "But I do have a bit of good news. You aren't stuck with Jack and me anymore."

Perking up at that, I raise my head to see Sasha burrowing under Ledger's arm into the room.

"My KitKat!" he yells, and I jump into his arms.

If I have to be locked up, at least it can be with my cousin. He smells like comfort and familiarity, and I'm so damn glad to see him.

"I'm so happy to see you!" I say, muffled into his shoulder as I squeeze as hard as I can. Jack and Ledger leave to go bring us more food, and Sasha sits down on the desk chair to face me with a serious face.

"Alright, KitKat. You've been keeping shit from me. Time to tell me everything."

"And so Henry is going to murder Uncle Ivan because he thinks he's behind all this, and he wouldn't listen to reason when I tried to tell him I don't think it's him. He wasn't really listening at all, though. He kinda went full caveman after the threat to me arrived," I finish, having caught Sasha up to date fully on all the happenings.

He's giving me a serious look, almost guilty, and I wonder what he knows that he's not telling me.

"It's not my dad, KitKat. You're right about that," he sighs, eating another cookie off the plate Jack brought before dramatically spitting it out into a napkin. "Fuck! What is that?"

"Danish wedding cookie," I reply primly, popping one into my mouth. "I've grown fond of them."

"Ugh, Jesus. More for you, then."

Swallowing, I ask Sasha a question I've been wanting to for some time.

"I just don't understand why he would push so hard to get me back. He made Henry so mad, and for what? Knowing it could hurt the business, when Ivan and I were never particularly close. I just don't get it."

Sasha gazes past me at the wall for a minute before shaking his head.

"He'll tell you one day, Kat, and probably soon, with all this craziness going on. I'm sure he'll answer all of your questions then," he finishes, and I can tell he's done talking about this for right now.

I stand to pace.

"I'm not happy about Henry going to see Uncle Ivan alone, either. Not that I think he's a threat, but clearly, our compound isn't safe. Someone was able to get to Father, and you *know* how tight Taranov security is, Sasha. The redundant keys, the stupid ID badges to get in and out..."

"Fuck," Sasha says, running his hand down his face as guilt overtakes his expression. "I actually have a confession to make. When I came to visit you, I actually flew in a couple of nights early to...umm, well, never mind that. But I was at a, um...club, and I think I was robbed."

I'm out of my seat before I know it, checking him for any injuries, like I would be able to find anything after so much time has passed. "Oh my God! Are you okay? Were you hurt?"

"I'm *fine*, really," he says, shooing me back to my seat. "Nothing happened, but I woke up the next morning without my master key. I must have drunk more than I thought I did..."

"Do you have any idea who it might have been?"

"No clue. The only person I really talked to that night was some lady at the bar. And before you ask, no, nothing happened. But that was just barely before Pavel passed away, and I always wondered..."

"Wondered what?"

"Well, what you said about him not being one to commit suicide, and I agree. I don't think he was the one who ended his life. And I've felt this twinge of guilt that it has something to do with whoever took my key that night."

"Please don't blame yourself. You would never hurt anyone in our family. I know you wouldn't."

"Yeah, I know, but it's not just Pavel now. Someone's been targeting *you,* and I can't help but feel like I've let you down," he says, looking down at me with fierce remorse.

"It's fine—"

"Henry told me about the break-in and the note." He interrupts. "I can't just sit here and act like everything is fine."

Sighing, I retreat to my chair and sit down. "You don't think I want to figure this out too? Name someone you know who's better at solving puzzles than I am. If I could only get a moment to look at my room, maybe I could find a clue or *something...*"

Sasha flashes me a grin I've seen way too many times growing up. "I can get you out of here, you know. What do you say? Wanna have some fun?"

I stare at him long enough to make him uncomfortable, or at least I hope it does. After nineteen years of being stuck in my family's compound, *now* he offers to sneak me out? All of the times I *begged* him to take me to the movies, or a theme park, or for just a coffee.

"Fine. Let's do it."

"Wow," Sasha says, looking around at the destroyed room. "Whoever's behind this really hates you, huh?"

"I suppose so."

Standing here again feels different from before. The adrenaline of sneaking past the Sinclairs has faded, and I'm feeling a mix of yearning to be back home laced with suspense and fear. *Sneaking out* is hardly the word for what happened. I walked right out the front door while Sasha fed the family false tales of his life in Russia. I honestly don't even think he's ever even visited there.

In a more relaxed state, I'm able to take in the condition of the room much better than I did right after the shock of it all. Walking Sasha over to the creepy adjoining room, I show him the window used as the entry point.

"And you really have no idea who it is?" he asks, measuring his stride back to my old room, as if that's going to help us catch the intruder.

"Our only suspect turned up dead a few days ago," I say, making my way back into the room and trying my best to notice anything helpful. It's hard to tell if anything is missing because I moved most of my important items into Henry's room weeks ago. Anything left behind would be easily forgotten.

"Oh yeah? Who did you have in mind?" he asks, following me.

Turning around, I watch as my cousin inspects every surface I walk by. "There was a man I ran into a few weeks ago who posed as our fill-in groundskeeper—"

Sasha freezes, the color in his face gone. "What was his name?"

"Tommy, or Timothy, I think."

"Goddammit," he whispers, running a hand through his hair before bringing it to cover his face. I stand frozen as well, not having the slightest idea what to say. Sighing, he continues. "I hired Tommy, Kat. He was just here to keep an eye on you. To make sure you were safe. *Fuck!*" he yells, kicking a pulled-out drawer that was lying on the ground.

"Oh, I'm...I'm sorry..."

I'm still immobilized as I watch my cousin mourn the life of this man who essentially died watching over me, feeling a bit of remorse for him as well. Not only that his life was taken while his job was to keep an eye on me, but because I judged him so poorly.

Sasha pulls himself together with a renewed ambition in his stance. "We need to find out who this fucker is and stop them," he says, bracing his hands on my shoulders and looking intently into my eyes. "I need you to think *really* hard while we walk through here and see if you can find *anything* that is out of place."

I shake my head, swallowing at the sudden importance of my role in this outing. With a deep breath, I center myself and look through my room.

Were they just here to hurt me? If so, why would they have made such a mess? And Henry mentioned coming in here earlier to lock the window. So they had been here before and left things tidy.

Were they trying to send a message? If so, why not leave a similar note to the one they delivered to Blanche's house?

There must be *something* in here they were looking for. But *what*? All of my valuables are in the room I share with my husband.

"What about this?"

Sasha points at the bookshelf in the corner of the room. Henry had it stocked full of first editions of all my favorite classics before I moved in but left room for me to make additions. I mostly read on my tablet now that Margot and Sloane have me in their spicy romance book club, so I didn't think to move anything from this shelf.

"What about it?"

As I get closer, he points at a shelf with a book leaning slightly onto the next one, where a gap has formed. "I've known you all your life, and I *know* you don't leave your books like this."

He's not wrong. I look at the shelf in front of me, perfectly neat except for that one gap. "Why destroy my *whole room* for a book that was so obviously on the shelf? And why didn't they mess this up too?" *And why haven't I noticed how weird this is?*

"To throw you off," Sasha says with a shrug. "So what kinda sorcery books do you have that are so important, KitKat?"

Rolling my eyes, I look at the shelf again. "These were just some books from the archives in the library. I was reading up on the estate's history in my free time before Henry and I started fu...when I was bored at home by myself. There's no telling what it was about."

Sasha steps back, his attention going from me to the missing book. "Well, whatever is in that book must be fucking important."

Chapter Thirty-Five

My call to Sasha calmed me enough to think a bit more logically as I made my way to the Taranov compound to meet with Ivan. He assured me that his father had nothing to do with the threat to Katarina, but refused to give me any information to support his claim. That's why I'm still mentally workshopping ways to get rid of my wife's uncle. *Just in case.*

Sasha insisted on being with Katarina during this time, which is a relief. As much as I trust my brothers, they have their own wives to worry about. And there is one thing I'm certain of—if I can't be at her side, her cousin is the best option.

Thankfully, he worked out all the arrangements for my arrival with his father, including a driver waiting for me when I land to escort me onto their property. I would normally like to have my own, but on such short notice, a paid car wasn't high on my list of priorities.

Pulling up to the main house, I see Ivan waiting, worry painted on his face. We've barely parked when he's opening my door, reaching a hand in to help me out.

"What's going on, Henry? Is she okay?" he asks, wasting no time for pleasantries as he pulls me out of the back seat. His genuine concern is most definitely throwing me for a loop. "Henry?"

"My apologies. Yes, Katarina is alright. She's surrounded by my family and the combination of all our security. Sasha is on his way to her as well…I'm sorry, but why are you so concerned? No offense intended, but my wife hasn't exactly had many fond memories of you."

Ivan takes a deep breath, and I can see the conflict in his eyes before he sighs, patting me on the back and leading the way into the house. "We should be sitting for this conversation."

He ushers me into the sitting room, directing me toward a plush set of chairs. I grow impatient as he stares into the fire crackling in the hearth. There are a million other things I could be doing right now, and I'm sitting with this middle-aged man looking at a damn fire. I'm about to insist we get this show on the road when he finally speaks.

"I wanted to tell her first," he says, still staring into the dancing flames. "You see, Katarina isn't my niece, Henry. She's my daughter."

The room seems to freeze at his admission. Her *father*. Well, damn. I guess Sasha had a good reason for not blaming Ivan. Not that it automatically makes him innocent. Looking up, I see Ivan looking at me with guilt, waiting for my response. "I'm sorry, I'm afraid you're going to have to give me more details than that."

Ivan half grins and takes in a deep breath before continuing with his confession. "Let's see…where to even begin. I guess I can start with her mother, Irina." His grin transforms into a full smile at the mention of Katarina's mother. "She and Pavel had an arranged marriage, much like you and Kat. I think she tried at first to love him. But he wasn't the devoted husband that you are. He was much more like my father, Dmitri. He never cared for her or even tried to. He always enjoyed multiple women and was never interested in settling down with just one.

"She had spirit at first. Katarina is much like her mother in that regard, but after several years, she learned to lower her head around my brother. Luckily, he was away often whoring about, or with my father dealing with business. That was when she and I got so close. I was mourning the loss of Sasha's mother, and Irina just needed someone. Over time, our friendship grew into something beautiful.

"When she found out she was pregnant with Kat, we were both so excited. We had a plan in place to run away. Of course she never made it out of that delivery room." Ivan looks down, trying to hide the tear falling down his face.

"You see, her actual conception date was a month later than what she told my brother. And in normal situations, it would've been fine. Babies are born late all the time. The problem was that we had forgotten all about the marriage contract. It had been years since the drama with your father and my sister." He stops to chuckle. "Around eighteen, to be exact. Oh, my father was thrilled when he found out *they* were having a girl. If they had known her actual due date, he would've arranged for a scheduled C-section. As it happened, they did not. They induced her the day before your birthday, but she wasn't progressing. Eventually, my father and brother had enough, insisting she go in for an emergency C-section. She didn't make it out.

"Neither Father nor Pavel cared, of course. And my father never made him remarry. He had everything he needed. An heir in Sasha and a way into the Sinclair family with Katarina."

This time, Ivan doesn't hide as he wipes a tear from his eyes. "She looked just like me when she was born, you know. I mean, she eventually took after her mother, thank God. But at first, she was all me. I got to hold her once. That's all I allowed myself. I snuck into her nursery one night and held her until dawn. I knew I couldn't have anything to do with her. If Pavel ever got suspicious enough to do a paternity test...I had Sasha to think of as well. He would have figured out a way to kill us all, consequences be damned.

"No, I kept far away, but always encouraged Sasha to look after her. It warms my heart how closely they grew up together."

He sighs, turning his attention back to me, staring fiercely into my eyes. "I dreaded the day we came calling to collect on the contract. I had no idea what kind of person you were and had already seen what harm an arranged marriage could do to a woman. Sasha told me you seemed to be a good man, but there was no way of knowing. I had been working with someone to get her out of the contract, but it was airtight. That's why I offered to buy her back. I certainly wanted to spend more time with her, but from all I knew, you were trying to get out of the contract as well."

"Excuse me? What would lead you to believe that?"

"I was in contact with someone who said they were a representative of yours. Oh, what was their name..."

I can feel my face redden, as I squeeze the arms of the chair so tightly that I'm surprised they don't crack. "Mr. Taranov, I can assure you, nobody was representing me."

We stare at each other, realization hitting us at the same time. Whoever this person is, is likely our killer. "Do you have any way of finding their name?"

I follow Ivan as he jumps from his seat and rushes out of the room. He speeds through the house before we make our way into a messy office, and Ivan immediately starts rummaging through papers in a box stacked on the cluttered desk.

"Sorry, I know it looks like a tornado came through here. This was Pavel's office, and I'm trying to go through his things while simultaneously moving mine in. Like this." He pauses to pick up a fruit basket, filled with green fruit, in the early stages of rotting. "I don't even know how long this has been here, or why it's *still* here!" he yells.

I feel useless watching Ivan sort through papers, trying not to panic at the disorganized state of his filing system. Moving to a box in one of the chairs, he finally finds success. "Aha! Here it is. *Dilan B. Sims.*"

The name sounds somewhat familiar, but I can't for the life of me remember why. Taking the paper from Ivan, I search for anything that might jog my memory. If I'm ever going to figure this out, I have to get out of this pigsty. I need my organized office, my calming home, and my goddamn wife sitting on my goddamn lap while I work.

"Pack a bag, Ivan. You're coming back with me, and we're all going to put our heads together until we figure out who the *fuck* is after my wife."

Before walking into the den, I look around the room at the entirety of my family waiting. Mom rocks a sleeping LJ in the corner while reading a book. Ledger and Jack bookend their wives on the sofa, passing phones back and forth, no doubt discussing nursery decor. Sasha is perched on the edge of a chair, braiding Katarina's hair while she sits on the floor beneath him.

The moment Ivan and I step into the room, everyone straightens up, their attention on the two of us. Katarina is the only exception. She jumps up from her spot on the floor and throws herself into my arms. Suddenly, we're the only two people in the room. I'm filled with guilt remembering how I left her.

I pick her up, holding her weight with one arm while my other hand digs into her hair, pulling her head to mine. "Kitten, I'm so, *so* sorry—"

"Shhh." She interrupts, her finger covering my lips. "It's okay. I know you were worried."

"It's no excuse. I should never have behaved that way toward you, and I swear to you, I never will again. I love you so much, darling."

"I love you too." She brings her mouth to mine. *Fuck I've missed her.* I deepen our kiss, as if I'll never get the chance again, and she returns every ounce of passion I give.

Someone clearing their throat breaks us from our little bubble of bliss. I place one more chaste kiss on her forehead before setting her down on the ground, turning her to face the room, then pulling her back into me, my arms securing her in place.

"Alright, everyone, lock in. There's something here we're missing. We're all intelligent enough individually, so there's no reason we shouldn't be able to put our heads together and figure out who is after my wife."

I'm about to walk us over to an empty seat when Ivan speaks up only loud enough for Katarina and me to hear. "Before we start, would you mind if I had a moment alone with Kat?"

She looks up at me with pinched brows, then at her uncle. *Fuck*, father.

"Ivan, I know this is a tender moment, but since this pertains to our case, I think we should all hear it," I say. "Let's just go sit down. Sorry, darling, this is going to be a lot."

I pull Katarina into my lap, holding her close while Ivan sits beside us, retelling the account of him and her mother. She's being strong, but can't stop her tears from falling. A quick look around the room confirms she's not the only one. In fact, except for Ledger and me, everyone has tears in their eyes. I was expecting this from the women and Sasha, but Jack...I have to force myself not to laugh in the middle of this incredibly emotional story at the sight.

As Ivan wraps up his story, I give Katarina a pat on the outside of her thigh, signaling her to hop up and hug her father. I sit patiently waiting for their embrace to end as the rest of the family continues blubbering, wondering how we are ever going to reel this back into business, when Katarina snaps around, narrowing her eyes at Sasha.

"You knew this, didn't you?"

Sasha opens his arms, trying to bring humor to the situation despite his tearstained cheeks. "What? Your long-lost brother doesn't get a hug too?"

I watch as Katarina walks over to Sasha, her smile obviously fake. As she gets closer, she raises her arms as if to return his hug, but at the last minute, she smacks him on the side of the head.

"Ouch!" he cries, backing away from her slowly with his hands raised in surrender. "I promise, I only found out when Pavel died, and Dad made me promise not to tell you until he could. Meanie." He sits slumped over in his chair, pouting with his arms crossed over his chest.

With my hands rubbing my brows, I sit back down in my seat, pleased as my wife finds her spot on my lap soon after.

"Okay, everyone, let's get it together. We're wasting precious time. Let's start with what we know. Someone is obviously after Katarina, and they have taken extreme liberties to get to her. We *know* someone broke into her room and ransacked it. We *know* they were able to hack into our security system. We *know* it's someone who had easy access to my mother's home and who knew Katarina would be here. We also discovered that someone using the name Dilan B. Sims was collaborating with Ivan to release her from our marriage contract and posing as my representative. Does anyone else have anything to add to that?"

"I do," Sasha says, his voice hushed. He's no longer pouting, instead sitting straight with a deadly gleam in his eyes. "Two things, actually. One is that the groundskeeper who died was planted there by me. I wanted someone to keep an eye on Kat and make sure she was doing all right. I know he isn't a suspect of yours anymore, but I just wanted to clarify. He was in excellent shape and basically an expert in martial arts. One of the best security units I had. I would also be shocked to hear of him causing any harm to himself.

"Two, I lost my keys one night while I was at your club," he says, nodding his head toward Ledger and Jack. "As you guys know, we made plans for me to check out Rendezvous when I visited Kat a few weeks ago. I never made it past the bar, though. I chatted with a lady and then felt way too intoxicated to play. I remember getting to my hotel room, but when I woke up the next morning, I was missing my key. This was shortly before Pavel died. I never said anything, but I've always felt like there was a link between his death and that key."

Sasha pauses, giving my wife a look. "And actually, there is a third thing. Kat?"

Katarina turns to look at me, and mouths, "Sorry," before turning her attention back to the room at large. "Sasha and I snuck out yesterday. I don't know how you guys didn't catch us." She pauses when I squeeze her thigh, a warning to her that there will be consequences for that. *Hopefully some we both enjoy.* "We went back to search through my room for any clues and found one. A book was removed from my shelf. I can't remember what it was, but I know it was related to the history of the Sinclair estate. I'm sure we were in too much of a shock to notice it before, but the bookshelf was actually the only thing in the room that hadn't been destroyed."

"So whoever this is wants Kat out of this marriage, either dead or alive. And was after a book about the property?" Jack asks, looking up from where he had just been writing in his notebook like a proper detective before turning to Ledger. "Did you notice anything strange about the footage from the library when you went through their system?"

"Hmm, nothing stuck out to me, but I wasn't exactly putting a ton of focus on the library." My brother, who is pure genius when it comes to any software hacking, pulls his arm from around Sloane and gets up to grab his computer. The room is silent as he runs footage, and although the suspense makes it feel like much longer, it takes him no time.

"I found something! I went back to several hours before you found your room, and there's a cut in the surveillance from your library feed. Unless someone was looking *very precisely* at the library time stamps against that of other feeds, you would never notice it. But it's here."

"And you don't have any idea what it could've been about?" I ask, as my wife shakes her head.

Everyone is quiet as we take in all the information. We need to determine which book is missing and who it was that contacted Ivan. We can't do either of those things from my mom's house, though.

With a deep breath, I break the silence lingering in the room. "Sasha, Ivan, Katarina, and I will leave tomorrow morning to go back to the estate. We'll have the Taranovs' security with us. The rest of you should stay here until it's safe."

Chapter Thirty-Six

Since our huddle last night with the whole family, I've been itching to get back home. Something about us all coming together made me feel like a real-life detective. All of my fear and anxiety about the danger of the situation is gone, and I'm ready to solve this puzzle.

The car ride here was dreadfully silent, with everything confessed last night still hanging in the air. Ivan is my father. It's still so strange. I never knew much about him. Sasha never had anything but positive stories about his, *our,* dad, but he was always so reserved around me. I promised him we would work on building a relationship, and I plan to do so, but I'm still a bit nervous about the whole thing.

The only positive thing about the quiet car ride was the chance to daydream about the makeup sex Henry and I had last night. It had been over twenty-four hours since he left, which is by *far* the longest we've been separated since I moved in. Needless to say, we didn't get much sleep last night.

After taking a moment to change into something appropriate for a hike, Sasha and I split away from our father and Henry. Our plan of action is for the two of us to explore the area where Tommy was found dead while they look into figuring out who was working with Ivan to find the loophole in our contract.

By the time I make it downstairs, my *brother* is already waiting for me with my gloves and scarf in his hands. "Henry threatened my balls if I let you get cold," he says, handing over my cold-weather gear. "So if you don't mind, please make sure you stay nice and toasty."

An awkward silence hangs in the air for the first half mile of our hike, which is unusual for Sasha and me. It's normally hard to get either of us to shut up when we're together, but I don't know what to say at this moment, and I'm sure he's feeling the same.

"This is killing me, KitKat," Sasha says, finally breaking the quiet. "I'm really so sorry I didn't tell you, but I swear I've only known for a few weeks. Dad made me *swear* not to say anything, and it was hardly something to talk about on the phone."

"It's fine. I'm not mad at you, Sasha. It's actually pretty cool. You've always felt more like my brother anyway. Now I don't have to pretend," I say, throwing my arm around his waist. Smiling down at me, he wraps his arm around my shoulders as we walk farther into the woods. "It's me who should be apologizing, though. I really am sorry for what happened to Tommy. Were you close?"

He shakes his head with a sigh. "No, not particularly. He worked for our family, but answered to me. I feel responsible for any of my men's deaths."

I freeze suddenly, making us both stop in our tracks, and whip my body around to face Sasha. "Your men? Since when do you have *men?*"

His eyes scrunch together in confusion, and I can practically see him recounting his words in his mind. "Kat, what do you think our family does for a living?"

"Imports and exports? I don't know everything we trade! Why should I even bother trying to keep up with all of that?"

He shakes his head slightly, fighting a grin, before throwing his arm around my shoulders. "That's all you need to know, KitKat."

Rolling my eyes, I let it go, allowing him to guide us farther down our path. With our conversation running smoothly again, the next half of the journey goes by much faster. Before we know it, we're coming up on the area still taped off from when they found Tommy's body.

There isn't anything suspicious at first glance, nothing that would indicate a fight or violence. In fact, everything is peaceful with the songs of the winter birds combined with the sound of wind weaving through the pine trees, causing the wooden door on the greenhouse to open and shut with every gust.

"No sign of blood," Sasha says, finishing his scan of the area. "No personal effects lying around that might tell us anything either, but maybe he left something in there."

Sasha takes off for the greenhouse, and I follow. "Why is this even here?" he asks, looking around at the tropical plants thriving in the hothouse, safe from the wintery weather outside.

He's looking at something that seems as if it came from an alien planet when I walk up beside him, elbowing him jokingly in the side. "There's no reasoning behind the purchases of rich old men."

After a good chuckle, we walk side by side through the space, looking for any signs Tommy could have left behind, to no avail. We're about to leave when Sasha reaches for a fruit hanging from a tree in the corner.

"Stop!" I yell, swatting his hand away, "Aleksandr Taranov, you *know* better than to touch any fruit you don't know! Honestly, did the whole *don't eat the berries* speech not stick with you? That's an *extremely* poisonous plant. It's called Cerbera odollam, but it's often referred to as the suicide tree because the fruit...oh my God, that's it!"

I take off running back toward the house, desperate to tell Henry that I know which book was taken from my room. That particular volume of the estate's history focused on the vegetation planted around the property over the years. I first pulled it out when Henry and I were looking at the different maps over the land dispute because it listed the year the peach orchard was annexed.

Sasha chases me, eventually giving up on asking questions as I make the mile trek as quickly as I can. Thankfully, I'm in decent shape from years of endurance training and am able to reach the house in no time.

Both Henry and Ivan startle as I burst through the doors into the study. "I remember the book!"

"You couldn't have told me that before we sprinted all the way here?" Sasha says, panting behind me.

Henry stands from his chair behind his desk and walks over to me, pulling me into a warm embrace. "You did such a good job, Kitten," he whispers, tucking loose strands of hair behind my ears before raising his voice for the room to hear. "Can you tell us about this book?"

"Like I told you before, I knew it was from the archives pertaining to the history of this estate. I just didn't know which volume it was." I pause a minute as Henry leads me over to his desk chair and pulls me to sit on his lap. "As you know, Sasha and I were surveying the area for any clues from where Tommy's body was found. There weren't any, by the way. But during that search, we took a walk through the tropical greenhouse nearby. We didn't find anything pertaining to Tommy, but Sasha did almost pick a very poisonous fruit from a tree in said greenhouse. I realized then that I had learned about it from a book about the history of the vegetation on the property. Our missing book!"

"Wait a minute," Sasha says, sitting in front of the desk with his head propped in his hands. "You called it a suicide tree. What if *that's* what killed Tommy. We didn't even look to see if there was any half-eaten fruit lying on the ground anywhere."

"There's no time like the present. We can all go back and look," Henry says, helping me to my feet before standing himself and placing a kiss on the top of my head. "I'll carry you if you want, Kitten."

"I am quite capable of walking by myself, thank you."

"Ugh, can you carry me?" Sasha says, slumped back in his chair.

Henry huffs a laugh, and I forget about the seriousness of the moment, imagining a future of happy family gatherings with Sasha trying to make my husband laugh. Before I can think any more about their potential for hijinks, Henry gently tugs me toward the door. *Right.* We still have a mystery to solve.

"Here," Sasha says, leading everyone to the tree. "Although I don't see anything left on the ground. That pretty much confirms he didn't eat it by mistake."

"You know, I can't say I've ever actually been in here," Henry says, walking up to get a closer look at the green fruits hanging from the branches. He reaches to pluck one, stopping before he touches it. "Katarina? Is it toxic to the touch or just ingested?"

"Safe to touch. It's the seeds that are dangerous," I reply as he pulls one from the tree and turns it in his hand.

He's deep in thought, his brows furrowed in concentration. "Ivan? Does this look familiar to you?"

I can see the moment realization hits them both, "Is this what I think it is?" Ivan asks, stepping back from the fruit Henry has held out.

"I believe so." My husband replies, "Is there anyone who could send you a picture of the basket?"

Sasha and I watch on with confusion as Henry and Ivan go back and forth, almost as if speaking a different language. They're holding Ivan's phone up, looking back and forth between the fruit and his screen when Sasha finally breaks the silence. "Can someone tell me what's going on?"

Henry drops the fruit and runs his hand through his hair, sighing as Ivan flips his phone to show us a picture of a fruit basket in Pavel's old office. "I don't think Pavel committed suicide," Henry says as Sasha and I continue to study the photo. "And I don't think Tommy did either."

The walk back is much more melancholy with the weight of our discovery outweighing our adrenaline, and when we get back to the study, we're all quiet. Like magic, Mrs. Potts waltzes in to save the day with a tray of refreshments and the mail.

I'm in Henry's lap again with Sasha and Ivan both in a chair across from us. Henry's alternating between feeding me, feeding himself, and sorting through the mail. I would have thought I would be shy about letting my husband feed me like this in front of my dad and brother, but it's still the most natural feeling.

Their plates are almost empty when Henry speaks up, holding a letter in his hand. "Wait a minute. Ivan, do you still have that letter from the person posing as my representation?"

Ivan nods, pulling the letter out of a folio he had on the edge of my husband's desk and handing it over. Henry studies the two letters before turning them around to show my father. "Do these names seem a little too similar to you?"

I'm half leaning over the desk, trying to look at the papers, when Henry pulls them back. "Oh, I'm sorry, darling. Here," he says, placing them in front of me instead of Ivan.

Dilan B. Sims.

Simon L. Dixon.

When I've finished looking, Henry gives the papers back to Sasha and Ivan.

"That's a bit too coincidental if you ask me," Sasha says, handing the letters to Henry.

Henry pulls out his phone and snaps a photo before sending a message to Ledger. "Well, I don't believe in coincidences, and especially not ones on this scale. I do believe that this Dilan/Simon is our guy. I'm going to send this to my brother to see if he can dig anything else up, and then tomorrow I'll go into my office and see if any of our investigators can help as well."

Turning his attention to me, he cups my cheek, resting his forehead against mine. "I swear to you, I'm going to find whoever is doing this, love. And when I do, they better hope I'm in the mood for an easy death."

I'm wrapped in a blanket, staring into the blackness engulfing the trees behind the house, when Henry finally finishes his business with my family.

"Kitten? I thought you were in the library," he says, wrapping his long arms around me and resting his chin on my head.

Sighing, I turn to bury my face in his chest hair, delighting in his warmth and the smell that's so uniquely him. "I missed you, and I got restless. I was going to take a nap, then I thought about you coming to find me after I was already asleep."

His eyes darken as he realizes my meaning.

"And then I got even more restless, so I decided to read, which didn't help. I've only been standing here for a couple of minutes. I was about to come looking for you."

Henry picks me up, and I wrap my legs around his waist instinctively, letting the blanket fall to reveal my minuscule lounge set.

"I sincerely hope you weren't about to come looking for me dressed like this," he teases, nuzzling into my neck. He's just as ravenous for me as always, but I can't help but think about the parts of his past that I haven't fully experienced. Before my brain can go totally fuzzy with need, I decided to be brave and ask a question I've been pondering as we've continued to strengthen our relationship.

"Why don't you tie me up or make me kneel?" There. Straightforward, easy peasy. He stills, pulling back from my neck to look into my eyes with concern. Gently, he sits down on the edge of the bed and arranges me back on his thighs so we can see each other better.

Rubbing gentle circles on my upper arms as he holds me, he tilts his head to the side. "Why do you ask? Is that something that you want?"

I can't help but bite my lip, then smile as his eyes immediately track the movement. "I don't know if it's something I want...maybe?" *Ugh. Time to be very, very brave.* "I just don't understand why we don't do that stuff. I know you used to, with the other women. The shibari, or whatever it's called. It seemed like a big part of your life."

My voice is so quiet by the end that I'm not sure he heard me until he lifts my face back to his with one finger under my chin.

"It was a big part of my life, particularly when I wanted to feel in control. If you're curious, we can try it and see if you enjoy it," he says gently, tracing my bottom lip with his thumb.

The thought has me wiggling in his lap. "Please. Can we?"

He holds my jaw and gives me a stern look. "We can, but it's serious, baby. If I bind you, you have to tell me if anything feels too tight. And use your special word if you want to stop. Can you promise me that?"

"Yes, Daddy. I promise."

Less than twenty minutes later, I'm kneeling on a cushion on the floor, wrists and ankles securely fastened to the bedpost behind me. The ropes crossing my skin feel soft and warm, but are a constant tease, keeping me on edge. He's left me here to rummage around in the closet, and I keep my eyes down when I hear him return.

"Look how prettily you wait for me, Kitten. You deserve a reward."

I can't hold back a gasp as he reaches down to slide something into me, a vibrating portion remaining outside and resting against my clit. He gives me a little pat on the thigh as he stands and sits in a wingback chair he's dragged across the room. He's only five feet away, but I spend so much time in his lap these days that the distance feels like a mile.

"Look at me," he says quietly, and I see that he's fully dressed himself in a suit, looking so handsome I have to bite back a moan. He's sitting with a small book in his lap and a glass of liquor in his hand, the picture of masculinity. "How do you feel? Is your position good? Does anything hurt?"

"I feel good, Daddy. Nothing hurts," I reply sweetly, deciding to tease him a bit. "Except my pussy."

His responding grin is sinister. "I assure you it's only going to get worse."

He pulls a remote from his suit pocket and clicks it twice. My abs clench as I try to bend over from the sensation, but my binds to the bedpost keep me upright. I'm forced to hold my position as the vibrator begins buzzing on each end, inside and outside, and I'm thrust toward a screaming orgasm. Just as I prepare to fall over the edge, everything stops.

Henry sips his scotch and eyes me hungrily. I pant but don't complain. If this is what he likes, I'm going to do it *better* than all the dumb women who came before me. I'm not a quitter, and I'll be the best at...whatever this is, if it's the last thing I do.

After two more rounds, though, I'm questioning my sanity. Sweat beads at my hairline, and my thighs quiver with the pain of being dragged away from my release again. Henry isn't as unaffected as I'd assumed he'd be, either, bent at the waist and staring at me intently. His suit jacket has been removed, and judging from the buttons open on his shirt, he's feeling the heat in the room as well. He clicks the remote, and I heave out a sob of pleasure and pain when he stands suddenly, throwing the liquor glass against the far wall of the bedroom where it shatters.

Immediately, I'm released from the bedpost, and he quickly pulls the vibrator from between my legs. I barely start to wheeze out a question of what he's doing when he pushes me onto my back on the cold hardwood floor. His eyes are manic as he rips his shirt off, buttons flying across the room. His pants are shoved down his thighs, and then he's inside me, my soaked core welcoming him with as little pain as is possible for me to feel with his size.

I can barely catch my breath as he drives into me, deeply and steadily. His hands are on either side of my face, holding me in place and ensuring I can't look anywhere but at him.

"I'm sorry, little girl. Daddy couldn't take it anymore. I need to be in you. I have to feel your skin on mine. You were too far away, Katarina. I *needed* to feel you," he captures my lips with a moan, his thrusts becoming more frantic and uncontrolled. One hand finds my clit and rubs in my favorite pattern immediately, as if he knows he's on borrowed time before his completion.

"You have to come for me. You *have to*. Now!" His final command is growled into my ear, and the feeling of his warm cum sets me off. I'm dragged under with him, the feeling of my orgasm overwhelming after the earlier denials. Trembling slightly, Henry pulls me to his chest and relaxes back against the bed. He holds me tightly as our breathing slows, only moving when I shiver to reach for a blanket to wrap around us.

I can tell that he has something important to say, so I patiently wait until he meets my gaze.

"I prefer you in my arms," he says quietly, softly kneading my hips where he holds me. "I prefer the feel of your skin on mine. Your sweat, your goose bumps...the raised scar on the back of your left knee from falling in the woods chasing Sasha, and the little hairs you always miss when you shave around your left ankle."

My mouth drops open indignantly at that, but before I can defend my skills with a razor, he silences me with a tiny shake of his head.

"It was, of course, very erotic to have you tied to my bedpost. And I'll do so anytime you wish, if you like it. But I don't enjoy denying you pleasure, Kitten. I vastly prefer giving it to you. Ideally, with my hands all over you."

I rest my forehead against his for a moment before replying.

"It was fun. And I came so hard once you actually let me," I tease. "But I agree. I prefer being in your lap to being on the floor. As long as you're sure you don't miss the lifestyle. All the bondage and submission aspects of it. I don't want you to give up anything for me."

I know he sees the vulnerability in my eyes as I admit my insecurity. In return, all I can see is the love in his.

"Katarina, I haven't given up anything for you. What we share is more profound than having you kneel at my feet or bound before me. It might be something we play with, but it's not as important to me as feeling you and pleasuring you. I just need you. That's all."

We're quiet for a moment as I snuggle into the crook of his neck and melt into his embrace.

"Also, for the record. Our free use arrangement is an incredible act of trust from you. That's the most exquisite submission I've ever experienced, and I'll never take that for granted. So instead of thinking that you've pulled me from the lifestyle, I would actually argue that you've elevated me to a higher plane of pleasure. It's nothing I've ever felt before, baby."

When he puts it like that, it does seem like I'm the BDSM queen over all his past partners. Petty of me, but a win's a win. I'll take it.

"Does the higher plane of pleasure we're on include midnight snacks?" I ask, nibbling at his neck and enjoying his rumbling laugh. He stands effortlessly, still holding me, and finally pulls his cock free before setting me on the bed, wrapped in the blanket.

"I think you've earned a snack. I'll bring sweets, but you have to eat some fruit first," he says, giving me a stern look as he pulls on clothes to go forage for food.

Eyeing the snack I actually want, barely hidden by the gray sweats he's wearing, I wink.

"Yes, Daddy."

Chapter Thirty-Seven

I take a minute to look out my office window at the sunrise over the city before settling in for some research. I left especially early this morning to try to make it here before anyone else, hoping for several hours of peace. Not many people should be here since it's only a few days until New Year's, and almost everyone is off for the holiday week.

I'm lost in a trail of files pertaining to the land dispute when the lights in the main office turn on, and a glance at the time confirms I've been at it for a couple of hours.

"Good morning, Henry!"

I look up from my stack of papers to see Linda at my door, looking to be in good spirits. Smiling, I tell her good morning, hoping that will suffice and she'll leave me be. Of course she doesn't. "How was your Christmas?" she asks.

With a sigh, I place the papers I've strewn in front of me neatly back into a file and give her my attention. "It was wonderful, Linda. And how was yours?"

Somehow her grin grows even bigger. "Fan. Tastic," she says, breaking the word apart in a way that has me grinding my teeth.

I know my time of peace has come to an end. I stand to leave, grabbing my file and keys from the desk. "Well, if that's all, I'll be on my way. I just came in to grab a few things."

I expect her to move from the doorframe to let me pass, but the closer I get, the more I worry a conflict might arise. I could just push past her or ask her to move like a nice normal boss. *Excuse me* usually does the trick.

"Oh!" she says, thankfully unblocking my path as she runs over to her desk. "Here, this is for Kat, erm…Mrs. Sinclair. I feel like the two of us might have gotten off on the wrong foot. I just wanted her to know I'm very happy she's around to deal with your grumpy self now instead of me."

Linda laughs as she hands me an elegantly arranged gift basket filled with assorted treats and…fruit.

Green fruit.

Green fruit I've become quite familiar with over the past twenty-four hours.

Cerbera odollam.

The entire world stands still as everything runs together. Linda S. Baker. I've only ever seen her full name a handful of times on official documents, but I remember it well enough. Suddenly, her strange behavior toward Katarina makes sense. But *why?* In ten years, I've never had the slightest reason to suspect her of having any romantic feelings for me. Even when she was dealing with the applications and correspondents with potential submissives, not once did she demonstrate the slightest bit of jealousy.

"Is something wrong?" she asks, bringing me back to the moment.

Every ounce of restraint I have is being tested as I look up to see an obviously painted look of concern on her face. My instinct is telling me to end her life right now, but I know that would be a nightmare to clean up. No, I have to contain myself. She's still going to die for her attempt on Katarina's life. But in the light of day, in the middle of the heavily surveilled office, is not the time or place.

Luckily, thirty years of business training have taught me how to think quickly in situations like these. Well, not necessarily *this* type of situation, but still.

With a pained expression of my own, I sigh, "Actually, Linda, Katarina and I aren't on good terms..."

"Oh, I hate to hear that," she says, with a frown.

"Yes, I'm afraid whatever short stint of hope I had for our union to work was only ever that. Hope. Maybe we could discuss it later tonight? Over dinner?"

She reaches up to touch my shoulder, and it's a fight for my life not to cut her hand off letting her touch linger on my chest. "I would *love* that."

"Wonderful," I spit out, removing her hand by her wrist as gently as possible, not wanting to give away my charade at the moment. "I'll have a car pick you up at seven."

"Well, lovely to see you too, brother...hey! " Ledger yells as I pull him through the door.

As soon as I was safely in my car, I called him, letting him know to get his ass to the estate. Since Ivan and Sasha are already there, I thought it would be an easier base as we figure out everything before I meet with Linda tonight. I should've told her tomorrow and given us more time to get our ducks in a row, but she's already lucky she has the extra ten hours to live.

I lead him through the house to the study and guide him behind my desk. He looks at me with suspicion as I push him into my chair. Ivan and Sasha are already sitting, so I pull up one of the more plush chairs between them and Ledger and waste no time cutting to the chase. "It's Linda."

Minutes pass as all three men look at me in confusion, until Sasha breaks the silence. "Who the fuck is Linda? I swear to God, Henry, if you're cheating on my sister, I'll kill you."

"I suggest you take back that threat right fucking now," Ledger growls. "I don't give a damn if you're the bratva or not, I'll beat you to a pulp if you try to lay a hand on my brother."

Any pride I had in the way Ledger defended me is short-lived as he turns his attention to me. "Now, you better have a good explanation for who Linda is because if you're cheating on your wife, *I'll* beat you to a bloody fucking pulp."

I look between the three men. Ivan is sitting with his hand over his eyes, massaging his temples, while Ledger and Sasha are both practically fuming. "Linda is my PA, you idiots," I say, shaking my head. "And if *either* of you ever questions my devotion to my wife again, I'll beat you *both*. Understood?"

I look between the two of them as they nod. "As I was saying, Linda is behind this. I don't know *why,* but I know it's her." I pause, getting up to go grab the basket from the corner of the room before setting it on the desk in front of us. "She gave me this and told me it was a gift for Katarina. If you'll notice, it's identical to the one in Pavel's office, so I'm all but certain she was behind his death as well. I don't know what reason she would have to kill him, and I don't know why she would target Tommy either, but I plan to find out. We have dinner this evening at seven, so Ledger, you need to find anything and everything you can on her in the meantime. Sasha, Ivan, I'm going to need your more...*nefarious* skills. She's not making it out of this evening alive."

I've been sitting around useless while everyone else does their jobs. I've decided the most poetic way to kill her is with the fruit she used for her own victims, so there's really not much left for me to do at this point. Ledger is finding out everything he possibly can about the woman, while Ivan and Sasha arrange the logistics of the evening.

Ledger called the girls to come keep Katarina company while we worked, which is good because I'd be much more inclined to abandon the guys and go fuck my wife if my mother and sister weren't in the same room. As it stands, with my current level of angst, that's still not entirely off the table.

I'm unraveling more with every passing hour. The Taranovs have pretty much figured out their end of things. We are going to meet at an upscale restaurant where I'm going to use every acting skill I've ever developed during my life and *"woo her."* I'm to make her *really* believe that I've always had feelings for her. Then I'm going to suggest she come home with me to a secret property of mine, a.k.a. the Taranovs', that my wife "doesn't know about." Give her a drink with the toxin from the plant, and get her confession.

The problem is, Ledger hasn't found out anything that would lead us to believe Linda to be a cold-blooded killer. Her record is crystal clean and her accomplishments exemplary. Something I knew when I hired her. In fact, she wouldn't have been hired in the first place had those things not been true.

"Guys..." My brother's face tells me he's found what we're looking for. "I think you're *all* going to want to sit down for this."

The three of us walk back to the desk where he's been working and sit as suggested. A glance at my in-laws confirms they are just as confused as I am.

Ledger looks between us, his eyes wide. "Linda isn't her real name. It's Simona. Simona Linden. And her mother's name, well. It's Natalya Dmitrievna Taranova."

"Sorry for the state of things," I say, walking Linda, *Simona,* through the door to one of Taranovs' burner houses. "I had to have some place to go since I made the mistake of letting Katarina know about my other properties, so this is a very recent purchase, and I haven't had much time for renovation."

"That's fine. I'm just thrilled to finally have some time with you *alone.*"

"Why don't you go get freshened up while I pour us a drink." I'm flooded with relief when she takes the bait and leaves me to fix up her concoction. I opt for two different drinks to avoid any chance of a mix-up. After almost ten years of working so close together, I know she won't think a thing about me pouring her a glass of wine while I nurse some scotch.

Taking a breath, I ground myself as I wait for her to get back. Having to pretend to care for the person I hate the most in this world has been grueling tonight. I barely fought the urge to slit her throat right in the middle of the restaurant. Every word out of her mouth had me ready to throw up my meal. My only saving grace was thinking of my revenge.

"Now, where were we?" I'm broken from my thoughts as Linda tries closing in on me, her hands reaching for my chest.

"Actually, I wanted to get your advice on something first," I say, holding out her glass to block her from putting her hands on me and leading her to one of the chairs in the sitting room.

Sitting in the chair across from her, I take a sip of my scotch and breathe an internal sigh of relief when she mirrors my action with her wine. I'm not sure what all Sasha put in the vial he gave me. All I know is that it is supposedly super potent and only requires a sip or two. I know it has some of the seeds from the Cerbera odollam, but he said not to worry about it when I asked if there was more.

Hiding my smile with another drink, I continue with the rest of the plan. "This is a delicate subject, but there's nobody I trust more than you, Linda. I need advice on how to get rid of my wife. As you know, the contract is airtight, or I wouldn't have married her in the first place. To be frank, I need to make her disappear permanently."

"Oh!" she says, the shock on her face is genuine as I make my request.

"The problem is her family. You see, although they hide it well, the Taranovs are a *very* dangerous family. Their ties to the bratva make it almost impossible to get one over on them. I need a way to get rid of Kat that will look like an accident. One the Taranovs won't dispute."

Linda searches my eyes before gulping down the rest of her wine. "Alright, Henry, but I have a little confession of my own."

"Let's hear it!" I say with as much enthusiasm as I can muster.

She stands and walks over to the bar table. "Did you give her the basket?" she asks, her back to me as she pours herself another glass of wine.

"No, I haven't seen her. Why?"

Turning to come back, she flops down in her chair. "Have you ever heard of the plant Cerbera odollam?" she asks, pausing as I shake my head before continuing on. "It's a tree native to Southeast Asia, also known as the suicide tree. And I know from experience that it works."

"Oh?" I say, leaning forward in my chair as if this is brand-new information. "And what experience is that, you naughty thing?"

While I'm fighting the urge to throw up over my words, I reach for the red satin rope planted beside my chair. "Speaking of which," I say, holding it up with a forced smirk on my face. "Well, you know my proclivities."

"Oh course," she says, giving what I assume to be her attempt at a seductive smile before answering my first question. "That's the thing, I've also solved another one of your problems. I've successfully fooled the Taranovs. Well, their leader, to be exact. If I can get rid of Pavel Taranov without them being suspicious, I can surely help you get rid of his whore of a daughter."

Luckily, I'm behind her, tying her wrists together, so she doesn't notice the way I ball my hands into a fist to keep from knocking her out cold. "Oh?" I manage to breathe out, my actual loss of breath making it sound extremely convincing. "And how did you do that?"

"*Easy.* His fool of a nephew got chatty at a bar and didn't notice the light dose of Rohypnol I slipped in his drink, making it all too easy to swipe his keys from him. From there, I was able to get into the Taranov compound. I posed as one of the maids, gave him the basket, then talked up how rare and wonderful the fruit was. He ate one immediately, of course."

I finish securing her wrists and move to her left ankle. "And the others? I assume there were others."

"Of course," she says, rolling her eyes. "I wasn't going to experiment on him. I tried it on some less important individuals in my way before moving on to Pavel. There was a lawyer who helped my uncle with contracts years ago, Burnam or something or another. An old neighbor of yours—sorry about that, by the way—but, well, let me backtrack. The tree is on *your* land. I was trying to get possession of it so I wouldn't have to keep sneaking around. It all would've ended up both of ours in the end anyway."

"Ah, your uncle, you say?" I say, finishing the tie around her ankles.

"Excuse me?"

"So Simon L. Dixon *was* you, then." My grin this time is sincere since I have her bound in front of me with no way to escape. "And why did you kill Tommy, Simona?" I ask.

She narrows her eyes at me, realization starting to sink in. "He got in my way," she deadpans.

I stay on my haunches, my eyeline level with hers as I stare at her. "Your way of *what*, Simona?"

"You!" she yells, pulling harder on her restraints.

I walk back to my chair, sipping my scotch, relieved that I don't have to act anymore. "I wouldn't do that. You, for one, should know how practiced I am in shibari. Not that you've ever experienced it firsthand." I pause to take a sip of my drink. "Katarina has, though."

If looks could kill, I'd be dead before her poison takes her out.

"What? You thought I was actually trying to kill my wife? Tsk, tsk, tsk. That was very silly of you, *Simona*. Katarina is the love of my life. She *is* my life. There are no lengths I wouldn't go to keep her safe, and nobody I wouldn't burn who might cause her harm. Plus, she is a beautiful little thing, isn't she?

And let me tell you a secret." I pause to lean closer. "She's got the most amazing little pussy."

She's practically frothing at the mouth as my words hit their mark. "You were supposed to marry me!" she screams. "If it wasn't for that cunt Pavel telling his father about my mom getting knocked up, she wouldn't have been disowned from the *precious Taranov family. I* should have been the one to take her place in that stupid contract! Not that *teenage* whore! While I fought to keep food on the table for my addict mother, she got to grow up like a little princess in her gilded palace. She took *everything* from me, and I swore she wasn't going to take you too. She has *no* business fucking around with a man *twice* her age! I know what you like, *Henry.* I spent the last decade making sure every partner you had was qualified enough for your bed, and there is *no* way that *perfect* virgin girl knows what to do to please you."

I stand, sending a text to Sasha, letting him know to send in Kat for the next stage of our plan. "I guess you're about to find out."

Chapter Thirty-Eight

When Henry, Sasha, and my dad formed this plan, it sounded so straightforward. Lure Linda under the guise of Henry wanting to be rid of me. Give her a sob story about how he was sorry he had fallen for my "teenage whorishness," then bring her back to a property that Sasha owns to question her, get a confession, and turn her over to the police. Whatever this old house is, it's creepy. I'm with Sasha and one of his "men," sitting and waiting for Henry and Linda to show up. I thought briefly about asking Sasha why he owns a house in the sketchy part of town, but I think I finally get the picture. I *really* do not want to know what Sasha gets up to.

I'm trying to stay strong and stay mad at Linda, but I'm starting to have second thoughts about all this. Maybe she's not necessarily psycho, just misguided. Or she *is* psycho, and that's really not her fault. I certainly know firsthand how awful our family can be. She might need a mental hospital instead of a jail. I tried mentioning this to Henry, but he wouldn't hear of it. To him, she needs to be punished accordingly for attempting to kill me. Not to mention the murders she successfully committed. Sasha, similarly, wouldn't hear of showing any mercy. Ivan, when I tried to broach the subject, mumbled something under his breath in Russian about the police being the least of her worries.

While Sasha, Ivan, and some other very large men wait in one of the back rooms of this house for Henry's all clear, I try to remind myself that he will handle this, and once it's over, we can live in peace. I turn my attention back to chatting with Sasha about his plans for the new year. He's being vague, but it sounds like he might spend a lot more time here, so I'll get to see him more.

"I had to kill her before she could ruin you by getting pregnant! The last thing you need is a half-whore abomination of a baby, Henry, can't you see!" Linda screams, and I see red.

Oh, this bitch. Any hint of sympathy I may have held for her is gone in an instant. She wasn't just coming for me. I completely understand Henry's point of view now. She deserves no mercy. Sasha and my dad see my clenched jaw and nod at Henry, each kissing the top of my head as they leave the building. Whatever they saw in my eyes showed them their work is done here. Henry's obviously heard enough as well, as he places a piece of duct tape over her mouth.

One of Sasha's men pulls a bottle from his pocket before yanking Linda's head back and placing a few drops in each of her eyes. She tries to close her eyes before screaming under the tape.

"What is that?" I ask, happy that this monster is feeling some pain after all she's inflicted on my family.

The man replies in a thick Russian accent. "To keep eyes open. Will hurt more to close."

Henry thanks him and pats him on the back as he exits, leaving only the two of us with Linda, who clearly wants to close her eyes but can't.

Arranging the furniture in the room, Henry moves one chair into the center, facing Linda but ten feet away. She eyes him warily, and I have no idea what he's going to do next. I've seen him almost lose control—on the plane when Ivan offered to take me back. I've seen him actually lose control—when he left in a fury to go accuse Ivan of being behind the threat to me and Pavel. Now, he seems very *in* control, and it's more intimidating than anything I've seen before.

He sits in the chair, patting his knee in a gesture for me to come. I perch myself on his lap with my arms around his neck, and he takes a long inhale of the crook of my neck before facing Linda. His voice is steady, calm, and utterly terrifying.

"I'll level with you, Linda. You've killed multiple people, in cold blood, with no regard for their families or the lives you were destroying. I could give a fuck about any of them. In fact, by killing Pavel Taranov, you allowed my wife to meet her true father much earlier than she likely would have otherwise. So thank you for that, I suppose," he says conversationally.

He's rubbing soft circles on my back with one hand and my thigh with the other, and I find myself soothed that he's safe and here. With Linda tied up and obviously no longer a threat, I feel safe for the first time in too long. I know Sasha and Ivan are outside with their men, and hopefully, this will all be over soon. Henry's hand starts moving up my inner thigh, and I tense. He squeezes to reassure me, and I relax further into his embrace.

"Your mistake was thinking that you knew better than me, and that you deserved to have any say in my life whatsoever. Your life was forfeit the moment that you decided to try to murder my *wife*!" His booming voice at the end of his sentence is the only thing that betrays his anger, and I'm still considering the fact that he said "forfeit her life" when he continues.

"The wine you drank contains the same poisonous fruit you've been using on your murderous rampage, the same kind you sent to try to take my wife from me," he says, and Linda screams beneath her duct tape. "That's right. At most, you have two hours left now, so we'd best get started. Whatever pathetic jealousy you've felt is about to be magnified, because the last thing you're going to see before you die is how beautiful my wife is when I fuck her. If we're lucky, tonight will be the night we make the baby you were so enraged by. That is, if she's not pregnant as we speak."

Before I can even process what he just said, he's flipped me around to straddle him on the chair, my legs dangling on either side of his. I can feel his dick throbbing underneath me, and despite myself, I squirm, chasing the friction.

"She tried to take you from me," he whispers. "And she's going to die for it, soon. She was delusional and wanted me, and I'm ensuring that she's in misery for every last second of her pathetic existence. We're going to ignore her completely, and you're going to take me right now, in all three of your little holes. Because you. Are. Mine. Isn't that right, little girl?"

I see it now, buried behind the dilated black of his pupils. Henry hasn't loved before me, and he never would again if I was taken from him. He's given me every bit of himself, and in return, he demands all of me. He's killing for me, defending our future family, and I have no doubt he would again. I knew when he told me he loved me and he'd burn the earth for me that he meant it, and now he's showing me. I'm not sure what it is within him that needs to make Linda suffer in this way, but I can see in his eyes that he's begging me to trust him. It doesn't matter to me why he needs this. He wants to claim me here, end this nightmare, then put it all behind us so we can go home. I give him the only answer I'll ever feel, because I am his.

"Yes, Daddy."

His eyes roll back, eyelids fluttering with pleasure as he squeezes my hips. When his gaze meets mine again, it's playful, and I find myself excited for the pleasure I'm about to receive. Even with a dying audience in an uncomfortable room, being in Henry Sinclair's arms is worth any price.

"On your knees, Kitten. Help Daddy get his cock wet," he purrs, and I swear I can already feel my wetness threatening to slide down my thighs. I love it when he's bossy, and tonight, he's getting whatever he wants.

Sliding to rest between his knees, he stops me before I touch the ground. Unbuttoning his shirt, slowly, and dropping his cuff links to the floor, I revel in the sight that's displayed for me.

It doesn't matter how many times I see his defined shoulders, dark chest hair, muscular waist...the view never gets old. He crumples his shirt and places it on the floor for me to kneel on, removing his belt to make my job easier. I make quick work of getting his hard cock out of his pants, immediately licking up the precum that's dribbling from the tip and getting to work.

"Fuck. I'll never get over your mouth, little girl. You know exactly how Daddy likes his cock sucked, don't you?" he says. I pull off his dick to spit on it, saliva leaving a trail from my tongue to his tip when I lean back. I continue to work him, but he stops my hand before I can play with his balls.

"If you make me come down your throat, I'll be very upset with you, Kitten," he warns, and I lick around his crown before murmuring into his tip.

"Sorry, Daddy."

That's all it takes for him to snap, taking control and fucking my throat deeply as I moan around him, gagging every few thrusts, which seems to spur him on.

"Such a thirsty girl, loving my cock down her throat like this. My good fucking girl."

I moan louder, knees wide and searching for any friction at all on my clit before he stops and pulls me up into his lap, straddling him again but facing away from him. He pulls me flush against him with one big hand around my throat, and squeezes.

"Look at my cock, Kitten. If I hadn't already been inside you, I'm not sure I'd believe it's going to fit," he says, voice raspier now, before nibbling behind my ear.

I look down, and he's right, sitting on him with his dick standing proudly against my stomach, it almost reaches my breasts. It's definitely past my belly button. I clench around nothing, knowing exactly how good it feels when he fills me. Wiggling my hips, I rub my clit against him, desperate for anything at all.

"Mmm, yes, that's my sweet little wife, taking anything she can get. You're just desperate to be filled, aren't you? It hurt so much when you were learning to take me, and now look at you. Always ready for me. Go ahead, Katarina. Take what's yours."

I'm lifted and placed on his cock, whining at the stretch like always. It's too much and not enough all at once, and I brace my feet on his thighs to bounce. Throwing my head back, I ride, his hands on my waist holding me steady.

"What a sweet girl, milking my cock. You always spread so perfectly for me, Kitten. Your little body shouldn't be able to take all of me, but you do, because you love me, hmm? You take the pain for me. Such a good girl," he growls into my neck before biting, and I yelp, falling back against him.

He takes the chance to take over, thrusting up with my legs held wide over his forearms. He's hitting the perfect spot inside to make me detonate, and it's only a matter of time.

"Fuck yes, that's my girl. Tell me what you want. You know I'll give it to you."

"I want your cum! Please, Daddy." I sob, shaking with the pleasure that's on the brink of hitting me head-on.

"Where do you want it?"

"Inside me!" I scream as I come, clenching around his girth and shaking with pleasure. I let myself collapse entirely into him, knowing that he can hold me up and use me without any strain.

"That's right, Kitten. You want me to come inside, don't you? You're the only woman who's ever gotten it there, and the only one who ever will. Look at me, Katarina," he says.

I turn, eyes glassy, to try to focus on him above me.

"You want my cum to make me a baby, don't you? I know you do, darling. You're the only one who's ever deserved it. Such a good girl, letting me use you like this because you love me. *Fuck.* You can have it. You've earned it. I love you too," he whispers the last part, just for me, as he groans and fills me, staying as deep as he can. Holding me tightly, he lifts me just enough to turn me to face him, holding me up to watch some of his cum leak out before plugging me back up with his still hard length.

I'm hoping we can go to bed soon because I'm so, so tired. But his voice is serious again, and when I look up there's desperation in his eyes. .

"I need all of you, Katarina. Please say yes. Please," he begs, and I know what he's asking for. We've been working on it, and he always speaks of it with such reverence, knowing and owning every part of me.

I nod, and he pulls a small bottle out of the pants he's still wearing. Prepping me with his fingers first, I whine at the loss when he lifts me off his dick, then moan at the sensation of him positioning his head at my other entrance. A pinch of pain and then he's inside me, the final piece of me claimed as Henry Sinclair's.

This time, he's slower, barely advancing with each thrust, and the sensation is so overwhelming that I can feel myself shaking.

"Darling, it's okay. You're doing so well. Look at me, Katarina," he whispers.

I do, and I see that I'm not the only one with tears in my eyes. His ferality is gone, replaced with tenderness as he sinks deeper and deeper inside me. The rage he was filled with earlier has subsided, and all that's left is the man I adore.

"I'm yours," I say, and his eyes close as he breathes out a heavy sob. Pressing kisses from his temple down underneath his ear, across his jaw, then capturing his lips, I feel him approaching his breaking point.

"I'm yours, I love you, I'm safe, and I'm not going anywhere. Let go for me, Henry. Come for me, please," I whisper, and with a groan, he does.

He peppers kisses across my chest, then up my neck to my lips. After a moment, he gently pulls out of me, pulling me even closer and banding his arms around me like he's never going to let me go.

"You don't have to," I say. "You never have to let me go, Henry. Actually, I'd say you're stuck with me. Legally. I have the paperwork."

With a watery chuckle, he pulls back to look at me. "I didn't intend to say that out loud."

Gazing into each other's eyes, eventually we both realize the room is silent. He peeks over my shoulder, then looks at me again.

"Dead."

Shrugging, I can't find anything nice to say. "Good riddance."

One more kiss and I'm up, being carried into the adjacent room where a bag has towels and a change of clothes for each of us. Giggling, the absurdity of the situation hits me all at once. Henry turns to look at me with a bemused expression, which just makes me laugh harder.

"I'm sorry, it's just..." I wheeze. "What do you think pushed her over the edge? The breeding talk or when you...when you..." I can't breathe, I'm laughing so hard. "When you put it in my ass!"

Sighing, he pulls a sweatshirt over my head before helping me into the pants and putting on my socks and shoes. I've rendered him speechless. But now that this is over, I do have one question.

"What's going to happen to all this? Pretty sure we just left quite a bit of DNA evidence all over this crime scene," I say, a little nervous now that I've said it out loud.

Henry finishes dressing himself and picks me up again.

"Well, darling, this is the type of thing your family excels at. Your father will arrange for a suicide-esque disposal of Linda, we'll work with authorities to ensure families of her other victims know the truth and get closure, and Sasha will probably torch this place, if I had to guess," he says matter-of-factly.

I blink, thinking again that I really don't know too much about what the Taranov empire is about, before smiling. It's not my problem, and I don't have to worry about any of that. I have a husband, *a Daddy,* and I get to go home to my house, which is now safe, and spend time with my family, which keeps growing.

"Sounds perfect," I say, because it does. "Let's go *home.*"

Epilogue 1

If I thought I was prepared for Valentine's Day as the object of Henry Sinclair's affection, I was sorely mistaken. We've spent most of the morning wrapped up in each other, with breakfast in bed quickly devolving into more sordid activities involving pancake syrup, followed by a shower to rinse away the stickiness. This, obviously, also devolved quickly into debauchery. We finally stopped for brunch before collapsing lazily back into bed.

Sighing, I stretch myself out like a Kat who's got the cream, and honestly, that's how I feel lately. Although we've just passed our four-month anniversary, it feels like we've been through at least a year's worth of married life. Henry has proven himself to be my perfect partner again and again, and I still can't believe that this beast of a man who would kill for me is also such a big softy, walking toward me now with two mugs of steaming hot chocolate.

"Don't you dare think of doing anything sexual at all with the whipped cream on these drinks, mister. I need at least an hour break before you try anything again," I tease, accepting the quick kiss I'm given as he sits down with me on the edge of the bed. At some point, he's dressed himself in his usual outdoorsman attire, and I consider that I might be ready to go again in thirty minutes.

With a quirk of one eyebrow, he sets a timer on his phone for one hour and then winks at me. I've told him that his winks should be outlawed for inciting sexual eruptions, which of course means he now winks at me all the time. Sipping our hot chocolate, he finishes first and rubs my feet while we enjoy the quiet of the afternoon.

"Thank you for not making me leave the house for Valentine's Day. Or much at all, lately. I promise I'll be ready soon—"

"Katarina." He interrupts. "We will continue onwards at a pace dictated by you and your therapist, darling. I promise you I am not in any rush. You know exactly where I stand on this."

And I do. When we returned home after everything happened, I had a...minor breakdown, you might say. I became obsessed with security, making Henry show me all the cameras, all the redundant backup cameras, all the dummy cameras, and the software that would fool even the most experienced hacker. We hired full-time staff to monitor them and the alarm system, and our suite of rooms has its own code that changes regularly, so that if a door opens, I know it can only be Henry.

I knew deep down that I was going slightly overboard, but I didn't think it was irrational. Henry agreed, but when I started refusing to leave the estate, then the suite, he suggested perhaps we should talk to someone. That's how Dr. Benedict came into our lives. She specializes in post-traumatic stress disorder after home invasions and has helped me tremendously. Apparently, my upbringing put me at very high risk of being negatively affected by the attack, and I attribute an unhealthy amount of comfort to maintaining my own space, since it's all I've ever had any control over. I've recently been able to visit Margot and Sloane, which was especially nice, considering I don't think Margot will make it much longer carrying the twins.

Smiling at Henry, I agree.

"Yes, I do know where you stand," I say quietly, which is the truth. He doesn't begrudge me our time at home. In fact, he seems to relish it. But equally, he refuses to let me sink in on myself and become a hermit. This is why he and Dr. Benedict have me following a plan to systematically get out more and more. But I haven't been ready to leave our little reclaimed love nest to travel or vacation extensively yet, and he's been patient with me.

Giving me a soft smile, he pulls me to my feet and sets my empty mug on my nightstand.

"Let's go for a walk and stretch our legs after our lazy morning. Maybe fuck against a tree," he says, kissing my temple. "I'll go grab a picnic basket with some snacks and a blanket."

As we wander farther from the house, I notice that we're taking a familiar route, winding around toward the greenhouse. I tense slightly, not really wanting to see it, and Henry stops, blocking my path.

"I know it doesn't hold fond memories for you right now," he says quietly, rubbing my upper arms in a very soothing massage. "But I've done some renovations, and it doesn't look quite the same as it did before. Will you take a look at it and see how different it is? If you don't like the energy or you don't want to go in, we don't have to."

Taking a fortifying breath, I nod. I've had nightmares of Linda kidnapping me and bringing me to the greenhouse, dark and pulsing with sinister vines of evil plants. Dr. Benedict says that because the plants grew here, and I associate them and death with Linda right now, it makes sense to be a foreboding place of peril in my dreams.

Henry moves from blocking me and takes my hand, leading me around the final curve to the clearing where the greenhouse...*was?* It's not there anymore. At least, there is *a* greenhouse, but it's not the old one that's been haunting my nightmares. This is a glass architectural dream, reminiscent of a larger version of the orangery from my childhood home. I'm immediately at peace, and none of the negative energy I was worried I would feel is present.

Leading me inside, Henry shows me the replanted species from the old greenhouse before assuring me all of the harmful plants have been completely eradicated. He moves us to a back corner where a swing sits facing west, and we watch the sunset as he pulls out the finger foods he packed earlier. Polishing off the entire basket, he surprises me by pulling out a much smaller box, just as the sun is setting. Tears fill my eyes as I realize what I'm almost certain it contains.

"Henry..." I whisper tearfully.

He says nothing, but as he meets my gaze, I see that I'm not the only one emotional at this moment.

"You," he says so softly, I can barely hear him, "are the greatest gift that I have ever been given, and the one I was least expecting. It's unfathomable to me that someone got so close to taking you from me." His voice cracks, and he stops, head bowed before taking a deep breath and continuing.

"I know that legally, we're married, but I want..." He stops to clear his throat before continuing in a stronger voice. "I want you to have your dream wedding, whatever that looks like, in front of only our families, people who matter...although I suppose if you want to invite two hundred people to this one as well, I won't stop you."

He laughs as he moves to one knee and opens the tiny blue box he's been holding. Inside is a dainty gold wedding band half-encircled with diamonds.

"Your engagement ring is your mother's, and I would never presume to replace it. Plus, you don't like to wear it too often since it gets in the way of your shenanigans as you gallivant around here and cause mischief," he says, giving a watery laugh. "But I would very much love to give you something shiny for everyday wear."

Looking up, he finally asks me the question that has him so emotional he's trembling, ever so slightly.

"Katarina, I love you, and I want to give you the world. Will you do me the honor of marrying me again, by your own free will?"

I can't help but laugh at that, giggling before reaching down and holding Henry's precious face in both my hands.

"Yes, you romantic man. Yes, I will marry you. Of my own will," I squeal as he stands, picking me up off the bench and spinning me around. The gorgeous ring fits perfectly onto my finger as he places it, matching the gold of his wedding band. I can barely tell it's on, and even though during my daily activities I usually don't wear jewelry, this won't bother me at all.

Finally stopping his spins, but not putting me down, he kisses me until I'm breathless, then gives me the goofiest grin I've ever seen on his face.

"Well, Mrs. Sinclair. Let's plan a wedding."

It's early April before my plans come together, and my tiny wedding is finally upon us. We waited for Margot and Sloane to each give birth, although I don't think any of us expected them to go into labor on the same day. I thought Blanche would faint from joy the day all three babies were born. The funniest part of the day was watching Jack and Ledger sobbing, holding their own daughters, then swapping to hold each other's, then panicking as they tried to remember who was who. Of course, Margot and Sloane had both put the girls in coordinating outfits, so the risk of baby swap was low.

Now, a knock on the door tells me that Ivan is here.

"Come in," I say, smiling when I see how handsome he looks in his suit. We've been spending more time together, bonding over trying to sort through the family records in the Taranov archives that Pavel had neglected for years. It was hard to hear about my mother from him, and both of us cried over how much we missed her. But it's been healing as well, and I think before long it'll be natural to call him Dad. He's already given me more love than Pavel ever did. And I can't imagine anyone else walking me down the aisle today.

"You look absolutely stunning, Katarina. I'm so proud to be on your arm today," he says, kissing my cheek and wiping a tear from his eye. "I actually have something for you, as I was recently informed you're missing something blue."

I roll my eyes teasingly, knowing immediately that he and Blanche must have been in cahoots about my something blue. She had promised me a bracelet of her mother's, but suddenly she had "misremembered" this morning, and it was in fact a gaudy citrine rather than a sapphire. Now I see that she had been keeping Ivan's surprise.

He pulls a box from his inner suit pocket and produces a dainty sapphire and diamond bracelet, understated and perfect for my wrist today.

"This was the only piece of jewelry I ever gave your mother. It was thin enough that it was usually tucked just under her watch band. But every so often, it would catch the light just right and sparkle, and we would both smile to ourselves just knowing it was there," he says, clearing his throat as he clasps the bracelet around my wrist.

"You've inherited so many of her positive qualities, Katarina. And as I've gotten to know Henry, I've realized the two of you are a truly special match. I'm so happy for both of you." His voice cracks on the end as he pulls me close for a tight hug. Finally asking if I'm ready, I nod as I hear my processional swell, indicating it's time for us to start our short walk down the aisle.

This wedding is entirely different from our last, with a guest list consisting of only our closest family members and favorite staff. My dress, a far cry from the puff ball that Mrs. Nixon picked out, is a sleek silk number with barely there spaghetti straps and a nonexistent back. It's cut with no forgiveness to my body, intended to show off my toned shoulders and back, and I feel gorgeous and strong, just what I had always wanted for my wedding dress. My thoughts quickly focus back in as Ivan and I reach the beginning of the aisle.

Henry waits for me at the end, in front of the fountain in the garden, flowers surrounding him, with a quack now and then reminding me of our resident ducks that are thriving these days. Our friends and family turn to look at us, and I can see Sasha's beaming smile from here, but my focus is on my Henry. He's not even pretending not to cry, letting his tears track down his face as he smiles at me. Reaching him, Ivan shakes his hand and whispers in his ear, before I hand my bouquet to Sasha and take Henry's hands.

Jack was already ordained, so he proudly begins the short ceremony we decided on as Henry and I melt into each other's eyes. Before I know it, we've arrived at our vows.

Clearing his throat, Henry begins.

"Katarina, my love. Thank you for making me the luckiest man in the world not once, but twice, by agreeing to marry me all over again. I've told you before that you are the greatest gift I've ever been given, and I feel that's doubly true today." He gives me a soft smile.

"I'll follow you wherever you lead, and I promise to always be your protector and haven, to love and cherish you above all others. There will be no secrets between us, and there is nothing that we can't face together. The world is ours, and I intend to take it on with you by my side until my last day," he finishes, tearing up again by the end as I squeeze his hand.

I'm lost in his stormy eyes when he returns my squeeze, reminding me that it's my turn to speak. Taking a deep breath, I try to get through as much as possible without tears.

"Henry, my love," I begin, my voice breaking immediately, betraying the emotion I've been trying so hard to keep contained. "You rescued me unintentionally but completely, and I cannot imagine my life had you not barreled into it. It's impossible to think of any day without you because you are woven into the fabric of the magic of a life that I never thought would be possible. I'll follow you wherever you lead, and I promise to vex you as often as possible. And to keep you young."

This gets a laugh from the crowd, and my desired effect: a grin and an eye roll from Henry.

"I vow to love and cherish you above all others, and face life as a family regardless of what comes our way, until my last day," I finish, enjoying the predatory gaze in his eyes because he knows what's coming.

"Ladies and gentlemen, may I present to you Mr. and Mrs. Sinclair. You may kiss the bride!" Jack exclaims, and Henry is immediately on me like he's never kissed me before, as if I'm an oasis in the desert.

After way too long, he pulls away and gives me a look of such pure love that my heart feels like it's going to burst. *I can't believe this is my life.* We turn, and everyone cheers from where they've already spread out to the snack tables. We must have been absorbed in our kiss for longer than we thought.

I see Ivan cooing over one of the *two* newborns Margot is holding, Ledger trying to help LJ walk, Mrs. Potts laughing with Sloane, and Sasha deep in conversation with Blanche...

As Henry and I quietly sneak back inside, I know that nobody will miss us for a few minutes. I'm going to defile my husband, then laugh the night away with my family. Kat from six months ago could never have dreamed things would end up this way, but I wouldn't change a thing.

I have my family, and I'm *home*.

Epilogue 2

"You look perfect, darling. Although I'll admit I'm not pleased at other men seeing you so scantily dressed," I say, trying to soothe Katarina's nerves.

She's more excited than nervous, but I can tell she's feeling a bit out of her element as we drive toward my brothers' club, Rendezvous, in the city. Tonight's party is themed to "A Midsummer Night's Dream", and she looks divine in a minidress of her signature periwinkle, with flowers woven into the braid down her back.

"I'm excited, more anticipatory than nervous, I think. I just can't imagine your brothers or their wives in a sexual context at all, so I hope it's not weird," she explains, and I understand the sentiment. Anyone's first time at a sex club is going to be daunting, and more so if you're there with family who are also the owners.

Squeezing my hand on her thigh as I pull the car in and park at the back of the club, I'm more thankful than ever that I drive almost exclusively automatic vehicles these days. Shifting was forcing me to remove my hands too often, and keeping one hand on her at all times while driving is a much better alternative.

"I think you'll be pleasantly surprised. Ledger and Jack have outdone themselves with this place, and we'll move from the bar area gradually into the more explicit areas. But I have to tell you, darling. We might run into women from my past in here tonight," I say, absolutely hating that I didn't think to have Ledger ensure there were no tickets available for any of my past partners.

"You own my heart and my soul, and I don't even remember their names now that you're in my life. You've completely erased anyone who came before you, Katarina," I finish softly, looking at her so she can see the truth in my gaze.

She smiles sweetly back at me, squeezing my hand. I search for any hint of discomfort, but I don't find any.

"Thank you. But I think I'll be okay. I knew it was a possibility once you asked me if I wanted to come, and while I would obviously rather never see those women, it's bound to happen. I actually discussed my jealousy with Dr. Benedict, and she thinks it's rooted in the disparity between our experience levels as well as the number of partners. She actually suggested it might be healthy to explore more partners for me to be able to..."

"*She what?*" I yell, feeling the steering wheel crack in my grip as I squeeze as hard as I can to try to dispel some energy.

"Gotcha," Katarina says with a wink before continuing. "You're very easy to rile. But I did talk it over with her, and I think I'll be okay."

She leans over the console to give me a soft kiss, and I blink, my heart rate barely coming down as my rage subsides a bit. I crack my neck back and forth and get out of the car, moving around to the passenger side to open her door. My little wife has a pleased expression on her face, looking far too happy about her joke. *She won't be happy when her ass is so raw she can't sit for a week.* I remind myself we aren't here to play, necessarily, and we both agree that's something we need to talk about after she's experienced the club and had time to digest. We're going to start with drinks in the VIP area with the family, then perhaps indulge the girls with time on the dance floor.

When I lead Katarina through the private back entrance straight into VIP, we see Margot and Sloane sitting in a large semicircular half booth, facing the dance floor but set back enough from the balcony railing that we aren't easily seen by patrons. It's nice to see both of them out and looking well rested, considering they both have babies at home. I give Katarina a kiss on the temple and a smack on the ass, letting her know it's fine for her to leave me and go join the girls. They squeal when they see her and hop up to envelop her in a hug and squeeze her between them, immediately including her in whatever discussion they're engrossed in.

I walk past them to take the stairs down to the bar, hearing Sloane say, "I swear! I did! I rode him right there in the middle, in front of everyone...I know! But it was really..."

Her voice fades as I shake my head, letting the security guard know that I've added additional men to the perimeter for the night and making sure he has the updated plans. Although the immediate threat to my wife's life was eliminated, her family's...unique activities led me to hire additional security staff full-time. She hasn't outright said it, but I know their around-the-clock presence at the estate makes her feel more secure.

Finding my brothers at the bar, I see I'm just in time to say hello before following them back up to VIP.

"Big bro!" Jack cries, wrapping me immediately in a bear hug. Ledger joins in, ensuring that all eyes are on us as we have a way-too-long group embrace.

"I'm glad you made it out tonight, brother," Ledger says, wiping a tear. He's been very emotional since his daughter was born, and has been prioritizing family life over everything else. I've seen more of him and Jack since our mystery was solved than I have in the past twenty years at least, and I can honestly say I've never been happier. Game nights, cookouts, family vacation planning...it's been a family-centered whirlwind in the Sinclair household lately.

Following the server carrying our champagne bucket upstairs, I look around at the throngs of people clearly having a great time before taking part in any debauchery this evening. It feels so different to be here with Katarina. *My wife.* Whether this ends up being something she's interested in or not, I couldn't care less. Our life together, largely consisting of being homebodies while fucking all around the estate, fulfills me in ways I never expected. If we never cross the threshold of a club again, that's fine with me. Especially with the play we have planned for the first time this weekend...

Finally making our way back after being briefly waylaid by a business associate of Jack's from New York, the girls' animated discussion falls silent as we approach the booth. Scooping

Katarina into my lap, I bury my face in her neck, inhaling deeply before biting down hard.

She lets out a hiss of displeasure, squirming in my lap and making my already half-hard cock come to life even more.

"Do I even want to know what you three were talking about?" I murmur into her ear as I trace light circles on her thigh. A glance to the other side of the booth reveals my brothers similarly bewitched with their own wives, nobody paying attention to anyone else.

"You really don't," she whispers in reply, then giggles. "Although, let me just say...you measure up *very* well." I can't control my exasperated sigh, and she laughs even harder, drawing the attention of the group.

"Did you convince him to let you play tonight?" Sloane asks, as Ledger looks ready to drag her out of VIP and into the exhibition hall that I've yet to show Katarina.

Jack pipes up, "Sloane, you know it all has to do with how many eggs the chickens laid today! Does that mean it was less than five eggs, Henry? I can never remember the cutoff..."

"Have you ever seen a single chicken at the estate, Jack?" Margot asks, giving him a bemused look as she sips champagne.

Ledger's brows furrow in confusion as he chimes in. "Well, no, but...I mean. Chicken coops aren't big. They could be anywhere. Where is the coop on the estate, Henry?"

After a few beats of pregnant silence, everyone but Ledger and Jack bursts into laughter.

I finally regain my composure.

"There have never been chickens at the estate, to my knowledge. At least not since Mother moved out. The two of you were just starting out planning your club, and you *would not stop* badgering me about my lifestyle. I had to say something outlandish to get you off my back, but instead of putting you off, it just made you ask more questions! The legend grew from there," I explain, sipping my champagne.

Jack looks at me like I've just shown him his favorite superhero is just an actor, and drains his champagne, mumbling about how he doesn't believe me about the chickens. Ledger laughs it off and starts to drag Sloane to the exhibition hall before Margot speaks up, asking about Sasha's whereabouts.

"So, Kat, where is Sasha? Ledger, wasn't Sasha spending a decent amount of time here in the past few months since he moved down full-time? He was helping Blanche with the programming while you looked for another full-time manager, right?" Margot asks, and I give my brother a very subtle shake of my head.

"I'm not sure," Katarina says. "I think since Ledger finally hired someone, he's been helping Blanche with other business things, and not spending as much time at the club. I won't see him before we leave for our honeymoon next week."

Ledger clears his throat before answering Margot himself.

"Yeah, he was here for a couple of months helping Mom ensure everything ran smoothly. I think they figured out that they work pretty well as a team. You know she loves directing people to do her bidding. But once we hired Brad to join the floor management team, she took a step back and took Sasha with her. Angel," he says, thankfully changing the subject and looking at Sloane. "Want to come explore?"

Sloane beams up at him and takes his hand before he whisks her away.

"Princess?" Jack asks Margot with a waggle of his eyebrows, and with a wave, they're also gone.

"Well, Kitten, what do you think of the place so far?" I ask as she sips her champagne and resumes squirming on my lap. It's a little uncomfortable, considering this is one of the longest stretches that I've gone without being inside her in the past few months. Both of us have been insatiable, enjoying our honeymoon period and feeling like true newlyweds after our ceremony. Especially with the threats over and that monkey off our back.

"It's a lot more beautiful here than I expected," she says apologetically. "I kind of thought it would feel seedy in some way. I should have known that Jack and Ledger would never."

"Hmm, yes," I agree, kissing her neck to try to rile her up the same way she's torturing me with her wiggling. "Some members come for the ambiance of the bar and the dancing without even going to the hall each time they visit. But what do you think? Want to go take a look around?"

She's a little flushed, and I'm not sure she'll make it much longer without being fucked. But I do really want her to get a little taste since we're here. I think it'll make her absolutely feral for me tonight and potentially open her up to playing in new ways.

"How about this, little girl," I say, letting her know that I'm serious. She perks up to sit primly on my lap.

"Yes, Daddy?" she asks sweetly, and *fuck me.* It's almost impossible to remind myself why I'm trying to avoid taking her into Ledger's office and fucking her on his desk. After a few deep breaths, I offer her a choice.

"You have two options. One is that we can go home right now and start our weekend as we discussed," I explain, and her eyes immediately brighten. "Yes, that's right. Instead of tomorrow morning, we'll begin as soon as we arrive on the property."

She opens her mouth to say she wants option one, but there's a catch.

"But," I warn, "There will be no touching on the way home. Not even my hand on your thigh. No crossing your legs, either. I know all your tricks. You'll have to control yourself all the way home."

A whine escapes her sweet little mouth. "What's option two, Daddy?"

"Option two is that we spend thirty minutes walking the exhibition hall for you to see some of the things people are presenting tonight. Then I'll fuck you before we leave to go home. But when we get home, Katarina, you're taking a bath like a good girl and going to sleep. No more once we're at home. You'll need your rest for tomorrow."

She tries to hide her smirk, but I see it and smile. My kitten knows she's getting fucked at home regardless of which option she chooses. But I am curious if she'll try to please me by being patient and seeing the sights while we're here.

"Option two please, Daddy," she says sweetly, and I stand so she can wrap her legs around my waist. I don't see any reason for her to walk tonight. By the end of the night, she won't be able to anyway.

"A wonderful choice, my love," I say, pressing a sweet kiss to her lips.

We wander toward the hall, both knowing we won't last thirty minutes. I'm ready to get my wife home and start our weekend activities that we've been discussing for a little while now. An entire weekend together to play, no interruptions. She shivers in my arms, and I see that she's caught sight of the first room.

Oh, Kitten. *Just you wait.*

Missing the Sinclairs already?

Dying to know what Daddy has planned for his little girl when they get home? Sign up for our newsletter for an exclusive *Caged in Desire* bonus chapter and find out! https://dl.bookfunnel.com/lj21ytqgpr

Be the first to know about T.K. Drake's new releases and receive exclusive content! www.tkdrake.com

Instagram: @tkdrakeauthor

Also By T.K. Drake

Available now!
Ledger and Sloane's story
Redeemed in Crimson
Book One in Sinclair Affairs Series

Margot and Jack's story
Masked in Deception
Book Two in Sinclair Affairs Series

I never thought I'd be so happy to arrive home to a one bed, one bath cottage, but here we are. After a weekend back home to sign paperwork for Dad, I'm ready for a little peace this afternoon and a solid night's sleep before filming starts tomorrow. *Filming.* Since apparently now I'm an actor. *Yeah right.* I take a deep breath, reminding myself it's an honor that my sister's mother-in-law was so impressed by my fucking at her son's sex club that she cast me as her late husband in her film. *Right.*

About the Authors

T.K. Drake is a dynamic duo of best friends who couldn't find the perfect romance novel and decided to write it themselves. As only children, they spent their childhood entertaining each other with elaborate stories and games. Reuniting as adults has inspired them to unleash their creative energy into contemporary and dark romance, bridging gaps in the genre and writing books they longed to read. Based in the Southeastern United States, when not writing they are usually reading, lounging on the beach, or planning their next international vacation.